FORKED

THE WICK CHRONICLES
BOOK THREE

BLUE BOX BOOKS

FORKED
THE WICK CHRONICLES
BOOK THREE

Published by Blue Box Books
www.blueboxbooks.com

ISBN 978-1-932461-42-8

Printed in the United States of America

FORKED

THE WICK CHRONICLES

BOOK THREE

MAX THOMPSON

FORKED

1

Finn pored over the logs he'd been collecting from the day he first stepped through a portal at the edge of Union Square. He was looking for specific trips he had made through time, moments when he escorted people from a doomed San Francisco of the future into different points in the past, where they could safely live out their lives. Over a period of twenty years he had personally relocated at least a thousand people, and his technicians had taken thirty thousand more—a fraction of the lives that could be lost to the meteor that was speeding toward the earth. The numbers had overwhelmed him then because it was impossible to save everyone in the city, much less the world; the numbers overwhelmed him now because it was impossible to track down everyone and offer to take them home.

That was why he opened the logs in the first place. He wanted to look for people who had been scattered throughout half a millennium, people who might want to return to the timeline in which they were born. He made notes as he scrutinized the records; he needed to hire someone to research the impact each relocated person had on history, and if they hadn't been integral to the overall progression—or regression—of civilization, he could send someone to make the offer of home.

He especially wanted to search for those who had died soon after being transplanted. Time did not like people moving about and tried hard to flick them off the wrong timeline, and not everyone would have survived. If he could find the people whose anchors failed them, those who succumbed to the progression of illness that came with relocating to a new When, he hoped he could save them.

He'd given very few people access to the portals. Only twenty of his technicians had transponders, and they intentionally stranded those they relocated. That seeming cruelty was to prevent them from hopping through time and causing chaos and to keep anyone from using the ability to move through time for personal gain. With so few people having access, he hadn't expected to find any recent activity in the logs; he assumed that his son, the Emperor of San Francisco, had made a few trips that he had been unaware of, but Will should have been the only one.

Instead, when he opened the logs, he was presented with dozens of recent incidences of activity. Nearly every one of them originated from the portal on Union Square in the current timeline, with a designation heading twenty-five years into the past. He hesitated; it was none of his business who had used portals they clearly had access to, but the trips were clustered close together, often three and four nights in a row. He checked the time stamps; with few exceptions, the portal activated at two in the morning, with a return trip just a minute later.

He reversed the search and found that the portal that opened on the other end was reactivated three to four hours later for the return trip. That wasn't enough time for most of the things Will used the portals for, and when he did spend only a few hours in another When, it was always during the day.

So he opened the individual logs to see who was taking the series of quick trips. And when he saw, he debated whether he needed to tell someone or not. He was torn; it was none of his business, but he could also see how the continued use of the portals for personal diversion might become a problem.

Someone running from their own demons just might be tempted to go through, and not come back.

2

"Drew needs a transponder."

That was the first thing out of Finn's mouth when he met Will on Union Square. He didn't say hello or ask how Will had been in the three days since they had seen each other; he didn't even give Will a chance to kiss him on his cheek, which he generally did every time he saw his father. Will was leaning in, and Finn popped out with it. Drew needs a transponder.

Will kissed him anyway, and let him go on talking.

It made sense; Drew was a fixture in Oz's life, and she was not going to stop portal-hopping, not until she became Queen, and even then she might not want to stop. Neither one of them was afraid to take risks, and because of that, there might come a time when Drew found himself sitting on a bench two hundred years in the past, not knowing where she was. "If he has a transponder, he can get to the closest portal and come home. If she's not waiting for him here, we can locate her signal. You know they're going to go play and who knows? They might get separated."

"All right," Will said, waiting for Finn to say more. He knew when his father was on a roll, with bits and pieces of data spinning through his head at once. Sometimes he took the long way around when he was trying to relate information, and Will knew he had to wait him out. Finn had something to say, and his lead statement was not what he really wanted to talk about.

"You know, they should have fun. They're young and this is the time for them to make the most of it. They might even want to go see things that aren't you at seventeen, all cranky and... mean."

"I was not mean, Dad."

"Fine, but you were intensely serious. And I know they've gone back to watch you."

"And that was *your* doing," Will reminded him. "It wouldn't have occurred to them had you not suggested it."

Pretty sure it was Drew's idea. Finn just got him to think of it.

"And he went with them, Wick. Seventeen-year-old me didn't know who Oz or Zed were, but I damn well knew what my own father looked like."

"I wasn't your father then," Finn said.

"Yeah, you were. You just didn't know it yet."

Finn's eyes crinkled at the corners the way they did when he smiled. "Really now. Are you sure?"

"Reasonably. And we're getting off track. I don't think Oz and Drew want to go back and spy on my teenaged self again."

Sure, they do. They just don't want to get caught.

"Yes, well, there are other things they might want to do."

Will nudged him toward the closest bench. "Such as?"

Finn had no idea; they might want to sit in the sunshine on a cool February morning and watch the ferry boats come and go, but a few centuries back when they could be an average anonymous couple instead of the Princess and her future consort. Or perhaps they wanted to spend an afternoon riding the cable cars around town in the nineteen-sixties, when the city was loud and colorful, filled with hippies and wildly painted vans.

He listed half a dozen reasons why they might want to take a few field trips, but danced around the point.

When Will was sure he'd caught the direction Finn was heading, he asked, "Are they using the portals often enough that you're worried about the statistics of something going wrong? Oz knows to be careful."

"Things happen, that's all."

"And you're not answering the question. Are they?"

Finn gazed at the balcony of the royal house for a long minute. "I noted several weeks' worth of late-night portal activations in the logs. They always leave after midnight, and they stay gone for several hours. They don't even go back that far, Will, just a couple of decades."

"Are they making a straight jump to the same date and time, or are they heading for specific times?"

"Most of the time they're going from two in the morning to two in the morning, same date."

Will thought that meant they weren't going back to spy on him, nor were they lurking around, trying to watch her parents as they fell in love, the way Jax had done with his own parents when he was young. "There's nothing to see at two in the morning. Nothing to do."

Maybe they don't want to be seen. They just need to get away.

"Do you know something, Wick?" Will asked me. "Are you going with them?"

No. But Oz hasn't slept well since, you know. The war.

Will thought about it for a moment and then asked, "Have they gone in the last five days, Dad?"

Finn shook his head. "Not since the day before your birthday. I found that odd, as well, given how often they were going prior to that."

"Wick, has Oz been sleeping all right this week?"

She's been in bed.

"That's not what I asked."

I know. You said the rest of it wasn't any of my business.

"Indeed, I did. And I would guess that if she hasn't slept much in the last few days, she doesn't care."

Finn had to think about it. "Ah. All right then. The distractions of young love and all that. But I still want to give Drew a transponder, just in case. Will you talk to him?"

"Any reason why you can't?"

There wasn't a specific reason, but he was buried in work, trying to find a missing variable in an equation that might help him figure out why the transporter he was trying to build wasn't working. Everything he sent through it turned inside out, and everything Richard—Drew's father and Finn's new playmate—sent back simply fell apart. Finn knew that once he went back to his lab, it would slip his mind, and he counted on Will to relay the message.

The variable bothered him so much that he asked Will to look at it; Will took one look at Finn's equations and snorted, "You're just making things up now, aren't you?" It wasn't math; he didn't know what the mess on Finn's clear-board was supposed to be, but it bared no resemblance to the structure of math as he knew it.

Now he wanted his son to act as his messenger, but he hadn't considered how distracted Will had been since his birthday party. Will's brain was stuck on one thing—Aisha Okuda—and everything else he was thinking about had to swirl around thoughts of her. He'd even zoned out during a security council meeting with the King, unable to focus on anything other than all of the worries and doubts percolating in his head.

She kissed him on his birthday, but they hadn't repeated it, and he really, really wanted to.

He was also really, really afraid to.

When you can hear inside someone's head just by touching them, a simple kiss can get very complicated; he'd been practicing touching without listening—Oz touched him a lot, trying to help—but he'd never had to balance it while his hormones boiled over.

Will promised his father that he would speak with Drew, but by the time Finn was back in his lab, he'd forgotten. Instead of going to find Drew, he stayed on the bench and engaged in a flurry of text messages with Aisha; Zed's seventeenth birthday was in two days, and there was going to be a family dinner to celebrate. Aubrey had invited her to come, and Will wanted nothing more than for her to say yes.

When she did, any thought of Drew was effectively erased.

*

He remembered on the way to the restaurant. We walked there with Oz and Drew, who agreed to help keep an eye on me—I had to promise to keep my feet off the floor and not whine about sitting in a high chair during dinner, which seemed like it was three kinds of unfair, but dead delicious things were being offered so of course I promised—and after he'd greeted his parents, which was mostly just his mom whining about his beard, he pulled Drew over to the bar to fill him in on Finn's idea.

Will thought that it was a good idea; having a transponder jammed into Drew's head would relieve Oz of a distraction she didn't need. If he had one, keeping track of him was one less thing she needed to worry about. He didn't tell Drew he knew they had been going on late-night field trips and didn't lecture him about time travel safety; he just did what his father asked him to. Tell Drew.

Still, while he said it was a good idea, he also made it sound painful and in no way appealing. What Finn wanted to do, he said, was take a long needle and jab the transponder into a tender spot behind Drew's ear where it would then integrate into his brain, and if he didn't cry, then he and Oz would teach him how to use the portals.

Drew didn't promise not to cry, but he agreed to the transponder. It would be a very Oz-like thing to wake up at four in the morning and decide it was a fine time to jump through a portal to watch her parents paw at each other while they sat together on a blanket under a tree in the park, or even to go back a few years to get hot chocolate and watch the fog swallow the Golden Gate Bridge.

Will leaned back a touch and considered that Drew had told him exactly what they'd been doing. If she couldn't sleep, if her nightmares had returned and she was restless, it would be very much like them to go somewhere they could be alone, and do nothing but sit together, watching the fog roll in, waiting for her disquiet to fade. If he wanted to ask, he restrained himself. They were both adults, and if they needed his help, they would come to him.

He could stop her nightmares; he could touch her as she

slept and replace the horrors invading her dreams with happy things, like dancing at her birthday party or snuggling in a sleeping bag with Drew in the winter woods near Denver. It had been a long time since anyone had asked him to do that, and he was aware that he could no longer slip into her room at night to check on her.

She might not be alone now.

Still, he was curious.

What was brewing in Oz's brain? Jax wanted her to see a counselor because his gut told him she wasn't dealing with all of the emotional fallout from having been abducted and abused by the First Minister of Florida, not as well as she wanted everyone to believe. She was easily frustrated and sometimes short with people, and she cried more often than she had before the war, which was especially not Oz-like. He was aware that Jax intended to employ Drew in his effort to get her to admit she needed to see someone. She resisted the idea; seeking help now could be used against her later, when she held the throne.

Oz dug her heels in; she would deal with it on her own.

Before he could press Drew on the matter, the King and Queen arrived, and the topic withered. Will spent the rest of the evening dodging advice from Jax—make a move already, she clearly wants you to—and working up the nerve to confess his deepest secrets to Aisha, all the things he thought would make a difference to her. He struggled for a way to begin; how could she possibly believe that he hadn't even been born yet, or the reasons he never went home?

And there was the body count; he thought that would matter to her.

Drew came to his rescue. After dinner, Will and Aisha sat at the bar while he fumbled over a way to tell her that he was basically an alien displaced by the physics of time. Every word that clung to the tip of his tongue tasted wrong. When he couldn't find a way to start Drew said, "What's that you say every now and then? Just rip the bandage off? Try that."

"Go away," Will grumbled.

"I will. And Aisha, whatever he says, as bizarre as it sounds… it's the truth."

He still didn't know where to begin, so Drew went on. "Aisha. Will hasn't even been born yet. That momentous event is still a couple of centuries away. He can travel through time. Twenty-five years ago he came here to help save the world, and he damn well did it. Now…have fun."

It took the rest of the evening to tell her the things he wanted her to know. He showed her pictures of him and Jax, taken when Jax was six and he was fifteen, and then others when he was seventeen and Jax was eighteen. He explained his reasons for staying in this When—he needed to be here to help thirty-year-old Finn when he popped up with no memory of who he was or why he was here—and glossed over some of the things he'd had to do in order to protect the timeline. He made it clear there was a body count. He told her everything he could, every detail he'd been afraid would send her running, but she said that she believed him.

The complexities of his life changed nothing; she already knew that with a simple touch he could hear her thoughts or give her admission to his own. It wasn't a stretch to believe he had access to time travel. And once she made it clear that his truths were not a barrier that she had a problem jumping over, no matter how wild they were, and that she was unwilling to let him make another excuse, she kissed him so deeply that I was afraid his mother was going to throw things at them. Jo had a dinner roll in hand and it wouldn't have taken much effort to chuck it at them.

She would have aimed it at Aisha, but if it hit Will instead, that would work, too.

After Aisha let him up for air, she grabbed him by the tie and then led him out the door. He had just enough time to set me down on the floor I had promised to not set a paw on and to tell me to go to Drew, and then he followed her like an eager puppy.

They left without saying goodbye to anyone.

Jo was not happy. Finn, on the other hand, would have

chased after Will to high-five him if he could have. I went straight to Drew, who was amused at how she dragged Will from the restaurant, and happy enough to sneak more meaty things to me.

3

They didn't sleep together. Will made that clear to anyone who asked, and Jax, Drew, and Finn couldn't stop themselves from asking.

Jax and Drew were hopeful; they wanted Will to get the girl and were oddly excited that he might. Finn—while he wanted Will to get whatever it was that would make him happy—was more practical and had no problem poking his nose into his son's non-existent sex life. "She's at least a dozen years from menopause," he told Will. "You should absolutely not reproduce."

He was painfully aware of that. No one knew why his brain worked the way it did, and it was something Jo, especially and emphatically, felt was better off left alone. Will had a miserable childhood because of it, and if his abilities were genetic, the risk of passing it along was not worth it. Why saddle someone else with his misery?

Drew sat on a stool in Finn's lab, eyeing the tray lined with needles of increasing length and diameter, knowing one of them was about to be poked into his head, and the thing that bothered him most was the idea of Will never having a child of his own. "You'd be an awesome dad," he said.

Will had long accepted that he would never have children of his own. He intended to co-opt any that Drew had, the same way he had Oz and Zed. Caring for them had fulfilled any need he felt towards parenting. He assumed caring for their children would do the same thing for him; he didn't want anyone to feel bad for him because there was nothing to feel bad about. It was also a nonissue; he was a long way off from stepping any further into a relationship than he already had. He'd deal with it later.

After Finn implanted the transponder—Drew did not cry, which meant he was going on a field trip with Oz and Will—Drew turned into Proactive Great Grandpa and declared that if there was even a slim chance that Will would engage in activities of the bouncy kind, he needed to do something about it. He dragged Will to the doctor, and I sat in the waiting room with him while Will was taken to a back room and given an implant of his own, one that would prevent any unexpected tiny Emperors.

And afterward, while they sat on a bench on Union Square so that Will could whine about how much it hurt, he continued to hold his position that it was far too soon for him to consider a physical relationship. He was barely at the point where he felt comfortable presuming she wanted anything at all from him.

Drew thought that was all bullshit.

He could call it whatever he wanted, but he was in a relationship. She was going to expect things from him sooner or later.

He also thought that Will needed to invite Aisha to come along while he learned to use the portals. She might believe you, he said, but there's nothing like going through one to drive the point home. They were only going to spend a couple of hours hopping from time to time, just enough to make sure he could navigate without help, and it was a chance for Will to share that part of himself. At least ask her; she might get a kick out of seeing San Francisco in the past. We'll only take her to safe times, and we won't stay for long.

It was the idea of relative safety that convinced her to go; it was an opportunity to see a part of Will's life that was difficult to imagine, where she could see the city through a fresh lens, and be back just two minutes after they left. The worst thing that might happen was Drew barreling through a portal and knocking someone over on the other side.

Again.

She agreed that it sounded like fun, and what was the harm?

That might have been the jinx.

4

Because it was the most private of the portals closest to home, Oz wanted Drew to practice with the one behind the old Hyatt hotel on the Embarcadero. It was tucked into the space between two buildings that were so close together that it was rare anyone even used it as an alley, which meant it wasn't likely that anyone would see us disappear and less likely that anyone would notice us coming out on the other side. And, as the Emperor pointed out, "It's a spot where Drew won't be plowing into any elderly fake monks."

"Hey, I apologized," Drew mumbled.

Aisha was puzzled but seemed to be getting used to that. "Probably not the point of the story, but how do you know it was a fake monk?"

"The number of expletives and high volume were a significant clue," Will said. "If it happens, if you bump into someone on the other side, just apologize and move on. Don't give them a chance to think about how you appeared out of nowhere."

She would be a step behind him, holding onto his hand, so if there was any accidental plowing over of people, he'd be the one doing it. He didn't have a habit of apologizing—the few times it happened he kept moving and didn't look back—but she didn't need to know that. Not yet. There was plenty of time for her to understand how rude he could be.

"All right, hot stuff," Oz said to Drew. "I'm not holding your hand this time. Using the portal is simple: think of a specific date and hold that thought in your head as you step through. You'll wind up when you want, at the same clock time. If you're going through during the day and want to get there at night, think of the time, too. Like, August fifteenth, twenty-two-ten, thirteen hundred hours."

"Use the twenty-four-hour clock," Will added. "Specificity is important."

"What if I just want to follow you but don't know what day you're headed for?"

"If you're right behind me, just think 'follow Oz.' That will also work if you're using a portal you know for sure I've been through within the last couple of hours. If you're not sure, think 'home,' and it will bring you back to a minute or so after you left."

That was Drew's failsafe. If they became separated, he only needed to find the nearest portal and head for home. Will pushed the point: *home is your safety net*. It shouldn't be the last thing you think of, but the first or second.

"What if she used a different portal? How will I know if she made it back?"

"Call me when you get back," Oz said. "Or text me. If we can't find each other on the other side, I'll head for home, too, and should be there within a minute of you. Just get in touch."

"And if you can't get in touch with her," Will said, "find me or find my father. He can access the computers that control the portals and pinpoint her last entry. That goes for you as well, Oz. Don't waste a lot of time looking for Drew. Come home and find Finn. He'll locate Drew's signal."

He turned to Aisha. "Stick with me, always. You won't be able to get through a portal without one of us, but you can go through as long as you have skin-to-skin contact with me, Oz or Drew. Hell, Wick, too. If you have to, grab him, tell him to think about home, and step in the direction you think the portal is. He can get you there."

"Just think 'follow Will' as he pulls you through."

Now's the time to tell her, dude.

"That's not necessary, Oz. It only matters what I'm thinking. Or in that case, what Wick is thinking."

She scowled. "Then why was I always told to think 'follow Dad' or 'follow the Emperor?' I was always holding someone's hand until I was twelve or thirteen."

He gestured to her ear. "Because you've always had an active transponder. If you'd been thinking anything else, you might have wound up in the wrong When. That was to protect you."

She would have been wishing for Disneyland. It's not like she would have wound up there.

"She could have wished for a trip to Disneyland tomorrow, Wick," Will said. "It would have mattered."

"Well, now I want to go to Disneyland," Drew said. "It doesn't work like that, though, does it?"

"You're limited to moving through time. Dad hasn't quite perfected moving through space as well, not with the portals or the gate. The most he can do is transport to his ship."

Oz wanted to get back to it. "All right, so it really does matter what you're thinking. Good to know. I'll go first, and you just think about following me. Nothing else, just 'follow Oz.' You might feel a little tingle behind your ear as the portal locates you, but don't worry if you don't. It's a subtle sensation."

"And how will I even find a portal if you're not with me?"

"Listen carefully," Will said. "You should be able to hear it now. It's a very faint crackle or sizzle."

Drew leaned in the direction Will pointed, straining to hear. "Huh. Like a drop of water on a hot pan."

"Eventually I'll show you where all the portals are," Oz said. "Once you know where to expect them, it'll be easier to hear when you're near."

"You can show him all the ones you know about," Will said.

"Seriously? I don't know them all?"

Look in the back of your closet.

"What about Wick?" Aisha asked. "How does he even know it's there?"

Will took me off his shoulder and slipped me into the pouch of his sweatshirt. "Like Oz, he can see them. But still, we protect him. His transponder is programmed to default to whoever is carrying him, and he will always be with either me, Oz, or Drew. That way, if his brain hiccups and he starts thinking about shrimp he had at the Ferry building ten years ago, he won't wind up somewhere alone." He tapped the top of my head with his pointy finger. "Your backup transponder is gone. So pay attention."

Drew argued against letting anyone other than Will carry me. "You need him. If I were to get lost, you would still need him."

"If you get lost, I'll find you."

"Just don't get lost," Oz said to Drew. "I kind of need you just as much."

Barf.

Do we have to do this again? I just ate.

Will set one hand under me to keep me steady, and reached for Aisha's hand. "Ready?"

I don't think she answered, because Oz stepped in, Drew followed, and the next thing I knew we were near the fountain on the Plaza, watching her four-year-old self push six-year-old Drew into the water.

*

"Really," Drew snorted. "You had to pick a day when you were being mean to me."

Will directed us toward the back side of the fountain, where it was less likely that Aubrey and Shazia, who watched the whole thing happen but did nothing about it, would see us. Little Drew was balancing along the retaining wall, paying no attention to Oz—which was probably what set her off—and she reached up with both hands, planted them on the back pockets of his jeans, and shoved.

He came up sputtering, took one look, and then chucked the toy truck he'd been clutching, missing her face by only an inch or two.

Little Oz ran to Aubrey, wailing about how mean he was,

but neither mother bent to her will and neither did they allow a guard to step forward to help. Aubrey scolded Oz for starting it, which made her even madder, and within thirty seconds she was whining because Drew got to play in the fountain and she didn't.

"This is what I was telling you," Will told Drew. "Most of the time she was the one starting things. You wouldn't have thrown the truck if Oz wasn't such an instigator."

"I didn't really believe it," Drew said.

"Now wait and watch," Will said. Little Drew climbed out of the fountain, leaving a trail of wet footprints as he went to retrieve his truck. Oz was still pouting; she sat down on the ground and refused to move, stubbornly folding her arms, scowling hard. He picked the truck up, sat down in front of her, and offered her a turn to play with it.

"How'd you know that would happen?" Oz asked Will.

"Because it usually did. You'd pick on him until he couldn't take it, he'd get yelled at for throwing something at you, you'd milk it for all it was worth because it wasn't fair, and then he'd do something to try to make you feel better."

"Remind me again." Drew nudged her shoulder with his. "Why did I fall in love with you?"

"I think because when you were thirteen I promised that when we grew up I'd let you touch my boobs."

"Wait." Will stepped in front of them, blocking the view. "Did you really? This—" he gestured to Drew and then Oz "—began that far back?"

"Sort of, and yeah she did," Drew said. "Now I'm thinking it was just an apology for getting me into trouble so often."

"Maybe," she allowed. "It was definitely rooted in a whole lot of hoping on my part. I wanted boobs and that was not happening fast enough. Then puberty finally exploded all over the place for both of us and you had to get all serious and mature on me. 'Let's be friends. Friends is *good.*'"

"Shut up," he said, trying to not laugh. "Besides, I also said we should get married someday. I still wanted to touch them."

"Not right now, please," Will said.

Little Oz had stopped pouting; she rolled the truck toward

little Drew, and he scooted back so that they could send it speeding between them. After the truck had exchanged hands a few times, she was laughing and he looked relieved.

Aisha hasn't said anything. Maybe she's scared.

"Are you all right?" Will asked her. "First time through can make a person a little queasy. Drew threw up."

"I did not!"

"I'm fine," she said. "It's just—I can see that Aubrey is so much younger, but this doesn't feel any different to me than this morning did. It's like we wandered down the street and we're watching someone who looks like her. Nothing has really changed since then."

She wasn't wrong. This wasn't like going back a few hundred years to when the city was so crowded we would have been jostling against other people. I didn't mind going back when it was like this; I liked seeing little Drew and little Oz picking on each other. But the view was no different than what we saw day to day. The fountain was cleaned regularly, but it hadn't been renovated in the last fifty years. The Ferry Building looked the same. Even the shops that dotted the edge of the Plaza were mostly the same.

"I get that," Oz said. "But I really did want Drew to see this. Want to go see something that will give you warm fuzzies?"

Aisha smiled. "Sure."

We followed Oz again, this time into night. Once we were through the portal, she grabbed Drew's hand and led Will and Aisha down Market, turning a block ahead of where she normally would to get home.

"We need to be on the north side of the Square," she explained. "And we'll need to hang back a little bit, to stay out of the way."

"What are you up to?" Will asked.

She headed up the corner steps to the Square. "I want her to see you when you were the happiest I've ever seen you."

"Oz. When are we?"

Drew turned. "She's right. You were damned happy."

We stopped near the planter on the east side, where we

had a good view of the entry to the royal house. She'd taken us two nights back, hours after Will and Aisha ditched everyone at the restaurant; we were on our way home, and they were near the front door waiting for a taxi. As we crossed Powell Street, she grabbed the front of his shirt and pulled him close for a kiss that went on a lot longer than I remembered.

Drew and Oz were walking down the street toward them, and I was perched on his shoulder; none of us looked like we believed what we were seeing.

Aisha let him take a breath but locked lips with him one more time before getting in the cab.

"Right there," Oz said. "The look on his face. I've seen you happy before, Emperor, but not anything like that."

We lingered a few more minutes, until Jax and Aubrey had arrived, and Jax was pointing Will and Drew in the direction of Fuzzy's bar. He looked our way once, and I thought he'd missed us, but as he trailed behind Will and Drew, his arm shot up over his head.

"Did your father just flip us off?" Will asked.

"I think he flipped *you* off." Oz laughed. "I don't think I've ever seen him do that before. I kind of want to tell on him now. Mom would not be pleased."

"Does that happen often?" Aisha asked. "Not him flipping someone off, I've seen him do that before. You see yourselves lurking about?"

"Not often," Will said. "I did catch these two spying on me when I was eighteen or so. They thought I wouldn't notice, but my father was with them. It didn't take much to make the mental leap to who Oz and Zed likely were."

"Finn had no memory," Oz said. "And thinking about it, that was before he was your father."

"That he knew," Will said. "I'm fairly certain my mother was a week or two along when he showed up in our When."

"Teenage Emperor ordered us to go home...I don't know why, but we did. And guess who was waiting for us on the other side," Oz said, gesturing to Will. "I did it enough times that he finally got pretty pissed off with me."

"You were being nosey," Will said.

"We were curious, that's all. I'm still tempted to go spy on my mom and dad some. They were cute together."

Aisha thought about that. "I could have seen you when I was your age and never had a clue. Are you ever tempted to go back and change something?"

Oz looked away. Tightly, Will said, "Tempted, yes."

Don't tell her about that. Not right now.

"All right," Oz said to Drew. "Your turn. You're leading the way through. Think 'twenty-sixteen, noon.' That's all. It will take us to this date, that year." She turned to Aisha. "It'll be a lot noisier and the number of people will quintuple. Just keep hold of Will until you get your bearings."

I pushed myself deeper into his sweatshirt because I knew I wasn't going to like where we were going. And I was right; as soon as we were through the portal, my ears began to ache for all the noise, and a woman pushing a giant baby stroller was yelling at Oz for not paying attention to where she was going. "And where the hell did you come from?"

Oz shot back, "If you were watching where *you* were going, you'd know!"

"Oz," Will started.

"Well, I'm not wrong."

"Your behavior still matters."

She raised an eyebrow. "Fine, *Dad*."

Drew was more concerned with Aisha. "Too loud?"

"This is like Vegas on New Year's Eve," she said. "But—" she squinted, looking past Will to the street. "Are those *cars?*"

"Awesome, aren't they?" Drew made a beeline for the stairs that in our own When were in front of the royal house. In this When, the building had a giant MACY'S sign on it, and the balcony was four floors higher. It was part of a restaurant that Oz liked to go to; she enjoyed sitting outside at a table, sneaking pieces of food to the pigeon gangs.

Oz hurried to catch up to him. They walked ahead of us, dodging grumpy tourists and pushy panhandlers, and twice Oz had to yank him back before he walked out into traffic. He was headed for Chinatown, which meant being shoulder to shoulder with exhausted tourists not happy about yet another hill to climb. I was all right with the idea as long as I stayed in the sweatshirt, but Drew was practically skipping along and was one inattentive moment way from getting lost or squished by a giant delivery truck.

She made him stop before going past the decorative gate that marked the start of the commercial part of Chinatown so that Will and Aisha could catch up.

"This is the tourist magnet," Will told him. "If you truly want to see the cultural side of Chinatown, we need to go back a block or two."

Drew wasn't after culture. He was caught up in all the colors and sounds and the paper lamps that were strung over the street, tethered between buildings. It was a long stretch of shops that sold the same souvenirs alongside small restaurants that sold nearly identical dishes, and it was exactly what he was looking for. It was part of the charm that drew people to the city by the thousands, and it was far more exotic than the same street in our own When.

"We *are* tourists," Drew reasoned.

"Yeah, we're headed for Pier Thirty Nine," Will grumbled.

He was probably right, because the Pier was a very Drew thing to go see, but Drew kept stopping to admire the cars parked along the street and he was overly thrilled to come upon a line of motorcycles parked one after the other, rear wheels to the curb. It was everything he could do to keep himself from touching one, and it seemed like he was about to until Will told him to take a few steps back.

"Touching another man's motorcycle is considered to be very much the same as touching his girlfriend," Will warned him. "You don't touch, you don't drool, and for God's sake, you don't straddle."

Aisha laughed for the first time since we landed in this When; she leaned into Will, clutching at his arm.

You let people sit on your bike.

Does that mean you'll let them sit on Aisha?

"That's not up to me, Wick."

"Do *not* ask him to tell you anything about these," Oz said. "We'll be here all day hearing about the differences between Japanese and British motorcycles, and why he thinks they were better than the American-made bikes of the same time. And then he'll tell you all about his Triumph and the year they moved from drum brakes to disk brakes, and I hate that I remember any of that."

"Drew and I have had that discussion before," Will assured her. He looked at Drew. "We could ponder the benefits of a two-wheeled Vespa scooter over a three-wheeled Piaggio instead. The Piaggio had an articulated front end which allowed it to lean equally as well as a motorcycle. It was also automatic—"

"Oh my God, no," Oz groaned. "Can we just keep moving? There's more to see than...this."

"But this is amazing," Drew said, pretending to be upset.

We moved on; when Oz reached California Street she turned right, and I thought we would wind up at the Ferry building, but then she got to Sansome and turned left. Will chuckled under his breath, because he knew what she was doing: Drew wanted the sights of the city, and he was about to get a whole lot more of the smell.

"This is certainly...aromatic," Aisha said.

"Sewer line runs along here. But truthfully, a lot of San Francisco smells the same right now. If you stay long enough, you get used to it."

No you don't.

This was off the beaten tourist path, and there weren't nearly as many people walking along here; while there were businesses and cars lining the street, there were also a lot of apartments and nothing to attract someone looking for San Francisco culture. It was quiet, which made arriving at the Wharf even more abrupt for Aisha and Drew.

Pier 39 was a major tourist attraction; it was an outdoor mall stretched out on an old pier, and a definitive part of twenty-first century Fisherman's Wharf. It was brightly colored and had an amusement park feel, and there was no escaping the odor of the seals that had taken over the water on the side of the pier. They'd shown up one day in the nineteen-eighties and refused to leave, becoming almost as much of a draw as the pier itself.

It felt like every person who had ever visited San Francisco was clustered onto the pier at once, and the deeper onto it we were, the quieter Aisha became and the closer to Will she walked.

Drew was bubbling with excitement and wanted to go into every shop he passed; she just wanted to stop and turn around.

The far end of the pier was open to a view of the bay, with Alcatraz in the distance. It was also cold and windy and Aisha was shivering, so after looking out over the water for a few minutes and musing over how different Alcatraz was with the old prison still standing on it, Will told Oz to head for the picnic tables behind the clear acrylic wind barrier. Before he sat down, he took his wallet out and told her to take Drew to get drinks for everyone, because it was time for a break.

She waved him off. "I have cash for this When. Chances are I got it from you, so I'm spending your money anyway."

He pulled me out of the pouch and let me sit on the table. "Are you all right?" he asked her again. "We can go home once they're back. There's a closer portal we can use."

"I think I just need a little more time to adjust. I'm fine."

"It takes some getting used to. I think that's partly why Jax can't get Aubrey to go with him anymore. The adjustment can be a bit unsettling. Well, that and the last time she went with him, they stayed for two weeks and she went home pregnant."

"Well, if that's a side effect—"

"I'm pretty sure Jax had something to do with that."

"All right. Note to self, never do this with Jax."

"Please don't. Well, that, not the portal. Not that—" He took a deep breath. "Wow, I am really not very good at any of this."

"You're better than you think. And you're adorable when you get nervous."

No, you're not. She's being nice. But keep talking because she's not shaking as much.

"Look, I'm sorry Oz chose the other night as a destination. I don't think she considered that it might be intrusive."

"I'm not sorry." She turned on the bench seat but still kept her hand on his arm. "At least now I know it wasn't my imagination telling me that you didn't want to let go."

"I did not. And I owe you thanks."

"What, for pinning you to your own sofa, then getting you all worked up before I went home? I thought that was a bit mean of me."

"I rather enjoyed that. The entire time…I didn't hear a single thing spinning around in your head. And since you didn't roll off the sofa laughing at me, I assume I didn't project anything."

She inched a bit closer. "Why would I laugh?"

"Because half of what I was thinking ran along the lines of 'I have no idea what I'm doing. I have no idea what I'm doing.' And really, I had no idea what I was doing."

"Trust me, hon, you did just fine."

I bet she's lying to you. Ask Oz, she'll be able to tell.

"But it is the truth. I have no idea what you expect me to do. Or want me to do. Or when. Or how. And if I figure it out, I doubt it will meet expectations and may be borderline disappointing."

"Will." Her hand slid up his shoulder, and she toyed with the hair that was just starting to curl near his ear. "I know this is all new for you. You'll tell me if I touch you too much, won't you?"

He leaned into her hand. "Don't stop. I mean that. If I twitch away, it's only because I'm not used to it, but…I don't think you can touch me too often. I will always welcome this from you."

"If you only realized," she said lightly.

"Serious question?" he asked.

She nodded.

"Where do you see this going?"

She stopped playing with his hair. "Oh, no. I did that once and it backfired so hard that I wound up in Las Vegas. This time around, you have to tell me what you want. The other night is as much as I'm willing to risk right now, not until you figure out what you want. I'll give you time, Will, but the first real move is yours."

Great, you'll be a virgin until you're ninety.

"I know what I want," he said, tapping me on the head, "but

I'm also concerned that this is just something we need to get out of our systems, and if it's that?"

"No. It's not that. Not for me. But, God, tell me now if you honestly think it is for you. I'm not going through losing you again. I'll be your friend, Will, but not after being with you and falling all over again."

Kiss her, dude.

He didn't. He ignores all my great ideas.

"Are we starting over," he asked, "or picking up where we left off?"

"This doesn't feel like starting over."

"I'd like to pick up about fifteen minutes before we left off, and I'd like to go with the impulse thought I had before the coldly logical part of my brain decided it would be a fine idea to break your heart."

She waited.

"I wanted everything you did, absent having a child and that only because I never should. I wanted every single thing you said you wanted with me."

"And now?"

"I think I still want that."

Like you're not sure. Tell her you're sure.

He didn't tell her. He waited for her to say what she wanted.

I think he tensed up a little bit, in case what she wanted was going to upset him.

She rubbed her hand over his arm and sighed. "Will, I never stopped wanting that. Even through my marriage and a dozen relationships, it's really all I wanted. When I moved back, a huge part of me hoped that somehow you'd find your way back to me." She laughed lightly. "I knew the woman you were dancing with at your birthday party wasn't your wife. I kept up with the public details and all the gossip websites that named you as the country's most eligible and most mysterious bachelor."

"The websites." He rolled his eyes. "I never understood that. Why is there any interest in someone known to be so stiff and outwardly irritable? And for some inexplicable reason, there was a win-a-date contest once. No one bothered to clear it with me first. I don't know who won, but I'm afraid they were disappointed when I didn't show."

"I entered that contest," she confessed, laughing at herself. "But I can tell you who won."

He raised an eyebrow.

"A guy named Dennis Broadman, and if I remember correctly, he was a mechanic in Portland and wanted to spend an evening talking motorcycles with you. He was also offering you a ride, though it was never clear whether he had a motorcycle or not."

"I'm sorry to disappoint him."

"You are aware that some of the gossip surrounding you is whether or not you're gay?"

"I'm aware. I've never addressed it because it's not something that needs to be addressed. But no one has ever asked, to be honest."

"And if they had?"

"I take that back. My father asked, before he was even my father. I told him I was not relationship material. But had I been asked publicly? I most likely would have answered that while I consider the inquiry inoffensive, it's unimportant. I'm celibate."

"Oh, sweetheart...that just would have sent the crazies into overdrive, wanting to be the one you gave that up for. You would have had men and women trying to get past the royal guard at home, just on the chance they might get to talk to you."

"Then I'm glad they never asked."

"And now?" she asked. "Are you still committed to being celibate? I don't think I can do the whole relationship thing if you are. Friends, yes, but sweetie, there are so many things I *really* want to do to you. With you."

"I'm not. But..." He sighed sharply. "I am so far out of my element here, and there are things you still need to know."

"We'll deal. Stop worrying. We can go as slow as you want, as long as we eventually get there."

Now would be the time to kiss her.

He didn't.

I know he wanted to say more, but Oz and Drew were back, and he was carrying a tray loaded down with food. "I'm hungry. I figured you might be, too."

I'm hungry.

"I got you some fish, Wick. The only shrimp they had was fried, and I know that's not your favorite."

Fish is fine. I enjoy fish.

"It's grilled, so you don't have to worry about the coating. And I asked, they didn't use garlic or onions or even pepper. There might be a little salt, but not too much."

I think I love you now.

Of all the things the Emperor ever translated for me, that had to be one of them. I couldn't even take it back because Will would just shrug it off and not tell him.

It was good fish. Almost worthy of a declaration of affections.

The burgers he bought for everyone else must have been good, too, because he ate his and then half of Oz's, and the only reason he didn't finish Aisha's was because she started ripping apart what she couldn't eat, and she tossed it to the seagulls before she knew he was more than willing to sacrifice his stomach in order to not waste food.

"You don't throw away meat in front of him anymore," Will said. "And when he's dead, if there's an afterlife, he's going to find every animal he consumed in his lifetime, and thank them."

Oz scowled. "Don't make fun of him."

"I'm not, truly. He's made me more conscious of what I do with the food I have. If I wouldn't waste Wick's life on an impulse, then I shouldn't waste the food that came from the life of another animal."

"And Drew made you see that."

"Indeed, somewhere near the Colorado-Kansas border, a lesson made more poignant when he ate the fish I'd caught and killed, even though he hates the taste. Though he did beg me to not kill a bunny. Cute furry things apparently cross a line."

"Why didn't I know this about you?" Oz asked Drew. "And do you understand the concept of leftovers?"

He gives me leftovers sometimes.

"We're not at home right now," he said, shrugging. "If we were, I'd have set the rest of your burger aside to give to Wick as a snack later. And I don't want to be a dick about it, so I'm not going to make a big deal over three uneaten bites of your lunch."

"Well, now I feel a little bit guilty," Aisha said.

Drew shook his head. "You didn't throw it in the trash, you fed it to the birds. That wasn't wasteful. That was kind."

"Tell that to the people sitting two tables over who now have seagulls pestering them for more," Will said. "All right. Where to now, Andrew? This will be your pick and your lead."

"How far into the future can we go?"

"Not at all, and you know that," Will said. "But not only for the reasons we told Oz when she was little."

"Then why?" she asked.

"We don't know the condition of the equipment that keeps the portals open past the most current date of my father's When. It's likely that they're open and functional at least fifty years beyond that, but we still don't know what we'd be walking into."

"So it's possible, just not a good idea?"

"We could revisit my childhood or a few years beyond when I left, but I would rather not. Although I did tell you I would take you there one day, if you wanted, and I still will."

Drew shook his head. "Going into the future would be trippy, but let's not pick scabs open today. Let's shoot for something fun. Or different. When did San Francisco look like something else?"

Will thought about it for a minute. "Early nineteen-eighties," he said. "Our clothing would still mostly fit in, but you'll be horrified at the sight of the freeway that cut the Embarcadero off from the city skyline."

"Well, sure, make it sound like a lot of fun," Oz deadpanned.

"It's worth seeing. If you like, I can give him the date of the earthquake that nearly brought it down. That at least would be of historical significance."

Oz tilted her head. "Aw, that's cute. Your history teacher side is coming out to play."

"Ozzie, I swear—"

"You bring it on yourself," Drew said. "But yeah, no earthquakes. What date do I think of?"

"Nineteen-eighty," Will said. "That's all you need. It will bring us to this date, that year."

"Nineteen-eighty," Drew repeated. "Simple enough."

We headed back to the portal behind the old Hyatt—which wasn't old anymore, it was still operating as a hotel—and when Oz gestured for him to go first, Drew said again, "Nineteen-eighty," and stepped through.

5

Water lapped at the Emperor's heels and fog swirled around us. It was eerily quiet; instead of the chaotic noise of fifty thousand people jostling their way through the financial district of San Francisco, there was the gentle pull of water splashing onto the shore. Floating through the fog was the song of birds that sounded nothing like the fat pigeons that normally reigned over the streets and claustrophobic alleyways. That angry cooing of feathery beggars had turned into a soft, lilting melody, and I didn't trust it any more than I did the pigeons.

The city was in ruins; buildings that should have reached into the sky were broken down into crumbled bricks, with dust and stones left to outline the graves of their decay. The old Hyatt was a line of scattered pebbles that spilled into the water. The Ferry building was gone, along with the Embarcadero. Behind us was the bay and we stood at its new shoreline, and ahead was a forest that stretched impossibly into San Francisco's downtown district.

"Drew," Oz said, her words floating on breath, "where did you take us?"

To a beach with no sand.

We stood on dirt that was inexplicably dry for being at water's edge. Will looked down, and then out to the bay. The Bay Bridge—the Emperor's Bridge, the place where he had once saved the life of the young prince who would become king—was a skeleton, bent and broken with ragged beams that ended only a mile out from the city. Treasure Island was a faint outline etched behind the fog. Drew spun on his heels, looking in all directions, and was as confused as Oz; this was not what he expected.

"Tell me exactly what you thought when you stepped into the portal," Will said. He was calm, but I wasn't sure that would last.

"What Oz told me to think. Nineteen-eighty."

"What else?"

"Emperor," Oz said. "He knows better."

"What else?" Will insisted.

The color drained from Drew's face as his thoughts came back to him. "I stepped in, and thought it was too bad we couldn't go forward a thousand years. It was super quick, though. I was muttering nineteen-eighty over and over."

Will let out an exasperated sigh.

"We're in twenty-nine-eighty?" Oz blurted. "How?"

"Further." Will said. "It was abstract enough that the portal would have moved us a thousand years beyond Drew's When. We could be in thirty-four-sixteen."

"Oh my God." Drew's hands went to his head. "I am so sorry."

Oz reached out and pulled his arms down. "Relax. We turn around and go home. No harm, no foul. And now we know the world is still here in a thousand years, even if it isn't what we might have hoped for."

Someone broke San Francisco. Earthquake?

"It could simply be the erosion of time," Will answered. "We would need to explore further inland to know for sure, but I don't think that's a good idea."

"If we didn't stray too far from the portal—" Oz started, but Will was shaking his head before she could get the entire thought out.

"We have no compelling reason to stay. This—" he gestured in a wide circle "—is enough. We can see that the city is gone, and we would truly be better served to port to a time when we have a fundamental understanding of the political and cultural climate."

"Finn would be thrilled to know there's a future," Oz said. "You know he'll want details."

He wasn't yielding. Without a good enough reason to risk everyone's safety, we were going home.

"Then what's the point of being able to travel in time?" she pressed. "We already know what happened five hundred years ago, and it's just as risky to pop into the past."

He was not happy. "Oz."

"Come on, you know if it were just you and Drew, you'd explore."

"Drew is not going to be my queen someday," Will said evenly. "I will not risk anything more than is necessary—"

"I wouldn't be here if that were true."

"*Oz.*"

There was more, I think, but Aisha tugged on his sleeve and whispered, "Will. Will, we're not alone."

I felt his muscles tense, and his hand went into the pouch of his sweatshirt and under my chest, in case he needed to pull me out quickly. I was ready to jump; once he started to pull, I intended to get out of his way. Oz and Drew parted so that Will could see behind them, and blocking the entry to the portal was a teenaged boy with wild black hair and a scant line of peach fuzz over his upper lip.

If not for the sword in his hand, he would have appeared entirely nonthreatening.

He tilted his head to the right a touch, grinning. "Magicians? Wizards?" he asked hopefully. "Warriors?"

"Travelers," Will said.

Disappointed, the boy sighed. "Useless, then."

Oz took offense. "Don't be so sure about that."

Will exhaled sharply.

"What?" she asked. "We're not wizards but we're not exactly useless."

"We need to go," he insisted.

Oz was still looking at the boy. He was thin and not as tall as she was, and he made no move to lift the sword. He let it dangle in his hand, as if he'd forgotten he was carrying it. "We can at least hear him out."

"Oz!"

The teen took a step closer. "Oz. That's an unusual name for a pretty girl. I've heard it before but I never pictured an Oz as being so pleasant to look at."

"Back off, sword boy," Drew said. "She's taken."

He grinned again. "I wasn't flirting. But she is pretty." He looked at Aisha. "So are you. Quite beautiful."

"Great," Drew said, half under his breath. "We tumbled a thousand years just to meet Don Juan."

The boy finally sheathed his sword. "No, I'm not Don. I'm Shivan." He cocked his head a touch. "That rhymes."

Amused, Drew said, "I stand corrected."

Shivan looked up, squinting against the light. "It's nearly evening. You should get indoors soon."

"Why?" Oz asked.

Puzzled, he answered, "The rain."

"Okay," Drew said. "A little rain never hurt anyone."

"Not a little rain. *The* rain." He looked at Oz uncertainly. "The nightly rain. It will peel your flesh and then melt the meat from your bones."

Again, Will pushed Oz to go home, but she resisted, too interested in the boy to listen to him. "How long until this deadly rain begins?"

"Ten minutes?" he replied. "Could be as much as fifteen. I can take you to shelter if you have none."

"Appreciate the offer," Drew said, looking past him to the portal. "But we don't know you at all, and I'm not apt to trust someone the first two minutes after meeting them, especially someone who walks around with an unsheathed sword."

Shivan's hand rested on the hilt of his sword. "I don't hurt the innocent. I protect them. On the honor of my family, I will not harm you."

"And you are?" Will asked.

"Shivan, son of Yeosof. I am the last of the House of Blackshear."

Oh yeah. We're staying.

*

There was a path that cut through the woods, heading in the same relative direction as Market Street. Shivan led the way along the worn trail, not checking to see if we followed. There were piles of rubble and crumbled half-walls where buildings once stood—a jutting of metal here, stones in untidy stacks there—all lost to centuries of slow decay.

This feels like history.

"Indeed," Will said. "It reminds me of hiking near the ruins of old castles in Scotland. I half expect my grandfather to appear ahead, poking at the stones with his cane."

"Your grandfather likes to vandalize old ruins?" Oz asked, amused.

"Your grandfather is usually right there with him," he answered. "Don't worry about them. I've established a bail fund, just in case."

Oz laughed, but Drew was horrified. "Seriously? You're prepared for them to get arrested?"

"Do you remember my grandfather?" Oz asked. "Of course there's a chance he'll get arrested."

Drew remembered him, but the only certainty he held was that the old king had frightened him as much as the Emperor, and he'd avoided crossing his path.

"Oz is quite a bit like him," Will said.

"Hey. No scaring the fiancé until after he has a ring on his finger," she warned. "Let's just follow the newest Blackshear and find out what the hell is going on here."

"All right, but he should know there's a bail fund for you, too."

Shivan led us to an old hut that seemed as if a sudden sneeze would knock it over. It was framed in fractured metal bits that were folded together to hold walls in place, walls that had been rebuilt with stones taken from the ruins. There were three window wells along the front wall, with wood shutters that opened and closed from inside. The hut leaned a few degrees to the right, propped up by the half dozen water tanks lining the side and back, and on the left side was a thick tree that looked sturdy enough hold it in place if the wind caused it to shift.

Oz mused that based on the distance and direction, buried under the ground a few feet out was the Powell Street transit station. And in the place of the hut Shivan had brought them to, there was a sandwich shop in their own When.

"It's a dojang in my youth," Will said absently.

"Dojo," Oz said.

"Dojang. Taekwondo. I spent several years training here. My dojo was on the other side of Union Square, not far from where you trained."

Shivan's hand was on the doorknob. "I don't understand what you're saying, other than this place is familiar?"

"There's a similar location at our home."

Inside, the hut was dim, lit only by cracks around the wood that covered the exposed windows. There were blankets hanging from the ceiling to the left—made to create private spaces where there were none—and there was a small kitchen to the right. The iron sink had a pump-handled spigot, and there was a large pantry at the end of the counter, its wood door splintered and bowing in the middle. Baskets of fruit lined the counter; apples and pears and grapes, and the sweet aroma was almost strong enough to cover the stench of old grass that slapped at us the moment the door was opened. The rest of the space was a room with a planked wood floor, and instead of furniture, there were crates and bales of hay topped with towels and blankets.

Shivan closed and locked the door and then moved to the far side of the room, where there was a narrow shelf lined with candles. As he began to light them he called out, "Hagar! I brought guests."

From the other side of the closest blanket came a grumpy, "Why?"

"To keep them out of the rain," Shivan said. "Come out, and be nice."

"Your father?" Drew asked.

"No, just a grumpy old wizard with no manners." He lit the rest of the candles, and as he unbuckled his sword's sheath, he gestured to the crates and hay bales. "Sit. It's not comfortable, but it's functional."

Will pulled me out of his sweatshirt before he sat next to Aisha on one of the covered bales. He cocked his head at the same time I did, hearing the first drops of rain ping off the metal roof. Within seconds, the ping became an onslaught, a million wet nails being poured onto the hut.

"Now we wait," Shivan said.

"For how long?" Oz asked.

"It will be safe to go outside in the morning."

"Seriously?" Drew blurted. "My bladder will explode before then."

Shivan pointed to a door that was partially hidden by a blanket hanging on the far wall. "We have modern facilities. Well, mostly modern. You'll still need to pump water...but don't use a lot of it. We'll capture some tonight, but it takes a while to clean and we usually save it for drinking."

The blanket near us fluttered, and from behind it came a much older man. His hair was white and his beard was flecked with spots of black, and his overgrown eyebrows arched angrily. He reminded me of the old king in the days after his queen passed away; there was a sadness that clung to him, and a weariness that pressed him down, making him hunch over to allow for the pain.

Hagar carried the same weight of grief as the old King, as if another loss would shatter his bones.

"There's plenty of water, Shivan." His tired voice rumbled deeply. "That awful horse hasn't been by for several days. The main storage tank is full. We shouldn't bathe, but there's enough for consumption and hand washing."

"What about food?" Shivan asked.

"More than enough. We have a dozen loaves of bread and twice as many chickens. There's fresh butter and at least four jars of jam. I counted thirty eggs this morning. We're fine."

The wizard wore a long, bright red shirt with a brown belt clasped at his waist, and his pants were rough twill that made me itch looking at them. He reminded me of something familiar, but it wasn't until he sat down that I realized.

Give him a hat. He'll look like a garden gnome.

"This is Hagar," Shivan said. "He's almost always in a bad mood."

"I'm in a bad mood because I'm locked in here every night with a fifteen-year-old boy who thinks he can save the world yet cannot fathom that his clothing doesn't belong in a heap on the floor." He told Shivan to bring a pitcher and mugs from the cupboard. "Truly, ignore the boy. There's enough drinking water to last for a week or more."

"Until your horse returns," Drew ventured.

Hagar snorted. "He's not my horse."

Shivan brought the pitcher in on a tray, and set it on a hay bale in the center of the room. "I'm sorry, I didn't get all of your names."

Before any of them could answer, Hagar waved him off. "I know who they are." He gestured to Aisha. "Except for you. You are a pleasant surprise."

"All right," Will said, skeptical.

Hagar pointed at them one by one. "The Emperor. The Princess Oz. The Prince Andrew." He tapped the side of his head with his pointy finger. "I know things. I'm a wizard."

Shivan was quick to add, "He's a Wizard of Light. He's not like Tobias."

"And that is?" Oz prompted.

"Evil wrapped in flesh."

"I've met evil wrapped in flesh," she said. "I'd rather not do that again."

"Tobias is a Wizard of Dark. He's the one who brings the rains every night."

Sounds like a fun guy.

Will's curiosity finally began to bubble. "Why? What's the purpose?"

"He uses the rain to control the elves," Shivan explained, as if of course that made sense.

Drew choked back laughter, trying to cover it with a cough.

"The rain destroys most of their work," Hagar added. "It becomes a daily struggle to survive. Tobias flattens their crops each evening and by morning the food has rotted and returned to earth. If he's in a reasonable mood, there's new growth by mid-morning. It's a tortured existence, trying to carry on and harvest enough to survive. It keeps them on the slimmest edge of survival—the mortality rate is high, especially among the foundlings. The adults are frail and the foundlings...they no longer thrive."

"And the waters," Shivan reminded him.

Hagar nodded. "They have such a short time to fish before he begins to churn the waters in the bay. One elf can bring in a catch large enough to feed two or three families for the night, but will lose it—and his life—if he doesn't dock and get to shelter in time."

"Why hasn't anyone blasted this tyrant from power?" Drew asked.

Hagar reminded them of Tobias's magic and the frailty of the elves. He looked at Oz and said, "Imagine a small band of sickly, ill-armed men storming your King. How far would they get?"

"They'd never get close," she said. "The royal guard alone could stop them."

"And yet, one person trained well enough, with the right people at his side..." Hagar looked to Shivan. "We have the one. We need those who can strongly stand with him."

"Killing him is my purpose in life," Shivan said. "I'm not strong enough yet, and Hagar's magic is becoming weak. I won't give up, but... We need help."

6

Hagar and Shivan offered their beds, but Will—knowing he was not likely to sleep—declined. Drew and Oz thought they'd be fine on the floor, and Aisha said nothing. She'd said a lot of nothing all day, and once Drew and Oz were asleep, Will sat on the floor close to her and asked if she was all right.

It was overwhelming; she knew she was feeling a mixture of curiosity and excitement, but there was a part of her brain that refused to engage and believe this was real. That disconnect frightened her. "If I'm overly quiet...I also don't want to say the wrong thing. I don't know what to make of any of this, Will. I'll leave the talking to you."

"Once the rain lets up we can go home," he said. "This was supposed to be about letting Drew practice with the portals, not about stirring up fear or placing you in an uncomfortable position."

She slid her hand down his leg, ignoring his sharp intake of breath. "You'd take me home and then come right back. You want to know more, I can feel that. So do Oz and Drew. Those two are excited about this. I'm almost surprised Drew didn't start squealing at the idea that there might be some adventure coming his way."

He admitted to curiosity and wanted to stay long enough

to see what the real issue was. "Hagar knows who we are. I want to know how."

"Books may exist still, you know," she said. "If I can pick up a book and read about King Henry the eighth, they can read about King Jackson and his Emperor. You'll each be part of history."

"Yes, but he showed no surprise at our presence. Knowing who we are is simple, but expecting us? There has to be a reason."

"Ask him."

She's right, you know. Stop making things complicated.

"Your input is not required, Wick."

"What wise thing did you tell him?" she asked me.

"He agrees with you," Will said.

She patted her lap, inviting me onto it. "I knew there was a reason I liked you so much, Wick. You're very smart." I head bonked her, because compliments should always be acknowledged, otherwise it would just be rude. "You know, somehow I always thought you were Jax's cat. How did I not know you were Will's?"

"It's a little complicated."

No, it really isn't.

"He was our family pet, until my dad realized who I was. Then he lived with Jax...now he spends his time where he chooses, and lately it's been with Drew. So really, he belongs to no one. He takes care of us all."

I'm your anchor.

"Yes, you are."

But maybe not for much longer.

"What do you mean?"

All you need is a strong attachment. Aisha might be your next anchor. That's a good thing. I mean, I think I'll always be here for you but it would make me happy if you had more.

"I would like that, too, Mister Wick. As long as you stick around."

Aisha tucked a finger under my chin to rub it. "And what words of wisdom did you have now?"

"He's rooting for us," Will said.

"Funny enough, so am I."

Drew's sleepy voice cut into their moment. "Oh, my God, Will, just kiss her. Now I know how Zed felt. Kiss her and then go the hell to sleep."

Better do it before Drew gets up and does it for you.

On a scale of one to ten, I rated him a 5.6—mostly for effort.

"I rarely sleep," he told her, whispering to keep Drew happy. "You should at least try."

She wanted to know if he'd be all right staying with her or if proximity was an issue. She understood if he wanted to not-sleep across the room, but she'd be happier if he stayed where he was.

An hour later he was flat on his back with her head on his shoulder. I curled up on his chest, so that he could hear me.

Don't plant dreams in her head. Not yet.

"I had no plans for that," he whispered.

Maybe not, but if you wish something when you touch her...

"It wouldn't hurt if she heard my truest wish."

Will, you're the one who needs to fly. Don't risk burning her.

"I don't know what that means."

Yeah, you do.

*

As abruptly as it began, the rain stopped. The final drops of water exploded off the roof and the sudden quiet startled me enough that I twitched off my spot on the Emperor's chest and slid to the floor. It would have been easier if not for the fact that at some point during the night I crawled under his t-shirt to steal the warms from his skin. I was trapped between his ribs and his shirt, on my back, and the quickest way out would have drawn blood.

I wiggled around, trying to keep my face out of his armpit and my back claws from digging into his ribs. He peeled the shirt away just far enough for me to slide out, and then carefully slipped his other arm out from under Aisha's head. His sweatshirt was tucked around her; I was cold, but he seemed fine, even with his arms bare and shirt pulled halfway up.

Oz and Drew were wrapped around each other so tightly I wasn't sure how they would ever become untangled. It was like the sleeping bag all over again; they might have spent part of the night playing baseball, but more than that she was trying to steal warms from him the way I leeched them off Will.

He put a finger to his lips—be quiet, don't wake anyone—and slowly got up. The front door creaked as he pulled it open, a soft moan of an old man trying to get out of a chair after a long, unintended nap, and he hesitated, listening for an unhappy sleeper being disturbed. When no one yelled or threw anything at him, he opened the door the rest of the way. I tapped his leg—pick me up—and he carried me outside. He wanted to see the damage from rain that had fallen that hard for that long, and stepped onto the path to get a good look around. I wanted to steal more warms from him and as long as he was holding me, at least part of me wouldn't be cold.

Leaves were still firmly attached to the trees and the ground was dry under Will's feet; there was no sign that it had rained at all. I inhaled deeply; there was no hint of petrichor, no wafting aroma of wet dust and dirt, no scent of newly washed grass. The ground was dry and there were no puddles along the path. He looked toward the bay, peering through thin fog as baby waves lapped onto the shore, and if he heard Aisha step outside, he didn't react.

She slipped her arms around him, and then just as quickly stepped away. "I'm sorry," she started.

He turned around. "You can touch me, Aisha. From you I welcome it, and I need to get used to it."

Yeah, well, didn't that sound clinically romantic?

You need practice. Tell her that her bedhead is especially attractive.

"Good." She lifted his arm and made him put it around her shoulders. "Now what are you looking at so hard?"

He pointed out how dry the ground was, and how little moisture clung to the trees. She did the same things he had—

checking up and down the path—and noted that the ground gradually sloped toward the bay, which might allow for some runoff, but that did nothing to account for the moisture the ground should have absorbed and the puddles that should be spotting the landscape.

"Hard rain leaves puddles," she said. "Rain that hard should have left deep pockets in the dirt."

Shivan's voice cracked behind them. "Dark magic."

"Magic," Will repeated.

"Well, do you have a better reason?" he asked.

"There must be a scientific explanation."

Hagar was right behind Shivan. "Science. Magic. What difference does it make? It happens every day. Whatever the cause and no matter the effect, Tobias controls it and is irritatingly punctual in his daily delivery."

"Do you actually know this, or is it a guess?"

"A well-educated guess," Hagar said. "Now come back inside. I'll make something to break the fast."

Shivan stopped them before they could go inside. "Fair warning. Hagar's idea of breakfast food is questionable. Every morning he consumes the unborn children of the chickens Kilfin raises."

"So," Will ventured, "eggs?"

Shivan's nose crinkled with disgust. "I know, and I'm sorry. But it's his house, so we eat his food. If you put salt on them, or even sweet syrup, they go down easier."

I'd eat an egg. Can I have an egg?

"I'll share with you," Will said as the followed Shivan back into the hut. "And don't worry, we'll find something more cat-food like for you today."

"I have food for Mister Wick." Hagar said. "Fish stew. Bits of rice, a tiny bit of potato, but plenty of fish. Is that acceptable?"

I head bonked him.

"Thank you." Will set me on the floor, near his feet. "He's always hungry, and I appreciate that you considered him."

"The inimitable Mister Wick must be kept well fed. It's my honor."

Finally, someone appreciates me.

Take notes, Emperor.

When the food was ready and they were all sitting together on the floor, using the hay bales as tables, Will asked Hagar how he knew of them. "We're not of here," he pointed out.

"But you are. You're not of this time, but you are of here."

"Yeah, we're gonna need more to go on than that," Drew said.

"You're part of the prophecy," Hagar said. "Shivan is the Lord of Prophecy. You are the Trident. Without you, he has no hope of victory."

No pressure.

"I *might* be part of the prophecy," Shivan added. "I might just be in the way."

"And the prophecy is?" Will prompted.

Hagar closed his eyes and recited it from memory.

The Lord of Prophecy stands not alone, the Trident by his side
The warriors of time long past; the head, the heart, the brawn
The evil rains of darkness fall, to peel the flesh from bone
One man, noble, light of heart, will stand before the Dark
A bloodless sword he wields with might and battle skills not won
The Lord will draw the life from Death, and freedom then will fall.

Drew muttered to himself, "Well, that needs work." Will was more curious about the particulars. What does it truly mean?

It was simple, Hagar thought. He, Oz, and Drew were clearly the Trident, the warriors from another time. Oz balked; what made him think they were from another time?

He gestured to their clothing, an eyebrow raised.

"Hey," Drew said. "We could be from Canada. You don't know."

"I do know," he said. "You're not that polite."

7

Down the path from Hagar's hut there was a clearing, and near the center of it was a tall stack of hay bales covered with a thick canvas tarp that was tucked in at the bottom, with rope around the base to keep it tight. Shivan repeatedly lunged at it with his sword; he stabbed, withdrew, spun about on his heels, and struck again.

We stood at the clearing's edge and watched as he demonstrated his skills. Oz had one hand over her mouth, amused, and Drew scowled, confused. Will was less obvious in his assessment until he asked—not as kindly as he likely meant—if Hagar really thought *this* boy was the one meant to fulfill the prophecy.

There were no others to consider. "He's the last of his House. He was born from a line of nobility and is as eager and innocent as they come. He wants nothing more than freedom for all in Saint Francis, in spite of the risks to himself. He's quite willing to have the Blackshear name die with him if it means extracting Tobias from power."

That would suck.

No more sticky little Oz or Zed people?

"He's truly the last?" Will asked.

"There are others, but it's not likely that they would admit to it if they even know they're part of the family. They certainly have no idea they descended from kings and queens. Most live as members of the Adomondai clan. And regardless, Shivan is the last direct royal Blackshear descendent."

"Where did Adomondai come from?" Oz asked.

"It was a name taken by Yeosof's great, great grandfather to hide his children from the darkness he felt coming. His children knew the truth and have passed it on, and one day Shivan hopes that he can find them all, to bring together the family that has been lost to both fear and exodus." He urged Oz to look at him closely. "You know I speak the truth."

"Maybe. Lie to me."

He considered it. "I find the disruption of the rain every night to be quite pleasant."

She shrugged. "Half lie, half truth, I think."

"All right. I know much about you."

"Okay."

"You're quite vile, and Prince Andrew only wants to marry you because no one else will, and the royal line must go on."

She grinned. "There it is. Your lie is aggressively blue. It swirls like India ink dropped into water."

"And my truth?"

"Pink, actually," she said. "More magenta, with that same watery swirl."

"I find that lovely," Hagar said. "Are we all the same, or does each person have their own colors?"

"Everyone is unique."

Aisha broke her stretch of quiet. "I am so confused right now."

Welcome to my world.

Will tried to explain Oz's synesthesia; she saw every sound as a color, and we were each surrounded by a cloud of swirling hues generated by our heartbeats and breath, and she could especially see the changes in colors when anyone spoke. "Lie to her, and the colors in which you speak change."

"Wow. That's...good to know." She gestured to Will. "What are his colors?"

"He keeps a steady pale blue," Oz said. "It's almost like the sky on a really clear morning. He doesn't seem to lie."

"You caught me in one recently," he admitted.

"Ah, yeah. When you said you didn't want us to celebrate your birthday. Aren't you glad now we did?"

"Very."

"And it's orange," she said to Aisha. "His lie is the prettiest candy orange."

What about me? I want to know.

"I always see wisps of white around you," she said when Will told her what I wanted to know. "But you don't lie, do you?"

I don't know if I can.

"Give it a try," Will urged. When I balked—lying makes the Queen sad, and part of my job description is making her happy—he promised she would understand. It helps Oz to see both sides of people, and for this, I was people.

I watched Shivan swing the sword over his head and then fall clumsily forward, bouncing off the hay stack.

He's very talented.

Oz crouched next to me, and tickled me under my chin. "That's very unusual, Mister Wick."

I don't have a color?

"You have a beautiful, soft rainbow of colors. I've only seen that in one other person. My mom has the same wispy white, and the rare times she lies, she has the same wonderful rainbow."

"Maybe because she only lies to protect someone's feelings," Drew ventured.

I like being like Aubrey. Maybe we're related.

"Maybe it's because you're very much alike," Will said. "Although you're kind of a pain in the ass sometimes."

You and Drew are shades of the same color. But he lies in red.

"Perhaps if I practice, I can elevate my lies from orange to red."

Probably. It might be genetic.

He considered that for a moment. "Oz...what are Jax's colors? And yours?"

Jax was a pale yellow and soft orange. Oz's were smoky blue and fuchsia. "Why?" she asked.

"Wick was curious if there was a genetic thread. I'd be interested in plotting it out sometime. Drew and I have a similar color pattern."

"It's possible. Finn—"

She lost her train of thought when Shivan raised his sword over his head and it flew out of his hand, skittering on the ground. It stopped only a few feet near me, and Will finally said something.

"The first order of business is teaching this boy to fight. Flailing about is going to get him and whoever is near him killed. Minus his enemy."

"The prophecy does say he has no battle skills," Drew pointed out.

Shivan ran to pick the sword up, muttered, "Sorry," and ran back. He was clearly tiring, and when he tried to swing the sword over his head again, the weight of it pulled at him and he fell, landing on his backside.

"Perhaps now is a good time for an explanation of how you intended for this boy to defeat someone you paint as being a powerful wizard. It would take years to hone his skills with a sword well enough to serve him even a small measure of success. I presume Tobias has guards?"

"He surrounds himself with Shedu warriors," Hagar said. "But we're not alone in this. Kilfin has been roaming the provinces near Saint Francis to raise an army of our own. He made a dozen trips last year, and a dozen the year before and has gathered more than a thousand willing fighters. I expect him to return soon with news of one more band of men and women who have fallen outside of Tobias's reach, but who want him gone regardless."

"And Tobias? Where is he?"

Hagar pointed west, toward the ocean. "He's taken the ancient white house on the hill. It should have crumbled a hundred years ago. I have hopes that some of his magic is being diverted to keep it intact."

"The Cliff House," Oz guessed.

"The restaurant?" Drew asked. "Isn't that the place I was

going to take you on a date but we wound up getting pizza with Zed instead when Sophia had to go to France instead of visiting here and he was super depressed about it?"

"It is, and not exactly relevant right now."

"Well, yeah, but you have to admit, he's gone bat crap crazy over her."

"Focus, Drew."

Will wasn't paying attention to the musings about Zed and his long-distance love life. "It would be a reasonable place to hide. Unless the geography has changed, there is no approach from any side that could easily be hidden. The fewer attack zones, the fewer he needs on guard." He gestured to Hagar's hut. "Is there a specific purpose to having your home here, in the woods and close to the bay?"

"It's been my home for decades, long before Tobias took control," Hagar said. "From here, I have ready access to all the quarters in Saint Francis. I can observe areas where the elves are held. They work from the Marina, through Castro and Haight, and some reside in Sunset and Richmond. Many have homes in Presidio, but the distance to the orchards and wheat fields is too far for most to endure on foot every day. I have privacy, but I am not secluded."

Aisha scowled. She was thinking the same thing Will was: wheat and orchards, in San Francisco? Vineyards, perhaps; there were wine grapes grown on Treasure Island, but the city itself was not especially habitable for crops. The trees could be explained; as people moved away and the population thinned, as buildings crumbled to dust and made way for nature, the trees took over. Active orchards made little sense, even to me.

Bet he's gonna say it's magic.

Shivan sat in the dirt, staring at the canvas-covered hay, willing the whole thing to explode.

"How far does Tobias's reach extend?" Will asked.

"He controls the rain over all of Saint Francis," Hagar said. "He controls the people only in the western quarters. There are very few left on the eastern side."

"Can we move about freely?"

"Cautiously. There are Shedu who patrol in the eastern quarters."

Will wanted to reach the marina, get as close to it as they could get without falling into any gray areas of Tobias's control. If they could travel within the city and left soon, they could get there and back before the rain began.

Hagar didn't share his sense of travel time. "There are places for shelter near the water. Old inns and abandoned homes. We could be there by late afternoon and take refuge in the converted cannery. It hasn't been overly long since people lived there, so it should be comfortable for the night. We'll have water, but will need to bring food."

Will seemed dubious that it would take that long to get there; he could jog it in half an hour, and that would be if he took his time. If he walked, pacing for a casual stroll, he could make it in less than an hour and knew that Oz and Drew could match his stride. And Aisha, even if she wasn't as fast, wasn't going to take that long.

He didn't account for Hagar's age and physical condition, though, and the only thing that kept him from picking the old wizard up to speed up the process was not wanting to embarrass him. We walked slowly, and Shivan pulled a wooden wagon loaded with food behind him.

It was late afternoon when we got there, to the place we knew as Ghirardelli Square. Water lapped at its foundation; the aquatic park where Zed parked his skiff after work was long gone, Fort Mason was under water, and the Marina had moved inland by half a mile.

We were separated from the water by a waist-high brick wall. Shivan leaned over it to look down, and commented casually, "No swimming. There are sharks down there."

I backed away.

No one else acted like he was serious, but I wasn't taking any chances. Sharks bite, and I am not food.

8

Oz had a hard time processing that the spot on which she stood was once part of Ghirardelli Square. The old chocolate factory once stood high above the water line, with the aquatic park ahead of it by a quarter mile. Gone was the park and the municipal pier, gone was Fisherman's Wharf, and gone was the picture she had in her mind, the vision of what her city would always be.

"This geographical shift was expected," Will told her. "In fact, it was expected long before you were born. It was largely an artificial construct that was ill-maintained."

"Built on a lot of silt and rock," Drew added. "It was rebuilt a few times, but if technology failed..."

That didn't make her feel any better. "It's just sad to think that if it keeps up, San Francisco will be gone someday."

"I wouldn't worry about it becoming completely submerged," Will said. "I suspect that long before then, it will fall to an earthquake."

"Thanks," she grumbled. "That makes me feel so much better."

I would worry about the sharks. What if they've evolved and have feet and can walk up here now?

"That would take considerably longer than a thousand years, Wick," Will said.

Aisha picked me up. "Are you worried about something?"

"Being eaten," Will answered for me. "He has an unnatural fear of pigeons. And now, apparently, sharks as well."

The pigeons formed a gang. You know they did. They're just waiting for the right time to get me.

"I'll hold onto you," Aisha whispered into my ear. Her breath tickled, but I didn't want to pull away, so I rubbed my face against hers instead. "No one is going to eat you. I don't care how hungry they get."

Will reached over to scratch my head. "We established last year that he is not food. It was a concern while we hiked through Colorado. He knows we would starve first."

Shivan couldn't have cared less about my fears. "You spend a lot of time talking to that cat. He doesn't understand you, you know. He's just a cat."

Hey. And I thought I liked you.

Hagar's hand was on the door to the building he planned on using for shelter. "You don't know as much as you think you do, Shivan," he said. "They understand each other quite well."

He'd taken us to an old, abandoned inn that had been remodeled from an equally abandoned cannery, which long ago was a chocolate shop frequented by tourists. It was not as dirty inside as I expected, and the lack of dust made me think someone used it often. There was a large common area with overstuffed chairs that were not constructed from hay bales and towels, and there was a squat, round fireplace in the center of the room. Best of all, nothing smelled stale. Once we were all inside, Hagar reached behind the door to flip a switch, and the lights came on.

"Not all technology is lost," he said. "Places with plenty of sun still have light."

But where do you get the light bulbs?

I blinked and then tried to look at one with my eyes squinted. It was like one of the tiny bright lights that illuminated the royal house; the ceiling at home was peppered with them so that any level of light desired could be selected. Those bulbs were supposed to last a long time, but a thousand years seemed to be stretching it.

Will heard when I asked—his ear twitched—but he didn't relay the question.

Oh. It's arithmetic time, isn't it? Things aren't adding up for you?

Ask Aisha. She teaches math.

He wanted to get back outside; the entire point of being there was to see for himself what happened as the fishermen's boats came in. He was most interested in determining what made the bay water churn, and why they weren't able to simply escape by boating to the Marin County side.

With most of Fort Mason under water, the new shoreline began somewhere near where the walking trails and bike paths behind it used to be. Marina Green was gone, along with the ancient, beautiful houses that looked out onto the bay. Now there were jutting divots in the dirt, with heavy posts dotting the water's edge.

There were a dozen small boats out on the water, far fewer than Will expected. There were only one or two people aboard each one, and none of them were designed for ocean fishing. Will watched quietly for a while, then murmured that at best he would take one of those boats onto a calm lake, and never one that generated any sort of wave force.

"So that's probably why they don't cross the bay and make a run for it," Oz guessed. "It's risky, and they'd be leaving their families behind."

"They probably don't catch much, either," Drew said.

That's sad. So little fish to eat.

Hagar shared his fish stew with me, and now I worried that it was a real sacrifice. If people were only bringing in a few fish at a time, it was probably valuable food.

I can eat something else. Fish feels like gold now.

Tell him, Will. Tell him he can keep his fish.

The old wizard smiled warmly when Will relayed my concern. "I catch my own fish, Mister Wick," Hagar said. "I have plenty because I cheat with magic. You don't need to worry."

"But those guys do," Drew said. The water was beginning to froth. It bubbled at first, like a pot of water on the stove, simmering until enough heat built up that it became a rolling boil. The boats sped toward the shore, until the water was shallow enough for someone to jump out and haul it the rest of the way in. In just a few minutes, every post had a boat tethered to it, and men and women sprinted toward home with heavy, wet bags on their backs.

There was no wind and there had been few waves, but the boats bobbled up and down hard enough that one turned over.

Hagar sighed. "If they stay on the water, the choppiness eventually flips the boats and sends them overboard, and they sink like stones."

"No time to swim for shore?" Oz asked.

"That depends on Tobias's mood. Sometimes they make it, often times they don't."

"Once," Shivan spat. "Only one time has an elf made it to shore, and that was because he thought to jump before the water churned too hard."

Aisha watched as the fishermen disappeared in the distance. "I thought they would be elves," she muttered.

"They are," Hagar said. Then, realizing her confusion, he asked, "Did you expect tiny people with pointy ears who live in trees?"

She laughed at herself. "That's exactly what I thought."

"The elves are simply the working class," he explained. "Foundlings are the youth who are too small to enter the workforce, and the elves are the adults. But they are human, as we all are."

I admit, I was disappointed.

"And those not caught in Tobias's net?" Will pressed. "Such as Shivan's father?"

"Outliers," Shivan answered. "There aren't many in Saint Francis, but my father is one. He raised me in Dogpatch, and then moved into Soma to be closer to help."

"Yeosof is an active outlier, make no mistake," Hagar said. "He would be by his son's side if he could. We have a greater need for his skills."

"He's creating leather armor," Shivan boasted.

That'll certainly stop a sword.

He went on, bragging about his father's shop, where he was piecing together chest plates and leg armor. Aisha only half listened; while he excitedly babbled, she stared out at the Golden Gate Bridge, and I tried to follow her gaze to see what had caught her attention.

Near the center of the bridge, running along the outside edge of one of the towers and jutting far above it, was a thin spire. It was a bluish-gray color but was beginning to turn red, the color creeping from its base upward.

She turned to look east, her eyebrows furled together as she spotted another in the distance. It was sticking up from a spot where the Ferry Building used to be, which meant it was sticking out of the water.

There are glowing sticks in the sky.

Will asked me to be specific; Aisha pointed to the spire in the east, and then said there was another on the bridge. Hagar could not explain either of them; he'd noted the one in the eastern quarter before, but it seemed to have no purpose. "I've always thought it was simply an old relic."

"That old relic is glowing," Aisha said.

Will was curious and wanted to see what would happen, but Shivan pointed to the sky and reminded them that the rain was coming. "Look from the windows if you can, but we have to get inside."

*

The fireplace in the inn was a lot like the fire pit on the roof of the royal house; it was circular and had a stone lip all the way around that I could walk on if I wanted to, but it had real flames where the pit did not. I was not walking on it. I wasn't even getting close. Hagar had flames licking the air above it, and he'd set a heavy metal grate on top so that he could heat up the kettle of stew he'd made Shivan cart from home.

Down the hallway to the left there were rooms with actual

beds, which meant no one had to sleep on the floor. There were also two bathrooms—the facilities, as Shivan insisted on calling them—at the end of the hall, with running water and actual toilets. Will questioned that when I wandered down the hall with him: how is plumbing even possible, given the condition of the city, and who maintains it all?

I wanna know where everything goes when you flush.

"My best guess is into the bay."

I almost felt sorry for the sharks waiting just beyond the retaining wall, but then I considered what they would do to me and decided it wasn't worth the energy.

After he had explored the inn, Will settled into a chair by the fire. He pulled it close to Aisha's, and I had to decide whose lap I wanted most. Drew and Oz were sitting on the floor together even though there were plenty of comfy chairs, and Drew didn't have a squishy lap anymore. Neither did Will, so I jumped onto Aisha and hoped she would be all right with that.

She didn't complain; she also didn't have a squishy lap.

You people have to stop exercising. It's ruining my comfort levels.

"What's the overall plan?" Will asked when Hagar finally sat down.

He looked pained and reluctant to answer. When he hesitated, Shivan jumped in enthusiastically. "I keep practicing with my sword while Kilfin gathers the army. Once everyone is assembled, we fight our way into Tobias's lair, and I kill him."

I expected Drew or Oz to laugh. Aisha's fingers twitched against my back, but she didn't laugh, either. And Will was too composed to insult Shivan's eagerness.

"Sometimes simple is the most effective way to approach a difficult task," he said. "But consider the bigger picture. You kill him and then what? Can Hagar undo whatever it is that brings the rain every night? Have you considered that it's possibly not generated by magic after all? And worse—what if you don't survive long enough to get to him?"

He didn't bristle at the idea but instead pointed to Oz.

"Oz is of noble blood," Hagar said. "She is light of heart."

"That could easily be Drew."

"Prince Andrew is not truly of noble blood."

"Not anymore," Drew agreed.

"And you, Emperor. You are of noble blood."

"But not light of heart," Will said.

I looked up at Aisha; she was confused but waiting to ask what he meant.

"There are shadows. You aren't consumed with the dark, but no, you are not pure. You have killed—"

"Yeah, well so have I," Oz said.

"To protect yourself," Drew pointed out.

"And the lives the Emperor took were to protect us. He's never just outright killed someone. There's always been a damned good reason."

Hagar stared at Will for a good, long minute. "Then it's something else." He leaned forward and grabbed Will's bare forearm without asking, and gripped hard enough that he couldn't easily pull away.

"Ah," he sighed. "Your heart was tattered and torn but is newly healed. The shadows will fade. Perhaps it could be you."

"Let's just keep Shivan alive." Will pulled his arm back. "In the morning we should go back to your hut, and we'll begin teaching him to fight without relying on his sword. Oz and Drew can start him with some basic techniques—"

Shivan protested. "But I can fight!"

"—and while they begin, I'd like to explore the eastern side of the city. My gut tells me there are important things in that quarter."

"Really," Shivan went on, "I know how to fight. Kilfin showed me how to wield my sword. I just need more practice."

Oz got up and gestured for him to do the same. She led him away from the fireplace, to a space behind Hagar's chair, and when he was close, she lunged at him, tossing him to the ground before he could react. "Get up," she ordered.

He did, and she quickly slapped her hand against his forehead. "If you can't stop me from doing even that, how can you stop someone from punching you? How can you expect to dodge something like a bat or an axe?"

"I'll have my sword."

"Unsheathe it. Swing it at me."

His eyes went wide, and he looked to Hagar, who simply nodded. He hesitated, but finally pulled the sword out, and with both hands swung it at her head.

Oz ducked, and then came up sharp, plowing the heel of her palm into his stomach.

"Don't rely on that sword, Shivan. You have several weapons on your own body. Learn to use them."

He picked the sword up again and lunged at her, but she spun out of the way and caught his side with her foot.

"Enough," Will said. "You can't beat her, Shivan. But you can certainly learn from her."

He wasn't embarrassed; he was impressed, and suddenly eager to find out the secrets she knew.

Zed would have cried.

Will leaned over to whisper to me. "He would not have. But I agree, Shivan surprises me."

Later, after we'd eaten the stew and they'd cleaned up, Shivan didn't argue when Hagar told him it was time for bed. He needed rest if he planned on keeping up with Oz and Drew. He simply got up, said good night, and then headed down the hallway toward the bedrooms.

"He is the most agreeable kid, like, ever," Drew mused.

"He understands his purpose," Hagar said.

Oz pushed herself up from the floor and reached for Drew's hand. "And I understand the purpose of a bed, and I intend to use it. Shivan isn't the only one who's tired."

Will stopped them before they could leave the room. "Please consider that the walls are thin. If you're not going to sleep—"

"Hey, keep that in mind for yourself," Drew said, grinning.

Doesn't matter. You're going to hear something.

"Wick."

Oz snores sometimes.

He laughed at that. "Are you sure it's not Drew? I know he occasionally snorts in his sleep."

No, I've been right there. She sounds like angry bees.

"The way you communicate with him fascinates me," Hagar said. "How do you do it?"

"Magic," Will said.

"As good a reason as any."

"And you," Will said. "Where does your magic come from?"

Hagar tugged at a thin chain hanging around his neck and pulled a small medallion from under his shirt. It was a bit bigger than the bottom of a beer bottle, and rainbow prisms of light from the fire reflected off of it as he turned it over in his hand. "The ability to harness the magic, I was born with. I apprenticed under the wizard Tereska, and during my first days she gave this to me...it aids in focusing my innate abilities. As I learned, its power grew stronger, and through it I've been able to use the magic I was born with. But as I've aged, its power has grown weaker, and with it my abilities are beginning to falter."

"And Tobias?"

"He was my apprentice." He sighed sadly. "He was a good boy and eager to learn. Very strong, the kind of strength which is only found in those whose bloodlines have magic on both sides. He mastered his gifts long before most do."

He'd been a bright, funny, and gentle child, and was destined to carry on as a wizard of light. Hagar had never looked for any shadows that might be lurking in his soul. Then on one horrid day, he lost everyone he loved. His wife and children, gone in a horrible explosion that brought the distillery showering around them, killing nearly everyone in and near it.

"He was with me when they died. I had insisted he accompany me to meet a young girl who might become his apprentice...he never forgave me for keeping him from them that day. He blames the elves because it was a mistake made by workers that took them from him. In the years since, he's held them hostage to his grief. The elves and his memories."

Will didn't feel sorry for him at all, but he could feel the anguish wrap around Hagar.

"Is there any way to destroy his magic without killing him?"

"I wish there were," Hagar whispered.

Aisha felt the compassion Will did not. "Who is he to you?"

"I've known him since the day he was born. He began his apprenticeship when he was less than ten years old. He married my daughter, fathered my grandchildren. He cried with me when my wife died and carried her body to the priests when I could not. He was a good man—I never once thought to make sure he was *truly* in the light."

Maybe he was. Bad things happen and make good people hate.

There was a beat of quiet; Aisha looked away from him, but Will did not and he made the mental leap over the idea that a part of Hagar was rooting for Tobias.

"We need a concrete plan," Will said. "Kilfin is forming an army. What about the elves themselves? Are they aware?"

"They know war is coming. They know the prophecy."

"Can we get to them?"

"If it's just the two of you, yes. I wouldn't want to take Shivan and Oz and Drew into the fields or the orchards. That many people would be easily noted."

Will decided that in the morning Shivan could take Oz and Drew back to the hut and begin his training, and Hagar could show them the way to the elves.

Hagar agreed, and told them if they wanted time to go there as well as explore the eastern quarter, they needed to leave as soon as the rain stopped. He offered to tend the fire, make sure it was out, if they wanted to retire.

I followed them down the hall to the first open door and sat at Will's feet while he tried to tell her goodnight. He was probably hoping for a kiss before finding a room of his own, but she grabbed his hand and pulled him inside, saying, "Oh, hell no, I am not sleeping here alone."

I ran in and jumped onto the bed before he could scoop me

up and tell her no. He didn't know what to say, but he closed the door and leaned against it, having no clue what to do after that.

"Relax," she said when she realized he was uncomfortable. "Just sleeping."

With a deep breath, he pushed away from the door and stepped over to the bed. He kicked off his shoes and socks and started to get in fully clothed, which would have been at least four kinds of uncomfortable with his jeans and sweatshirt, and I was about to tell him he wasn't going to be happy when she said, "I didn't realize you were that shy."

"Neither did I," he muttered.

"Come on. Drop the pants. I won't look." She tossed her jeans across the foot of the bed and then threw her sweatshirt on top of them.

While she pulled off her socks, he sighed and quietly said, "It's fine." He peeled off his sweatshirt and t-shirt, and then reluctantly took off his jeans.

She'd never seen his tattoos; I don't think she knew he had any to begin with. "Impressive," she said, sliding under the covers. "The tattoos, too."

Ha. She said she wouldn't look.

When he was in bed, she rolled onto her side and put one hand under her head, and the other on his stomach. He sucked a breath in sharply, and she said lightly, "Will, really."

"Your hand is cold," he said.

"Liar." She laughed through her nose a little bit. "Don't worry. Your virtue is safe for the time being."

He set his hand on top of hers and traced a finger over her wrist. "I'd be lying if I said I wasn't at least a little bit disappointed. And a tiny bit relieved."

"Is this really when and where you want us to be together for the first time? I mean, I'm flexible and would happily keep you up all night, but this doesn't feel like what you would want."

"I honestly don't know. But it's a moot point, I think." He took a deep breath. "I—proactively, and as a matter of just-in-case, not that I expect anything, ever—got an implant two days ago and I don't trust it yet."

"Did you really?"

"Drew thought…" He considered what he was saying. "Yes, I took the advice of a twenty-year-old whose sex life started all of ten days ago. He suggested I not wait, and even took me to the appointment."

"He's a wise twenty-year-old. Where is it?"

He guided her hand down to the spot near his belly button. "It's still a bit tender, so please don't press too hard."

She ran a finger over it, making him inhale sharply again.

I don't think it hurt, though.

She pulled her hand away and told him to roll over and kiss her. "Just a kiss or two. Let's start out by seeing how you handle sharing a bed, okay? Wake me if you hear anything rolling around inside in my head."

"All right." His voice sounded thick. "Let me know if you have any dreams that don't feel like they're your own."

I can listen if you want.

"There's that, too. Wick can listen to your dreams. He just needs to be able to put a paw on your head."

"Sleep, Wick," she said. "If he hears my dreams, he hears my dreams. It's all right."

She kissed him again, until I wasn't sure either of them could breathe. When she finally let him up for air, he rolled onto his back and she set her head on his shoulder, closing her eyes.

Will.

Will.

Will.

"What is it?"

Something under the blanket is twitching.

"Shut up, Wick."

9

The wheat fields fit neatly into old city blocks and stretched out in front of us, fuzzy yellow squares that waved in the breath of the breeze. We stood at the edge of the Castro—or just Castro, according to Hagar, who seemed wholly unimpressed that his pockets of Saint Francis bore the names of neighborhoods in San Francisco—watching as a dozen men and women threshed grain by hand. Others carted baskets down the beaten paths, and in the distance, there were guards armed with laser rifles.

That was not the weaponry Will expected. He expected swords and possibly old rifles, but not 25th-century laser ordinance.

Hagar explained simply, "The Shedu have the advantage of Tobias's magic, as well as access to data from long past."

Aisha twitched at the word "data," and it made the Emperor pause, too.

"Aradyn and Lerym," Hagar said, pointing to two of the elves working in the closest of the wheat fields. "Brothers. They're the most likely leaders we will find." He looked a bit longer and then pointed to two others. "Krisf and Jesf, also brothers. They were storytellers who passed along the tales of knowledge until Tobias had their tongues removed."

"Teachers," Will mused.

"In a manner of speaking, yes. Each storyteller had a

special line of history to pass on. Krisf will know of you, of your father, his father, and his father's father. He studied the lines of the nobles, and knows you all."

Maybe better that he can't speak.

Not unless you want to tell Aisha who you and Oz and Drew are.

"How will you be able to talk to them with the guards present?" Aisha asked.

There were four within our sightline. He raised his right hand while clutching his medallion with his left, and began mumbling—it was either Latin or Elvish or Russian for all I knew—and then said that they had at best twenty minutes. For that long, the guards would be unable to move or to speak; they wouldn't realize anything was amiss.

Well, if it's that easy, tell the elves to run.

"It's likely not that easy," Will told me.

"My magic is fading," Hagar said. "I wish it was that easy. Were I fifty years younger, I could match his magic with my own and be done with this."

Aradyn was thin, and not because he was trim and athletic. His thinness was the sort of the long ill-fed, and dripping from him was frailty that hinted of bones easily broken and exhaustion that would cut his years short. His blond hair was cut at odd angles, and he had a short, clipped beard that was patchy near his chin. I felt like he was around the Emperor's age, but he could have been younger and was just beaten down by fatigue and poor nutrition. He startled when Hagar called out his name and lifted his scythe protectively, to ward off the blow he expected. When he realized who was calling him he relaxed, but glanced over his shoulder to make sure there were no guards nearby.

He met us at the edge of the field; Hagar started to introduce Will, but Aradyn cut him off. "Which part of the Trident are you?"

Hagar said "head" at the same time Will said "brawn."

"Remains to be seen, then," Will said.

"And Kilfin? Is the army complete?"

I think he knows more than just the prophecy.

"He hasn't returned."

"Soon, then. Tell him we'll need weapons. Real weapons. Our scythes and sickles won't match the guards' guns."

While they discussed the types of weapons Aradyn thought would be more useful and then how to get them into elfin hands, Aisha stared off into the distance. There was another thin spire of bluish metal. I thought it was in the heart of the Haight, but long distances were never my strong suit so I couldn't be sure.

I used to worry about that, until Will told me that most cats can't see even an eighth as far as I can. Or as many colors. But then he reminded me I think everyone is a shade of pink, and he was chuckling when he said it, so I'm not sure he meant any of it.

I was perched on his shoulder but decided to reach out to Aisha to see if she would let me sit there for a bit. He noticed and carefully moved me over, reminding her that she could set me on the ground if she wanted. I tried to get comfortable on her narrower shoulder and then set a paw on her head. I wanted to listen; it was trickier than listening to peoples' dreams, but every now and then I could do it. And while I could help a bad dream get better, I couldn't put a thought into someone's mind the way Will could. I'd tried that a hundred times, hoping to convince someone to feed me something they shouldn't, but it never worked.

All I wanted was to get an idea what she was thinking. She was noticing odd things around us when Will wasn't. Even walking into the inn, I felt like she saw a puzzle there but wasn't sure what the pieces were or how to connect them. If I could listen, I might be able to help.

She was distracted by me wiggling around on her, so whatever she'd been thinking while she stared at the tower was gone. She reached up to pet me and said I was cute, so I did the only polite thing I could and licked her ear.

"I'll be back tomorrow," Hagar said to Aradyn. "The Emperor and I will discuss the weapons available, and we'll come up with a way to distribute them. I can bind the guards for a time, but how long is uncertain."

Will reminded him the twenty minutes was nearly up and Aradyn needed to return to the spot he'd been earlier. Unlike his abrupt greeting, Aradyn lifted a hand as he walked away, and thanked Will for coming.

We headed east, toward the heart of the financial district, where Union Square and home once were. We stood on the spot where home should have been, surrounded by trees and a few dilapidated dwellings that were barely large enough for a single person to live in. Sloppy wood constructions, held together by a few nails and a lot of hope, listed to the left or the right, and they were plunked down in a semi-circle that at one time had wanted to be a neighborhood.

I wondered where the people had gone. Were they elves, now trapped working the wheat or fishing for dreams on the west side of the city? Or were they outliers who scurried south to make sure they weren't caught in Tobias's net?

Will looked down at his feet. "My remains are likely under where we now stand," he mused. "Wick's, too. If the building decayed and fell and was covered by layers of dust and dirt, we could be pressed into hard stone just feet from here."

"That's a little creepy, Will," Aisha said.

He looked up. "You could be there, too."

"And that makes it so much better."

"Would you like to know?" Hagar asked.

They blurted out "no" together.

They lied; they both wanted to know but were afraid of the answer.

There's a tiny house where the elevator used to be, Will. I think that's where the elevator was.

Hagar dismissed it as nothing special; it was once the hut of a single man who fled rather than chance being forced to move west and join the elves' village. He'd been in it before, and there was nothing left but a shelf on one wall, and a worn, dirty rug on the floor.

Will wanted to see it anyway.

It was big enough that we all fit inside and we could move around a little bit, but it felt like it had never been someone's home. There had never been a kitchen, or a bedroom, or even facilities. It was built to be that single room, though perhaps at one time it had a chair or a small bed. Whoever had lived in it never intended to stay.

Maybe it's not just a shack. Maybe it's like the barn over Richard's lab. Hiding something.

Don't forget, there's always a downstairs.

Will flipped the rug back, exposing a small hole in the splintered wood floor. He peered into it, looking for spiders or snakes or anything else that might bite back, and when he was sure it was all right, he put a finger into it and pulled.

A square of the floor opened with a loud groan, and there was a staircase leading down. Or it led up, who knows. I suppose it depends at which end you're standing. There was a lot of dirt but no cobwebs, so he decided to inspect it closer.

"Stay here," he said as he headed down. "If I scream...run."

"That's not funny," Aisha snapped.

"It's stairs. I'll be fine." His footsteps faded, but within a minute he was on his way back. "There's a locked door with an electronic keypad. I may need Drew's help getting in."

"Andrew knows locks?" Hagar asked.

"Andrew knows computers," Will said as he moved the carpet back into place. "He has a better chance of finding the right combination to get in than I do."

"Then tomorrow or the next day, you can bring him back. My magic does not include the ability to hack into a computer."

This time, Aisha's eyebrow went up noticeably, and it matched Will's almost perfectly.

*

When we returned, Oz was showing Shivan how to block a punch. She demonstrated with Drew, deliberately, letting him see how she connected to his arm, and then they went faster, until Drew threw a punch toward her face at full speed. Neither worried that he would hurt her. She could block faster than he could hit, and if by chance she missed, he'd developed enough control to stop just short of her nose.

When Shivan thought he understood, Oz showed him how to block a front kick, and then how to spin away from it. She went slowly, demonstrating over and over, which made Will wonder why they were still working on those two very basic things. It was mid-afternoon; surely by now she had shown him a few more techniques.

He stopped at the edge of the clearing to watch. Once I was sure Shivan wasn't playing with the sword—it was resting against the haystack—I wiggled until he set me at his feet. Oz had Drew step aside and told Shivan to block. First she would throw a punch, slowly, and then they would speed up.

He blocked lazily, and the faster she went, the worse he looked. When she punched at full speed, his arm was nowhere near hers, and she stopped her fist just a breath away from his face. Drew shook his head and backed away until he was standing near us.

"Ah, that's why," Will said. "He would learn to move faster if she connected. He would certainly want to after that."

"She hits hard?" Aisha asked.

"She is hard, fast, and accurate."

"And she's the only person to have ever racked him," Drew said. He sounded proud of it, too.

"Racked?"

With a sigh, Will said, "Had I ever planned on having children, it's quite likely that I would no longer be able to. I'm surprised at least one testicle isn't lodged in my lungs."

Laughing, Drew added, "He threw up."

"The point is," Will grumbled, "she's very skilled."

She was also very frustrated and asked Aisha to help show him something a little different. They'd been going over the same three things all morning, and she hoped a shift in perspective would help. Aisha was taller than Oz, and she wanted to show Shivan that it was possible to get inside the length of an arm or leg on a bigger opponent.

Drew was also taller, but perhaps a bit intimidating.

Oz promised Aisha there would be no contact—just a slow demonstration—something to make Shivan pay better attention.

Hagar mumbled to himself; getting a fifteen-year-old boy to pay attention in the presence of two attractive women was like grabbing a thread width of water and expecting to be able to tie a knot. He excused himself; if they would keep an eye on the boy, make sure he didn't get hurt, he would prepare food for later.

Drew sat down and leaned against a tree to watch, and Will followed. Oz had changed the block she was showing Shivan; instead of just batting Aisha's arm out of the way, she pushed it up, and then spun close to elbow her in the ribs.

"All he's going to see is boobs," Drew mused.

"As if you don't."

"Hey, I paid enough attention to get further along than he has."

"And initially I was your instructor. Every time you work with Oz it devolves into…kissing."

"Fair enough." He snorted when Aisha reached over Oz's head to slap the top of Shivan's head, trying to make him listen. "So. You slept with her last night."

"Sleep was all it was, Andrew."

"Yeah, I figured as much."

"How?"

"I recognize the frustrated longing."

"It was an uncomfortable night," Will admitted. "But I'm far more happy that she's here than I am frustrated."

"But…?"

"I have conflicted feelings, that's all. I still don't know what I'm doing."

Shivan was pinned between Oz and Aisha, laughing as he tried to figure his way out.

"You don't need to. She knows exactly what she's doing. And I don't mean physically."

Finally, Oz threw a fist at Shivan, and he ducked.

"How so?" Will asked.

"She's making you seriously want her, Will. Enough to push past all the doubts. Right now you're the instrument she's tuning, and then she'll play you like a pro."

"That sounds a bit manipulative."

"Manipulative would be not bothering to tune the instrument first, just plucking away at the strings without caring that the song was off-key."

Unless you're a horn, and then she would just—

"Wick!"

Drew laughed. "God, I wish I could understand him."

"Lately, I've been quite happy that no one else understands him."

"Aisha, mostly?"

"Especially Aisha." He sucked in air through his teeth when Shivan's foot missed Aisha by mere inches. "I'm going to need your help in the morning."

"Pretty sure she'll take care of that for you if you ask nicely."

"Really, Andrew?"

"Fine. What?"

"I found the entrance to a possible bunker under the remains of Union Square. There's a door with a keypad, and I'm hoping you can get in."

"I don't have the tools to bypass the lock, but I can try."

Something with Shivan clicked, and he was moving closer to the speed Oz wanted. She pointed to Drew and beckoned him to come back, and Aisha looked like she was a couple kinds of relieved for that.

Will got up when he did, and as soon as she was near enough to reach him, Aisha grabbed his hand and told him there was something she wanted him to see. It had bothered her while they were walking back from meeting Aradyn; she stopped at the spot where the path Hagar's hut was on intersected with the one they'd returned on.

"Does this path follow Powell or Stockton? Can you tell?"

"Powell."

"Then shouldn't it incline? Seriously incline? It stretches on, perfectly flat. San Francisco has always been hilly—this path shouldn't be flat, not even after so many years."

While he thought about it, she gestured to the trees. "The leaves are still there. That rain is supposed to be hard enough to strip someone's skin off? Why didn't it take the leaves? Or the bark? Rain hard enough to peel a man like a grape should whittle the trees into toothpicks."

"Perhaps for the same reasons they're able to grow wheat so close to the ocean. Orchards, perhaps, but the wheat makes no sense to me. There has to be a reason."

"So it's not just me," she said. "Something is off."

He nodded. "We play along until we figure it out. And then we hope that whatever it is, we can fix it before I feel like I have to drag Oz and Drew home. And it will be dragging them, because she, especially, will not want to leave until the bitter end."

10

By dusk, everyone wished for the familiar comfort of the inn; we had moved inside the hut before the rain started and Shivan lit all the candles, but the furniture was still comprised of a bunch of itchy hay bales, and sleeping would be done on the ground. Hagar lit a fire this time so I had high hopes that I wouldn't have to sleep under Will's shirt, but it was still cold and the air felt damp on my fur. Will was the only one even close to feeling comfortable; the rest of us were doomed to shivering until dawn.

Once the rain started, Will listened with his ear cocked toward the ceiling. When it was steady and as hard as it was going to get, he went to the front door and pulled it open. Shivan tried to stop him—he was inviting the danger in—but Will grunted that he was only going to look. Hagar was curious, too; he stopped what he was doing in the kitchen and watched, wanting to see how horrible it could be.

Dusk had barely begun, leaving him enough light to see by, and he leaned against the doorjamb to watch the nearly solid sheet of water three feet away from where he stood. Nothing ran from the roofline to the door, and there were no errant drops splashing at his feet. Aisha stood next to him, slipping an arm around his waist, and they watched together, quietly.

"I really want to get used to that," Drew whispered to Oz. "Seeing him so comfortable with someone else."

"So I do. He deserves it."

He can probably hear you, you know.

"So we get this thing figured out as fast as we can, so they can go home and, you know, date."

"Date." Oz chuckled. "Why do I think you want them to do something other than date?"

"Hey, we had a lot of fun just doing stuff together while you were recuperating. Remember that frozen car exhibit at the Modern Art Museum? That was kind of cool. And when we went to Treasure Island to map out the spot for Zed's future imaginary castle, we had a great time."

"And borrowing the Emperor's car to park on Treasure Island. I almost caved then, you know. I might have if I hadn't remembered you being very specific once, not wanting it to happen in a back seat."

"Yeah, but tormenting each other like that was fun. He needs that kind of fun. I want to see him get completely stupid over her."

"Mister Romance," she laughed.

Shivan dropped onto the hay bale that Will and Aisha had abandoned. He wanted to know what the Emperor was doing, taking such a risk, inviting the rain in along with Tobias's dark magic.

"He's probably calculating how hard it's actually coming down," Oz said. "It doesn't look like it could literally skin a person."

It's like looking through a portal but without the pink.

Drew peered over Aisha's shoulders and agreed. "We could test it if we had, like, a piece of raw chicken and a long stick. Shove it outside and see what happens."

Shivan popped up and went to the cupboard. There was an icebox on a middle shelf from which he pulled out a chicken leg, and then he grabbed a strand of twine from a drawer, snatching up a broom that had been left in the corner.

"Here," he said as he held it out to Drew. "Science it."

After Drew had tied the chicken to the broomstick he took it to Will. "Shivan says to science it," he said, chuckling.

"Interesting," Will muttered as he took the broom from Drew. He held it out as far as he could without letting the rain hit his skin. He waited nearly five minutes, the force of the water making his arm quiver. Shivan bounced on his toes behind them because he wanted to see as the meat was ripped away and then destroyed as it fell to the ground, but then Will pulled the stick in.

The chicken was wet and bulging on one side because water became trapped under its skin, but it was intact.

"Where did the idea come from?" Will asked Hagar. "That it would kill someone."

"I've seen it!" Shivan blurted. "The bones of men in the morning, shattered on the ground."

"But did you actually *see* it happen?"

After a strained beat, Hagar answered. "No. We've heard the screams in the dead of night, and then found remains in the morning." He took the broomstick and handed it to Shivan. "Wash the chicken carefully. I'll cook it for Wick."

Aisha glanced out the door. "How did the people whose bones you found survive until late at night? They would have been screaming long before they were anywhere near here."

From the pantry, Shivan said, "The prophecy—"

Before he could finish the thought, Will stepped outside. Aisha gasped his name, but she didn't try to stop him and she didn't beg him to come back. He turned to face the hut, his arms extended from his sides, and said, "It's just rain."

"You have to come in!" Shivan yelled across the room. "We don't know—"

Hagar turned from the door. "Just go get the Emperor some dry towels and a blanket. He'll need to warm up by the fire while his clothing dries."

Shivan wanted to argue and in his irritation he slammed the chicken leg into the sink, but he did as Hagar told him. By the time Will was inside he had two towels ready and then he held the blanket up for privacy while Will stripped down just inside the front door. He dried off with one towel and wrapped the other around his waist, and thanked Shivan for his thoughtfulness.

"I had intended the blanket for warmth," Hagar said. "But, yes, thank you for your consideration, Shivan."

Will scooped his wet clothes up and took them to the sink to wring out. "The rain is very cold, but there's nothing about it that should keep you in hiding when it starts." He sniffed at his arm. "It has quite a bit of salt. I wouldn't drink it."

"We clean it before we drink it," Shivan said.

There was a large tank behind the hut. It collected a significant amount of the daily rain, then filtered it into smaller tanks that lined the outside back corner. As they consumed water, more dripped through the filters, so they almost always had enough. The only time it was an issue, Hagar said, was when that horse, Kilfin, was there. He drank enough for five men, sometimes more.

"Not that he stretches the truth," Shivan offered.

Hagar sat near the fire and stared at the flames. "Perhaps we've been wrong all along. For years we've blindly followed the prophecy, and if that part of it is a lie, all of it might be."

"Or it's just a guideline," Drew said. "Like a riddle or a puzzle; there's truth in it, but truth hidden behind embellished layers."

"And they came, Hagar," Shivan said. "The Trident came. The Emperor, the Princess Oz, the Prince Andrew. You knew who they were before you saw them. One of us will stand before Tobias, and when it's over, there will be freedom."

"Perhaps."

Will sat down next to Aisha and Drew grimaced. "Legs together, Will. Jesus. You know this means the elves aren't penned in or pinned down by the rain."

"Indeed," Will said. "It provides the opportunity for many of them to be taken to safety under cover of night. Those who cannot fight, run. That leaves the strongest to face the Shedu instead of needing to protect the others, and then Shivan can go after Tobias."

"Perhaps it doesn't have to be Shivan, after all," Hagar ventured.

He sounded hopeful; win the fight, save the boy.

Aisha disagreed. "Doesn't your prophecy speak about battle skills not yet won? I'm not positive, but I think it's fair to say that that all of them—" she gestured to Oz, Drew, and Will "—have tested their skills."

"Oz fought for her life," Drew said.

"And Drew fought for her freedom," Will said.

Aisha looked right at Shivan, her deadly serious mom-stare. "You're still the one. So learn from them. Take it seriously when Oz tries to show you how to defend yourself. Your Trident may very well save your life."

*

Dawn was still an hour away when Will woke up; he opened his eyes and looked at me with surprise as I sat on his chest and stared at him. He'd actually slept, and more than in short snatches here and there. He was the last to fall asleep, but once he heard Oz and Drew settle and quiet, and Aisha was pressed up against him for warmth, he let himself fall.

He was slow to get up, not wanting to wake anyone else. For nearly an hour he listened to the rain while rubbing my head right behind my ears and the spot on my chin where I liked it the most, and then he carefully slipped away from Aisha. He wanted to watch the rain again, but this time it wasn't to judge how hard it was really coming down. He wanted to see how quickly it stopped.

When light began to poke through the trees, the rain abruptly ended. "It's like someone flipped a switch," he murmured. He took a few steps outside and crouched down, touching the ground. "Dry."

There was no runoff. He turned to the bay, where the path sloped down, and there were no errant threads of water slipping toward the ocean. The water in the bay, rolling and churning just a moment before, was suddenly calm. "That shouldn't be possible."

He walked toward the path that should have been Powell Street. As Aisha noted, it was flat when it should grade higher; even if the centuries had worn it down, there would still be something more than a long, wide dirt path that stretched out as far as he could see. "That shouldn't be possible, either."

Neither should he.

"What, Wick?"

That dude. That really big dude.

Cutting across the clearing, from behind the haystack Shivan used for stabbing practice, was a man over a head taller than the Emperor, with broad shoulders and thick, heavily muscled legs. His clothing was similar to Shivan's, but was dirty and torn, his sleeves straining against his arms, and his long hair and beard were unkempt. I ducked behind Will's legs, just in case.

He raised a hand in greeting. "Good morning," he said cheerfully, his voice deep and gravelly. "I am likely known to you as 'that horse.'"

"Kilfin?"

"One and the same. You are the Emperor?"

Neither man offered their hand. "Call me Will, please."

"Aye. And please, I am not 'that horse.' Kilfin will do."

Are you sure about the horse thing? You're really big.

"I half-believed that you were exactly that."

"The old wizard was drunk off his ass when he met me," Kilfin explained. He was leading a horse across the clearing—before the haystack was assembled—and in his late-afternoon inebriated state, Hagar looked up from his spot under a tree, and decided he had met the world's first Centaur. "He claims the sun was in his eyes and all he saw was my ugly mug and the backside of my steed. Since then, I have been 'that horse.' He refuses to give it up." He looked over Will's shoulder, and his smile broke into a wide grin. "Well, hello. I wasn't expecting you."

"I wasn't expecting you, either." Aisha, still blinking sleep from her eyes, leaned against Will as he introduced them.

"I-ee-sha," Kilfin said slowly. "It's a very nice name, one I've never heard before."

"Well, you're my first Kilfin," she said.

He watched as she slipped her arms around Will and rested her head on his shoulder. She wasn't ready to be awake, and closed her eyes when he pulled his arms around her.

"You must be the hand that guides the Trident's shaft," Kilfin said.

"Honey," Aisha breathed out, "I haven't laid a hand on this man's shaft."

Kilfin's laugh boomed louder than his voice. It was enough to bring Hagar and Shivan out of the hut; Shivan was eager to see him, but Hagar didn't bother saying hello. He scowled and asked, "What took you so long?"

"I returned last night but fell a bit short before the rain. I had to stay in the chicken shed until morning."

"And the army?"

"There are men and women waiting just outside of the range of rain. Some are near the lake, some at Twin Peaks, and many are hiding between Soma and Dogpatch. Yeosef is fitting as many as he can, though there won't be enough armor for all. It takes too long to weave the metal through the leather. He would need a dozen more years."

"He doesn't have even one. Not even a week."

"The Emperor stood in the rain, Kilfin!" Shivan said excitedly. "And not just for a second or two. He was in it for ages, and not one scratch!"

Kilfin looked dubious. "Is this true?"

"It's nothing more than hard rain," Will said. "It's not comfortable, but it won't hurt anyone."

Kilfin went straight for the bigger picture. "This means we can move under cover of night. We'll have surprise on our side."

Will's enthusiasm was a bit more constrained. "Perhaps. The Shedu surely know about the rain, and they may have patrols out at night. Once we know for sure...yes, we move at night."

"Send your men out tonight," Hagar said. "Watch them. Be sure."

Drew and Oz shuffled out of the hut. "Be sure of what?" he asked.

Neither of them seemed surprised at Kilfin. Drew knew who he was without asking, and Oz assumed. "Big guy, loud voice. Of course the wizard thinks he's a horse." She blinked a few times, thinking about it. "I apologize. I will never say that again."

He wasn't offended.

"Practicing with the sword?" he asked Shivan. "Can you lift it now?"

"I suppose you could call it lifting. I can swing it around, but that doesn't mean I can hit anything with it."

"Weeks ago you told me you could."

"Weeks ago I hadn't seen real fighting," Shivan said. "Now I have and I know I was wrong."

"Oz is helping him," Hagar said. "She'll teach him to fight without the sword."

"But he needs—"

"He needs to stay alive long enough to face Tobias."

Oz nudged Shivan with her elbow. "Are you ready to start?"

"Now? Before we break the fast?"

Drew chuckled. "Yeah, she's going to wreck you today. You don't want anything in your stomach."

Kilfin was still stuck on the sword. "He won't get far without his sword. He needs to be able to swing it, and hit his target."

"More than that, he needs basic defense skills," Will said. "Without those, the sword does him no good. He doesn't have endurance or adequate strength to wield it properly, and he has no clue how to use it to deflect blows. He's been training himself, which has left him with the ability to stab hay, and nothing more.""

Kilfin turned to Hagar. "Can the Trident battle?"

Hagar shrugged. "See for yourself."

"You two should spar," Drew suggested, gesturing to Will and Oz. "Let them see how well you fight."

Will peeled his shirt off and dropped it onto the ground next to me. They began fighting as soon as they were inside the clearing, and it was fast, furious, and so loud that it made Aisha put her hand over her mouth to keep herself from yelling at them to stop. After seeing Will kick Oz twice, and then landing blows that slapped her arms away, she leaned toward Drew and asked, "Will he hurt her?"

"She'll be bruised, but so will he."

Will scrambled to the edge of the clearing, using a tree to get height, and leaped over Oz. She immediately dropped to sweep him as he landed, but he barely touched his toes and was in the air before she could get her leg on him. When the sweep failed, she pushed off the ground with her arms and kicked out, catching his hip as he landed.

He went down. Oz popped back up, ready to continue, but he stayed on the ground. He sat up, his arms draped over his knees. "I did not expect that, Oz. The move made you vulnerable had I been able to twist away, but it worked. Instead of waiting for me to get up and continue the fight, what else would you have done?"

"Depends on whether or not I was armed."

"Presume you were not."

"Stomp kick, crush your throat. Or if you were on your belly, drop a knee into your spine, then break your neck."

He got up and brushed the dirt from his pants, and told Drew to come over. "Have you done any multiple partner sparring yet?"

"We were waiting until she was healed up. But I guess she is."

He told them to both attack him. "As hard as you want, but if I tell you to stop, you stop. Right where you are."

"For feedback?"

"Either that or I'm hurt."

"Or," Oz went on, "it's because you found a point where you could seriously hurt one of us."

"Indeed."

Oz peeled her shirt off, and when Will questioned why she pointed out that they could wind up grappling, and she wasn't giving him the advantage of having her shirt to use as leverage.

"You just want me to be distracted," Drew said as he took his off.

"There's that, too. And I don't care what the situation is, the bra straps are off limits."

I couldn't make heads or tails out of what happened once they started. It was arms and legs flapping around, and dozens of sick, sweat-wet slaps as they made contact with each other; I couldn't tell one punch or kick from another, until Drew used Oz as a vault. He flew toward Will's head and almost got there, but Will ducked and lunged for Oz, putting her in a headlock.

"Stop."

Drew stopped where he landed, and Oz didn't move.

"I just broke your neck," he told her. "You're out."

She scrambled out of the way and stood by Aisha. Shivan was glued to the fight, and Kilfin mused to Hagar that if the boy could be taught even a small bit of that, it very well could save him.

Aisha leaned toward Oz and asked quietly, "Are you all right? This looks...brutal."

"The Emperor has a lot of control. It looks like he's hitting hard, but he's really not. I think if he hit me full force, I'd drop like a rock." She nodded toward Kilfin. "So would this one."

Kilfin laughed. "Is that a challenge?" He shouted to Will, "Can you best a horse, Emperor?"

Drew was out of breath, and grateful for the break. As Kilfin took his place, Drew muttered, "Finally, someone who might be able to beat him."

Instead of running into the fight, Will backed away. He shuffled his feet as he ran in reverse, first in a line and then in a circle. He wasn't taking the first strike, and when Kilfin realized that, he laughed loudly and lunged.

Will sprang up and caught him in the head with a front kick that snapped so hard it made my ears twitch.

The giant of a man went to his knees and then face-down into the dirt, and as Will walked away, he shrugged and said, "Simple is often effective."

He picked his shirt up and tossed Oz's to her. As she turned it right side out, Shivan noticed the scar that ran down her back from her shoulder to her waist and excitedly asked her what battle it was from.

Before she could answer, Aisha stepped between them. "No," she snapped. "You don't ask that of people. You don't ask them to remember their pain."

"I'm sorry." He seemed genuinely contrite. "Every warrior I've met likes to boast about their battle scars."

Drew stepped next to Aisha, to shield Oz as she slipped back into her shirt. "Some battles are better left behind," he said gently. Then he poked his thumb over his shoulder, toward Kilfin. "But this one? You can tell *everyone* about it."

Aisha turned to Oz and asked if she was all right.

"I'm fine." Her voice was soft, and she was not fine. "But thank you. I'm not ready to explain it."

"I am truly sorry," Will said. "I didn't think about it."

She hugged him, hard. "You hadn't seen the scar yet."

When she started to pull back, he tucked his hand under her chin and made her look up at him. "But I saw the raw wound. And I am sorry."

I sat near Shivan's feet and tried to tell him it really was all right. Oz knew he didn't mean anything by it.

"Why was she so abrupt?" he asked Hagar about Aisha.

Hagar looked over Shivan's shoulder. Aisha was brushing a stray lock of Oz's hair from her ear. "The woman is somebody's mother, Shivan. Protecting them is her nature, as if they were her own. Remember that. She may not be a tine on the Trident, but she is fierce and as sharp as if she were."

Kilfin finally made it onto his feet. "We will never speak of this again."

Shivan snorted. "Oh, yes we will."

Hagar agreed. "Frequently."

11

The keypad was like a hundred others that Drew had seen; it was the same type that his father used to secure entry to both of his labs and his offices, and the same type routinely used to protect homes across the world. His apartment door locked with one, as did Will's. It was a ten-digit keypad backlit well enough that it served as a flashlight in the dark space at the end of the stairs, bright enough that he and Will could see each other as they examined it. Oz and Aisha sat together four steps up while Will and Drew stared at the numbers.

"Only four of the numbers have been used routinely," Drew said. "Two, three, four, and seven. They're dirtier and more worn than the others. But that still leaves an impossible number of combinations. I can guess the first digit, but the other three?"

"Which is the first?" Will asked.

"The number three pad is the most worn. People tend to really pound on the first digit. If I had the tools, I could pull the entire thing away from the wall and try to bypass it, but all I have is my phone and like, six sticks I could gather up outside."

Stab it with Shivan's sword.

"That's not helpful, Wick," Will said. "How many guesses do you think you'd get before it locked up?"

"Five?" He was not certain. "Maybe ten. It's a fairly standard-issue access panel, so I doubt it's booby-trapped. I think the worst thing that would happen is that it would lock up and we'd have to wait until tomorrow to try again."

"Then take the chance. Start in numerical order and go from there."

I jumped to the third step so I could watch. He pressed in order, 3-2-4-7. The keypad made a clicking sound, but nothing happened. He tried 3-4-7-2, with the same result.

"You know," Oz said, "if it's a bunker like the safe house, this far underground and protected, and being right *here*, it might be what's left of Finn's lab. At some point he would have had it retrofit to the same standards as the safe house, wouldn't he? So that it would survive a major earthquake or fire? Maybe it held up to time."

Drew stopped playing with the keypad.

"Go on," Will said.

"Well, come on. There's still power running to parts of the city, and he would have made sure that there was a way to keep the utilities attached, right?"

"But his lab is much deeper than this."

"Well, yeah, the lab he started under Union Square. But at some point he spread out, I'm guessing. And if he took over all levels of the garage, he would have had to protect the whole thing."

"Huh."

"Think about it. His work is going to get even more complicated. He has to take over every level under the Square and then some. The construction for the portals is massive, isn't it?"

"Massive is an understatement. And yes, the final one did overtake Union Square, as well as the underground transit tube from Powell up to the Civic Center, where then it looped back. Much of the later construction extended to space under the Westin Hotel."

"I saw the tunnel in a dream, didn't I?" Oz asked. "You were in a room alone, studying. I looked out a window, but instead of seeing outside, I saw a freakishly huge metal tunnel with a row of red lights."

"That was it."

"We got here...so this really could be his lab if he built it under Union Square. Take away all the years between his death and now, and maybe it's his. It would have been built solidly, for no reason other than to protect the portals through time."

It seems to be the right spot. We didn't use the elevator when you were little. We used stairs.

"Three, two, seven, four," he said to Drew.

"Any reason?"

"On a standard numeric and alphabetic keypad, it spells 'Dash.'"

"Good a reason as any." He punched the numbers in, and the door beeped. Will was careful to push it open—who knows what waited beyond—but it opened easily and led into a room that wasn't as big as the safe house, yet was still large and sterile-looking. Lights popped on as he stepped in, and dust motes danced in the beams.

Why dust? Dust is mostly people-skin flakes. There haven't been people here, right?

"Presumably," he muttered. "Everyone tread carefully."

Directly in front of the door was a large island with dozens of little drawers and a steel countertop. On the far wall behind it, a long storage cabinet. There were smaller rooms to our left—offices, Will mumbled—and a tiny kitchen area to the right. It had a small stove, a sink and faucet, and a neat little row of cupboards mounted to the wall over the counter. There was also a smaller storage cabinet in the corner and another door to our immediate left.

"That should lead down to the actual lab," Will said, pointing to the door. "This area was more of a break room and a place to sleep on nights that ran long." He moved further inside and headed for the closed doors on the left wall. "There were a lot of those. There were times we stayed down here for a week."

"You were stuck down here with them?" Aisha asked. "What about school? Or hanging around with friends?"

"I had neither," he said, pushing the second door open.

"This is the room in your dream, Oz. It's where I did most of my studying."

"It looked a lot grimmer in the dream," she said. "This is actually kind of nice."

"It looked grim because that's how I felt about it," he said. "I loathed it. Most of the time, it felt like a cell that was closing in on me." He went to the window. "It looks the same. Those shadows on each side, the ones that resemble entryways—those are the actual portals. You step in, take a step, and move through the next opening. And the red lights are why it always looks pink. The mist diffuses the light."

"What's the mist for?" Oz asked.

"It's water vapor to keep the tunnel cool. The machinery runs at temperatures too high to support human life, so there's a freezer built around it." He tapped at the glass. "This isn't an actual window, it's a projection. Finn wanted to be able to see into the tunnel without having to leave the lab."

Drew looked over Oz's shoulder. "It looks like it goes on forever."

"The curvature of the tunnel makes it seem that way." Will said. "In truth, if you were to run the length of it, it would be less than five miles. But it's several stories tall—definitely massive."

"And still here," Drew said softly.

Will stepped aside so that Drew could get a better look. He left the office and Aisha followed, leaving Oz and Drew to stare at it as long as they wanted to.

"You didn't go to school?" she asked.

"I did, preschool through year two. After that my mother decided I was better off being home schooled. For better or worse, she became my teacher. And she was a formidable teacher."

"Will—"

"My abilities, whether viewed as a curse or a gift, terrify other people. I had little control when I was a child, and it made being around others my own age difficult."

"So you spent your time with adults."

"For the most part. I did have two to three hours away from them almost every day, when they weren't too caught up in work. They realized the level of torment I endured when I was still a toddler, and my father insisted I learn to defend myself. My daily escape was karate and taekwondo."

"With kids who were afraid of you."

"Indeed. Although their snubbing made it possible for me to focus on the training. I was far less distracted than the children who their time socializing instead of working. And yes, I understand that it explains quite a bit about me."

Lightly, "It explains why Oz teases you about sounding like a history teacher."

"I truly don't intend to lecture. Or sound as if I am."

"It's the accent. It makes you sound all-knowing. Kinda sexy, too."

"Sure, flatter me, take the sting out of how stuffy I am."

"You're not stuffy."

He pulled the door open on the storage cabinet near the sink. "I am, and I know it. I am also aware—" he coughed at the spray of dust that flew out at him "—that it's a bit of a defense mechanism. I'll work on it."

"Not for me, you won't. I like my Emperor all stuffy and wise."

He pulled a large plastic container from the cupboard and pried the top off. "Yes, but I would prefer to not speak to you as if I were lecturing Oz or Zed." He set the container down. "It may be hopeless." He pulled another container out and opened it. "Air mattresses and blankets," he said. "As well as a pump. And not as dirty as I feared. They've been sealed up all this time."

When he tried turning the faucet over the sink on, it sputtered and belched, but then clear water began to flow from it. "All we need is food, and we could stay here instead of sleeping on Hagar's floor."

Aisha leaned against the island. "Maybe if we beg the food fairy, a loaded refrigerator will magically appear."

"It seems that way, doesn't it?"

When the wall-width storage unit on the far wall wouldn't

open, he cocked his leg and slammed through the door with his foot, then reached inside to flip the latch. It sprung open just as Drew and Oz came out of the office, and Drew muttered, "Damn."

The cabinet was lined with neat rows of laser pistols, and there were three canisters that were about six inches long and four inches around. Drew started to reach for one, only to have Will slap his hand back.

"No. Those produce a burst of energy not unlike the laser pistols, and the last I knew of them, they were not easily controllable and could blow out half a wall."

"But the guns are manageable," Drew pointed out. "Are the ammo packs charged?"

"There are only enough for what, fifty people?" Oz asked.

"There are enough here that we need to explore other levels of the lab," Will said. "He would have only had these if he felt he needed to protect his work, or if he expected to have enough people in here who could do it for him. And as overly-prepared as he tends to be, there are probably weapons on every floor."

"Why?" Aisha asked. "Why this level of security?"

"The world was about to end in his time," Drew said. "People can lose their damned minds when they know something catastrophic is about to happen, and he had to protect his work if he had any hope of it succeeding."

"Indeed." Will closed the cabinet as much as he could, and headed for the door. "So let's see how well armed the lab was after I left home. If there are more weapons and recharge packs, we may have a fair fight on our hands."

*

Hagar wasn't angry, but he was more than a little surprised to come home from a meeting with Kilfin and Aradyn to find Shivan loading things from his pantry into the wooden pull cart. It was parked outside the front door, and he arrived just as Drew was helping Shivan carry the icebox to it.

"They found a safer place to sleep," Shivan explained.

"This has always been a safe place," Hagar said.

"That was before discovering that the rain isn't harmful," Drew said. "Once more people know, there could be anyone crawling around outside at night. No one's getting into Finn's lab."

"Finn."

"My father," Will said. "The door I could not open yesterday leads into the remains of his lab. It's still there and appears to be fully functional."

"Everything we need except food," Drew grunted as he loaded the icebox onto the cart.

What convinced Hagar was when Will told him about the weapons. He wanted to see them for himself.

"There aren't enough guns to arm everyone, but there are a sufficient number of them to make a significant impact."

As he expected, there was a weapons cache on every level of the lab. Finn had taken over not only the space that was the Emperor's workshop but the other 5 levels, as well. Overall, he estimated there to be 250 laser guns, with twice as many ammo packs.

"That's only enough for a day, perhaps two," he said. "But the packs can be recharged."

"And the elves can do this?"

"As long as there's sunlight."

Great. Jinx us into darkness.

He didn't argue about abandoning his hut. Whether curious or practical, he followed Will to the lab, leaving Drew and Shivan to pull the cart. They lugged it along, the weight of the contents making it drag, and when we reached the little hut, Shivan groaned at the idea of hauling it all down the stairs.

Drew didn't say a word; he picked up as much of it as he could, and began taking it down. Oz followed, carrying almost as much as he did.

"Whether you enjoy it or not, complain or not, or delay or not," Will said, lifting the icebox by himself, "work always has to be done. It's up to you how difficult it feels and how long it takes to complete."

He'd said the same thing to Oz when she was younger, and

Zed when he was about Shivan's age. Dread it or not, you still wind up having to do it. You might as well get it over with and then get on with your day.

Oz took to the idea more easily than Zed did, and he still had to work at it, but he understood.

Once Shivan was downstairs, Will pointed to the weapons cabinet. "No touching. And don't open that door—" he pointed to the downstairs door "—unless I'm with you."

There are things that bite.

"Exactly, Wick. Things down there might bite."

And go BOOM.

He left them to load the food into the cupboards and headed for the office that he loathed so much. Aisha followed, so I ran to catch up, and he held the door even though he'd planned on leaving it open.

"No one is setting your tail on fire, Wick."

I jumped up on the desk, just in case.

You don't know that. Hagar's magic could go wonky and he could light us all on fire with one bad sneeze.

"You have that look," Aisha said. "I remember it well. That 'I don't trust this, but let's see what the hell happens anyway' look. Most of the time it was reserved for Jax, but I remember it."

"I could say the same for you." He opened the top desk drawer and dug around until he found the remote control for the video panel on the wall across from the desk. "You look like your gut is screaming at you."

"Because this place makes no sense, Will. Wizards and elves—and the elves are human, thank you very much—with crops being grown where crops should not thrive at all. And every building we've been into..." She stopped, as if she just realized something. "Hagar's hut. The Inn. Here. You walk in the front door, and it's the same basic layout. They all look different, but they're essentially all the same. Rooms and bathrooms to the left. Kitchen to the right. Common area in the middle."

"To be fair, we've only been inside three habitable structures."

She sighed. "I know."

"But...?"

"Powell Street," she went on. "The paths just outside here. I'm willing to bet if we looked hard enough, we'd see that they run along the same lines as the streets at home. But they would all be flat. This place is laid out like a grid, Will."

He nodded, and then glanced out the door. "Keep this between us for now, all right? My gut is telling me the same thing, but I want to see how this plays out for a bit longer."

"To humor them or keep them from being afraid?"

"I'm not worried about Oz or Drew being afraid, but it was Drew who brought us here, and I need to understand why."

He sat against the desk and pointed the remote at the monitor. Once it clicked on, he pressed a few more buttons, and a keyboard slid out from a spot just beneath it.

"That still works?" Aisha asked. "How?"

"Magic," he said, trying to not laugh.

He was looking for working security cameras. At one point Finn had at least ten set up around the Square and other downtown points. Three of them appeared to be at least partially functional, working but obscured by dirt. He had a spotty view of the Bay Bridge remnants, and another view that looked west but didn't have the range he hoped for.

There wasn't much to see, other than clouds rolling in.

"Right there," Aisha said, pointing at a spot over the Bay. "One of those towers. What the hell is it?"

It was another spire and was glowing red, starting from the bottom up. When the red reached the tip, a thin white line of light shot across the sky and held steady, a rope of never-ending lightning. Will leaned in, squinting to see past the dirt, trying to figure out which direction it pointed. It crossed where the Embarcadero should be, at an angle that aimed it away from the heart of downtown, and he wasn't sure exactly where it headed.

From the other camera, slicing through the sky was another thread of light.

He changed the angle on the bay side camera, and the water was already churning hard, a rolling boil. They both jumped to their feet and stood close to the monitor when they realized what was happening.

"It's raining upside down," Aisha said, her voice hushed.

"Pulling water from the bay. It's the source of the rain."

"Whatever fuels those towers, if we can find the source, maybe we can stop it."

Will stepped back, and leaned against the desk again. "Stop the rain, and what happens? Tobias knows something is coming. What would he do?"

"Unleash hell," she guessed.

"But we need to find out if we can, indeed, stop it. Something to have in our back pockets, so to speak."

The rain became a wall of water, and there was no longer a way to tell which direction it was going. The thin strands of lightning were still visible, but when Will switched to the third camera, all he could see were trees.

The leaves aren't drooping.

"I see that, Wick. Rain they believed would destroy a man, and the leaves on the trees are dancing as if it were nothing more than an easy breeze."

Aisha sat next to him on the desk and watched him flip between cameras and the view that was no longer changing. "I know you said that when we went home, you could take us back to just a minute before we left."

"I can. I will."

"This will be our fourth night here, Will. I can't help but feel like Jimmy is at home, panicking and wondering what the hell happened to me."

He turned on the desk so that he was facing her, and reached up to push a strand of hair from her face. "I promise you, he's not. Because to him, you never went anywhere. Even if you think of this When as occurring long after we're gone, it still happened in that singular minute between stepping into the portal and stepping out. Think of our When as being frozen in time. It resumes when we go home."

"Still."

"Aisha, when I stood outside and said our remains might

be under our feet, I wasn't kidding. When I die—when I died—my cremated remains will be pressed into stone and laid to rest in the royal house. So as long as the stones of those who had passed weren't moved and were allowed to decay into the earth, I'm right across the Square. We'll get home, Jimmy will never be any the wiser, and we'll live out our lives as if we had never been here."

"I can't even think of you being dead." Her breath caught. "Not after getting you back."

"You could be there with me."

That's an awkward proposal.

"Well, if I have to be dead," she sniffed.

Kiss her.

Seriously. Kiss her.

This time he did as I said. It wasn't a long and drippy kiss, just enough to make her smile.

So. When are you gonna marry her?

That is the plan, right?

"We should go through the rest of the lab," he said, sounding regretful. "See what else here might be useful."

Answer me, dude.

When?

"What are you upset about, Wick?" she asked.

"He's hungry. He's always hungry."

Liar.

12

The Emperor's best guess, after having merged several maps together and then measuring angles against old city blocks, was that the light emitted by the spires merged at Coit Tower. Presuming, he added, that Coit still existed.

"The tower stands," Hagar told him. "I've expected it to topple for the last three decades, but it stands."

"Only one way to know for sure if those beams are converging or not." Will dug into the island drawers and pulled out two headlamps and a body camera. "We'll go look."

Shivan was horrified. "You want us to go out at night?"

"When else will we be able to see where the lights converge?" Will handed one of the headlamps to Drew. "But you're staying here. This doesn't require everyone."

"Need me?" Oz asked. "More eyes on it?"

He wanted her to stay in the lab and watch on the monitor. He paired the camera with the computer and said that he would flip the switch on it as soon as they were up the stairs. "Make sure the junior swordsman doesn't get too curious about the weapons locker," Will said to Oz quietly. "He seems to do what he's told, but he's also curious."

So is Oz.

Wait, I don't have to go, do I?

"You stay and watch the monitor with Oz and Aisha, Wick. And listen carefully to everything going on around you, all right?"

He emphasized *everything*.

I could do that. While he and Drew headed up the stairs, we went into the office. I jumped up onto the desk so I could get a good view of the monitor, and Oz sat at the desk behind me. Aisha settles into the comfy chair near the desk, but Hagar and Shivan stayed in the other room. They were playing with a headlamp that Will left on the island, flicking it on and off as if it were magic.

They have light bulbs. Why would that interest them?

"The Emperor will turn his camera on in a minute," Oz said. "Don't worry."

"You still can't call him by his name, can you?" Aisha asked.

"Ingrained habit, I think. Plus it annoys him, and I enjoy annoying him."

You do it because you love your Emperor.

The image on the screen changed. Will turned the camera on and clipped it to the band of his headlamp, so everything we saw was from his point of view. It was dusk, so there was still some light to see by, but because of the rain it was like looking through a frosted pane of glass. When he and Drew started in the direction of Washington Park, the image bounced up and down with each step.

"They're going kind of fast," Aisha mused. "Shouldn't they conserve energy?"

"They are. Otherwise they'd be going at a dead run. Both of them could run to the Golden Gate Bridge and back and not be tired."

"And you?"

"I used to be able to. I can do the distance, but I'd be wiped out after. I'm slowly getting back into shape."

Drew was running ahead of Will, darting between trees that had overtaken Little Italy.

"I can't imagine that's been easy."

"It's not horrible, but I get frustrated," Oz admitted. "I got it into my head that after the pain was mostly gone that it would take a few weeks, tops, and I would be right back to my fittest. When that didn't happen? I'm annoyed with myself. But...Drew and Will have been working out with me and it helps to have one of them running next to me. Drew keeps my pace and Will pushes me. It's a nice balance."

Oz might have had nice balance but Drew didn't. The camera stopped bouncing when Will stopped running, and he stopped running because Drew tripped and fell face first into the dirt.

"That's gonna leave a mark," Oz muttered.

He popped back up. I wanted to know what Will said to him because he turned around and flipped him off before he started running again.

"Well, that was rude," Oz said, chuckling. "Wouldn't have happened a year ago."

"Will says he's gotten very comfortable with Drew."

Oz nodded. "They went through a lot together last year."

"He's hinted at that," Aisha said. "He says Drew is more like a friend now, but it feels like it's a little deeper than that."

"He trusts Drew with his life. Not many people get that close to him. My parents might be the only other ones."

"He loves you. Hell, Oz, he gave you his memories."

"I know. But I'm not someone he would confide in, not the way he would with my dad or Drew. He and I will never go sit in a bar to have a drink together unless he needs to talk to me about something specific." She thought about it for a moment and then added, "And that's all right. He feels a little too parental toward me to be friends. I still need that from him."

Aisha fixated on the monitor. They were nearing Washington Square Park; there was a clearing just beyond it, and in it what was left of the church. There was a front façade and part of a side wall, but the rest was gone and overtaken by weeds.

"How much has he told you about himself?" Oz asked.

"Enough, I think. The important parts, the things he thought I wouldn't believe or would scare me off. I choose to believe him, no matter how out-there it all sounds."

"You know, he didn't even tell my dad most of it until last summer. Dad guessed at a lot, like the fact that the Emperor had to be from another When, but even as close as they are—Dad didn't even know his name."

"The secrets he had to keep," Aisha murmured.

"Just so you know, it wasn't just you that he kept everything from. He kept it from Dad, too, and my dad is the one person he would have told if he could."

Aisha smiled softly. "You don't have to defend him, Oz. He and I are okay with each other."

"I just want him to be happy."

"I know. So do I."

If he wasn't happy at the moment, he was at least amused. Drew tripped a second time, sliding a few feet before coming to a stop.

"I swear, Drew is coordinated," Oz said.

They were headed for Telegraph Hill, where Coit Tower stood. Will pointed Drew in the next direction to go—they were taking the long way—and we watched quietly as they made their way close.

By the time they reached Telegraph Hill it was dark, but there were lights around the base, leading up the street; they turned off their headlamps and waited behind the trees, crouching low. Will slowly looked around the tree; there were guards standing at the path that led up to the tower, men in black flak jackets, armed with laser rifles.

He looked at Drew and pointed up. Above them, coming from six directions, were thin white lines of electric light that met at the top of the tower like wheel spokes. Just above the tower there was a swirl of fog that lifted a good twenty feet over and then ended abruptly. It was flat, as if someone had sliced off the top of a cloud.

How is there fog during rain?

"What the hell is that?" Aisha wondered out loud.

"Seriously," Oz said.

Will pointed Drew to the direction they had come from, and he started running back.

Don't slip again, dude.

We watched until they were close to the bunker entry. Oz turned the monitor off and got up, rubbing the top of my head before stepping out from behind the desk.

Hagar and Shivan were still at the island, playing with the headlamp. They were no longer turning it off and on, but spinning it like a top.

"Have they moved?" Aisha asked. "They've been doing that for almost an hour."

"Apparently the light is fun to play with."

Oz went into the bathroom and grabbed towels for Drew and Will, but as soon as they were through the door, Aisha said, "Hot showers. Now," and shoved Will in the direction of the first bathroom.

Drew's sweatshirt was covered in mud.

"Just stand under the shower with it on," Oz said. "That'll sort of clean it."

"Washer and dryer in the other bathroom," Will called out as he opened the door. "Wait for my clothes."

Oz snatched the headlamp away from Shivan. "Seriously. It's a flashlight, that's all."

She might as well have kicked his puppy. "I've never had one before," he said. "My father had one once, the long kind you hold in your hand and wave around until your wife barks at you to stop being an ass, but I was never allowed to touch it. It was only for night, and finding his way around his shop."

She looked at it; it was an ordinary headlamp, something she never would have thought twice about when she was little. She tossed it back to him. "All right. Keep it. Just don't keep flicking it on and off or you'll drain the battery and it'll be useless."

He took it to the other side of the room and sat on the floor, unable to resist turning it back on.

"Jimmy used to do the same thing any time he got his hands on a flashlight," Aisha said. "But he was also only four years old."

"Look at it as the quieter version of someone clicking a pen. Fun to do but annoying as hell for everyone else."

"Holy hell, pens. My ex used to do that all the time. I

literally grabbed one out of his hand once and chucked it out the window, twenty stories up. It was probably halfway down before I worried about whoever it might have landed on. But the clicking, oh my God."

"If only I'd know that when I was still in school."

"Oh, I'd have failed you," Aisha said. "Really. You might have gotten all of the test questions right, and I'd have deducted ninety percent of your points for the incessant clicking."

Oz snorted. "Zed has you for the summer term, right?"

"Don't you dare."

"Note to self," Oz said. "Crash the school's computer system on a test day, thereby requiring the use of pens and paper, and remind Zed to click, click, click."

"I swear, I will retroactively fail you."

Oz might have been willing to take that chance.

Shivan was still sitting on the floor playing with the headlamp when Will came out of the bathroom. He had a towel wrapped around his waist and dropped his wet clothes on the floor just outside the other bathroom. He noted Shivan with amusement, but his eyebrows knotted together just a touch when he noticed Hagar standing at the island, leaning on the counter on his elbows.

"Want a blanket?" Oz asked him. "So you don't get cold."

"It's warm enough. Unless you're embarrassed and need me to cover up, I'm fine."

"Just don't drop the towel."

He headed into the office, but I'm pretty sure he heard when Aisha mumbled, "I'd be fine if you dropped it."

I was going to tell him because if he hadn't heard her, the look on his face would have been funny, but she followed me into the office and ruined my fun.

He sat against the desk with the remote in hand and turned the monitor back on. He wasn't interested in anything going on outside; he wanted to dig through the contents of the storage drive.

"Has Hagar moved at all?" he asked Aisha.

She looked over her shoulder; he was still standing by the island, resting his elbows on the shiny metal top. "He and Shivan were playing with the flashlight, but I don't think he's budged from that spot."

"All these new things and no exploring, no asking questions. Interesting."

She came all the way in and sat on the desk next to him. "What are you looking for?"

"For all intents and purposes, this is my father's lab. I'm looking for the files that will tell me for sure if we're where we seem to be. Something only he would leave as a breadcrumb."

"The code to get in here was pretty specific."

He nodded. "Yet it's also something many people would know. I find it hard to believe that everything in this place would be so close to what it was when I left at seventeen. How do we have power? Water? How is the computer system still functional?"

"Why didn't your parents move things around?"

"Exactly."

She glanced down at his towel and then back at the screen. "I don't suppose that if they left everything in place, you somehow have extra clothes here?"

"My clothes will be in the dryer within half an hour."

"If you don't put some pants on soon, I'm taking the towel."

He stopped scrolling through menus.

I know what happens if she gets the towel.

"It's very distracting," she said after a quiet beat, when it seemed like he was going to start drooling instead of talking. "I'm working very hard at looking at all that data flying past on the monitor instead of sneaking a peek. Just so you know."

"I'm not exactly shy."

"Will." She took the remote from him. "We can spend the entire night combing through these files, but if you stay here with just the towel...I will do things to you, and I know this isn't where you want that to happen."

He blinked rapidly, trying to get his brain to engage. "My resolve may be crumbling."

Aisha's fingers went to the hem of the towel. "As tempted as I am to slam the door shut and whip this off you? And I am very tempted...it would just be sex, I think. And I honestly don't want that. I want privacy, and I want enough time to make love with you, without worrying about who's on the other side of the door or who might barge in. So please, if there are pants around here, find them. Because my resolve is crumbling, too."

He thought there was a box with old sweatpants and karate uniforms in the storage cabinet, along with the air mattresses and blankets. Everything he found had once fit him at fifteen, when he was two inches shorter and fifty pounds lighter, but at the bottom of a box marked 'Dash' there was a pair of black cotton uniform pants that he was able to get into. After slipping them on he grabbed a stack of mattresses and tossed four of them onto the island—Hagar twitched, but he was still standing in a stupor—and took two into the office.

Aisha cocked her head when she looked at him. "Those really don't leave much to the imagination, Will."

He shrugged lightly.

Yeah, you knew that when you picked them.

But that's proof, right? No one else would have known they were here.

She helped him shove the desk toward the wall and then unfold and fill the mattresses. They used the desk as a headboard and he sat leaning against it in the dark, combing through the storage drive, until all the lights in the common area of the lab went out.

"Are you all right with the mattresses being this close?" he asked.

"I should be asking you that."

"We've slept together this closely and I haven't lost control of my brain. But if we're both teetering on the edge—"

She felt safer being next to him at night. I curled up between them, and Will continued his search through the storage drive while she fell asleep. He wasn't entirely sure what he was looking for, but knew that when he found it, the chattering little voice in the back of his head, the one that was telling him something wasn't quite right, would quiet down.

Unless he wound up with more questions.

That was an entirely people-like thing.

He should expect it.

13

Dolores Park was a long, sloping meadow nestled on the periphery of a wheat field. We stood at the top of the hill—the first truly non-flat place we'd seen—looking down on the places where Jax and Aubrey used to picnic, and where Will and Aisha often sat together on a blanket to read quietly; while she studied, he devoured textbooks that Jax lent him. When they'd been quiet for too long, they quizzed each other on the material; Will wanted to affirm he understood, and Aisha wanted to cement everything into her brain. When they were sure they knew what they'd been studying, they fell quiet again.

I had a vague memory of being stretched out on the blanket between them, a furry buffer to keep them from touching.

The park was also where they went to drink beer that Jax appropriated from the staff kitchen, and where Will had to rescue him from a drunken fountain of vomit that he refused to tell Drew and Oz about.

"He was unreasonably inebriated," Will said. "Leave it at that."

Aisha laughed but conceded. It wasn't a story to tell, not yet. She pushed hair out of her eyes, a losing battle because the breeze kept plucking strands and laying them across her face, and told him that one day she was going to tell them all sorts of things he didn't want her to.

"Teenaged Emperor was a lot of fun sometimes."

The wheat field was laid out much like the last one; there was a path that cut through the middle of it, likely 19th Street. Aradyn stood in nearly the same spot as he had before, but this time he was with one of the Shedu guards. Drew thought they were arguing; Aradyn gestured wildly, his arms flailing about as he pointed to elves who were dragging over-filled baskets behind them, and as he gestured toward the sky. When the guard glanced away, Aradyn reached out and slapped at the rifle slung across his chest.

The guard did nothing.

"Damn, that took nerve," Drew muttered.

"The guard is Erich," Hagar said. "He's outwardly sympathetic to the elves when there are no others present. Aradyn knows there will be no punishment for bickering with him."

"And he's a leader among the Shedu," Shivan added. "We don't want to do anything to give him away."

Erich Greeley was once one of the working class; he joined the guard when he was very young, and it was as he reached command ranks that Tobias took control of Saint Francis. He remembered life before the rain and the terror and did not favor the conditions the elves were forced to live under. He followed the orders he was given, but did not approve, and left to his own devices treated the elves fairly.

"Is he merely a sympathizer or is he an ally?" Will asked. "Can we count on him?"

Hagar thought he was an ally, but also would not entrust him with all of their plans. "He can't repeat what he doesn't know."

"We kind of need plans first," Drew pointed out.

Aisha wondered out loud where the rest of the guards were. From where we stood—which gave us a wide view of everything below—there was only the one guard, and he was still arguing with Aradyn.

Oz counted the working elves. "Under a dozen. If they're friendly with the guard, that may be all that's needed."

Will wasn't as sure. "One might assume the need for additional guards for no reason other than to assure the work is done."

"When you're hungry, you do what you have to in order to eat," Oz said. "They don't need the threat of guards. They have the threat of starvation."

"Man, it is so much easier to just go raid your mom's fridge," Drew muttered. "Everything they're doing today might get them fifteen loaves of bread, if they have the ability to grind it all for flour."

He left the question hanging: what do they do for everything else? The oil, the yeast, the sugar. They had the grain, clearly, but what about the ingredients to turn it into food?

"How many elves and how many guards are there?" he asked instead.

There was a beat of quiet before Shivan said, "We've never counted them all."

Oz scowled. "You're forming an army and you have no idea how many fighters you'll be up against?"

"The guards number approximately one thousand," Hagar said, as if he just remembered.

She crossed her arms because rolling her eyes would have been rude. "All right, but that still leaves us needing to know how many elves there are. And of that number, how many are willing and fit enough to fight? How many children need to be protected, how many are elderly or frail or infirm? Those are things you need to account for."

Hagar gestured to Aradyn. "We ask him."

"In broad daylight," Drew argued.

"Erich knows me. There will be no confrontation."

With a heavy sigh, Drew gestured for Hagar to lead the way, and he fell in step behind him, treading carefully so that he didn't fall down the hill. Oz and Shivan followed, but Aisha grabbed Will's arm to hold him back.

"Why wouldn't he know?" she asked him.

"Because he hasn't decided yet. Keep your eyes open.

Anything that seems even a tiny bit off, make note so that you can tell me later." He reached up and touched my back paw. "You, too, Wick."

We started after the others, and Will walked carefully so that I didn't fall from his shoulder.

There's a breeze.

"There's almost always a breeze," he said.

But the wheat isn't moving. It waved at us the other day.

He hesitated. The wheat should have been swaying with the air current, but the stalks stood perfectly straight. The only movements came where someone was chopping it down or pushing through it.

"What else do you notice, Wick?"

It's all the same people except for the guards. They're in the same spots they were before. And they're all wearing the same clothes. Everyone is skinny, like they'll break in half if they sneeze too hard. Aradyn's hair looks just like it did, too, like he combed it to look uncombed.

He quickly translated for Aisha, but they couldn't discuss it; we'd caught up with everyone else and were only a few feet from Aradyn and the guard.

Erich showed no surprise at our presence. He raised one hand in greeting and said, "The Trident."

"They are," Hagar confirmed. He then asked Aradyn about plans to move as many elves as possible overnight. He didn't ask about the numbers, there were no questions about how many would leave and how many would stay to fight.

"There are no plans because no one believes that it's safe to be out in the rain," Aradyn said. "No one is willing to be the first to step outside."

"So we come back after it starts tonight," Oz said. "Once they see for themselves that it's just water, they'll be willing to leave." She turned to Will. "Drew and I will go to Aradyn's and stand in the rain where they can see us. If that doesn't convince them, nothing will."

"He has a large family," Erich said. "Give them proof, and they can spread out to most of the village within half an hour."

"How many?" Drew pressed.

"Elves? At the last census, we counted seven hundred within the village."

"And how many of those are able to fight?"

"Able? Most are children, many are old. If I had to guess, I would say you have two hundred among the adults who are strong enough to do battle. That doesn't mean all are willing."

Aradyn agreed. "This is all many of my people have ever known. It's safer to survive under tyranny than risk dying for freedom."

"Count on one-fifty," Erich said. "It's not many, but they'll be the bravest of the lot."

"One-fifty." Drew did the mental math: a thousand guards versus one hundred fifty elves. "This will be a complete crap fest of a fight."

"We also have the army," Will reminded him. "But even if there are as many as Kilfin says, we'll barely outnumber the Shedu. And only a fraction of them will have decent weapons."

Erich gestured to his rifle. "My men are well armed, Emperor. There's nothing I can do about that."

"Exactly what *can* you do?" Oz pressed.

"Once you get into the stronghold, I can get you to Tobias." He looked to Shivan. "You'll only have one shot at him."

"He'll be ready," Oz said.

Will told Hagar to take them back so that they could work with Shivan; he wanted to get a better lay of the land, to determine where best to send fighters once the attack began. Hagar offered no argument or notion of where Will should look; he turned with a small wave of his hand and started back up the hill. Oz scowled—that was rude—but grabbed Drew by the hand and followed.

"Hagar knows where you live?" he asked Aradyn. "They'll need directions."

"He knows."

"Just after dusk," Will said. "They'll be there."

*

The trek was less like scouting the land and more like searching for oddities; there was a collective wrongness both of them felt, little quirks that Will wanted to investigate without Hagar or Shivan in tow. After skirting around the far side of the wheat field and walking for half an hour, we reached the perimeter of the orchard. The air was peppered with a heavy, sweet fragrance that hinted the fruit was over-ripe and that it was past time to harvest, but there was no one picking apples or tending to the trees. There were no elves, no guards, not even the clicks and chirps of insects, nor the subtle singing of birds nesting between the thin upper limbs.

The silence had weight and made my ears twitch.

Will followed the tree line for another half a mile, and then took a well-worn path toward the north that ventured into the Presidio woods. He often hiked there during winter when it was quiet, and sometimes—when he was willing to put up with a cadre of guards—he and Jax jogged the narrow paths. It was outdoor space they fought for; even when Jax was a prince, they battled the council every time someone had the notion that the woods would be better utilized as a housing development. The population wasn't dense enough to warrant the ruination of hundreds of years of careful care to the woods, Jax argued. Will pointed to the destruction of large areas of land to the east of California, where the earth was scorched from drought and scarred from deforestation; save what we can, keep what we can, and work at bringing new life to the things we've already destroyed. Cutting down the trees in the Presidio was a sacrifice that shouldn't be made.

The old King agreed with them and Jax would never let go; Will hoped that Oz would keep an eye open for the future, and fight just as hard to keep the woods, as well as the nature trails that wound through Land's End.

He pointed out various landmarks along the way, things that would mean nothing to other people, but were burned into his brain. The spot where he first found Jax with a smuggled case of beer and six of his fifteen-year-old friends. A Jax-crafted burrow where he sometimes took girlfriends. Logs they sat on when Will was sixteen and trying to decide if he should leave home. Logs they sat on when Will realized that the next time he came, he would stay forever, and how quiet Jax was when his now-best friend broke down and cried.

"He didn't say a word," Will told Aisha. "He waited until I was done, and then pulled out the beer."

The real marvel, she said, was that Jax never became a raging alcoholic.

"Ah, he drank less than our memories tell us he did. But truthfully, I loathed the stuff until that day. He taught me to appreciate a superior lager, and later I taught him to appreciate fine scotch."

"Sealing the brotherhood with booze," she chortled.

"That kind of closeness came later. But I knew then I had the best friend that I likely ever would, and leaving home became a bit less overwhelming."

"Losing a friend like that is my second biggest regret about running away to Vegas. I promised Aubrey I would call, and I never did. I kept telling myself I'd do it tomorrow, when I was less upset. One day I realized it had been six months, and thought it was too late."

"She would have welcomed—"

"I know," Aisha said. "I knew then. I can't explain it. It felt like a custody battle that I'd be on the wrong end of. Come on, tell me more about the things you two got into before we met."

They talked until we were at the village border. Will made sure they were back far enough to not easily be noticed and stood under the cover of old trees with heavily drooping branches as they spied on the village. It was close to Aisha's vision of tiny men in trees, and the largest tree on the border had a door carved into it that was tipped at the corners with sconce lighting, and it had several wooden slab steps leading up to it. The elves' houses were built between the trees, intricate dwellings that went on for a hundred feet or more. I counted twenty of them spread out in the woods, and each had several doors, each door painted a different bright color.

Aisha stared at the tree with the door, a tiny smile tugging at the corners of her mouth, before looking on. Unlike the orchard, the village center was filled with the timbre of voices and music of children's laughter. Of the two-dozen people milling about, most of them were very old women caring for very young children, and there were three guards with laser rifles slung casually across their backs.

There was no tension, no sense of fear. There was barely any movement as people stood near each other, rocking sleeping babies in strollers, engaged in quiet conversation.

"All right," Aisha said softly. "That's odd."

"Indeed."

"Where are the old men?" she asked. "There were none working in the wheat field. I can't believe only their women would live to be this old."

He thought it depended on their social structure. If they lived under a patriarchy, where the men felt duty bound to be the providers, it could very well be that few lived to see old age. "They work from the moment the rain ends in the morning until the moment it begins again at night. Day in and day out. I imagine that takes its toll."

They get lots of time to chill before bed. The rain starts at dusk.

"Family duties take time, too, Wick," he said. "A long day of hard, physical work, followed by hours of feeding and caring for children? There's not much personal time."

That's why you were a babysitter, right? You did feeding and bath time stuff so Aubrey and Jax could play with them at night?

"That was part of why I was Oz and Zed's caregiver during the day. Someone had to watch them, regardless."

"The Emperor nanny," she snickered.

"Indeed, and I'd be lying if I said I didn't miss those days. I've even offered my services to Oz and Drew when they have children. I get to indulge the part of me that wants kids, but I get to send them home at the end of the day when they're wound up."

You wound them up on purpose.

"Of course I wound them up on purpose, Wick. What's an uncle for?"

The Marina was next; it took nearly an hour to get there, skirting along the lines of the Presidio. Will headed for Ghirardelli Square, where he knew he could see the bay and still have a view of the bridge. The water was calm, which bothered him, but was probably ideal for the fifteen boats out there.

"There should be ripples and waves," he said. "People surf near the bridge. This isn't normal."

Aisha pointed out the retaining wall. The top was crumbling, when it had been in repair only a few days before. "No sharks, either." She peered over the edge. "I want to take a look in the building."

He forced open the door to the inn and went in first. It was dim, and he reached over to flip the light switch on, but the wall where it had been located was smooth. Aisha followed and took several long strides in, to the spot where the fireplace should have been.

"Nothing," she said, not sounding surprised. "It's one big empty room. No bedrooms, no kitchen, no furniture. All of that was here just a couple of days ago."

Bathroom is still there, I think.

"Where the hell did it all go?" she asked, not expecting an answer.

This is creepy. Even the dust is gone.

Will didn't bother closing the door as we left. He headed down the path formerly known as Hyde Street, looking for the Columbus intersection, and he was not any sort of happy.

Hold her hand, dude.

I bonked his head with mine to make sure he was paying attention. Within a few seconds, his gait changed and I looked down; he'd taken her hand and was walking very close to her.

Good job.

We walked all the way to the church near Washington Park; the lone wall that was connected to the façade had toppled, leaving a spray of bricks across the ground. Will stopped to inspect it, and while he poked around, Aisha looked up.

Across the sky there was a black splotch, like someone's thumb had smeared pencil lead over the blue sky and clouds. She told Will to look, and they stood shoulder to shoulder, and watched as the sky swallowed the smudge whole.

14

Hagar went in search of Kilfin while Oz and Drew worked with Shivan. They were sparring outside of the little hut that led down into the lab, using tree branches in place of swords, trying to give Shivan the feel for the weight of a weapon without risking anyone's life.

The branch was easier for him to swing, but he flailed about, with no sense of the people near him. Will watched for a moment, but then went down into the lab without saying anything. Oz didn't need his help, and his brain was too full of smudge-eating sky and an abundance of old people to want to insinuate himself into their training.

Aisha followed; they'd both gone quiet after seeing the sky swallow the black smear. Will was trying to fit that piece into the mental puzzle he was assembling, and Aisha was trying to understand it as its own thing. What could possibly be the cause? Was it a random phenomenon? Mutual hallucination? Aliens?

He had an idea that he wasn't yet willing to share. Aisha wasn't willing to give voice to the thoughts spinning through her head. I thought everything they needed to know was on the computer, but he was already leaning in that direction, spending a lot of time poking through it, so it didn't seem worth pointing out.

He either would have told me he'd get to it, or that he'd already thought about it, and neither would come with thanks or praise for my stunning intelligence. Besides, I had to pee, so the first thing I did was run to the makeshift litter box in the corner by the bathrooms.

Will opened the weapons locker and pulled out three pistols, setting them on the island, along with several recharge packs. He then led Aisha down to the next level, the main lab, which was filled with things that could bite or go boom, and at the far end of the room there was a small gate, like the one Will once built to send Finn back to his own When.

He kept the gate. Why?

"That one isn't functional, Wick. It's a prototype of the first one he built, and he kept it as a reminder." When Aisha looked at him funny, he said, "The big metal hexagon-shaped thing on the other side. It's a prototype for a transport gate."

"There was one on the Bay Bridge for a few months, wasn't there?"

He nodded. "I built it last year to get my father home. He used the plans for that to build a better gate, and this was the model."

It also gave him the means to build the new portal, the one we got stuck in.

"It did, Wick."

So that means it was your fault.

There was another locker behind Jo's cluttered desk. He glanced at the things spilled across her workspace—whiteboard with formulas written in black marker, computer tablets in which she stored her notes, and a framed drawing that he'd made for her when he was five.

The drawing made him pause. He picked it up, but it didn't seem to make him happy.

"What is it?" Aisha peered over his shoulder. "A rocket ship?"

"Indeed." His voice was soft. "I drew this for my mother when I was very young. She had asked me to illustrate my dreams, and I gave her a picture of me leaving the planet for Elysium. I told her I was going the day I turned sixteen, and I was never coming back. From there I intended to go to the Mars colony, and then deep space exploration. I think I even told her she needed to be nice to me since she only had a few years before I left."

"Ouch."

He set the picture back on her desk. "She understood why. I think she kept this to remind us both that there was something else out there for me. But yes, it had to hurt. I'd forgotten about it."

"You know she hasn't," Aisha said.

"And then I left when I was seventeen." He sat in her chair, fixated on the things she had left behind. "The day I left, my father walked with me to the portal on Market Street. He tried so hard to not cry and failed miserably...she stayed here, in the lab. I said goodbye to her from right about where you're standing now. She hugged me for the longest time, but she never once looked sad or even conflicted. She kissed me and told me it was all right because I was heading into a wonderful life."

Aisha moved to his side of the desk and leaned against it. "She'd known all along she was going to lose you. One way or another."

"She also knew that she wouldn't see me for twenty-five years, and then six months later I would be dead."

"Will, why? What was the point? You had the portals. You could have visited each other."

"It was too painful," he said. He couldn't look at her. Instead, he pushed the tablets around on the desk, moving them with a pained deliberation. "I was a stranger in my own life by then. Every time I came home, after weeks of not seeing them—" he took a deep breath "—it was difficult to make the metal adjustment of realizing that to them I was only away for a few hours at most. I missed them, while they often didn't realize I'd been gone. And when I stayed home for any length of time, they were so busy."

That upset her. "Too busy for their own kid?"

"The world was literally about to end, Aisha. I understood. They had a finite amount of time to find a way to save it, and I was a distraction, especially during those years. They wanted to spend time with me, but..."

"Bullshit." She crossed her arms angrily. "They had the goddamned portals, Will. They could have taken every scrap of research back a few hundred years and worked on it then, and come back to five minutes later with the answers. They could have taken long breaks and used the portals for a three-week-long, two-minute vacation. They could have made time for you with very little effort."

Tell her about the Old Mint.

"If it had been possible to do the work in the past, I'm sure they would have. Jax's father would have accommodated them, but many of the materials they needed simply didn't exist in their past. And time has a way of trying to fix itself." He reached up to pet me. "There's no changing it now. And she was right, I've had a wonderful life, and it feels as if it started at seventeen."

With practice runs beginning at fifteen.

"Yes, Wick. The seeds were sown at fifteen. I'm not sure how it would have been had the old King not embraced me."

He has a name, you know.

"I know he has a name, Wick. And you know why I avoid saying it."

Saying it isn't a jinx, dude. Aubrey says it. It's not like Oz and Drew don't hear it every now and then.

He pushed out of the chair and stepped over to the locker. From it he pulled out a length of metal that looked an awful lot like the pipe he'd convinced Finn to be a memory stick. This one was more elegant, polished blue metal with a real handle and the top end was closed off with fine mesh that protruded a couple of inches.

Pointing it away from them, he slid a switch on the bottom side of the pipe, and a bright bluish-white light extended two feet from the mesh. It hummed but didn't hurt my ears, though the light made me want to squint. It smelled like rain had moved through, the odor of dirt turned to mud, and water droplets dripping from blades of grass.

"Plasma energy," he said. "Untested as far as I know, but if it works as my father hoped, it's deadly. Cut off an arm or a leg, and it instantly cauterizes."

He turned it off and set it on the desk, then grabbed another, testing it as well.

"Bloodless sword," she murmured.

"Indeed."

When he picked the first one off the desk, he knocked some of the tablets to the floor, and with an annoyed grunt bent over to pick them up.

"Will." Aisha picked a tablet off the desk. "Look at this."

She handed it to him. The top front was labeled *William, 3-15* and when he turned it on, it was filled with charts and notes, and on the first screen was a disturbing photo of him sitting in a chair with electrodes taped to his head.

"You were a test subject?" she blurted out.

The little boy in the photo was laughing. "No. I remember this. It started as a game. One of the lab assistants was training in brain mapping, and when I saw what they were doing, I wanted to play. When it proved useful, they spent time trying to figure out if my brain worked differently from theirs. My mother especially wanted to pinpoint the cause of why I was able to hear inside their heads." He turned the tablet off but held onto it. "They were trying to help me, Aisha. I was not a science experiment. It was simply a matter of trying to find a variance in the anatomy of my brain."

I don't think she believed it, but she helped him carry the plasma swords upstairs and set them on the island next to the pistols while he took the tablet into the office.

You're gonna make her butt heads with your Mom.

"I have a feeling that will happen no matter what I do, Wick," he said, quietly. "My mother likes her, but my gut says there will be issues."

Will you have to choose?

"There is no choice."

He shoved one of the pistols into the waistband of his jeans and then handed her one, with the promise that he would show her how to use it, and then he scooped up the rest and carried it all outside.

Drew took the pistol Will held out to him, checked the safety and the charge pack, and then slipped it into his waistband, too.

Will held up the plasma sword to show Oz. "How long has it been since you trained with weapons?"

She glanced at the stick in her hand. "Thirty seconds."

"All right," he sighed. "When was the last time you formally trained with a weapon? And no, I do not count firing the practice guns in the bunker last year. You had staff and sword training when you studied karate."

"I was fourteen," Oz guessed. "Short staff, mostly. I only got to play with wooden swords a little bit. Enough to help Shivan, anyway."

Will pulled her away from everyone and turned the plasma sword on. "This will do a significant amount of damage if you so much as touch it to someone's skin," he warned. "A bare flick to a leg, and it's amputated. Touch someone's torso, and they're dead." He turned it off and handed it to her. "Don't turn it on, but get used to the weight of it. Wield it as if it was a blade."

He wanted to see if she found it natural to hold onto, and whether or not she would, without thinking, turn it on herself.

"Pick a kata," he said. "Add a sword to it."

She stepped away from him and began to move, turning the handle easily. She stopped abruptly twice, realizing that the next technique in the form would turn the blade uncomfortably inward, but she made the changes quickly enough that he stopped her and told her to turn it on.

"Whoa," Drew muttered when the plasma stretched out from the mesh.

"Now wield it like a sword," Will said. "And for God's sake, don't let the blade come anywhere near you."

She moved far more carefully but found a rhythm and smoothness. We watched as she lunged and spun, and when he was satisfied that she could handle it, Will picked up one of the larger branches they'd been fighting with and held it out.

"Strike," he ordered.

With a bare flick of her wrist, she cut the branch in half, and it dropped to the ground. The cut ends were blackened and smoldering and smelled like a spent campfire.

"Keep practicing with it," he told her. "When you're confident, teach Shivan how to use it." He turned to Shivan. "You don't turn it on until either Oz or I tell you to. This isn't a flashlight. It *will* kill you." He clipped the handle to Shivan's belt. "Can I trust you with this?"

Shivan nodded.

Drew was horrified. He tossed the branch he was holding to Shivan and told him to practice, then pulled Will aside.

"What the hell? He'll play with it, you know he will. He can't keep his hands off a damned *flashlight*. First chance he gets, he's turning it on, probably while staring at its tip."

"Perhaps," Will said. "I highly doubt he'll turn it on near any of us, though, and I want to know if he'll even think of it when he's alone."

"He could kill someone. Himself."

"Indeed."

They stared at each other long enough that I was uncomfortable. Aisha was, too, because she stepped over to Will and set her hand on his arm. "Come on. You promised to show me how to not kill myself with the gun." He nodded and took several steps back, and she whispered to Drew, "Something is brewing in his head. Just go with it."

"He probably thinks I'm having a stroke," Will said to me.

But you know what you're doing.

"I hope so."

He took her gun and removed the charge pack, and then went over all the same things with her that he did when he taught Oz and Drew to shoot. He showed her how to engage and disengage the safety, how to load it, and how to aim. When she said she got it, he told her to aim at a tree and then pull the trigger. It wouldn't fire, but he wanted her to feel the click. After she did that a few times, he put his hand under her wrist, and when she pulled the trigger, he tapped at her hand.

"That's what the recoil will feel like," he explained. "It's not significant, but the added weight of the ammunition plus firing gives off a tiny recoil."

"That's fine, but I still don't think I could hit anything."

"Just point and shoot. You'll hit your target."

"I don't want to kill anyone."

"I don't think you'll have to," he said, slipping the charge pack into the gun. "But I need you armed, just in case."

15

Before clipping the camera to Drew's headlamp, Will added a tiny microphone to its underside, tucked up against Drew's eyebrow. He didn't expect full clarity and assumed that the rain would cause interference, but he hoped to capture at least some of the things said when Oz and Drew arrived at Aradyn's hut on the periphery of the elf village. They tested it before the rain began, as Hagar and Shivan left to wait for the first group of elves at his hut; Will and Aisha watched from the office as Drew told them he and Oz would be there in two hours.

There was no way for him to check with Will to see if the sound was working once they were on their way, because it was a one-way system.

Oz stood in front of him before they took off and gave Will a thumbs-up. "We'll just assume you can hear everything from here on out." To Drew, she said, "Keep that in mind. If you want to complain about the Emperor, now is not the time. He doesn't need to know you ordered those giant tweezers to pull the stick out of his—"

"Jesus, Oz! Will, I never said anything like that."

"Yes, he did," she mouthed.

"Wonderful," Will sighed. "We get to listen to this for the next two hours."

"Our first fight," Aisha recalled. "I don't remember what it was about, but I know I told you to pull the stick out of your ass. Is this a recurrent theme in your life?"

"Annually, at least. But I'm quite comfortable with my stick."

Show it to her.

Instead of perching on the desktop, Will lowered the monitor so that they could sit on the air mattresses, using the desk as a backrest. Oz and Drew moved quickly, down the Market Street path, where the trees clustered together so thickly that there was barely any light sneaking through the canopy. Ten feet in, Drew needed the headlamp just to keep from walking face first into a tree.

Once dusk began, they were navigating their way in complete darkness.

"We need popcorn," Aisha said after a few minutes. "And this is the worst movie I've seen. Ever."

"Maybe the big bad wolf will pop out from behind a tree to liven things up."

Are there wolves out there? Wolves might eat them.

"I doubt there are wolves, Wick," Will said. "And even so, they're armed. They'll be fine."

Ozoo. The neat to eat snacky treat.

That made him laugh. When he repeated it for Aisha, she reached up to pluck me off the desk. "I don't like horror movies, Wick. Why don't we hope it turns into a happy fairy tale instead?"

I've read some fairy tales. Goldilocks was a thief. Pretty sure the bears actually ate her.

"If anything happens before they reach Aradyn, it will involve heightened teenaged existential angst. Or kissing. I wouldn't put it past them to forget about the camera and engage in inappropriate activity."

Ugh. Watching your great, great grandparents making out.

"Indeed. I don't mind it when they sneak the occasional kiss or two, but no, I don't wish to witness anything more."

"It would certainly turn into a whole other kind of movie," Aisha said.

Will frowned. "I would need eye bleach."

Your first porn.

"Wick." He tapped me on the head with one finger. "And no, I am not repeating that."

"Is Wick offering suggestions?"

"No, not really. He's just being an ass."

Someday she'll understand me, and I'm going to tell her about your porn collection.

"I don't have any porn, Wick!"

Ha.

Made you say it.

He turned very pink and closed his eyes as he leaned his head against the desk. "Andrew and Zed," he explained. "They take great pleasure in teasing me about a collection of pornography that they know I do not have, and have never had. Wick knows how to—"

"Wick has a sense of humor." She rubbed her hand over his thigh, which made him tense up. "It's none of my business if you indulge a bit, Will."

"But I don't. Seriously."

"You've never been a teensy bit curious about it?"

His face went beet red and he couldn't look at her. "Curious, yes. But I've intentionally limited my explorations of the subject to textbooks and written works of fiction, and nothing terribly graphic. I thought anything else would be torture."

"For someone who says he's not shy, you're actually quite modest, aren't you?"

"I've never seen a point in subjecting myself to something I could never do."

"Then it's not a moral issue."

"No. I don't have a problem with human sexuality, Aisha. Basic biology doesn't bother me. That doesn't mean I want to witness what other people do, especially not in a media where, I'm told, everything is exaggerated beyond realism."

"Where do you draw the line for yourself, then?" He started to answer, but then she added, "Feel free to tell me it's none of my business. I'm curious, but that doesn't mean you owe me an answer."

"The line is drawn where someone else would be involved," he said, not at all embarrassed. "Though I suppose I also draw the line at personal...toys."

For people who aren't bouncing around together, you sure talk about it a lot.

"Are we making you uncomfortable, Wick?" she asked.

"He started it," Will grunted. "She deserves to know what she's getting into with me, Wick. I am not uncomfortable discussing this, but if it bothers you, feel free to go in the other room."

Aisha reached over to brush a finger across his cheek. "Come on, you're a little uncomfortable. You're blushing. It's adorable."

It's freaking hysterical.

"You know," she went on, "we're close to the point where we would normally have the conversation about the people in our pasts. It's going to be a very one-sided talk, isn't it?"

"I don't need to know anything, Aisha. What you've done and with whom is none of my business."

"It is if you're planning on having sex with me. Numbers can be a deal breaker for some people. STDs can be a deal breaker. Freaky, wild sex can be a deal breaker."

"There's nothing you could say that would upset me."

"Come on." She turned a little, and I slipped off her lap onto the mattress. "If I told you I had a triple digit past, and the first number wasn't one, that would bother you."

He thought about it. "You're forty-three years old. Assuming three to four partners a year from twenty to now, minus the years you were married? All right, that doesn't add up to one hundred, even, but it doesn't mean anything. The only thing that matters to me is moving forward."

She gave him a kiss, and snickered a little. "Sweetie. Don't assume I was a virgin when you met me. But no, I have not slept with nearly a hundred different men."

"Women?" he asked lightly.

That sounded hopeful.

She thought so, too, and it made her snicker. "All right, I have not slept with nearly a hundred different people. I don't flit from partner to partner. I'm more comfortable with monogamy, and I generally don't have sex just for the sake of sex. One-night stands are not my thing. But I have indulged my curiosity on a few occasions, and there may be a woman or two in the lineup."

He wasn't sure how to respond. "All right."

"Don't get me wrong. I love sex, Will. But only with the right person. So no, I don't have triple digits. Barely double."

"I hope none of them broke your heart the way I did."

"I never loved anyone the way I loved you. So, no. Nice guys, fun to be with, but no one I wanted to spend the rest of my life with."

"And my inexperience? Does that bother you?"

"No. And I promise, I'll be careful with you. I understand you have more going on than still being a virgin."

"Perhaps."

"Will." She smiled softly. "You're like a partly feral kitten. You want to be petted and loved, and you want to trust the lady who's trying to get close enough to feed you, but it's scary as hell and a part of your brain is screaming 'run.' I just wish I'd known that years ago."

"I wish I could have told you."

It's raining.

I see lights ahead of them.

Oz and Drew were close to the village. Aradyn's hut was near the main path that cut through the village, just past the giant door-carved tree, and he'd promised to tie a strip of red cloth to the door handle so that they could be sure they'd found the right place. They passed three homes before finding one with a long, wet-blackened piece of fabric plastered to the door; Drew knocked and then took a step back, making sure everyone inside could see that he and Oz were thoroughly soaked by the rain.

At least twenty people clustered around the door after Aradyn opened it. Without a greeting of any sort, he turned and said, "Do you believe it now? This is truth. The rain won't hurt us."

Will turned the volume up; we could hear, but just barely.

Someone in the back of the hut yelled, "This is just more of Tobias's trickery. They're under his protection!"

I couldn't see it, but I could feel Oz's eyes rolling.

"I was afraid of this," Aradyn said to Drew.

"So prove it to them," Oz said. "Come outside."

Aradyn took a half step back, afraid. "It's been years—"

"Either you believe us or you don't," Oz snapped. "If you don't, then we're done here. Tell us now, and we'll go home."

"And she means our real home," Drew said. "We'll leave you to fight your own battle. There's no point in us risking our lives for people who have no faith in what we tell them."

An elf that was quite a bit shorter than Aradyn stepped next to him. He tapped his own chest and then gestured outside.

"No, Krisf," Aradyn said. "I agreed to this. I'll go." And with that he stepped outside, staring at his hands as the water ran down his arms and dripped from his fingers. He was soaked within seconds, his clothes plastered to his body and hair stuck to his forehead. When he was sure, he took a few more steps and then turned around. "It's very cold, but not painful. I won't die." He grinned. "I won't die!"

Krisf tapped his chest again.

"Come out," Aradyn told him. "You'll be fine."

Carefully, taking small, unsure steps, the silent elf stepped outside. He held his arms out from his sides, letting the rain pour over him, and grinned widely.

One by one, the others left the hut. They were quieter than I expected; there was no excited buzzing nor loud marveling about being out in the rain they'd been sure would kill them all.

They don't seem happy about it. Except Krisf and Aradyn.

"Indeed, Wick," Will said. "They're going through the motions, nothing more. One might expect a reaction to the cold if nothing else."

Aradyn turned to a woman near him. "Gather up the foundlings," he said. "One adult for each. Oz and Drew will lead them to Hagar, and he'll take them to safety."

"All of them?" she asked.

"Just a few tonight," Drew said. "The guards would notice if all the kids were missing. You need to have a strong presence tomorrow."

Oz agreed. "By tomorrow night you need to know who's staying to fight, and we'll take the rest to Hagar. A day or two more. That's all the waiting you'll need to do."

Will grunted, "Hmm," and then started to get up. "I need to get to Hagar's before Oz and Drew return. I have a hunch I want to address before they get there."

Within a couple of minutes, we were outside, speed walking toward Hagar's hut. It was brutally cold and even tucked into Will's sweatshirt with a layer over it, I got soaked. I was not any sort of happy about it, but complaining was pointless. Even if he took me back, I'd still be wet.

Will threw Hagar's door open without knocking. The old wizard and Shivan were sitting near the fire; Hagar sat on a crate with a book in hand, and Shivan was sitting on a bale of hay staring at the flames, but neither reacted. They went inside and Will slammed the door behind him, being intentionally rude.

Still no reaction.

Will swore under his breath and snapped, "Hagar!"

The old wizard looked up, but Shivan barely twitched. "Apologies," Hagar said. "I was lost in the story."

"Clearly. Oz and Drew are on their way with some of the elves. They should be here within an hour."

"Kilfin will be here soon to escort them to Dogpatch."

Shivan still hadn't looked up.

"When they get here, tell Oz and Drew to go back to the lab. Don't let them dawdle."

Hagar nodded and then turned his attention back to his book.

"What the hell was that?" Aisha asked when we were halfway back to the lab.

"I'm not certain, but I feel as if we're not in control of this, not the way we assume. Neither are they."

"Any explanation?"

"Not yet."

He needed to think about it. He also needed to comb through the computer a bit more. He still wasn't sure what he was looking for but suspected the answer was there.

Once inside, he rubbed me as dry as he could with a towel, and then changed out of his wet clothes into the too-tight uniform pants he'd worn before. He dug out a sweatshirt and sweatpants for Aisha, and then went back to the monitor to watch as Drew and Oz delivered the small group of young elves and their parents to Hagar.

The old wizard was far more animated with them, but he remembered to send them straight back and didn't allow them to even go inside the hut. Once they were at the top of the stairs, Will turned the monitor off, and he watched them both closely as they slipped their shoes off near the door, and patted dry as much as they could before heading into the bathroom to shower and then change into dry things.

"Which one of them is it, Wick?" he asked in a whisper. "It's one of them, I can feel it."

*

The Emperor's old sweatshirt looked like it was trying to swallow Oz whole. She kept pushing the sleeves up, and they kept sliding down. She rolled the legs up to her calves, but the pants still hung so loosely from her hips that she was afraid they were going to fall off. Drew had the opposite problem; he didn't even bother with a sweatshirt because it was too small, and the pants were tight enough that we were all bothered by them.

"Fourteen-year-old you was not bigger than I am now," Oz grumbled as she sat down to dinner. "What the hell?"

"I went through a phase," he explained. "My mother had hidden all my black clothing, so I settled for oversized gray things."

"Did it work?" Drew asked.

"It took a couple of weeks and a resolute refusal to shower, but yes."

"I thought you didn't butt heads with them when you were a kid," Oz said. "No time with all the karate and stuff."

"Generally, I did not. My mother and I had a difference of opinion regarding my hair and clothing, though."

"The Emperor's major rebellion," Drew snorted. "Gigantic sweatpants."

"Truly, I was a total badass."

That made both Oz and Drew laugh.

"Tomorrow morning," he said, changing the subject. "We're finding a way into Coit Tower. I want to see whatever it is controlling those towers and determine if there's a way to disable them. We may be able to stop the rain."

"But the rain gives us cover," Drew argued.

"It's also a distraction," Oz said. "For sneaking around, it's great. But when we get to fighting? It would make something miserable even worse. The elves aren't in great shape as it is, and fighting in bitter, wet cold might end them."

A sudden stop in the rain would also distract the Shedu, Will said. Their distraction could work to our benefit.

"Or it alerts them to our presence," Drew said. "They'll come looking for the cause."

"You take the chances you get," Aisha said.

Will also wanted to know if Oz thought Shivan could handle the plasma sword. She thought he could; the weight of the metal sword was too much and knocked him off balance, but he was agile enough and she had demonstrated how easily it sliced through things in order to drive home the point that he could kill himself. As long as he was held to swinging and thrusting, he'd be fine.

"Just give him a seriously wide berth."

Later, after Oz and Drew drifted to the other office, Will sat back down on the air mattress and picked up where he had left off, poking through the storage drive. After a while, Aisha sleepily asked what he was looking for, and he said "Confirmation. But if I'm keeping you awake I can use the computer downstairs."

"No. It's warmer with you here."

She thinks you're hot.

I curled up near him while he stared at the screen, and later, when Aisha was asleep, he muttered, "Come on, Dad. What are you hiding from me? Just let me find the file."

An hour later he turned the monitor off, and sat there, staring into the dark.

Did you find it?

"I did. And this is now far more dangerous than I presumed."

16

He needed a visual; poking through static files on a video monitor wasn't giving Will the mental image he wanted, and sitting in the dark with nothing to do made him feel twitchy. Once Aisha rolled over, pulling the blanket with her, he slid off the air mattress and carefully opened the door, making sure that light from the main room didn't wash over the bed.

You're not used to being quiet at night, are you?

"I'm better at it than I used to be," he said, voice low. "Before the safe house, I never felt like I had to be quiet simply because I couldn't sleep."

When he turned on the light over the stove I thought he was going to make coffee, and warned him it was a bad idea; Jax wasn't allowed to have coffee after lunch because Aubrey thought it made him obnoxious and cranky at bedtime, and too handsy for his own good. If it was bad for Jax, it was probably bad for him, too.

He laughed softly. "I'm not making coffee right now. Aubrey doesn't want Jax to be awake all night, that's all."

He had coffee at night with General Myers a couple weeks ago.

"Caffeine is often required to survive meetings with the military or the council."

She yelled at him at three in the morning.

"At Jax or at General Meyers?"

Jax. She rolled over and yelled 'Oh my God, stop talking!'

"And did he?"

No. He said 'sorry.' And then he tried to kiss her.

"Ah." He went over the island and slid a long piece of black plastic out from the underside of the counter. "By 'tried to,' I presume you mean she shoved him out of bed?"

She wagged her pointy finger at him and asked if he'd also had booze. So he made kissing sounds until she laughed. Then she let him touch her boobs.

"And that's where the story ends, Wick."

Not really, but okay. What are you doing?

"I can only learn so much by reading lines of code and programming notes. I now know what my father was working on, but I want to see his test program files with more clarity." He pressed a button on the bottom edge of the counter, and a red-lit keyboard appeared on the black plastic. When he tapped his finger on one of the keys, the edges of the counter slid outward an inch and then up another inch; a few more taps of the keys and the entire counter hummed, and hovering in the air above it appeared all the lines of code he'd been poking through.

Will it bite if I jump up there?

"You'll be fine, just stay in the corner. I can render the program in three dimensions with this," he explained. "The code will display as a hologram. I believe we're experiencing this program on a much larger and incredibly more intricate scale."

When he ran the test file, an image of San Francisco appeared in the air over the counter. He reached out with one hand, fingers splayed, and touched it, moving the image around until he was viewing it from above and with depth—looking directly down on Union Square—and then rotated it again, viewing from an upward angle that looked into the city from over the bay.

"There are alternate layers to the imaging processes," he said, gesturing to a rectangle that ran down the right side of the picture. "I've only accessed a single file, yet there are a thousand choices I could use to overlay the city. This one—" he dragged a pink dot from the rectangle and dropped it onto the picture "—is what the San Francisco outside the lab currently looks like."

Hand out, he pinched his fingers together and made the entire city fit in the space. He could see everything, from the broken Bay Bridge waterfront to Ocean Beach, to where the orchards and wheat fields had taken over city blocks and parks. He was tracing his finger over an imaginary line between the Presidio woods and the Palace of Fine Arts when the door to Oz and Drew's office opened.

"Holy—" Drew blinked, and then squinted as if he was having trouble seeing. "What is that?"

Without looking at him, Will said, "It's an interactive holographic display. And no, I had not intended for you to see it and would prefer that you forget you have."

"Yeah, not gonna happen." He stood on the other side of the counter, alternating between looking at the picture of the city and at Will on the other side. "I've seen a heads-up display before, but this is amazing. There's no transparent view-board or monitor, is there?"

Will pointed to the raised edges of the countertop. "There are projectors." He zoomed in on a tree. "Very carefully, reach out. You can touch the image."

Drew cautiously poked one finger at it. "Damn. That feels... real."

"I wanted a better view of the city. This is most likely what it currently looks like." He picked another dot from the rectangle and dropped in onto the picture. "This is our own When."

"Man," Drew breathed out. "It barely looks like the same place."

"Indeed."

"I suppose a thousand years will do that." He moved around the island slowly, trying to take in every inch of it. When he reached the other side and noticed the keyboard, he bent over, examining it closely. "No worries. I won't touch."

Will showed him how to move the display to engage

different viewpoints. Drew nudged it along in inches, until he discovered he could spin the entire city with a swipe of his finger. It only took him a few seconds to discover how to magnify, and he zoomed in on downtown, honing the image until he settled on a cluster of people near Market Street.

"Elves?"

"Possibly. This image could pre-date Tobias, or they could be outliers."

"What else can you do with this? The computer, not the city."

"Anything you can envision, basically." Will tapped at the keyboard and pulled up the list of files. He scrolled quickly, as much to keep Drew from reading the contents as he was looking for something specific, until Drew asked him to stop.

"That icon that just flew by. What was it?"

Will scrolled back until he found it.

"Lunch codes?" Drew asked. "Typo? Is it launch codes? As in military launch codes? Are we sitting on something huge?"

Will tapped on the icon. "Nothing so interesting," he said as the icon faded. "I believe that when my father was trying to divert his attention away from a work issue he could not solve, in order to engage other parts of his brain he organized local restaurants into categories, as if it would somehow later serve a greater purpose."

"Places that deliver," Drew read. "Places I'm sure spit in the food. Sandwiches that smell like sweat socks. Things William will eat without arguing about. Best pizza. Okay pizza. Pizza that tastes like sadness."

"His organizational skills may need work."

"He had an entire category for you. He could have named it 'Food that shuts the kid up.'"

"He could have also named the entire file as 'My wife can't cook.'"

"What, *he* couldn't cook?"

Will closed the menu and went back to the hologram of the city. "He could. Having the time, however, was another matter.

Do yourself and Oz a favor, Andrew. Learn to cook, and then make the time. There's a reason Aubrey insists on family meals."

"I can make grilled cheese."

Will sighed. "Yes, and that's exactly what you want to feed your Queen after she's spent thirteen hours dealing with the dictator of a small South American country who wants the lion's share of a lopsided trade agreement."

"I'll make soup, too."

"And that makes all the difference."

Drew poked at the cityscape again, spinning it to view it from the west. "I'll never be as good a wife as Mrs. B," he said, scrunching up his nose as he looked closer. "I'll try to be as good a mother."

"Perhaps concentrate on being a good partner first," Will said.

"Working on it. Hopefully she won't realize I'm not until after I've gotten good at it." When Will didn't make fun of him, he turned away from the computer. "It's a skill. It takes time like anything else. Practice. You're allowed to suck at first."

"It's not happening anytime soon."

"All right. Just saying. You know how Oz likes to tease you about basically being a teenager? Try that."

"I'll keep that in mind."

The subject was closed. "Come on," Drew said. "Show me something else this computer can do."

"All right." He cleared the cityscape and typed quickly. He hit the last key with a flourish, and then said, "Here."

In tiny red letters, small enough Drew had to squint and get really close to read, it said GO TO BED.

"Yeah funny. I could say the same to you."

"Why are you even up, Andrew? You went to bed hours ago."

"Oz is tossing and turning like a maniac. After the third elbow to my gut I decided to get out of her way and wait until she's settled down."

"Nightmares?"

"Maybe. She usually talks in her sleep when they're really bad, but she's not, so I dunno."

Will erased the message and turned his attention back to playing with the cityscape. He drew a line along the waterfront with his finger, then dropped another dot on top of the line; trees disappeared and in their place was a stretch of dark green grass. "It's been a while since I used this system," he said. "I'm trying to reacquaint myself with it by manipulating a test program my father wrote."

"How would he have known what San Francisco would look like eight centuries later?"

"As long as the exterior cameras collect imaging data, the computer can extrapolate the information and keep the maps updated." He looked at Drew sideways, and then moved another layer onto the city. "This is San Francisco at night, in my youth."

Drew's eyes went wide. Everything changed; the preserved charm of our When was replaced by dozens of metal and glass skyscrapers lit up like neon towers. The streets were filled with traffic, and there were hover cars held suspended between buildings. Will moved it around so that Drew could get a better look, zooming in close to downtown. Hanging in the air near Union Square were people wearing backpacks, and on the Square were teenagers on hoverboards.

"Are those freaking jetpacks?" he squeaked. "Like, personal jetpacks?"

"Essentially," Will said. "They operate on technology similar to hovercraft." He took the image down to street level. "Personal cars aren't that much different than what you're used to now. They can traverse several levels of air traffic, much like our air shuttles."

"Ugly as hell. Every one of those looks like a giant oblong... breath mint. Are they faster?"

"Considerably. A shuttle commute from San Francisco to Chicago? Less than an hour. A trip from home to Disneyland in a car? Half an hour if there's traffic."

"Damn. I still want to go there. Can I see more of this? Like, the Wharf?"

"It doesn't resemble the current wharf," Will said as he

rotated the picture. "Over the years it became less of a tourist attraction and more of a public use facility. A park, more or less."

Gone was Pier 39 and all the shops. The entire stretch toward Ghirardelli Square was covered with a bubble, and from the outside it looked as if it were filled with stars and wispy clouds of red and green with streaks of yellow. Will tapped a finger to the top of the bubble, and we were looking from the inside out. The ground was covered with soft grass that bled onto a thin strip of beach, and the landscape was dotted with tall trees that had long, drooping branches. Drew sucked in a deep breath at the sight of the sky.

"This is like that night in Colorado. When we saw the northern lights."

"Indeed. Over the years the natural northern lights became rare, and spots such as these opened around the world to show people what they'd lost. It's a place to be calm and reflect. One can reserve a space inside for a night or two."

"Private space? Or shared public space?"

"There are barriers that allow for private space. It's climate controlled and quite comfortable, so if one wanted, the night could be spent sleeping under the stars. If this computer was larger, I could place you right in the middle of it, theoretically speaking."

"You could go home and visit this anytime. Take Aisha."

"The thought crossed my mind." He poked one more time, and they were looking outside again. "We'll see."

"This is insanely cool," Drew muttered, his nose half an inch from the ocean. "Does Finn have this in his lab now?"

"This particular system won't be a reality for well over a century. He does have access to something similar, but the holographic capabilities are significantly less detailed."

"Damn. I would really like to learn more about this system. Are there smaller versions, like for home use?"

"Not to my knowledge. This has always been used for scientific and military research."

Drew has an excited.

"He's good with computers," Will said. "His interest doesn't surprise me."

"Is that cat making fun of me? This is seriously cool stuff, Wick. Think of everything you could do with it. If you had a bigger platform..."

Here he goes.

"Think about it. Oz could program a sparring partner that she could use as a teaching tool. We could plop Shivan into it and seriously teach him to fight without the risk of hurting him. Or she could have someone her own skill level to work with instead of fumbling around with Zed and me. And the entertainment values? With a big enough room and a few thousand holographic projectors, you could visit anywhere in the world without leaving home. Hell, Wick, you could use it to chase all those birds you hate."

"Consider the negatives, as well," Will said as he shut the program down. "You could throw someone into a program without their knowledge, and wreak havoc on their psyche."

"That can be controlled with base programming," Drew said. "It could be set to fixed parameters for home and entertainment markets and made insanely difficult to get around. Design the basic operating system to crash if certain scenarios are introduced. Anything that could harm a person."

"Perhaps that's on the horizon."

Drew sighed. "Yeah, long after I'm dead."

The counter pieces on the island slid back into place, and Will leaned against it, regarding Drew for a long moment. "You are not fixed to the timeline of my history, Andrew. If your ambitions are to learn more about the similar system my father can surely show you, there's nothing preventing you from building upon it."

"Yeah, but I wasn't supposed to see this."

"I hadn't intended for any of you to see it. But you have, so do with that information what you will. I only ask that it not become a topic of conversation among your friends. Speak with my father, but—"

"Yeah, no, I get it."

Neither of you gets it.

Drew's not the only one not fixed to your timeline anymore.

He heard me and considered it.

"Indeed, Wick, neither am I."

So tell him about the thingies you were working on before he even moved to San Francisco. Before Finn showed up.

"Is Wick ratting you out about something?" Drew asked.

"Encouraging me. I've had an idea simmering in the back of my mind for quite some time. Is your interest in computer science something you'd choose to pursue, or is it more of a hobby? There's no wrong answer."

"It's at the top of my list. I know Oz thinks I should write, and I enjoy that, but stuff like this?" He gestured to the island. "This is what really gets me excited. I can freaking *see* how I would want to make it work. And not even just for entertainment. What I want is to build the system that will..." He hesitated—would Will laugh at him or not—but decided to go on. "The one that will change the world."

"Who says you can't do both?"

Drew squinted, trying to figure out where Will was going.

"As I said, I've had something simmering in my head for a while, something I cannot do on my own. If your interests truly lie in forwarding computer science, I would welcome your help."

"But Finn—"

"I would prefer to not work with either of my parents. Andrew, it does mean that I would venture far from the history of my timeline, but neither one of us is joined to that any longer. Think about it. When we get home, we'll revisit the idea. It won't interfere with your studies, and will give you the employment you seek."

"Do I at least get a hint?"

"Time travel. An improved portal interface." When Drew looked confused, he added, "Moving through time *and* space."

"You're going to leapfrog over Finn's research," Drew said breathily. "And you're not telling him, are you?"

"There's no reason to. And I ask that when you tell Oz, remind her I would prefer she not mention it to anyone." When

Drew opened his mouth to speak, Will added, "I would never ask you to keep anything from her."

"Just from your parents."

"Indeed. Now, truly...go to bed. Rest even if you can't sleep."

"Take your own advice, old man."

Will turned off the light over the stove. "If Oz is still tossing and turning and you think it's a bad dream, come get me. She doesn't need to suffer."

"I'm not waking Aisha."

Will said he would leave the door cracked open. "Just whisper Wick's name. He'll hear you and tell me."

It was a good thing Drew didn't need him because he crawled back into bed and Aisha rolled back toward him and trapped him with a leg thrown over his waist. Five minutes later he was sound asleep, flat on his back, and he didn't move the rest of the night.

17

Will woke up alone; I waited near his head while he slept because his waking after everyone else was unusual and I wanted to make sure he didn't miss the entire day. After he had blinked a few times, I crawled onto his chest and sniffed at his face.

"What time is it?" he asked thickly.

I don't own a watch. But it's past food o'clock.

"You should have woken me. I would have fed you."

Aisha gave me food. She fed me after she carefully climbed out of bed. She had to crawl over him, and tried hard to not disturb him, even though she took the blanket with her.

Did you know she prays in the morning?

"No, I didn't know."

It was a short one, not like the times Aubrey prays. I think she was praying for you.

"Really." He sat up, scooting to lean against the desk, and he blinked a few more times, like he wasn't sure if he was actually awake or not.

I think she wants you to lose weight.

"What?" He finally looked at me. "I don't have any to lose."

I dunno, but she got out of bed and was kneeling there and she said 'Dear God, he's huge.'

Did you know she can kinda turn pink? I think telling that to God embarrassed her.

"Wick, holy hell."

Oh, look. You turn pink, too.

"Right now, I am very glad I'm the only one who can understand you."

I think Drew understands me sometimes.

"He's good at guessing. It's not difficult when most of the time you only want food."

Oh. I think Oz needs something. She said some things off the bad word list and now Drew and Aisha are looking through drawers and cabinets, and Oz won't come out of the bathroom because life sucks big fat hairy donkey balls and it's not fair that Drew doesn't have to suffer, too.

"Ah." He finally got up and put his jeans on. When he went out into the common area Drew started to say something, but Will held up a finger to stop him, and he headed down the stairs to the lab. He was back in just a couple of minutes with a white plastic bag and asked where Oz was.

Drew pointed in the general direction of the bathrooms.

"Here," Will said, tossing the bag to him. "Be her hero."

He sat at the table, still looking groggy.

"How did you figure that out?" Aisha asked him.

"Wick said she was in the bathroom, swearing. I assumed."

She poured him a cup of coffee and brought it over. "At her age, I would have never told anyone, especially my boyfriend."

You were her boyfriend then, weren't you?

Will didn't understand the embarrassment. "You're female. It's not a secret. If you wind up in the same predicament, there's an ample storage of supplies in my mother's locker downstairs. She was prepared to be stuck down here for months at a time."

"You know, you could just bring a bunch up here and leave it in one of the bathrooms, so no one has to ask."

"If I were more awake, I would have thought of that. But I did bring up a few days' worth. I think. It was guesswork. My experience is limited to fourteen-year-old Oz begging me to go to the store for her. That was also guesswork. I bought one of each. There are far too many options, and I have no idea how women figure it out."

"Trial and error," she said. "That didn't mortify you?"

"Why would it? Unless the act of stacking ten boxes of tampons on the checkout counter should have been embarrassing. It should have been clear that they weren't for me."

"The cashier probably thought you were stuck in a house filled with women and felt very sorry for you. What other words of wisdom did Wick have this morning?"

He glanced at me. "Just that it was food o'clock, and I slept through it."

"Don't feel guilty. I fed him," she said. "Oz made eggs for everyone else. I'll fix you some if you're hungry. I swear, there's a never-ending supply of eggs here."

"Thank you, but I'll get something later."

"It'll be chicken or eggs," she said as she headed for the other bathroom.

Why did you lie to her? I said more.

"There's no reason to embarrass her, Wick. That wasn't a prayer. Let her have her secrets."

Don't you want to know why she thinks you're fat?

"She doesn't."

Oh. But you're not that tall, either.

"You know damn well what she meant. Stop trying to goad me."

Drew came back out, went to the storage closet, and then back to the bathroom. He barely pushed the door open, tossed things to Oz, and then went into their office.

You don't get squeamish about this stuff, do you?

"There's no point. Basic biological processes are nothing to get squeamish about, especially when it's someone you love."

You love Aisha.

"Indeed."

But you haven't told her.

"It's a bit premature for declarations."

So?

"You don't tell someone you've only been seeing for a couple of weeks that you love them."

But you loved her before, too.

"I never stopped, Wick."

He startled when she slid her hands over his shoulders and then leaned down to kiss his cheek. "Neither did I."

"You knew she was back there, didn't you?"

I'm helping.

Now kiss her.

He leaned his head back. "Wick thinks I should kiss you."

"Wick is wise."

Let her breathe, though, dude.

"For the record," she said as she pulled another chair out from the table to sit near him, "I don't think it's too soon. I've waited nearly twenty-five years to hear it, Will. It hasn't been just two weeks."

So really say it. That wasn't saying it, that was admitting it.

"I'd hoped for more private circumstances," he told her. "And yes, I've pictured it in my head a few times. It was definitely not in my parents' underground lab, with Oz in the next room bitching about the horrible timing of menses, nor was it with the cat sitting on the table staring at us."

Oh, I'm gonna be staring at you two a lot.

"You're not the only one who imagined it. And no, not here. Though in my head neither of us was wearing anything."

He choked on the coffee he was swallowing.

Drew came out of the office and sat at the table with them, so if Will had something to say about how much he would be wearing when he told her he loved her, he swallowed it along with the coffee. Aisha set her chin on her hand, her fingers hiding her smile, eyes laughing at him.

"It might be a late start today," Drew said. "Oz feels gross and wants to take a shower before we get going."

"She can take her time," Will said. "The only thing I want to get done before tonight is scouting Coit Tower."

"She needs time to work with Shivan, too," he said.

"I doubt she'll feel like it. And if he can't fight by now, it's too late. You're taking more of the foundlings out of the village tonight, and the number remaining will be low enough to draw attention."

"Are we ready to fight?"

"*We* are," he said. "Whether Shivan and the elves are, I don't know. But I don't want to stay here any longer than we have to."

"We don't *have* to stay at all."

Will's eyes flicked toward the bathroom door. "I think we do."

Drew nodded as if he understood, but Aisha's eyebrows knotted together and she had questions she knew she couldn't ask yet.

"Spend a couple of quiet hours with her, Drew," Will said, getting up to rinse out his coffee cup. "Aisha and I are going for a walk. I want to see if there's anything left of the Embarcadero."

"For?"

"For the hell of it. I'm curious. We'll probably be gone a couple of hours, and you'll have privacy."

"Yeah, I don't think—"

"That's not what I meant. She doesn't feel well and she's cranky, and if there are any medications here that aren't extremely expired, we may need them later, so she's stuck with whatever discomfort she's in. A backrub and some attention will go a long way in making her feel better. We'll head for the tower after lunch."

"A backrub," Drew repeated.

"Trust me," Will said. "And keep your pants on. In fact, from here on out, unless you're in the bathroom, stay dressed and be considerate in how you demonstrate your affections. And don't ask why."

When we were outside, heading toward the shoreline, Aisha grabbed his hand. "Not arguing with your suggestion, but what makes you think the backrub will help? She may have the cramps from hell." Before he could answer, she added, "Poor kids. You just basically told them not to have sex, and that's one thing that might actually help."

"Huh," he grunted. "I was not aware. But for many years, once a month, I was tasked with procuring a particular brand of chocolate, a bottle of fairly expensive wine, and often an assortment of oils. Jax wanted to be prepared because the chocolate and the wine when offered after a long backrub did amazing things for Aubrey's frame of mind. He hated her discomfort and wanted to help...and I suppose he wanted to prove to her that his attention didn't always come with the expectation of something more. Drew doesn't have the chocolate or wine but it will do him good to learn to occasionally cater to her without expecting anything to come from it."

"And Jax no longer does this?"

"I'm sure he does, but they've built a small wine cellar, and he no longer needs me for that errand."

"Exactly what do you do for the King?"

He babysits.

Literally.

"Initially, my job was to keep the prince alive. His father was aware of the lengthy list of incredibly stupid things he was doing and tasked me to pull him away from his more dangerous impulses. Once Jax became king, the job has largely been to pay attention, learn most everything he knows and does, and then to protect Oz. If something happens to him, I'm to be her advisor. Zed has anointed me 'vice king.'"

"The shadow king," she said, amused.

"I rather like that. Perhaps just 'The Shadow.'"

"Ah, trying to add to your mystery."

"It's fitting, I think. I do stand behind the royal family, watching and guarding. Rarely in front."

She bristled at that. "Why not next to them?"

"In private, I am."

"But?"

"No buts, Aisha. My public persona is intentional and my own choice. It's easier to keep the extremists and activists at bay when they have a healthy fear of the man watching over the kids."

"They have guards."

"Several, and if they do their jobs well, you never see them. That gives Oz and Zed a sense of a normal life, but when there's a major event? I want people to see that there is, indeed, someone there, and that particular someone will not tolerate any untoward behavior."

History teacher, dude.

"I'm nosey, I'm sorry. But I hate the idea of you standing behind them if it's not your choice."

We were right at the edge of where Chinatown once was, with all the colorful lanterns strung on lines that ran between street lights, and where you could buy a live squid and a live chicken in the same shop. It was close to the waterfront now and smelled of salt.

Will stopped.

"In every way that matters, they're my family, Aisha. Oz and Zed are like my own, and Jax is very much my brother. I literally think of him and of Aubrey as my siblings. And as Wick recently pointed out to me, they chose me. They love me, and they chose me to be one of their own."

There's even paperwork. Signed by retired King Eli Blackshear, so it's super official.

"Yes, there's even a paperwork trail, Wick."

She still had hold of his hand and tugged it as she took a step forward. "I'm picking at a scab that isn't even there. I have no idea why."

Oh! I know!

"Perhaps for the same reason I know nothing about your ex-husband, but my visceral feeling is that I'd like to punch him on sight?"

Yep, that's it.

"All right, we're both protective. But you don't need to feel that way about him, Will. He and I are good friends who happen to share a son. Other than his husband annoying me more often than he should, there are no hard feelings."

"He could have told you right off the bat that he was gay."

"He's bisexual. But he does have a strong preference for men. And he did love me, please don't think he didn't. He loved me enough that he was sure he could be faithful."

"And then he met, what's his name? George?"

"George," she repeated. "But you really don't want to hear about this, do you?"

"I'm a bit curious," he admitted. "How long were you married?"

"Less than two years. The entire relationship lasted less than three. If not for Jimmy—"

"I'm grateful for Jimmy," Will said.

This time she stopped.

"You came back so that he could be closer to his father. If not for your son, you might still be in Las Vegas."

"Or I would have come home much sooner. But you wouldn't have been ready for this before now, would you?"

"No, I wouldn't have. I'm afraid of what I would have said or done if we'd reconnected before we did." He considered it for a moment. "I'm still afraid of what I'll say and do."

"You're doing just fine."

She has to tell you that a lot, you know.

We wound up in North Beach, where he and Jax sometimes went to have ravioli and wine while they sat on the upstairs terrace of Baldacci's and watched women passing by on the street below. The woods ended there, and just ahead there was a stretch of lush, green grass that started right where the last tree stood.

That looks soft. Can I roll in it? I won't run off.

He pulled me from his sweatshirt and set me down, and then took it off so that Aisha could sit on it.

"Ah, you're still a gentleman." She whipped her sweatshirt off, too. "You can keep me warm."

While I wiggled in the grass on my back, they sat together and leaned against the tree, and were about as close as they could get without sitting on top of each other.

The idea probably crossed their minds.

"Why are we here, Will?" she asked.

"I wanted some time alone with you. I wanted Oz and Drew to have some time together. There's no telling what we're headed into, and I just wanted...this."

"If I'd known you wanted to be alone, I'd have had you wear the towel."

"If I'd worn the towel, you would have wound up disappointed. It's a little cold out here. I'm not interested in demonstrating my shortcomings."

"And what are you interested in?"

Oh, Bast. Not this. Why didn't you leave me with Oz and Drew?

"It has been suggested to me," he said, toying with her hand, "that it might be worthwhile to embrace my inner teenager."

"We could have done that back in the lab. Just shut the door and cuddle up."

"With Oz and Drew on the other side of the wall. And a bed right there."

"And you don't think I'll try to go for it out here."

That surprised him.

"Deer in the headlights." She laughed and started to lay back, grabbing him by his t-shirt to take him with her. "If my hands go anywhere that makes you uncomfortable, just move them."

"If we keep our clothes on, your hands can go anywhere you want."

He started to kiss her, but she squished his cheeks with her hands and held him back. "You understand how easy it would be for us to both decide the hell with it, and go further, even out here? Because I haven't seen a soul, and we could get away with it."

"It would be easy," he admitted. "But I'm asking you up front, no matter what I say in fifteen minutes, don't give in."

"You're asking for a lot of frustration."

"I know. But what I'm really asking for are some of the experiences we should have had when we were kids. If I'm out of line, tell me."

"Not out of line, Emperor. We had a lot of fun on your sofa the other night. But I'm groping you this time."

"Just don't let me—"

"The clothes stay on. More or less."

"I don't follow."

"My bra unhooks up front, Will. If we're doing the whole teenage thing and dry humping under a tree, you get to shoot for second base."

Baseball again.

"I may get stuck at first..."

"Don't plan it out. Just kiss me."

I had nowhere to go.

While they pretended to be sixteen again, I curled up and closed my eyes, checking now and then to make sure they kept their clothes on. If not, I intended to jump on Will's back and yell in his ear and remind him what he said.

If needed, I could bite.

18

"I can't believe you bit me," Will grumbled. "What the hell, Wick?"

Well, someone had to stop you two. I wasn't going to bite Aisha.

"You drew blood."

Ewe droo blud. Scottish, dude. And it's just a tiny drop on your ear.

"That's not the point."

We'll get you an earring for it when we get home. Something dangly.

"Very funny."

You said you wanted to keep your clothes on. She was going to unzip your jeans. I was helping.

Drew and Oz were a few steps ahead, and he finally couldn't take it anymore. He turned around to walk backward and asked, "What are you arguing with the cat about?"

"He bit me."

"Did he deserve it, Wick?"

Yes, he did.

"I did not!"

"Aisha?" Drew said. "Did he?"

She was laughing. "Actually, I think the bite was meant for me, but Wick went for the closest target."

"What did you do?"

"No," Will snapped, jabbing his pointy finger in Drew's direction. "You will no' ask that."

You're rattled. You dropped your t and your accent is showing.

Drew chuckled and turned back around. We were close to Telegraph Hill, where Coit Tower stood. They'd debated for almost an hour before we left the lab about how to get past the guards and inside—Drew proposed climbing the far side of the hill, away from the road that lead up to the Tower, but Oz thought that was too dangerous, so we might as well just shoot our way in—when Will decided to just go and see how many guards were at the head of the road during the day.

"I'm betting there won't be any."

He told them to wait a minute and went into the office, and while he was poking around in there, Oz muttered that a zero-guard presence made no sense. If they needed to guard it at night, they needed to guard it during the day. Walking up was too risky.

"Aisha and I were near there earlier," Will said as he came out of the office. "That quarter is very quiet. We never saw another person."

"Come to think of it, we never saw a single living thing," she said.

"We'll be fine."

He declared it, so we were walking there hoping he was right. When we reached the path that led up the hill, there were no guards. Still, he ordered everyone to walk single file, with Drew in the lead, laser pistol in hand. Aisha walked behind Will, where he could protect her if needed.

Funny how there was grass right where you wanted it this morning.

"Hush, Wick," he whispered harshly.

Just saying. Funny how there are no guards here, either.

He tapped me on the head with his pointy finger. I knew what it meant: be quiet, just in case, but he was confident enough that I didn't think I needed to be. He'd left his gun tucked neatly into the waistband of his pants, and even though he had Drew ready to fire, he hadn't suggested to Oz or to Aisha that having their weapons in hand was a good idea.

I could sing, Will. It wouldn't matter, would it?

Aisha's voice from behind us was soft. "Is he all right?"

He turned and began walking backward. "He's fine. Just choosing to not do as I ask."

You're ordering me, not asking. And I'm not in the army anymore.

That made him pause, and Aisha almost walked into him.

"I'm sorry, Wick, you're right. But would you please be quiet, just in case there is someone nearby?"

Since you asked nicely.

There was no one. We walked right up to the unlocked front door and went inside without so much as knocking.

"Well, this has changed," Aisha murmured once we were all in. "Significantly smaller."

I'd never been to Coit Tower, so I wasn't sure how big or small or tall or short it was supposed to be. I'd only seen it from the distance, the parts of it that could be seen from the Embarcadero. We entered into a single circular space that was lined with large steel boxes and bundles of wires that connected them all. There was a panel with lights and switches where the wiring met, and Will muttered "computer array." In the center, there was a metal pole that was larger around than two people, and it went through the ceiling a couple hundred feet up. Will walked around it, dragging his hand across the shiny surface, until he found a panel to open. It was almost as tall as he was, but he didn't struggle to hold it as he peered inside.

Inside there were thousands of color-coded cables in bundles of twenty to thirty, held together with thick black plastic ties. He leaned close, trying to look up the length of the pole, but failing to see anything, he snapped the panel back into place and then turned to the computer array. There was a dashboard similar to the one in the Denver safe house, and a monitor above it; Will pulled the door open on one of the steel boxes and grunted, "servers," and then closed it.

Cold air rushed out at me as the door clicked shut.

Refrigerated computers?

"Yes, Wick. To keep them from overheating. It takes a tremendous amount of power to run a system that controls the weather of an entire city. That would run hot."

There was a staircase that wound up the side of the tower, curving along its stone walls. He took a quick look up and then told Drew to guard the front door, and asked Aisha to stay back and to keep the metal pole between herself and the door.

"And me?" Oz asked.

"You're going up to the top with me," he said. "Can you handle the stairs?"

"I'm not an invalid." She headed up first, not waiting to see if he followed. If going up all those stairs bothered her, she didn't show it. She wasn't out of breath at all and didn't put her hand on the spot on her back that sometimes bothered her when she and Drew ran up and down the stairs at home for exercise.

The stairs ended in a room at the top of the tower. The metal pole extended through the floor and perched on its tip was a smoky glass ball with fist-sized pipes protruding from its surface; inside it, there were thin moving lines of static that randomly jumped and twitched.

"This vaguely reminds me of a Van Der Graff generator," Will said absently. "Did you ever get the chance to play with one in school?"

"In eighth-year science," Oz said. "We used to get Marcia Yance to stick her hand on it. She had hair down to her waist. It was hysterical." She extended her arms out, hands near her head. "Poof."

He chuckled. "My mother demonstrated one for me the same way. Though it was more of an archaic toy in the lab than functional equipment. She frequently trained new technicians using ancient equipment, sort of a 'this is how far we've come' lesson in the history of science. And don't touch this one," he said.

"Yeah, not planning on it. I doubt it's the same thing."

Bites?

"It might bite, yes." Will walked all the way around it, examining it as closely as he dared. The six fist-sized pipes sticking from the top of it were aimed out the windows, which had no glass or obstruction of any kind. "I suspect this is what sends the signals to the spires."

Oz peered at it closely. "But how does it generate the rain?"

"Not a clue. But it was at the moment that all six spires activated that we saw water being pulled from the bay, and the rain began almost immediately."

And it was salty.

"Yes, it was also salty. My conclusion may be faulty, but I assume it's drawing water from the bay."

"Then why isn't the rain killing all the vegetation? The trees and the wheat, they should all die off in salt water."

"Indeed." He leaned over the edge of one of the windows, coming close to squishing me against the wall. "Immediately following the rain, the ground is perfectly dry. I'm at a loss as to why. I was hoping you might have some insight."

She hadn't considered it at all. "My brain has been fixated on getting Shivan ready to fight and then getting home. And the getting home part is starting to worry me."

He turned and leaned against the wall, waiting.

"I haven't seen any other portals, Emperor."

"Princess."

She sighed. "Stop it. Your name *was* Emperor for the first eighteen years of my life. *Will.* The only portal I've seen since we got here is the one we came through. There should be one near the lab entry. There should be one where Ghirardelli Square was, close to the inn. One where Market meets Powell. They're all gone."

"Then we'll go home the way we came, Oz."

"We haven't been back—"

"Aisha and I walked past there this morning," he said, stretching the truth. It wasn't a lie, exactly, but he hadn't looked for the portal. "Don't worry. Just concentrate on getting this done, so that we can go home with a clear conscience."

She didn't frown, so his color must not have changed. "You've thought about leaving, too?"

"This isn't my fight," he said. "I don't want to put any of you at risk simply to stay here and see what happens."

"But?"

"But I feel as if I need to. It's that important, Ozzie."

"For Shivan?"

"We do what we can for family," Will said gently.

"All right. But I kind of wonder who's descendant he is. Mine or Zed's? Or yours?"

"Not mine. No matter what you're thinking about Aisha and me, I will not have children."

"Then he's Zed's. Because my line ends with you."

"Oz." He gestured to the stairs and then started to follow her down. "Just because I'm the one you know about doesn't mean I'm the only one."

"What?"

"Do you recall, in the safe house, when Drew asked how many children you were having because he needed time to mentally prepare if it was a dozen?"

She stopped halfway down. "Oh, hell no."

Shrugging, he laughed.

"You're mean."

"Little bit, yeah."

"I am not popping out a dozen babies."

"That's not up to me."

"Maybe two. Three if he gets me drunk."

"Again, not up to me."

"What about Zed? I mean, no specifics, but does Zed have kids?"

"Zed will not spend his life alone."

"Come on, Will."

"Fine. You get bonus points for using my name. Without specifics, yes, Zed will procreate. And unless I've damaged the timeline too much, he will leave a legacy. Zealand Blackshear will fundamentally change how the world treats its dead."

"Finn said that time would remember him."

"Indeed."

No telling.

"She knows not to tell Zed anything, Wick."

Zed gets his castle, though, right?

"Now that would be telling."

When we reached the main floor, Drew was still guarding the door, but Aisha had turned the monitor on and looking at a picture of the bay.

"I'm sorry, I wasn't thinking," she said. "Who knows how many alarms I set off turning this on."

"Likely none," Will said. He tapped on the keyboard to access one of the drives. He scrolled through the file list, hesitated on one, but kept scrolling without anyone else noticing. "There's no clear-cut way to disable this," he said, mostly to himself.

Oz pointed to a spot on the wall. "Unplug it."

"It can't be that simple," Drew said. He was still looking at the door, waiting, just in case. "There's got to be a backup of some sort."

"Sometimes the easiest way through is straightforward," Will said. "But not right now. I only wanted a cursory look around. We know we can get in, and when we're ready, I'll come back and figure out how to take it offline."

Drew finally turned around. "No way to execute a self-destruct? It would only take a few lines of code. You could time it to shut down at a specific time, and then you won't have to come back."

Will's fingers were on the keyboard, but he hesitated. "We would need to know for sure when the battle begins."

"We're taking the last of the young elves out tonight," Drew said. "Aradyn will send as many as they're willing to risk. Tomorrow morning Hagar wants us to visit Kilfin's main camp between Soma and Dogpatch. I would guess that tomorrow night, they'll strike."

"Oz?" Will looked at her. "Do you agree?"

"Whatever he says. He's pretty astute. Go with his gut."

"Aisha?"

She shrugged. "I have no idea. I'd go with Drew's gut, too."

He pulled me out of his sweatshirt and held me up so that we were nose to nose. "Major?"

Ah, man. I'm in the army again?

"Only for a few days."

We both know, Emperor. Just do what Oz and Drew want. Is that what you're asking? If I figured it out, too?

"It is. Which is it, do you think?"

You know who it is. You know what this is.

He knew. He handed me to Aisha and opened the file he'd hesitated on, found the root directory, and began typing. He stopped once, to ask Drew about a time loop, but it took less than five minutes. When he was done, he turned the monitor off and gestured to the door.

Just before midnight on the next night, the rain would suddenly stop while the armies marched toward the Shedu dormitories, their houses, and the Cliff House. Whatever happened once that began, there was no stopping it.

19

On the way back, Aisha lagged behind, intentionally letting Oz and Drew get far enough ahead that she could talk to Will without them hearing. It took some serious not-walking to let them get that far because Oz was moving in slow motion compared to how she normally walked, and Drew wasn't pushing her to speed up.

He had his arm around her shoulders and kept bending his head down to say things to her, which made me glad I was with Will instead because Drew still hadn't gotten the hang of carting me around in his sweatshirt pouch without letting me swing back and forth while he kept his arm around her.

Will let me ride on his shoulder, so it didn't matter where his hands were. I was on the side closest to Aisha so that I could hear her, too, and if I thought it wouldn't surprise her, I could jump over to her shoulder.

"The Oz I know," she said, her voice still low, just in case, "does not defer. That Oz takes control and is both willing to think out loud and be wrong. Does she always give way to Drew?"

"She trusts his judgment," he said, "and they're working more as one than they used to, which is important for their future in leading Pacifica. But I understand what you mean. She's typically far more inquisitive and decisive, but I chalked the downturn in that to her focus on working with Shivan. His rapid development in skills seems to be very important to her. Telling me that he can handle the plasma sword? She's usually far more circumspect. It's as if she's hoping that by wishing so, he'll fight well with it."

"A lot of wish fulfillment here," she mused. "A lot of sameness, too."

"Indeed."

"What aren't you telling me?"

He glanced ahead at Oz and Drew, making sure they were still far ahead, and then stopped. He leaned his back against the closest tree and reached for her hand, asking her to make this look like it was personal, something they wouldn't stop for and then backtrack to see what the issue was. She stepped closer and put her other hand on his chest, and leaned in to kiss him.

"Personal enough?"

"I did not mind that one bit."

Oz and Drew stopped and looked but the smooching made Oz giggle and then she grabbed his hand and made him keep moving.

"I could repeat it a few times, but I don't want you to distract me from the point. What aren't you telling me?"

He'd had the feeling that nothing was as it seemed from the first night in Hagar's hut, but finding the lab was too convenient. The mix of old tech and new made some sense; time would erode technological advances if education and research stagnated, but some of it might stick around. He would expect that in a class system if there were an educated upper class and an extremely oppressed lower class, but there weren't enough people to support any sort of class system. There weren't enough people to support the technology at all, and no one to maintain it.

"The lab is real, it's my father's lab, but I suspect that it's time locked."

She didn't understand.

"A time lock preserves a slice of reality and keeps the things contained within it available in every point of time from its creation to its end, and I think this particular lock was activated after I left home. The thing that makes me wonder, though, is that we can remove things from the lab, because we shouldn't be able to leave with anything we didn't bring in, and the existence of the portal tunnel makes no sense."

"Sweetie, the portals make no sense to me."

"We should be able to see shadows moving through it. If it were functional, we would be able to see movement as people stepped through. It appears the same as it did when my father was fine-tuning it, after he added new portals and hadn't fully brought it back online. I'm betting if I climbed into its access ports, it would simply not be there."

"Will...where are we?"

He weighed his words before giving them voice. "We're in San Francisco, I'm sure of that. We've been sleeping in the lab, in the room where my mother once taught me and where I did most of my studying. But I don't think we went a thousand years into the future."

He thought that Drew had tripped a failsafe, and they were most likely in the When two decades after his teen years, just before his parents left to avoid being lost to the end of the world. Finn had frequently spoken of trying to find a way to keep people from porting to a time past the end of the world, which would result in certain death. The files he found on the computer storage drives while she slept were for a holographic simulator; he was certain that when Drew thought about going forward a thousand years, they were instead transported into a virtual reality designed to protect them from a critical mistake. "Either the computer deduced he had two different time destinations in his mind, or it made the decision to send us here based on his desire to jump so far forward. It defaulted to a simulation."

"Then none of this is real?"

"The portals are activated by our transponders. Those are wired to our brains. So this is all very real to whichever one of us has this brewing in our subconscious. I think all of us contribute to the goings-on, but only one of us is in control."

Maybe Drew has been writing a story and this is in his head.

"I'd considered that, Wick, that Drew has been writing and this is a story he has yet to tell. That it's still forming somewhere in his mind. But I don't think it is...Drew would pay much closer attention to details."

Well, it's not me.

"It's not me, either. I think this is Oz's creation and she's working through everything that happened to her last year. That's a tremendous amount of fear and anger to be tapped into."

"Does this mean we can't actually be hurt? If this is all simulated."

"We can be hurt. We can be killed. And if this playing out because of the things that are simmering in Oz's mind, if she's as terrified and angry as I suspect, it could become very, very dangerous."

"Will—"

"I want to send you back, Aisha. It's one thing for me to risk indulging her fears. You have a son...I could take you home, and before you could get turned around, we would be there, right behind you, no matter how long it takes."

She hit him on the chest, lightly. "Not a snowball's chance in hell, mister. I'm seeing this through."

"I would never forgive myself if something happened."

"I'm tougher than you think. You've armed me, and now that I know I won't be killing flesh and blood people I won't hesitate to fire on someone."

"But you could still be hurt, whether they exist or not. Your brain will interpret a deadly blow as being very real, and your body will simply stop. I can't—"

"My choice, Will. I'm staying."

She kept her eyes locked on his. He swallowed hard, and then gave in. "All right then," he finally said. "But that means I'm not waiting for some perfect moment that I've constructed in the back of my head or waiting for your...admittedly appealing unclothed ideal."

"For?"

"To tell you that I love you. If something does happen here,

I need to have said it. I don't want to die with it resting on the tip of my tongue. I love you, and I have loved you since I was a stupid, thoughtless teenager."

Aisha's soft smile crinkled the corners of her eyes. "I love you, too, Emperor. Always have, always will."

"I will protect you—"

"Hey. I can protect myself. Don't you dare let me be a distraction."

He laughed under his breath. "You exist. You're a distraction. But I swear to God, you're the most beautiful distraction I could ever hope for."

When she leaned in to kiss him, I stuck my face between them and got a smooch on my cheek.

"That was rude," Will said.

I wanted a kiss. I stole one. You can have me arrested when we get home.

"I'd kiss you, Wick. Just ask."

No, I wanted one from her. Tell her I think she's beautiful, too.

"Wick agrees with me," he said. "He thinks you're beautiful, too."

She reached up to rub the top of my head.

Like hot chocolate.

"What the hell, Wick?"

"What'd he say?"

Say it.

"Wick, it's racist."

No, it's not. It's nice.

He gave in with a heavy sigh. "Please understand he means it as a compliment. However...he compared you to hot chocolate."

"Damn right I'm hot," she said, laughing.

"I was not disputing that."

"If some random person on the street called me hot chocolate, I'd be offended by the implied racist tone. But from you or Wick? As long as you think I'm hot."

"Smoking." He went in for the kiss and this time I didn't block him. "We should catch up to them."

We should have, but it took a while for them to get moving. Damned forty-year-old teenagers.

20

We trailed Oz and Drew the next morning as we walked toward Soma. Will was still trying to convince Aisha to go home—she didn't need to put herself at risk for this—and she was still refusing to budge. If it was important enough to him, allowing it to play out for Oz's sake, then it was important enough to her to see it through.

They argued in hushed voices, practically hissing. "There's a boy at home who matters more to the woman I love than anything else in existence," he told her. "Don't stay for me. Go home for him."

"And you need to have more faith in my ability to cover my own ass," she shot back. "I love you, too, Will, but you damn well better get used to this. I can out-stubborn a toddler, for God's sake. I'm not missing any of this."

There was no way for him to win. He knew it, but that didn't stop him from trying until she was, as Jo would call it, proper mad. When she reached that point he finally shut up, but I could feel it bubbling inside him; he wanted to take her home and keep her safe, even if it meant picking her up and diving through the closest portal.

I hadn't seen one, anyway. I looked for them as we headed down the Market Street path, and even the one we came through was gone. He was counting on it still being available, but if Oz was blocking them all, I wasn't sure we'd be able to find it again. Even the quiet crackle was gone.

Proof to the Emperor of the simulation was cemented when we came upon the spot where the Old Mint should have been. Even if the building had been lost to the years, the lock would have still been there, creating an annoying disturbance. Oz didn't notice, but the green sheen was gone, and there was no noise to flatten my ears.

Will didn't mention it, but I felt him hesitate as we passed the spot where it should have been. If he'd thought to say anything, the abrupt end of the woods interrupted his thought processes. The trees ended in a neat line edging an open field that was cluttered with off-white canvas tents set in a circle around a small bonfire.

I didn't count the tents, but there had to be fifty of them, seven feet tall at the peak and eight feet wide. Men and women milled around, many of them waiting in a line that ended at a giant wheeled cart managed by a man wearing a heavy blue tunic and brown leather pants. His black hair and beard were clipped short, and he was sweating as he moved the merchandise in his cart around.

Hagar and Shivan were already there; Shivan was helping pick through the leather goods, but Hagar spotted us and left them, leaning heavily on a stick that was almost as long as he was tall.

"Did you injure yourself?" Will asked him.

"Old bones," Hagar sighed. He hefted the stick in his hand. "It's also good for hitting people."

"Teenagers?" Drew asked, amused.

"Aye. I'm getting too old to be in charge of children."

"Yeosef?" Will asked, nodding to the man with the cart.

He was helping a woman slip into a leather vest, and Shivan was digging around for a second one for her to try.

"Shivan's father," Hagar said. "He has enough armor for the men and women here, but no more. Kilfin's army waiting south of the lake will have to do without."

"It's leather," Drew said. "It's not going to stop anything."

"He's woven metal fiber into the leather," Hagar said. "Finely knit. It will stop a blade, but no, not the laser weapons. Go take a look. He can probably use some help."

They followed him over, and after a short introduction, Oz and Drew began helping to sort the armor. Hagar excused himself to go find Kilfin, leaving Will and Aisha to wander through the camp.

When they were out of earshot, Aisha nudged him. "Who does Yeosef remind you of?"

Will glanced back. Yeosef was a couple of inches shorter than he was, and his hair was flecked with a spray of gray. "Shave the beard, and he strongly resembles Jax."

"Leave the beard, minus the gray."

"Jax five years ago, with a beard."

She reached over and touched his cheek. "Will. Why am I just now seeing it? I wondered, especially when you mused about a genetic connection between the colors Oz sees, but you do look like brothers."

Tightly, he said, "We're not."

"No, I get that. But you are related, aren't you?"

He stopped. We were near the fire, and I could feel the heat rolling from it. Aisha waited, her arms crossed, but she looked amused and not upset.

He was upset.

"I can explain."

"Please do."

"Later?"

"How difficult can it be, Will? Jax is what to you? Several generations back he's your grandfather?"

See, it was easy.

"Jax and Aubrey have no idea, Aisha."

"And I won't say anything."

You don't need to complicate everything, you know.

"They're my great, great grandparents. Oz and Drew know, but they only know that my father is their grandson. I won't tell them anything about his parents. I wouldn't have told them anything, but..."

"Oz has your memories."

"She doesn't examine them, and she didn't tell him, I don't think that even crossed her mind. But when Drew and I were looking for her, there was a moment of clarity when he realized that I was related to Oz, and he worried that if she died, I would vanish."

Her eyes went wide. "Would you?"

"I don't think so. But I told him who we were to each other, and have no regrets about it. Trusting him with that knowledge has fundamentally changed our relationship."

"You got closer."

"Indeed. He can be incredibly paternal toward me. After telling him, he relied on me less and less for leadership and began taking the reins himself." He took a step, and she followed. "I had reached the breaking point on that hike and felt incredibly ill. I needed sleep, was too stubborn to admit it...he gave me no choice. He found shelter, kept it protected, and convinced me to sleep for Oz's sake. And after that, he became very much my equal and was no longer the boy I'd taken into hiding."

"That does explain why he seems so comfortable giving you a hard time."

"It's a far cry from the child who was terrified of me," he told her, chuckling. "He was seventeen before I could get more than a few words at a time out of him. And then it was to stammer that he wasn't going to be anything but respectful toward Oz when I caught him ogling her breasts."

"You're awful."

"Little bit, yeah."

"Your relationship with them sounds complicated."

"It could be. Oz and Zed feel much like my own, even knowing that I wouldn't exist without Oz having children. Drew is as close as a friend could possibly be now, even though we both understand he's my great grandfather. I think it fascinates him. The idea that I may have changed the timeline...it breaks his heart a bit."

"In case you won't be born."

"I suspect I will be. They remind me so much of Jax and Aubrey...I don't see anything getting in their way. They'll get married soon, and will have children down the line."

Aisha gestured to the tents nearby. "Unless we hose this up."

"Most of it is up to Oz."

"She's level-headed. She'll figure it out."

He reminded her that Oz was still a teenager, no matter how mature she presented. Her brain was flooded with hormones and angst, and wrapped around that were tattered layers of anger and fear. "She has no idea that most of this is her doing. The things we're noting as being a bit off, she's simply not seeing. Her subconscious is stretched thin, and muting the details."

"Like this." We were at the outer rim of the camp, and beyond that, the field went on as far as we could see. But close to us, in a cluster of ten, were soldiers engaged in combat training. Identically dressed in dark blue t-shirts and black pants, they practiced lunging techniques using wooden swords. We lingered to watch for a bit; Will wanted to know why they were training for blade fighting when everyone of them would be armed with laser weaponry.

Every move was choreographed; block, spin, lunge. Block, kick, stab.

"Kata," he said after a bit. "Of course."

They all look like twins.

Short black hair, neatly trimmed. All around five feet nine inches. In shape, thin, wiry, with hard muscles that stood out on forearms as they wielded the wooden swords. Every man and woman there was a variation of the same person, and that person, Will thought, was Zed.

"She's been training Zed and Drew," Will explained. "Drew's a little bit ahead of Zed in terms of skill and strength. It makes sense that she would be mentally working with her brother. He needs her help, but he will always be there to fight for her."

"What do you make of Yeosef?"

"Father figure, protective of those around him, while allowing them to fight for themselves. He'll give them the tools to defend themselves, and then get out of the way."

"I'm surprised she hasn't concocted a version of you."

"Let's hope she doesn't. Somewhere in her head is the realization that I was not there in the moment she needed me, and I wouldn't be the least bit surprised if she wants me punished."

"Surely she doesn't blame you."

"She doesn't, but that doesn't mean she's not angry. I swore to protect her, and in the one moment I should have been there, I was on the roof checking the damned solar charge lines." I heard his teeth grind, and he exhaled heavily. "I should have taken them all outside with me. In all those weeks in the safe house, I barely let them out of my sight, and the one time—"

She reached for his arm and pulled him a little closer. "It wasn't your fault. I saw the edited recording, and there were dozens of men. Oz was leaving with them one way or the other."

His anguish broke. "But she would have at least seen me there, she would have known I meant it when I swore to be there. She fought alone, Aisha. Thirty men or more, and once Zed went down, she fought alone. She could see them coming for her and knew she couldn't win, and yet she still fought as if she could."

Her hand went from his arm to his chest. "She kept herself alive, Will. You taught her well."

"But it's my fault." His breath caught, and I stretched forward to look at his face. His eyes were red and watery, and he was clenching his jaw, trying to bite back the pain. "It was my decision to take them to into hiding in the first place. I thought about moving them to a new safe house sooner, and I didn't. I could have armed her, but I only gave them access to practice guns. I even warned Drew that an attack would come with multiple assailants, and he needed to have her back. And still, I left her and Zed alone. And then he tortured—"

It ended the war, Emperor. You said so yourself not too long ago. It's why you didn't go back to change things.

"Whatever Wick is saying," she said softly, "he's right."

No one blames you.

"I will never feel as if it wasn't my fault."

"Then you help her through it. Beat down the dogs of war, Will, even if they are data points on your father's server. This is all real to Oz, and you're going to help her fight her way to the end."

"Shivan—"

"Is just a manifestation of her self-doubt. He's eager, but he's clumsy. He wants the best for everyone, but he doesn't have the skills to get it. Don't worry about the boy warrior, Will. Let Oz worry about him."

They watched the combat training go on, and Aisha purposely looked away from him to give him time to compose himself.

"I could rewrite the programming," he said after a time. "All of this could just fade away, and leave us inside the bare walls of the simulator. Oz can find another way through it."

"How? Talking to a shrink?"

"For starters."

"She's a fighter, Will. There's something she needs to do, so we'll let her do it. The counseling can come later."

"The risks, Aisha," he breathed.

She stepped in front of him. "If it were my son, I would damn well roll the dice. I would drag myself through hell if it meant pulling him out on the other side. We suffer for what our kids need."

"I know."

"You said she feels like your own. And you know who she is. Don't take this away from her because you're worried about me or about Drew."

"But I am worried about you."

"I'll be fine. I have incentive to stay out of the line of fire." She stuck the tips of her fingers into the pockets of his jeans and tugged him forward. "My reward for getting through this? I am murdering your virginity, mister."

"I think I am both afraid and a little bit turned on right now."

With a laugh, she leaned in and kissed him. "Come on, let's go back and rescue Oz and Drew from handing out armor and then we'll all go find Hagar. There's no point in putting it off. Whatever happens, it all starts tonight."

21

Late afternoon, after the last hot meal Will thought they would have until getting home, he and Drew finished emptying the weapons lockers and they hauled everything up the stairs and outside. While they hauled weapons, Oz helped Kilfin organize his troops on Union Square; those who were not yet armed were put in a line near the lab entry, and the others were lined up on the far side of the Square. As Drew handed guns off, Oz made sure that each person knew how to engage the safety and knew how to swap out the recharge packs. It was time the troops didn't want to take—they wanted to get moving and be near the Cliff House before dark—but it was something she refused to yield on.

No one was going to shoot their own foot or blow someone else's head off because she was sloppy in her directions. She didn't care if it took an extra hour; refuse to listen, she said, and you go unarmed.

There was a buzz in the air that grew more insistent as the last weapons were handed out. They were straining to begin the march toward Ocean Beach and the Cliff House, but Kilfin ordered restraint; five hundred people chanting marching songs were loud, and Saint Francis was not big.

"We don't want them to hear us until we're upon them,"

he said. "Walk without cadence, step quietly, but be wary. Be prepared."

Guns were tucked into belts and waistbands, while those without firearms secured knives and swords to their sides. Will watched as the massive group of fighters—people who were supposed to pave the way into battle—bounced excitedly on their toes, as if they were all five years old and about to head into the zoo for the day instead of marching toward dismemberment or death.

Shivan's enthusiasm, on the other hand, had abated. He waited behind Oz and Drew near the tiny house that stood over the lab, one hand resting on the hilt of the plasma sword while the other was pressed against the front corner of the hut, and he mumbled to himself.

He's praying.

"I see that, Wick," Will whispered.

Oz is not religious.

"No, but she has faith, and Aubrey taught her to pray."

Kilfin pushed his way through his army to get to Will. I was sitting on his shoulder, and Kilfin reached his giant hand up to stroke the top of my head. He could only use one finger. Otherwise he would have crushed my ears.

"You be well, Mister Wick," he said. "When this is over, I want to see you again."

"He'll be protected," Will promised.

"We'll march toward the ocean," Kilfin said. "The path leads forward, but we'll depart at the Square of Alamo and continue through the panhandle of the old gate park."

"Golden Gate Park?" Will asked.

Kilfin shrugged. "Call it what you will. I expect that we'll encounter our first battle there. We'll continue to the water and then march to Tobias's house on the cliff. The army coming from the lake should be a few hours behind, a second wave they should not expect."

"Don't count on that."

"I count on nothing, but hope for the best. And you should

take the north approach. You need a small presence, no more than ten."

Will nodded. "We'll go through the Presidio to Land's End, and approach the Cliff House from there."

Kilfin nodded toward Shivan. "He goes with you?"

"He goes with me. He'll do as Oz says, and we'll protect him."

Kilfin leaned closer to Will. "He isn't as meek as he seems, Emperor. He's not afraid to die, and I often fear he would welcome his end if it meant victory."

"We'll get him to Tobias."

"Aye, I know you will." He looked at Aisha. "You could stay behind with Mister Wick, protect him underground."

Aisha reached out and smacked Will in the arm. "You put him up to that, didn't you?"

"I'm glad that was you and not me." Kilfin chuckled, stroked my head once more, and then turned to push his way back to the head of the line.

"I am not staying behind," she hissed.

"I know. And I'm not certain you should, not in the lab. But—"

"No buts. And why not in the lab?"

"Because I'm not sure whether it's time locked or time shifted. From here on out, we need to stay together. If I left you in the lab, I could be leaving you in a place out of synch with the time I'm in, and I don't know how that would work spread out over several hours. And if I knew for sure that we weren't confined to a limited space and that the program running this was secure enough to not allow a battle to bleed into other scenarios, I'd leave Wick behind."

No, you will not.

"I would if I could, Wick. For all I know we're in the lab right now, or an offshoot of it where we're moving in small circles within a single massive space. Without knowing for certain...we stay together." He went over to Oz and Drew and told them the same thing: we stay together. No matter where it looks like the fight is headed, we don't stray.

"We'll fight better as a unit than on our own," he said. "Even if you think you see something you feel like you need to chase after, don't. I don't want you out of my sight. Give me that much."

Oz nodded. "All right, Emperor."

"Oz—"

She grinned, just a little. "Hey, if you're in charge, I get to use your title. Give me that much."

"Fair enough. Princess. But I am not in charge."

"No," Drew said. "Call her Australia."

My parents were high when they picked that name, weren't they?"

Will snorted. "It could have been Brisbane, you know."

"That's at least alliterative," Drew offered.

Will plucked me from his shoulder and settled me into his sweatshirt so that he could hoist his backpack on. "Andrew, while you're teasing her, you should know that your name was almost Gunther. Your father wanted to name you after his."

"Promise me we'll give our kids nice, normal names," Drew said to Oz.

"Gunther is normal. I bet we would have called you Gunner."

"Goon-ther," Will said, rolling the r. "We would have called him Goon."

We still can.

"Still. If we have a daughter, let's name her after your mom. It's normal and pretty. But if we have a son, we are not naming him after my dad. I'm not letting people call my kid Dick."

"How about we get married before we start picking out names for kids we don't even have?"

Drew put his hands on his hips and looked at her like, what the hell. "I'll get married tomorrow, Oz. Just pick a date already."

Kilfin had begun moving his men and women toward the Market Street path, and their feet produced a quiet rumble.

"We need to figure out where," Oz said.

Will gestured toward the path that headed up Powell Street, and told them to start walking and argue while in motion. We were heading in the same general direction as the others, but a little north, going toward the elf's village.

"Just pick something."

Oz sighed, hard.

"I did not intend to start a fight between them," Will said to Aisha, quietly.

"It's not a fight!" Oz called back.

"It sounds like a fight to me," Shivan said. "You sound like my mother and father. He wants her to pick something, she wants him to say what he wants, then he says he wants whatever she wants, and they wind up mad over nothing. If he'd just say his opinion, it would be fine even if he was wrong."

"Astute," Aisha said.

"He's wrong no matter what he says," Shivan chortled.

"Is that it?" Drew asked. "You want me to pick a date and a place?"

"I want your input! It's not *my* wedding, it's *ours*. Stop leaving it all up to me."

"All right. Small ceremony on Union Square. Family and friends only. We can block the roads off, but people could still watch from windows around the Square if they wanted. Or there's the roof. We get married there and have the reception downstairs."

"What if it rains?"

"We get wet. Pick a date."

"How soon do you want?"

"Soon. Before school starts."

"Well, that sounds adult. Let's just squeeze it in between art and gym class."

"Oz."

Who's Art and Jim? Are they invited?

"Let's get this done. Then ask my mom how quickly it can be thrown together. I'm not trying to drag it out, Drew, I just want to get to the part where we're married. The actual wedding isn't a big deal to me."

"All right, then."

"Elope," Aisha suggested.

"I'd do it if it wouldn't break my parents' hearts," Oz mused.

"And private or not, people would feel cheated if we announced a marriage after the fact."

"We're about to walk into a war that isn't ours," Drew mumbled. "So what do we talk about? Wedding plans."

Will chuckled. "It could be worse. You could be having the same discussions you had with Zed and me while walking through Colorado."

Drew spun around. "Sure. Let's talk about how Will gets off. And then ponder how Wick thinks everyone is a shade of pink, even though no one has been completely Caucasian for, what, a couple hundred years?"

Oz turned around, too, and they both walked backward. "You did *not* discuss whatever weird little solo practices you engage in."

"If I did?" Will offered.

"Ew." Oz grimaced and then turned back around.

When Drew snorted and turned around, Aisha said, "You didn't."

"I did not. Two teenage boys did not need me to paint a vivid picture. They asked what I do, and all I told them was that I do the same thing they do. It did not go beyond that."

She nudged his arm with hers. "I enjoy imagery. Paint me a picture."

"Please don't," Shivan groaned.

"And you have a notion what we're talking about?" Will asked him.

"Bouncing things."

That made him pause. He scooped me out of the sweatshirt to look at my face. "You did that, didn't you?"

You wanted to know if we were all contributing. I contributed.

He slowed down and held Aisha back a bit. "Wick is the only one I know of who refers to sex as 'bouncing things.'"

"I can see where he gets the context—"

"No. I meant that Shivan just made the same reference. Wick admits he contributed to Shivan's thoughts."

"So we can manipulate this? I was pretty sure you were why Kilfin tried to get me to stay behind."

He wasn't positive; he was more certain that each of them contributed details to the simulation, but didn't know if they could control the actions of all the players, or if Oz's deepest thoughts carried the most weight.

I just thought, Shivan hates hearing about bouncing things. Then he said it.

I wasn't sure if it was that simple, but he thought it was worth a try. He watched Shivan walk ahead of us, and whispered to himself, "Shivan is a bit clumsy. There are rocks on the path. He's going to trip on one."

Fifty feet later, Shivan fell forward. He didn't go all the way to the ground, but he lost his footing, and it took slamming into Drew's back for him to catch himself.

"Fascinating," Will murmured.

Shivan doesn't want the sword anymore and he wants to give it to Will.

I repeated that two more times, but he never reached for it.

"He thinks of me as the Emperor," Will reminded me, whispering.

Still, when I said it again, calling him the Emperor, Shivan didn't turn around and he didn't offer up the plasma sword.

Maybe Oz won't let him give it up.

I was just about to think him into tripping again, when Drew called back, "Exactly where are we heading?"

"Palace of Fine Arts," Will replied. "From there we'll head into the Presidio woods, and go into the village from behind."

"Is the Palace still there?" Drew asked Shivan.

He nodded. "It stands. Though no royalty has ever lived there that I know of. It doesn't even look like a palace, though it's pretty enough to be one."

"It was never meant as a royal palace," Will told him. "It was built in the early nineteen-hundreds as an exhibit hall for the Panama-Pacific Exposition."

"I don't know what that is."

The Palace was built not too long after an earthquake that devastated the city. A good chunk of the rest of the world was in economic upheaval—it would lead to World War I—and city leaders got the idea that they could bring the world together, and show them what the future could be.

Their idea of the future was Greco-Roman architecture. Still, the exposition went on; it was a showcase of trade and art, and while a large chunk of the buildings erected for the exposition were later torn down, the Palace remained and over the years had been everything from a military depot to a theater to a museum and in our own When, a place to relax and reflect.

Weddings were sometimes held there.

I told Will to remind Oz about that.

I remember when it was restored. There were hippies.

"That was a few years before my father found you," Will said. "I didn't realize you were that old then."

Me either.

"How old are you, Wick?" Aisha asked.

No clue.

"His memories are spotty the further back he goes. If something reminds him, he can recall specific events, but the time period in which my father found him is the furthest back he's been able to remember. But knowing he was around during the nineteen-sixties renovation puts him at forty-five, at least."

I try to remember. I hate forgetting.

"I know you do."

He told her about the stretch that I had forgotten, when he was a small boy and I was his best friend. I didn't remember until Finn turned on a transponder buried in my brain, just before Will stepped into a portal that he hoped would prove the world hadn't ended.

I feel bad about that, you know.

"It's all right."

You were my boy. I won't forget you again.

"Wick," he breathed. "You may live long after I'm gone. It's all right if you do."

Will I be Oz and Drew's cat?

"Perhaps. You may even be their children's cat, as much as you can belong to anyone."

Did Finn have a cat?

That threw him for a loop. He wasn't sure, but he knew that Finn had a pet when he was young.

"What's Wick so vocal about?" Oz asked, slowing down so that they could catch up.

"He's pondering the length of his life. And curious if my father had a cat."

"Wow." Drew reached over and rubbed my chin. "I hope so."

I wasn't as positive about that as he was; if I became Finn's childhood pet, that meant I was going to be dragged through time, and I was pretty content in the When I lived.

Finn would remember if he'd had me. Wouldn't he?

Man...there better be shrimp in Finn's When.

He didn't answer.

There's shrimp, right?

"I didn't grow up with shrimp on the menu, Wick. It was hard to come by, and very expensive. I don't think you had any until the old King gave you some after you started living with them."

But I remember food o'clock being happy with you.

"You got plenty of other treats when I was a boy. Lots of chicken and on special occasions there was beef. You also sat under the table and ate the food I dropped before my mother realized I wasn't eating."

Oz laughed. "He did that for me, too."

"Wick should weigh as much as I do," Will told Aisha. "He eats constantly. It's hard to tell him no."

I'm hungry right now.

"Are you really hungry right now, or just thinking about food?"

I considered it.

I was hungry.

He handed me to Aisha and fumbled with a side pocket of his pack. Folded neatly into a piece of foil was a wad of chopped up chicken, and he fed it to me bite by bite as they walked along. After he had given me the last piece, he said, "There's more, but we need to parcel it out, all right?"

"Did you cook for him before we left?" Drew asked.

"I don't sleep often," Will reminded him. "Much of last night was spent in the kitchen."

"Avoiding me," Aisha said quietly. She wasn't angry; she was amused and teasing him.

"There was no point in both of us being awake."

"Oh, there would have been a point," she said, slipping me back onto his shoulder. "It might have ended with you bolting from the room screaming like a little girl about your virtue, but there would have been a point."

She didn't say that as quietly as he would have liked because both Oz and Drew laughed.

"You're a fine one to laugh, Andrew," Will said. He raised his voice an octave and went on. "Oh, no Oz, I'm saving myself. Don't make me touch you there."

"Shut up, old man," Drew snorted. "If you hadn't burst in and ripped the curtain open..."

"You'd still be standing there with your hands in mid-air, wondering what the hell you were supposed to be doing."

Pot, meet kettle.

"I figured it out."

Oz stuck her hand behind her back, and wiggled it back and forth, gesturing, "Sort of."

Shivan is embarrassed. Shivan wants to walk ahead of everyone.

Less than a minute later, he pushed ahead; he needed to stretch his legs and wanted to walk a little faster, but he promised to not get too far ahead.

Drew looked back at Will, his eyebrows knotted together.

"He's fifteen and naïve," Will said when we were closer. "We made him uncomfortable."

I just wanted to see if he would do it.

"I know, Wick."

"Or maybe he's more mature than we are and didn't want to put up with it," Oz snickered.

"He's about as mature as the Emperor," Drew said.

"Hey."

"'I am *not* a teenager!'" Drew mocked. He almost got the accent right, too.

"Andrew."

"Little bit, you are," Oz said. "Twentyish per cent, Will. You and Drew both."

I stretched forward to see if he was turning red. He was trying to not laugh, but there was a tiny extra bit of pink in his cheeks.

"Andrew is not a teenager," Will reminded her.

"A whole seven months out of my teens. Ooh."

"I'll ground you both when we get home," he threatened.

"Ozzie," Drew said, pretending to be upset, "he's going to send us to my room. For days and days, I bet."

"Meaniehead," she sniffed.

When they stopped poking back at him, Aisha gave him a long look. "What does twentyish percent mean?"

"Were I living in my own When," he said carefully, "I would be at roughly the twenty to twenty-five per cent mark of expected years to live."

Dude, she's a math teacher.

"You could live to be two hundred?"

"Theoretically, one-seventy to one-eighty. I don't think I will."

She was still looking. "That explains a lot. Will, if I were just meeting you, I'd think you were in your early thirties at the most. Are you going to age that much slower than I will?"

"Is it a problem if I do?"

She finally looked away. "So when I'm in my mid-seventies, I could be walking around with someone who looks forty-five to fifty at best."

"Possibly."

A slight smile tugged at her mouth. "I am *so* going to enjoy that."

He hesitated. "You're truly all right with that?"

"Will, I'll be the old lady rocking life with the hot younger man. You're the one who'll be looking at a wrinkled old woman all the time."

He didn't know what to say.

Tell her she'll always be beautiful.

Trust me.

"Aisha, I don't care what age has in store for either of us. You always have been and always will be the most beautiful woman I've ever known."

She reached over to pet me. "Oh, thank you, Wick."

Ha.

"Dammit," Will muttered.

"I'm sure you said it more eloquently than he suggested."

"Indeed."

I was about to give him another smooth line, one that would get us a kiss, but Shivan was running back, nearly out of breath, and could only get out one word.

"Shedu."

22

The centuries-old houses that once encroached on the Palace of Fine Arts were gone; it was on the edge of the woods now, an oddly shining, dome-shaped beacon near the waterline. A millennium hadn't destroyed its luster nor decayed its structure. I would have stopped to consider that—which one of us expected it to still be pristine—but it was guarded by a line of men with guns, and they had spotted Shivan when he turned around to run.

The chance to withdraw quietly was lost to the eagerness of a fifteen-year-old constructed from data points stored on a hard drive somewhere in the future.

The Shedu closed ranks around us. There were six of us and thirty of them, and Will hissed to everyone to not draw weapons, not yet.

The guard who stepped closest was tall, taller than Will or Drew, and clad in all black. He gripped his laser rifle like a toy, swinging it back and forth as he gestured to Shivan and then Oz and Drew. "No one is scheduled to work here today," he said sharply. "Get back to the fields."

Will was sizing them up, and no one spoke.

"Well?" the guard said, leveling the rifle. "Fields or orchard, take your pick. You have ten seconds to turn around and head back."

"It's nearly dusk," Will said. "Work is done."

"Then go home."

Shivan's hand went to the hilt of his sword. "You have no idea who we are. You wouldn't talk to us like that if you did."

"Stop," Will ordered him.

"Well, he doesn't. He'd be running like the Shedu coward that he is."

Neither Oz nor Drew reacted; they were steeling themselves, ready to fight. Aisha stood firm next to Will, but she glared at Shivan, willing him to shut up.

If I were bigger I would bat them around like little mouse-shaped nip toys.

We need a giant kitty. I'd name him Fluffy.

A voice behind the guard, "They're not elves, Ramus. They're outliers."

Ramus aimed his rifle at Shivan.

"We are neither," Will said. "Simply travelers."

"Travelers," he repeated. "No one travels to Saint Francis. No one visits. No one comes to barter. There's nothing here a traveler would want." From behind him, there was the clatter of rifles being raised. "You come here, you work."

"I don't think so," Will said evenly.

The other Shedu moved toward us and Drew put a hand out to stop Shivan from pushing his way forward. His other hand went to his gun—as did Oz's and Aisha's—and they had nearly pulled the weapons from their waistbands when the low rumbling began.

It vibrated through the ground, buzzing through the soles of their shoes. To a man, the Shedu looked up, then over us, and Will turned slowly to see what had stopped them.

"Wick," Will murmured, "what did you do?"

Fluffy. His name is Fluffy.

Fluffy was a simple tabby cat with orange and yellow stripes and a white belly, and his tail flicked back and forth excitedly as he purred. He was only slightly taller than a horse, which was a bit undersized for my imagination, and he was long and lean, his muscles rippling under soft fur.

His head lowered and back side went up, wiggling in anticipation. The Shedu began to scramble; rifles were dropped as they scattered, and Fluffy pounced, trying to trap the closest one under his mighty paw.

"Don't move," Will ordered. "He thinks they're toys. Move and you're just another mouse to play with."

Don't worry, Fluffy won't eat them. Or us.

"That's not especially reassuring, Wick."

"What the hell is going on?" Drew demanded. "What is that?"

"It's a cat, Andrew," Will said.

Fluffy pounced again, his massive paw slamming Ramus to the ground. Then carefully, he snagged the guard's shirt with his teeth and brought him to us, dropping him to the ground at Will's feet.

Ramus was out cold.

He thinks you're hungry and you suck too much at hunting to catch your own.

"The others will sound an alarm," Aisha said.

"And say what?" Oz asked. "Hey, we were on patrol and got the complete crap scared out of us by a giant ginger kitty?"

Fluffy laid down, purring, one paw set protectively on Ramus's leg. His claws flexed, curling dangerously close to the guard's groin, and he sniffed his new toy curiously, the way I did Will's mouth when I knew he'd eaten something I liked but hadn't shared.

"Is that cat getting bigger?" Drew sputtered.

"Wick, stop," Will hissed.

Fine. I wanted a house-sized kitty but I'll settle for horse sized.

"He's bigger than a horse," Will pointed out. "Please tell me he's friendly."

He is, to us.

"You'd better start explaining, Emperor," Oz said. "Where'd the mutant cat come from and why isn't he eating us?"

Will's eyes flicked toward Shivan, who hadn't moved. He stood still, staring at Fluffy, eyes wide. He was breathing hard and still had his hand on the sword hilt; Aisha reached over and carefully pried his fingers from it, and softly told him it was all right. The cat was friendly. He could even pet it if he wanted.

Shivan twitched and then relaxed.

"He won't bite?"

His name is Fluffy. Tell him.

Will sighed hard. "He won't bite you. His name is Fluffy, and if he's anything like Wick, he'll enjoy having his chin rubbed."

"Fluffy," Drew grunted.

While Shivan braved his way closer to Fluffy, Will took a few steps in the other direction and motioned for them to join him. He explained, reluctantly, about the files he'd found on Finn's computer. "We're caught up in a holographic simulation, one that we're collectively creating as we go along. Our thoughts are adding detail to the simulation, and as you can see, Wick has figured out how to create...friends."

He explained the failsafe, relieving Drew of a bit of the guilt he felt about pulling them so far into the future.

He also expected them to be angry; instead, Oz exhaled sharply and said, "Oh, thank God."

"Seriously," Drew added.

"I thought I was losing my mind. I mean, this whole thing—"

"Yeah, a little off," Drew said. "It's like this bastardized version of a book we read a few months ago, only in that there were two kids trying to free their people from an underground city. I think we both said 'what the hell' out loud a few times. Trees dotting a cityscape several miles under? They grew crops, had fish, and freaking had cars. And not, like, solar powered. These were freaking internal combustion cars, and they had gasoline. Under-freaking-ground."

"The people didn't realize they were underground," Oz added. "Well, except for the mayor and part of the council. They were royal dicks."

"Elves?" Aisha asked.

"No clue where that comes from."

"Oppression," Will said.

"Floridians," Drew mused.

"Yeah, but why *elves*?" Oz asked. "And if we were going to create a class of people who are clearly *just* people, why would any of us label them at all?"

Christmas.

"Christmas, Wick?"

They read the book at Christmas. When Oz was still hurt and stayed in bed a lot. Elves are Santa's workers. Drew offered to dress up like one for her if it would make her laugh. She was still on a lot of drugs then...it made her laugh so hard she almost peed.

"I'll be damned," Drew muttered.

"Well, you could at least have made them tiny with pointy ears," Aisha said, pretending to pout.

Drew looked over to Shivan, who was leaning against Fluffy, half buried into his fur.

"We could just go home, then," he said. "If this isn't real, there's no one to save."

"He's a collection of carefully crafted data," Will said, "but he's real enough. We need to see this through, Andrew."

Oz wasn't listening anymore; she headed for Fluffy to rub his chin. He took his paw off Ramus and she dragged him out of the way, still out cold, and then reached up to tickle the spot on his chin that I liked best.

Drew watched her for a moment, and then asked, "What aren't you telling us, Will?"

He considered telling Drew everything, but instead said that Finn would not have created a simulator without purpose. If he had only meant to keep people from traveling beyond a safe time frame, they would have wound up in a room with a giant sign telling them to go home.

"Anyone who has access to the portals knows to not go forward. Someone who tries has either made a mistake or is running from something."

"He gave them a way to work it out."

When Aisha asked why, Will told her about Finn being lost in time with no memory and his conundrum of letting Jo jump off the Golden Gate Bridge. When he realized what he was willing to let someone do, whether it was right or wrong or simple indifference, he became somewhat focused on the things that drive people to desperation.

"He understood that in creating the portals, he was giving those with access a permanent way out. If you wanted to just disappear into non-existence, a portal to nowhere would be appealing."

"So he created a stop gap."

Will nodded. "I think so. And I think he finished it recently."

After we got stuck in the portal.

"Exactly, Wick. He had to have done this after we were suspended in the portal. No one should be stuck like that, not when it could literally last an eternity."

Drew let that sink in, and then quietly said, "He would have found a way to get you out."

"He would try."

When Oz was done petting Fluffy she left Shivan to cuddle with him and came back, and she wanted to know what was next.

"We move onto the village," Will said. "Stick with the plan, but be careful. Now that you're aware of what your thoughts can produce—" he tapped me on the head "—be judicious. Imagination run amok can get us all killed."

"Even though this isn't real," Oz said.

"Even so."

She patted the hilt of her sword. "Is this a data point, or is it real?"

"It's very real, and will kill anyone you use it against." He tucked a finger under my chin and made me look up at him. "Consult me before you do something like this again, all right?"

Fine.

Can I keep him?

"Yes, you can keep Fluffy for now. Keep him under control."

Fluffy got up, knocking Shivan to the ground.

"Calling it now," Drew said. "I am not scooping his litter box."

*

Fluffy brought up the rear, trailing as we hiked through the Presidio woods to the elves' village. Will stopped grumbling about him when he realized that Fluffy's enormous presence meant a significantly lower chance of being attacked from behind; if anyone approached, they were either going to become a plaything or a snack.

I wanted to ride on Will's shoulder for a while, but he was reluctant to keep me exposed. For all he knew, Fluffy would take me for food, and he wanted to err on the side of caution.

Fluffy thinks I'm God. God is not a snacky treat.

"Seriously, Wick? You made that part of the scenario?"

I created him from nothing. What else would I be to him?

"A programmer."

Maybe we're all just bits and bytes in someone else's computer program and don't exist to begin with.

"That theory has been floated around for hundreds of years."

He explained what I was talking about; Drew shrugged and said, "It wouldn't really matter if we were. We're real to ourselves and each other."

Oz wasn't buying it. "But then the God my mother prays to every day could be some thirteen-year-old kid who pops zits in between the manipulative wars he creates and the people he destroys.

"Come on," Drew said. "If this is all created by a teenager, he's sitting there typing one handed, not popping zits."

"You know from experience? Deep into some fantasy video game and just couldn't help it?"

He shrugged. "Hell, Oz, I may have been chatting online with you."

If it is some horny teenager, it explains a lot.

"And I have new insight into why my son locks his bedroom door when he's online," Aisha grumbled.

"Seriously?" Drew laughed. "You hadn't figured that out?"

Oz came to her defense. "Kinda like how my parents didn't realize Zed was sleeping with the school punchboard? Who wants to think about their kids doing that?"

"Zed and Rhonda?" Aisha blurted. "You cannot be serious."

"Don't call her a skank or Uncle Willie gets upset," Oz said.

From ahead, Shivan called back, "What's a skank?"

"It's a pejorative that should never be used," Will scolded. "Didn't we have this discussion, Oz? Don't blame the girl for your brother's behavior. And don't blame him for being human."

Aisha sighed. "Will, you haven't met this girl, have you?"

"I don't need to. She doesn't bear the blame for Zed's actions."

"I can blame him for not treating her with even a little bit of respect," Oz countered. "I don't care if she made the first move. He didn't have to use her. But the point was, parents don't want to know when their kids are having sex whether they're with someone else or not. Even if they were horny little monsters at the same age."

"That goes both ways," Will told her. "No one wants to think about their parents engaging in any sort of sexual activity."

Drew snorted. "Well, yeah. The idea of a couple of wrinkled old prunes getting it on?"

"Look at each other," Aisha said. "Tell me you think that in thirty or forty years you won't still want each other."

"That's different," Oz said.

"We're not getting wrinkled," Drew added, laughing.

"I've seen pictures," Will said. "Trust me, you're wrinkling like an old sheet left to dry in a heap on the floor. Your nose gets longer, your eyelids sag and your eyes become watery. You stoop when you walk and you shuffle your feet across the floor as if they carry the weight of the world."

"Your nose gets huge," Drew said to Oz.

"No, Oz remains youthful and vibrant. It's quite the shocker. She stands tall and regal, and you...your testicles bang against your knees."

Without thinking about it, Drew's hand went to his crotch. "You're really mean sometimes."

Oz reached for his arm, and then his hand. "It's all right. We'll hire someone to cart them around in a wheelbarrow for you."

"You'll have access to the royal guard," Will said. "It could be a position of honor. Protector of the family jewels."

That made Oz laugh, loudly, and Shivan spun on his heels and barked at them to be quieter.

Fluffy hissed back, his breath a warm, moist gust of wind that made them flinch.

"Don't tick off the giant cat," Drew mused.

Will glanced over his shoulder at Fluffy. "Wick, don't let him speak. I have a feeling his voice is loud enough to be heard all the way to the Cliff House."

His purr wasn't any softer. When we stopped at the edge of the elf village to see if there were any Shedu on patrol, Fluffy plopped down and began to purr. It rumbled under Will's feet and traveled up his legs, and I could feel the vibration as I hung in the sweatshirt pouch.

Elves scattered as the rumbling reached the village center. Men and women pushed against each other as they ran for tight spaces behind trees and between homes; Aradyn, who was on the periphery, crouched low, his arms shooting from his side as he felt for balance.

"It's just the cat," Shivan called out.

The few who hadn't fled backed up several feet.

"What the hell is that?" Aradyn asked.

"Fluffy," Will answered. "He won't hurt you."

Krisf stepped away and tapped his chest. He pointed at Fluffy and then made a petting motion.

"You can touch him," Will said. "He'll lower his head so that you can scratch under his chin."

Grinning, Krisf skipped over to the giant cat while others still cowered. I asked Will to set me on his shoulder and watched as Fluffy rubbed up against the elf. Krisf seemed younger to me than he had been before; he wasn't any older than Zed and was bubbling with eagerness.

I didn't like that. Most of the elves waiting for their orders were young, and that felt unfair. I asked Will about it while Aradyn assigned his people to groups; if we were controlling this, why were they all so young?

"Old men send younger men to war," he said. "It's a collective stereotype. It's not intentional on our part."

Old men cling to their futures while denying young men theirs.

Women, too.

Those are teenaged girls. Someday they would be mothers.

"I know. In the real world, we send our strongest people, knowing that many will die, and with them the progeny they would have created."

More than that.

"I know."

Why then? Why don't we stop right now?

Softly, so that only I would hear, he reminded me that Oz needed this. "She deserves to fight her battle, Wick."

She could get hurt.

"Look at the elves," he said. "What do they remind you of?"

Aradyn had broken them into groups of fifteen, and they waited in a long line, ready to spread out. Their faces were painted in determination and hope, a certainty that they were fighting for right.

It reminded me of something.

They were fighting for salvation.

Eight people back in the line there was a boy of fourteen, his collar skewed, and he carried a homemade bow slung across his back. I'd seen him before, dressed in blue slacks and a white dress shirt, marching across a dusty field on the monitor in the King's office. I didn't know him, but he was hovering there like a memory, and it made me sad.

The boy warrior, the one I thought looked younger than Zed.

Florida.

"Oz wanted their freedom as much as she wanted her own," he whispered. "She wanted them to fight for themselves. Now they can."

They fought for the First Minister.

"Only because they didn't have the truth. Had they known?"

They would have followed the Second Minister.

"Indeed."

Oz and Aradyn gave final orders to the elves; his brother Lerym would lead half of them toward the fields, where they would split. Another elf, Bramble, would lead all but three of the remaining elves toward Kilfin and his armies. Aradyn, Krisf, and Jesf would follow Oz past Baker Beach into Land's End, and they would attack the Cliff House from there.

Oz's intention was to swarm the Cliff House from all sides and secure Shivan unguarded entry; if all went well, Erich would be with the Shedu guarding the house, and he would make sure they were otherwise engaged when we arrived. Once inside, it was up to the rest of us to protect Shivan and get him to Tobias.

Aisha listened long enough to know what was expected, and then went to Fluffy and Krisf. She spoke to Fluffy softly and convinced him to lay down on his side so that Krisf could snuggle up to him, and she held Krisf's pistol while he buried himself against Fluffy's fur. Shivan followed her and leaned against Fluffy's chest. He looked almost sad and a little bit scared.

Drew was with Jesf, giving him dedicated attention as he pantomimed his thoughts.

I tried to keep track of them all. There was a heartbeat wrapped in every breath, and for one fleeting moment I thought I could see what Oz did, a soft rainbow of color that lifted over the elves like fog.

It came on quickly but lifted slowly; I almost told Will about it, but wasn't sure I could explain it, and then wasn't sure I wanted to. If Oz had given me that one moment, I was keeping it to myself.

Once Oz had given the final instructions and ordered the elves out, Aradyn came over to Will, who had been watching everything quietly.

"She's a fine leader," Aradyn said.

Will agreed. "And she's in charge." He clapped Aradyn on the back. "It's almost over."

"I'll get Krisf and Jesf, and we can go."

Oz saw Will touch Aradyn, and when he was out of earshot asked him what he'd heard.

"Clicking."

"So you won't be able to touch someone and plant ideas in their heads."

"Not likely."

He reminded her—and Drew—that they needed to exercise caution in any attempt to manipulate the situation. "Feel free to a degree, but we need to be sure we're not working at cross-purposes. We can still be hurt. If one of us thinks up a massive dog to counter Wick's cat...fur will be flying."

23

The sudden swarm of butterflies confused me. It wasn't so much that I didn't expect to see one every now and then while hiking through the Presidio woods—butterflies happen even if they are rare—but they descended from the trees in one fluttering mass that obscured the light seeping through the leaves and then circled around us in a horde of blue and red, the brightest butterflies I had ever seen.

Everyone stopped, hands on weapons, and they crouched low, ready to spring forward—except for Krisf, who dropped into a squat and covered his head with both arms. Oz was the first to realize what the thick mass was, and she let out an amused chuckle as she stood up straight. "Let it be known," she said with mock gravity, "that on this day, we were victims of the Presidio Butterfly Incident, and we survived."

"At least it wasn't bees," Drew grumbled.

Some of the butterflies were the size of the Emperor's little fingernail, others were as big as his hand. They flitted playfully, floating between trees and landing here and there on shoulders and heads, but when one chose Shivan's nose as a place to rest, he froze.

"They don't bite, do they?"

Oz slipped a finger between him and the butterfly, carefully removing it from his face. "Only if you ask nicely."

She held her hand out so that he could get a better look. Its wings were outlined in dark blue peppered with spots of lighter blue, and in the center of each wing were patches of brilliant red. It held still, allowing her to examine it closely. Will took a look and mused that were the colors different, and if we were a few hundred years in the past before they went extinct, it might be a Monarch.

Probably is. Those are Pacifica's royal colors.

The swarm lifted to a foot above Will's head and moved along the path, stretching out ahead and trailing behind us. It was a steady, thick line of fluttering wings with a happy few dancing around our heads, but a hundred feet ahead the line abruptly turned away from the path, heading deeper into the woods.

"Are they guiding us?" Aisha asked.

Aradyn went ahead to scout the direction they were flying; the butterflies spread out, creating a path through for him. When he reached the place where they turned off, all the ones that had been flying overhead surged forward and created a fluttering wall between him and the path forward. The longer he stood on the path, the thicker the wall became.

He was not going any further along the path.

"A shortcut, perhaps," he said.

Will caught up to him. "If we go in that direction, we'll pass by Immigrant Point and Baker Beach is not much further."

Maybe they want us to go that way so they can eat us.

"I don't think they eat meat," Will said.

"He's afraid of becoming lunch?" Drew asked. "Wick, we'll never let that happen. Oz has a killer plasma sword. She'll cook them alive before she lets them get to you."

Oz nodded. "Besides, they would eat Fluffy first. He's got more meat on him."

Don't let them eat Fluffy either!

There was no clear path worn into the ground, but we followed the butterflies through the trees, chasing the long line as they zig-zagged toward the coast. Will kicked through tall weeds and broken branches, stopping every thirty feet to listen;

there was a louder beating of wings riding above the gentle buzz of the butterflies, and he couldn't place where it was coming from. Oz heard it, too, and asked Drew to walk just ahead of her to clear her path, so that she could turn and keep an eye on the things behind us.

When we were a few minutes off the beaten path, a monstrous roar shuddered the ground and Fluffy dropped down, his ears flat.

Oz saw the giant fireball barrel through the tops of the trees we had just walked away from, saw as it devoured the trees that lined the path, and as we began choking on the smoke that powered toward us, she barked, "Run! *Run!*"

*

We ran until Aradyn could run no more. He could barely breathe and coughed with every step, and then stopped abruptly to grab onto a tree trunk to keep from falling over. It might have taken Will several minutes to realize he was no longer running behind him, but Fluffy stayed to the rear and when Aradyn stopped, he let out a tiny but magnificent meow.

The smoke was far behind us, and the woods were not on fire, so Will stopped and went back to him.

"My back may be strong," Aradyn gasped, "but I cannot run. I'm too old for this."

"You're out of shape," Will said. "You're no older than I am."

"But *you're* old," Shivan sputtered.

It was Oz Will glared at. "Funny."

Drew pushed past Aradyn and Fluffy to get a better look. "What the hell was that?"

"Fire," Shivan replied.

"No, really?" Drew deadpanned. "I thought maybe one of us had blown sunshine out their—"

"Andrew." Will patted Fluffy on his haunch and told him he was a good boy, and then ignored the tiny growl he got in response. "That was too big to be a flamethrower, I think."

"In real life," Drew reminded him.

"We would be thinking in real life terms."

"Would we?" Aisha asked when we were back underway, and everyone but Fluffy was ahead. "Wizards and elves. A giant cat named Fluffy. I don't think we're creating real-life objects here, Will."

"Fair enough."

One of you needs to create a chopped shrimp store. Right there on the beach.

"You cannot be hungry again, Wick."

Wanna bet?

"If we get there and find a massive Wick's Shrimp Shack..."

"He wouldn't," Aisha said, laughing. Then without asking, she dug into the pocket on his backpack and took out another foil packet with chicken for me, and held it for me as we kept moving.

"He wasn't really hungry," Will told her. "His asking for food is habit. A bad habit."

"Who knows when we can take the time to feed him again?" When I was done, she tickled the top of my head and asked if Fluffy needed to eat, too.

Fluffy hadn't even made note that there was something real live fresh dead and delicious in her hand.

Will wasn't about to stop and find out. "If that cat needs food, he can hunt for it."

As long as it's not me.

"You were certain that Fluffy would not eat his creator."

Maybe not, but that wasn't a chance I wanted to take. And I would have told him that, but Aradyn had clearly caught his breath and had taken off in a dead run toward the beach. Will paused, and then heard what the elf had: the sound of laser weapons being fired.

"There shouldn't be anyone fighting on the beach," he said, picking up his pace.

Aradyn stopped abruptly at the edge of the woods and then took a few steps back. There were fifteen Shedu guards on the beach, and from the detritus strewn across the sand, there had been quite a few more. They were yelling orders at each other, firing into the air, trying desperately to avoid the flying dragon that was picking them off one by one.

24

Shivan pushed past Aradyn and ran for the beach. He had his hand on the hilt of his sword and went straight for the cluster of men who were cowering under the shadow of the pitch-black dragon. Drew took off after him, which prompted Will to swear under his breath as he pulled me from the sweatshirt.

He set me down. "Stay here and guard Fluffy."

We'll take notes.

Before Shivan was halfway to his target, Drew tackled him to the ground, the sand puffing up around them. He stayed on top of Shivan, his knees and arms tucked around Shivan's body, hands covering his head, until the shadow was a little further down the beach. When Will reached them, Drew flipped Shivan over roughly and yelled at him, using things off of the Queen's bad word list.

By then the Shedu had noticed them, and half were running, arms drawn, while the others took aim at the dragon.

Bolts of energy bounced off the dragon's skin like marbles off a steel wall.

Zap.

Ping.

Zap.

Ping.

The dragon was like a flying cat, toying with its prey. They couldn't hurt it, and it was going to chase them like mice until it grew bored and hungry.

I sat between Fluffy's front paws. The thump of his tail reverberated through the ground, and the steady drumbeat of it grew faster. There was no guarding the growing giant kitty; he was going to do whatever he was going to do, and I didn't think I had enough control over him.

I know what he was looking at; the same thing I kept looking at.

There was a funny looking black bird in the sky, and it was so close he could taste it. If it hadn't been gnawing on a Shedu, bones and all, he might have pounced.

Will and Drew had not drawn their weapons; neither had the others, which worried me. The Shedu ran at them with rifles in hand, but they waited, ready.

Oz was the first to engage. When the guard was five feet in front of her, leveling his rifle at her head, she bellowed "Coward!" and leaped forward, slamming the palm of her hand into his throat.

The fight was on.

Oz and Will fought with fists and feet, getting in close enough to strike blows that made blood spurt from noses and mouths, splattering their shirts and their skin. Aisha pulled her gun out and aimed, but ran backward until the guard was nearly on her and she had no choice; she pulled the trigger, and then sat down hard as the laser engaged and blew a hole the size of her fist through the Shedu's chest.

It went clean through, and smoke puffed out from the hole, but there was no blood. Her mouth fell open and eyes went wide as his head snapped to his chest and then he slowly fell, landing on his back. She scooted in the sand, gulping air like water, yet kept an eye on the fighting in front of her. Who to watch? Who to worry about? She settled on Shivan, who had unclipped his sword from his belt, his face painted in determination until he realized he couldn't find the switch to turn it on. He fumbled with it, trying to keep his eyes on the man running at him, until he lost his grip and the sword fell to the sand. He dropped to his knees, grappling for the handle, and as he looked away, Drew came in from the side and plowed his foot into the Shedu's knee.

As it buckled and he bellowed in pain, Drew kicked again, catching him in the face with a solid round kick. The guard flew backward, a tasty unconscious morsel that drew the dragon's attention.

It flew closer, and Fluffy couldn't contain himself anymore. He sprang over me and galloped onto the beach, and as Drew pulled Shivan to his feet with an order to run, Fluffy leaped over them both.

Aisha was on her feet again, slapping her hands at a smaller Shedu who had rushed at her with nothing but his fists to fight with; they both froze when Fluffy launched into the air, long, sharp claws unsheathed from his giant paw, swiping at the black dragon. He found the weak spot where its neck met its body, and he scratched, leaving four long welts that oozed a thick, clear liquid. Will grabbed Aisha's hand and pulled her toward the woods and the others followed, where they watched as Fluffy vaulted into the air again, slamming the dragon into the water.

Fluffy waited at water's edge for the dragon to pull itself onto the sand; when it was lying on the beach, gasping and roaring in pain, Fluffy bit down, and that's when I looked away, because if it looked as gross as it sounded, the aftermath was going to be nasty.

"As dragons go," Aradyn said breathlessly, "that was a small one. An infant learning to hunt."

Will scowled. "Then where is its mother?"

We waited behind the trees, watching and listening for the beat of wings and waiting for the heat of breath that had likely been the cause of the fireball that sent us off the path. The beach was littered with bloody body parts and one lone living Shedu who had dropped to his knees at the sight of his men scattered before him.

Mom might come here for lunch.

We should leave.

Will wanted a moment for everyone to calm down and breathe. "You were literally slapping him," he said to Aisha. "He had no idea how to respond to that."

"Fight like a little bitch, you get slapped." Taking a deep breath, she added, "I couldn't bear to shoot someone again. That was...intense."

"You did well," he assured her.

"Anyone hurt?" Drew asked.

"Pride," Shivan said. "I apologize."

"That was your first real fight," Oz reminded him. "You're not in a bloody lump on the ground, so it's fine."

"It is *not* fine," he cried. "How can I face Tobias if I can't even draw my sword against a single distracted Shedu? I wasted time, and I didn't know what to do when I dropped it. I *panicked*."

She wasn't sure what to tell him. Will waited a beat, and then said, "The first time I fought, and I mean a real fight, not sparring in the ring, I quickly came to realize that I had no idea what to actually do. I fought inelegantly, and the only way it ended without harm was when I got in close and screamed as loudly as I could. I had the skills, Shivan. I knew how to fight, but in that moment had no idea what to do. So I screamed like a little girl. Literally."

"And you did know what to do," Drew said. "You drew your weapon, but you just hadn't had enough practice with it."

"I should be better than this," Shivan said. "Oz trained me well enough but...I opened my mouth to exhale, and nothing but *stupid* came out."

"Been there," Drew snorted.

Oz gestured to Will. "The first time I fought the Emperor, I didn't land a hand on him. We sparred hard, until I threw up. I began training when I was six years old, Shivan, and twelve years later a total of twenty minutes sparring with him made me hork my breakfast onto the grass. When we were done, I was a mass of bruises and hadn't landed a single kick or punch on him."

"But now?" Will prompted.

"Now," she said, looking at him, "I can hold my own. And he knows he won't necessarily win every fight."

"You will do what you need to in the moment required," Will said to Shivan. "Of that, I have no doubt."

There was still no sign of a mother dragon, so Oz decided to push on. She stayed in the lead, keeping the group closer to the trees than the beach, and Shivan was right behind her, with Drew behind him, watching.

Aisha and Will were the only ones walking side by side, and Fluffy stayed to the rear, licking dragon bits from his cheeks.

"Who was that for? Aisha asked. "Shivan or Oz?"

"Take your pick," he said. "She knows she can fight. I don't know if she has faith in her ability to rise to the occasion when it matters most."

"How could she not?"

He'd made sure her training was solid; he had no doubt that she could beat almost anyone. But after she was taken from the bunker, she knew what her odds were, and she didn't fight back. She used her wits to keep herself alive, but there was that lingering doubt. Did she do well enough? Could she have fought and won? Why didn't she punch Munson hard enough to crush his larynx?

"She thinks we saved her, Aisha. In her mind, she couldn't free herself and had to wait for the cavalry to ride in on proverbial white horses and save the day. She can't seem to embrace the idea that the fight wasn't physical, and that it was very much a battle that she won."

Aisha nodded, but I don't think she understood.

"Levi Munson would have killed her if she'd fought back," Will explained. "He would not have accepted this girl having the strength and skill to thwart his will. She's not focusing on that, nor the fact that she was continuously outnumbered and that her determined silence and refusal to give him the physical battle he wanted is what kept her alive."

There's a butterfly on her head.

One of the bigger blue and red monarchs had settled on the top of her head; Shivan giggled but Drew set a hand on his shoulder and told him to be quiet. Within a minute, five smaller ones landed on her, and she didn't notice.

Drew is doing that, isn't he?

"I believe so," Will said.

Soon her shoulders were covered, and when they landed on her arms, she finally noticed. She turned her head and smiled at him, and then kept on going.

Butterfly kisses.

"I don't think that's what the phrase means, but yes. I think those are kisses."

Why doesn't he just grab her and plant one on her?

"Circumstances, Wick. He's not going to insinuate his immediate wants into the situation. He found another way."

Good thing he only wants a kiss.

Oh, and we're being followed.

He slowed his pace and touched his hand to Aisha's arm to get her to slow a bit, too. "How close, Wick?"

Close. Maybe fifty feet behind Fluffy, off to the left. In the woods.

He turned his head a touch and listened. The footsteps were soft but not careful; whoever followed wasn't trying to hide and didn't care if we noticed. Hand on his gun, Will turned abruptly and stepped to the side so that he could see past Fluffy.

"Hagar."

"Your numbers have grown," Hagar said, gesturing to Fluffy. He had Shivan's silver sword, sheathed and hanging from his waist. The weight of it pulled the belt down over his hip, and he leaned ever so slightly in its direction.

"He's helpful. He killed and ate a dragon."

Shivan ran toward the old wizard. "Hagar! The butterflies!"

Hagar lifted a hand, extending his pointy finger, and one of the big ones landed on it. "The Blackshear Monarch. These are wisps from the soul of your family, Shivan. They exist for no reason other than to bring happiness."

"They pushed us off the path," Shivan told him. "Right before a fireball came screaming through the trees."

"Living made you happy, didn't it?"

"Keep moving," Will said, pointing for Shivan to get back into line behind Oz. "We still have light, and I'd like to get as far as we can."

Oz turned. "We have light," she repeated. "Why do we have light? We left just before dusk, so it should be dark now."

Hagar didn't answer, and Will shrugged.

You want light, don't you?

She wasn't done. "And the rain hasn't started. Your destruct code shouldn't launch until midnight."

"No one wants to do this in the rain," Drew said. "Let's just get there and worry about the details later."

Krisf wasn't ready to move on. He pointed to the sky, and then made a slashing motion across his throat, then pointing ahead of us.

"Perhaps," Hagar said. "The fighting has begun in the Square of Alamo and in the panhandle of the old park. Surely Tobias knows. Delaying the rain gives his guards as much of an advantage as it does the elves and Kilfin's army."

Krisf went over to Shivan and tapped him on the chest, and made a circular motion. He then pointed to each one of us and made the circle again.

"We still protect him," Will said.

"Gotta get him to Tobias," Drew added.

Krisf reached for Oz's hand and pulled her to Shivan until they were touching.

Will understood. "We protect her, as well."

"Like hell," Oz spat. "We get him in. I can take care of myself."

Drew carefully plucked a butterfly from his shoulder and put it on hers. "No one says you can't. The point is that we protect each other, all the way through. Like my brother would say, I've got your six."

Softly, Oz said, "I've got your twelve."

Bloody hell. I've got nausea.

"Hush, Wick," Will whispered.

As they started walking again, Shivan mumbled, "No one said there would be math."

"And that," Aisha whispered to Will, "is a very Oz thing to say. First day in my algebra class, when I was explaining what I expected of the students, she looked at the board and said loudly that no one told her there would be math involved. I didn't know if she was being funny or if she was going to be that one student I wanted to boot by the end of the week."

Will snorted. "Both?"

"She was challenging, I'll give her that. I have never had a student ask 'why' so many times."

That's your fault, Emperor.

"It probably is," he agreed. "When Oz was little, I told her that if someone who was attempting to teach her something couldn't answer the simple question of 'why' then they likely did not know the material well enough. I intended that for her karate lessons, but she made it a personal quest. Aubrey has never quite forgiven me for that."

"Gee. I wonder why?"

"Now, see, I am not a parent, so that knowledge is not required of me."

"You had a hell of a lot of fun with the kids, didn't you?"

"Little bit, yeah."

"Jimmy always comes home with Emperor stories, you know. The videos of you dancing at birthday parties?" She laughed. "I knew you had it in you and wondered if anything would ever bring it out."

"It used to embarrass them. It's not as much fun now that it doesn't."

Oz stopped abruptly, raising her fist. Drew's fist shot up half a second later, warning us they'd heard something. Will filtered past the elves with Aisha right behind him.

"Bright light," Oz said. "Coming out of the woods."

We were turning away from Baker Beach so that we could skirt around China Beach—which was more of a cove than a beach, and a place one could get penned in by enemy fighters—and were heading in a direction that would lead us into the entry of Lands End. Deep into the woods, there was a glow that swallowed the trees, a ball of light that was peppered with sparks.

You know Drew is itching to go see.

"Approach *carefully*," Will said to Drew.

He and Oz took the lead and moved cautiously toward the glow with Will and Aisha right behind. I heard the others behind us, but they stood at a distance safe enough to protect themselves. Fluffy wanted to bolt toward the bright giant-cat-toy-sized ball but managed to restrain himself when Shivan told him it might bite.

The glow was a curtain of light, thin tendrils that sparked and popped, and it stretched around the trunks of a dozen trees. Trapped in its center were hundreds of tiny flying creatures, miniature people with wings that glowed red and blue.

Tinkerbell laid eggs and this is what hatched, right?

They noticed us, and formed a wall just behind the curtain; they stared at us as we stared at them.

Oz took a step closer. "Hello."

She was answered with the beat of a thousand tiny wings; the buzz of it washed over us, and was warm.

"Sprites?" Drew asked.

Or the butterflies mated with people and these are the shiny offspring.

Will's fingers tapped my head, right between my ears.

Hagar walked around the circle, his hand on his medallion. "The magic is strong here. But it always is, in the end." Carefully, he set his hand on the curtain, and it sparked around his fingertips. "Why are you here?"

Everyone spread out, standing at curtain's edge. The sprites began to move, flying around the circle, keeping a wary eye on us.

"You're trapped, aren't you?" Oz asked.

They moved as a mass toward her.

"Can you fly over the top?" She craned her neck to look up; the curtain went into the canopy of the trees, but it looked as if there were openings.

One lone sprite jetted up and bounced off a barrier we couldn't see.

"This is very old," Hagar murmured. "I haven't seen this magic since..." He sighed hard. "Tobias."

Hagar and Will ran their hands over the curtain, looking for a seam or a lock. When they didn't find one, Will tried to plow his hand through with a sharp strike from his palm. The curtain pressed in as if he'd only been fluffing up a pillow, and a hard, fast front kick fared no better.

Drew considered firing at it but then worried it would actually work and he would kill some of the sprites. He also thought about aiming for one of the trees it was wrapped around, until Will pointed out that he could bring the tree down, killing them all. They needed something they could control, something more powerful than any abilities he had.

Oz pulled the plasma sword from her waistband and turned it on. The blade leaped to life, as bright as the curtain, and I could hear it buzz in her hand.

"Stand back," she told Will and Hagar. To the sprites she said, "Get as far back as you can."

Working with deliberate care, she pulled the blade down the trunk of the tree she stood closest to, burning through bark, and sparks flew at her. She squinted against the light but didn't flinch as they popped off her skin, leaving tiny red welts. When she had cut from the base of the tree to as high as she could reach, she turned the sword off and with Drew began working the curtain loose, prying it back until they could fold a large piece of it away.

When she stepped back, they swarmed to the opening, funneling out as quickly as they could.

I hope they're friendly.

What if they eat us?

"Look at their wings, Wick," Will said. "They wear the red and blue of the Blackshears." He thought they were harmless; I reminded him that pigeons look harmless, too, but that didn't mean that they wouldn't gang up on me one day and take me for a ride off the roof of the house, ending with a sudden splat on Union Square.

Oz and Drew stood perfectly still while the sprites flew in circles around them. Hagar whispered to Will that this was deep appreciation and what Oz and Drew were feeling was not unlike the warmth of sleeping clothes fresh from the dryer. The sprites were deadly but loyal and would consider their freedom a gift to be repaid.

Will was worried about what they would do once the gift was repaid; I was more curious how Hagar knew what clothes fresh out of a dryer felt like.

The sprites followed when we began walking again, which worried Will. They were a shifting wall of light, a massive signal that there were things moving about the woods, a sign he didn't want noticed.

"Dim," Hagar told them.

Oz added, "Please."

The glow dimmed bit by bit until the only light was daylight creeping through the leaves on the trees. They continued to trail Fluffy; the buzz was noticeable, but it wasn't loud enough to be mistaken for anything other than bugs in a forest.

"What did you mean, the magic is strongest near the end?" Oz asked Hagar. "We still have a way to go."

"Yes, you do."

She waited, but he didn't elaborate, and the years of dealing with the Emperor convinced her to let it go.

"How far have you walked?" Hagar asked Will. He kept glancing at Krisf and Jesf, who were slowing down.

"Perhaps eight miles. It's been slow progress."

"And how much further?"

"Three or four. Why?"

The two littlest elves are tired.

Fluffy grabbed Krisf by the back of his shirt using his teeth and settled the elf onto his back. Jesf tried to run—he wasn't sure if he was about to become a snack or not—but Fluffy stopped him with his paw, and then placed him behind Krisf.

No point in having to keep an eye on them. He won't mind if they have to hold on by his fur.

"If Fluffy begins to run," Will told them, "jump off. And it won't hurt him if you use his fur as a handhold."

It's a shame we can't take Fluffy home with us.

"We'd have to build him his own house," Will said. "And hire someone to clean up after him, because I'm certain I wouldn't."

But he's fun.

Will tapped me on the head again. "He's in here."

Big whoop.

"Do you want a cat of your own? I can arrange that. A kitten you can boss around. I would be willing to clean up after another cat-sized cat."

"Can Wick talk to other cats?" Aisha asked.

That gave Will pause. "I don't know. Do you know, Wick? If you're with another cat, can you understand him?"

Get me one and we'll find out.

"We're getting another cat," Will called out.

Drew spun around. "Fluffy? I told you, I'm not scooping that litter box."

"A kitten. We'll pick a day to be his birthday, and that will be his gift. A pet of his own."

"I thought you wanted a hover cart," Drew said to me.

I can't have both?

"You can have both," Will said.

"All righty then." Drew turned back around. "We're marching off to war, and instead of discussing what we might be facing, we're planning a birthday for the cat. There's going to be a party, too, isn't there?"

"Could be worse," Will reminded him. "Besides, would you deny Wick a birthday party? He truly doesn't ask for much."

"I'm all for a party once we're done with this. Hell, Wick, I'll get you an entire litter of kittens if you want. But right now we need to figure out how the hell we get into the Cliff House."

"What are we going to do?" Oz asked. "Knock on the front door?"

"That's more or less how we got into Red's compound," Drew said. "Will touched the guard, made him think we were expected, and they opened the gates up without any real fuss."

"That won't work this time." Will said.

He didn't get a chance to ponder what might work because blocking the path there was a massive plasma cannon aimed right at us, and standing on top of it next to the switch was a Shedu with a twitchy hand.

25

"Elves and outliers," the Shedu said with a twist of a laugh. "Wandering the woods, pretending to be stealth, while keeping company with the sprites and...that."

He doesn't like Fluffy?

"And a pocket kitty!" he said gleefully, noticing me. He slid on the backside of the cannon until he was straddling it, stroking it with his hands.

Dude. That's kind of obscene.

Will and Aisha formed a tight line with Oz and Drew, standing in front of the elves and the wizard. No one drew weapons; there was no reason to because if he fired that cannon, there was no defense against it. Body parts would fly, and the entire day would be ruined.

Oz crossed her arms. "And a tiny little man with phallic issues waits alone, to guard a tiny sliver of beach that isn't worth protecting."

"Aye, and we both know it's not the beach I'm protecting."

"Do we?" she pressed. "You don't seem all that bright, out here without a backup. Hidden in the dim light yet in plain sight, no one to save you."

He snorted. "Save me from what?"

"Nine of us, one of you," Drew pointed out.

The Shedu slapped at the cold metal of his cannon. "One of these, all I need."

"And yet," Hagar said, pushing between Will and Drew, his hand on his medallion, "you sit there blabbing like an old woman, without considering the danger you're in."

"Wizard," the Shedu grunted. "Go home. You're old and weak. This battle isn't for you."

"Don't underestimate me." He lifted his free hand, making a fist, and from behind us there was a sudden bright light and the buzzing of a thousand sprites. The guard squinted against the blinding glow, trying to make sense of what was swarming toward him. He didn't understand until they were upon him, spinning around him so quickly that they were just a blur, the buzz and whir loud enough that I flattened my ears against it.

He only screamed once. It was loud and piercing and ended before he was done.

A few seconds later the buzzing stopped, the light dimmed, and as the sprites flew back to their spot behind Fluffy, the bones of the Shedu tilted and then slipped from the cannon to the ground.

"They've been trapped for a long time and were very hungry," Hagar said simply.

"Gross," Shivan muttered as he stepped around the pile of bones.

They're expecting us, aren't they?

"I'm afraid so," Will said. He reached up to a panel on the side of the cannon and opened it, then pulled from it a thumb-sized chip that he snapped in half. "Keep your eyes open and listen carefully. We aren't alone out here."

Well, yeah, there are man-eating sprites. They won't eat cats, will they?

He asked Hagar, to be sure. The old wizard swore they wouldn't eat me and they wouldn't eat anyone else unless we asked, but that didn't make me feel any better. Those bones were picked clean, not even a speck of blood was left.

When we resumed the walk, Will made sure he was with

Oz, Drew, and Aisha, and quietly asked which one of them had thought that up.

"Only thing I was thinking about, other than what a raging asshat he was, is that I kinda need to pee," Drew said.

Oz didn't think it was her, either. "I've been stuck on how to get into the Cliff House. There's only one way in that I know of, and it's going to be blocked."

Aisha didn't have a transponder and wasn't transmitting to the computer, but even so she was also thinking about a way in.

"Had to be you," Oz said to Will.

"Nowhere in my brain was the notion that we would encounter a guard perched atop a cannon, nor the idea that the sprites would then viciously consume him."

"Come on. Cocky guy, inappropriately big gun, never tried to fire it. Totally you."

"Jesus, Oz." Drew snorted out a laugh. "That's mean."

Will hitched the backpack up a little higher on his back. "I concede. Perhaps it was me."

Oz wasn't done poking at him. "The Emperor's delusion."

"Perhaps it was I?" he went on. "What's the grammar here? It was me. It was I. I should know this."

"You're deflecting, Will," Drew said. "And I think it would be 'I' but 'me' is more natural for the spoken word. Saying 'maybe it was me' would be even more natural. One day, when you become a real boy, you'll speak like the rest of us, Pinocchio."

"Don't help him," Oz said. "He wants us to not think about his ego." She stepped ahead, taking the lead again, but called back, "It's not the size of the pole, it's the wiggle in the worm."

"She's trying to tell you something," Will said to Drew.

"Bite me, old man." He pushed Will with his shoulder, chuckling, and went to catch up to Oz.

"Was it you?" Aisha asked when they were out of earshot. "That was kind of gruesome."

He didn't think so. "I was also focused on how we might gain entry to the Cliff House, and pondering how well guarded it might be."

"Variables," she breathed. "The program could be learning, Will. The more it does, the less control we have."

"I don't think my father—"

"It's all math. The program he wrote boils down to math and logic, and if he programmed it to function the same way semi-sentient systems do when they're used to create evolving testing scenarios..."

"The graphic interchange game players will use their opponents' weaknesses to win."

"It's just a thought."

It was a thought he wanted to examine, because if none of them created the Shedu-eating sprites, then they had to be even more careful, lest they become dessert.

*

The trail that wound through Lands End was cracked and covered in dirt, with weeds popping up through the cracks, exposing the broken magnetic disks that controlled vehicles on the road. I would have thought that in a thousand years' time—or even two hundred years—the road would have washed away or been buried under layers of detritus, but no one asked me to consider what we would find once we set out on the path.

The tables and benches near the Eagles Point entry were gone, but the semi-circle space where hikers often rested or used as a turn-around point was still there. Will decided it was a good place to take a break, because the elves looked tired and he wanted a breather before getting any closer to the Cliff House.

He pulled the pack off his back and dug into it for sandwiches for everyone else and more chicken for me. Fluffy plopped down in the middle of the Point and allowed Hagar and the elves to use him as a backrest, and he purred so hard that Krisf vibrated. Krisf grinned and pushed himself against Fluffy even harder, and briefly turned his head to bury his face in Fluffy's fur.

The sprites settled on his back; they folded their wings and stretched out, rolling around in his soft fur.

"Roughly two miles to the Cliff House," Will said as he peeled back the wrap on his sandwich. "It could be a long two miles."

"We can hike that in well under an hour," Drew pointed out. "Half an hour."

"Normally. But normally we would not have a cat the size of a Clydesdale tagging along, nor would we need to stop to swat dragons from the air and then bear witness as a man is rendered into nothing but bone. These are not normal circumstances."

Oz leaned against Drew's side. "I have a new appreciation for how hard it was for you guys last year. Cramps are off the charts. My back hurts, my hips hurt, and my left foot isn't very happy either. You walked this far before daylight every day, didn't you?"

"Scale of one to ten?" Will asked.

She waved him off. "I'm just whining. I'm fine."

He didn't think she was fine. She was pale and sweating, and barely touched her food.

Send her home.

He rubbed the top of my head and didn't have to say out loud what he was thinking. He couldn't send her home now; even if he tried, she would refuse. The only way home for her was if he picked her up and carried her to a portal, and the only one he suspected was functional was the one we'd come through.

Eight miles of a screaming and kicking Oz was not happening.

"I have pain medication," he told her. He was digging in the bag again, before she could answer. "It's old and not strong and probably not even real, but it will take the edge off if you allow it to."

"Take it," Drew said before she could protest. He stretched his arm out toward Will and took the pills, and then handed them to her. She didn't argue; she swallowed them dry before taking a swig from the canteen, and settled back against the tree they sat under.

"It's at least an eight," Will whispered to Aisha. "No

argument. If she weren't in significant pain, she would have argued."

"From last year?"

He nodded. "I've never seen someone so physically damaged who survived. The truth is that she may always have some level of pain unless she allows her brain to be remapped."

"Why wouldn't she? Remapping just breaks the cycle of pain. It wouldn't change anything else."

Oz didn't think it would work; her pain wasn't constant, it flared from time to time but most of the time she felt fine. She was afraid that if she allowed someone to peek into her brain and essentially reset her neurons and synapses to forget how much she sometimes hurt, it would change her.

"She says that the pain she feels has helped shape her," Will said, still speaking softly. "She's afraid that if she forgets it, she'll be less empathetic."

"So?"

"She's going to rule over Pacifica someday. She knows she needs to be able to empathize with the suffering of other people. She's afraid that without it she'll lose some of her conscience, and will become less than...kind."

She was afraid she would turn into her maternal grandfather, so at odds with the real world that he went after what he wanted without regard to how much it hurt others. It didn't matter how often Aubrey or Jax told her she could never become like that; it wasn't a risk she was willing to take.

Something made him the way he was, and she wasn't taking the chance that part of it was owed to biology.

"How many thousands of years will we argue over nature versus nurture?" Aisha mused.

"Had my father not succeeded in his efforts? Only a bit over two hundred more years."

"It seems to me, the success was more yours and Drew's."

Mine, too.

"It was his mission. We helped." He glanced over at Oz and Drew. "If not for them, I would be dead. Wick and I both would."

Or just stuck in that portal.

"True. We could also have just been stuck in the portal for the rest of eternity."

"Well, there's a cheery thought," Aisha said.

At least we would have had each other's company.

"Truly, the notion of it makes me appreciate not being there all the more. You would have been fine company, Wick, but at some point I would have snapped mentally."

Drew was helping Oz get up, and she stretched, bending over to reach for her toes. When her hands went flat on the ground, her back cracked, and it was loud enough to make Aisha cringe.

"Much better," Oz sighed. She nodded toward a spot off the path and asked Drew to go with her. No one else got up to follow; they'd all taken turns throughout the night to guard each other while taking care of personal business. I didn't bother, I just squatted behind the closest tree and if they wanted to watch, fine.

When they came back, Shivan popped up, brushing crumbs off his shirt. "Are we going now?"

An explosion in the distance answered him. Will stood, counting under his breath, waiting for the ground to shake, but it never came.

"That didn't sound good," Oz said.

"They're taking the beach," Hagar said.

"What, with bombs?" Drew asked.

Will didn't think it mattered. Bombs or cannons or even relic tanks; there was fighting ahead, and we were walking right toward it. Oz wasn't concerned; if the explosion came from the beach, we were still at least half an hour away. The entire battle could shift three or four times before we got there, so there was no point in worrying.

"Unless they bring the fight to us," Drew said.

"Hey, we have two plasma swords, four laser pistols, a sword, and a giant cat. We'll be fine."

"I'd share your confidence if the cannon we passed was portable," Will said as he slipped the backpack on. He'd unloaded a ton of sandwiches from it, but it looked as filled as it had when we started out. I jumped to his shoulder and pawed at it.

You carrying someone in here?

"Food and recharge packs," he said.

I saw you make sandwiches. You didn't make that many.

"I didn't need to."

Ah. Pretend food for pretend people?

"Something like that. Now, do you want to ride up there for a while? Or do you want back into the sweatshirt?"

Here is fine. If something happens, I'll jump down.

"If something happens, don't just jump down. Get out of the way. Hide in the trees, or even behind Fluffy, but don't put yourself in danger."

There was nothing deep inside me that wanted to get in the middle of a fight. I agreed, not only because I didn't want to get in the way, but also because I didn't want him to worry about me.

And I meant it when I said I'd hide.

Good thing I didn't promise.

26

Oz warned Drew about the steps ahead of us in Lands End. There were dozens to ascend, and—she had counted them once—133 to descend. He didn't think it sounded like too many, so she threatened to introduce him to them later, approaching from the other direction at the end of a long run.

"The Emperor," she said, glowering at Will, "took me on a run with him from the old zoo, partway into Golden Gate Park, and then along the beach. We ran eight miles before we got to the hill leading up to the Cliff House. After that, he headed into Lands End and expected me to run up the freaking stairs. When you've already gone nearly ten miles and survived that hill only a few freaking minutes earlier...it's mean."

She had to stop four times going up the stairs. He didn't wait for her, either; he ran onto Eagle Point and turned around to catch up as she slowly made her way down the stairs on the other side.

"She called me names," Will said.

"You earned every one of them, too. The only saving grace that day was calling Zed to pick me up after I made it back to the Cliff House. He'd just gotten his air bike and was willing to take me anywhere if it meant riding."

"And you made Will run home alone?"

"Hey, he could have hopped on the bike, but he wasn't touching anyone then."

"I got to Golden Gate Park and took public transport," Will said. "For some reason, when you're that sweaty, no one sits next to you."

"You're the Emperor," Aisha reminded him. "It's common knowledge that you give the Emperor an incredible amount of personal space, even if it means getting off the bus."

That gave him pause. "I hope people don't disembark simply because I'm there."

Drew snorted. "No one wants to get beheaded because they accidentally fell against you when the bus stopped too hard. Being the hard-ass you are, and all."

"He's never had anyone beheaded," Oz said. "He just takes away their toys."

Will pretended offense. "I give them back eventually."

"Except my water balloons," Drew sniffed.

"Those went to good use. I lobbed them at Jax. Alcohol may have been involved."

They think you're joking. I know better.

"I would pay real money to see that happen," Drew said. "If I had real money. You know, if you do it again and let me record it. I could put it online with a commercial sponsorship deal and make enough to live on for a couple of years, I bet."

"That's exactly what Pacifica needs. The future Prince Consort selling family videos to the masses."

"We need a new title for him," Oz said. "Consort makes him sound like a hooker."

"You're thinking of 'escort,'" Aisha said.

"Maybe. It still sounds vaguely inappropriate."

"My dad always said he was the Queen's boy toy. I'd be all right with that."

"You are aware," Will said, "that he once introduced himself as just that at a reception for the new French President? 'Hello, I'm Richard, Queen Shazia's boy toy.' And again, yes, alcohol was involved."

Another explosion echoed from the distance.

"I could use a drink right about now," Aisha muttered.

"You don't have to do this," Oz told her. "Just because we're freaks and find this kind of fun doesn't mean you have to be dragged into it."

"I didn't walk all this way to sit down and watch like it was entertainment."

"No, but you could hang back and keep an eye on Wick," Will said. "And I'm not saying that because I think you can't fight well enough. I suggest it because I truly cannot survive without him."

"I thought that was hyperbole."

He needs me.

"Wick is my anchor in this When. Without him...I need him to not be injured. Or worse. It goes far beyond a broken heart. The aftermath for me would be brutal."

She looked to Oz. "Is he serious?"

Oz nodded. "Wick is the furry little talisman that holds him in place. Without him, he'll stop sleeping, become delusional, sick, and slowly die."

"It's time's way of flicking me off like a flea," Will explained. "I'm not asking you to walk away from this, but to care for him in order to help me survive once we're done here."

I don't think she completely believed him, but she said she would watch me. I rode on Will's shoulder, close to her, and he warned her that if I sensed it was time, I would make the leap over to her. "He's small, but his six pounds feels considerable when you don't expect it."

Drew's hand went to his stomach. "Tell me about it. At four in the morning, it feels like a thirty-pound dead weight."

He was wiggling his fingers. I thought he wanted to play.

"I was scratching, Wick. Cripes."

I lowered my face to Will's ear. *Did he hear me?*

"Inferred, I believe. But I could be wrong."

We reached the first set of stairs, which Drew proclaimed to be "not that bad" and headed up. Halfway, he declared himself a liar; after the miles already behind him, the stairs were torture, and he was ready to be done with the walking part. "At least going across Colorado there were no stairs. Barely any hills at that point. Remind me again why we live in San Francisco?"

Shivan snorted. "You live here because Oz lives here and she lets you touch things."

"There's that," he conceded. "But I'd still rather not be dragging my sorry ass up these stairs. Someone should have installed a lift by now. Can I petition the council for a lift? I can't be the only person who wants one."

"You're not that lazy," Oz said.

"I am, but, fine. Race me to the top. Winner gets a kiss."

She took off before agreeing to anything and reached the peak three steps before he did. Instead of kissing him, though, she dropped low and gestured for him to get down. She stretched out on her belly and slithered forward, peering down the stairs on the other side.

Will signaled for everyone to stop and we waited, until Oz stuck her arm behind her back and lifted four fingers. Drew pulled his gun from his waistband and released the safety, and then whispered to Oz; she slithered backward, until she could stand without being seen, and ran back to us.

"Four Shedu armed with laser rifles, and all are in exo-suits. They're waiting about thirty feet out, two are completely exposed and two are half-hidden behind trees. All are ready to fire."

"We surprise them," Shivan suggested. "Run and shoot first."

The exoskeleton suits, armor designed by Drew's father, made that a losing proposition. Will didn't dismiss the idea as ridiculous but told him that we weren't in the position to ambush. "The type of armor they have prevents most ammunition from making an impact. The only viable targets are where flesh is exposed."

"Neck, face, and armpits," Oz said. "Slivers of skin, that's all."

"Do we go back and find another way?" Aisha asked.

Oz didn't think so. "You're a good shot, Will. So is Drew."

"Perhaps not that good," he said. "And bonus points for using my name."

"We need a diversion," Oz said. "If they're distracted and not focused on us, we might have a shot."

Before she could ask, the butterflies lifted from Fluffy's back and gathered in a massive ball of blue and red that floated over our heads. Will set me down and then took the lead to climb the rest of the way up, telling Oz to follow and the rest to stay back. There wasn't enough space at the top of the stairs for everyone to cluster, and he didn't want anyone to get in the way.

He laid in the dirt on his belly next to Drew, his weapon ready. I ran past Oz and found a spot near Will where I could hide behind a hand post and still peek out to see. The butterflies bolted overhead, the ball breaking into streaks that flocked the Shedu. They covered the guards' faces and hands, vibrating layers that plugged their noses and choked the air from their mouths.

The Shedu couldn't see and couldn't breathe; as panic set in, each weapon dropped to the ground while they clutched frantically at their faces, trying to clear away enough space to suck in air, Will and Drew took aim and fired. Two arms exploded from their shoulders, a hand went flying, and then as if choreographed, four helmeted heads hit the dirt and rolled until their noses became fleshy little brakes.

Their bodies remained upright for a second or two and then fell, bloodless, onto their heads.

Drew muttered under his breath, *they're not real, they're not real, they're not real*, until Will rolled over and sat up. Shivan raced the rest of the way up the stairs to see the aftermath, and when he saw their headless bodies, he leaned over the railing and vomited his lunch onto the side of the cliff.

There's no blood or guts, dude. It could be way grosser.

Aisha rushed to his side; she rubbed his back while he continued to dry heave, softly repeating that it was all right. Just don't look. Hagar waited on the stairs behind us and sighed hard; he didn't have to say it—he'd already seen worse, and it wasn't going to get any cleaner. He needed to suck it up.

Drew and Will got up and brushed the dirt off their pants, and then headed down the stairs. Oz tugged at Shivan's sleeve to get him to follow but didn't say a word to anyone else. She walked past the bodies of the Shedu guards without looking down and didn't stop until she'd caught up with Will fifty feet beyond them.

Wait for me.

Aisha stopped at the foot of the stairs when she heard me call out, and she scooped me up, holding me close as she jogged toward Will. She offered to set me on his shoulder, but he stopped to pull his sweatshirt off, and told her to put it on.

"It won't be horrifically big, I think. Wick can ride in the pouch." When she balked, he added, "I may need to hit the ground fast, and I don't want to hurt him if I do. A hundred eighty pounds of me and six pounds of him—"

I could easily leap off his shoulder and he knew that, but he was officially making her Keeper of the Cat. A task, as it turned, suited her well. She scratched behind my ears in just the right spot, kept a hand on me so that I didn't slide back and forth, and when the proverbial litter box contents hit the proverbial fan, she didn't try to stop me when I exploded from the sweatshirt, claws and teeth bared, ready to kill.

27

Hagar unsheathed his sword as he followed Aisha; Krisf and Jesf slid from Fluffy's back and walked beside him, hands on their weapons. Everyone listened carefully. The path on this side of Lands End was wider than where we entered, and it was lined with trees gnarled in thick vegetation; there were places for people to hide, small caves made of leaves and vines, almost impossible to see until it was too late.

Shivan grumbled to Aisha that they should have taken the Shedu armor. It would have fit Prince Andrew and the Emperor and would have made other Shedu think they were part of their own. It was a mistake, one that if not made could have saved their lives.

"Some battles have to be taken on with the skills you have," she told him. "Hiding behind the armor doesn't help. It gets in the way, especially if it was never part of your training."

He didn't understand, and she didn't try to press the point. He let out an exaggerated sigh and complained that no one ever took him seriously.

"You didn't suggest appropriating the armor, Shivan. When we were still close enough to have taken it, you let Will keep walking without so much as a hint that you had an idea."

"But *he* should have thought of it!"

"Maybe he did and dismissed the idea. Or maybe he would

have been open to your reasoning. But don't be angry that he can't read your mind."

Drew and Will slowed; we were approaching the Lands End Trail exit, where there was a large clearing that sloped in staggered layers down a hill. There was a cliff to our right, with steps that led down to the ruins of the Sutro Baths; in our own When there would have been a street to the far left that curved away at the top of the hill; it was now rock and dirt that hadn't been beaten down into a path, and there was no easy traverse from that direction.

Will expected a fight; we were close to the Cliff House, where the sounds of battle on Ocean Beach pierced the air. Voices rose over the high-pitched whine of laser rifles, explosions from cannon fire thundered, and the rapid popping of pistols set to fire in short bursts came at us like sparks from a bonfire. As we came out of Lands End and surveyed the vista before us, the sands of Ocean Beach were painted in blood, and the Shedu outnumbered Kilfin's army by at least five to one.

There was no time to let it sink in. One layer down the hill there were guards dressed in black camo pants and t-shirts. Aisha did as Will asked; she lunged for cover to protect me, making sure Fluffy had space to squeeze between the trees with us. Her breathing was labored and heart rate raced as she peeked around the trunk of the tree; Oz and Drew ran ahead, and they began fighting hand-to-hand, while Will engaged the first Shedu to get past them.

Hagar and the elves sped down the hill; the old wizard swung the sword wildly, creating a path as the Shedu dove away from him, and the elves shot without aiming, hoping to hit their targets with luck. Shivan stood rooted on the first layer of the hill, watching with eyes narrowed and nostrils flared. I thought he had frozen, too afraid to move forward, but then he slowly unclipped the plasma sword from his belt, and without looking, flipped the switch.

When it roared to life, he marched with intense deliberation toward a cluster of four Shedu; he didn't guard himself and he held the sword like a flashlight until they turned en mass and ran at him. He stopped and waited, planting his weight on his back leg, and when they were close, he pulled the sword to his right side and swung it neatly to his left.

They dropped, one by one, sliced through their torsos, held together by their spines.

He marched on confidently and didn't look back at the bodies that fell in broken pieces.

Will was on the ground, grappling with a guard in an exo-suit. His hands slipped on the slick armor, his strength matched by the advantages the suit gave the Shedu fighter. He was on his knees, trying to get his arms around the guard's neck, feet slipping on the dirt as he tried to press himself forward. His legs strained against the effort and he gained ground in hair-width measurements, and with it his arm slipped around his opponent's neck.

He nearly had the choke hold and could hear footsteps behind him, but there was nothing he could do about the guard running at him. Aisha gasped and I sprang from the sweatshirt, growling, and together we bolted from our hiding place. I leaped for the face of the Shedu that Will battled, and she lunged at the man behind him, knocking him to the ground before he could reach Will.

As I bit down on the Shedu's cheek, as Will twisted and broke his neck, the sound of laser fire screamed from behind us. Will let go and spun, letting the body hit the ground; I scrambled out of the way and ran for her without looking because I didn't really want to see.

She was flat on her back, pistol in hand, and the guard who had tried to get to Will was three feet away in a twisted lump.

His face was gone.

*

Hagar's sword was on the ground next to him. He sat in the dirt, surveying the chaos, counting the bodies as the weight of loss pressed up against him. Jesf was scattered in charred fragments and Aradyn lay before the wizard, eyes closed and his chest quivering with each labored breath. Krisf was on his knees next to his elfin leader, head hanging and hands pressed against the wound that ran from Aradyn's right shoulder to his left hip.

Oz and Drew slowly returned; neither was injured but took deliberate care with each step, until they saw Will hunched over Aisha, his head blocking their view of her face. At the sight of her on the ground, with Will on his knees next to her and arms around her, they ran. Drew jumped over bodies and Oz ignored Aradyn. They ran until they were a few feet from us, Drew muttering *please, please, please* while Oz cried, *no, no. no.* Both hit their knees and reached a hand out, until Will said, "She's all right. She's just shaken." He sucked in a deep breath and added, "She saved my life."

"If you don't ease up," Aisha squeaked, "you're going to suffocate me."

Slowly, he helped her to her feet. She grabbed him and held on, burying her face against his shoulder. "I'm sorry, I couldn't stay back. I couldn't…" She sucked in a hard breath. "Where's Wick?"

Here. At your feet. I can see up your shirt, you know.

"Thank God." She reached down and snatched me up. "Why didn't you stay with Fluffy?"

You didn't tell me to, and someone had to bite that dude.

"Where *is* Fluffy?" Drew asked.

Fluffy was standing between two trees, on his back legs, and he batted at the branches above. When that didn't get him what he wanted, he pushed them with his front paws, shaking the trunks until three more Shedu fell to the ground. Drew reached for his gun, but Fluffy calmly reached out a paw and batted them over the edge of the cliff.

He peered over the side as they fell, and then ambled over to Shivan, who was standing near the bottom of the hill, staring at the war still being waged on the beach. He'd turned the plasma sword off but held it in his hand, arms relaxed at his sides.

He doesn't want to watch Aradyn die.

"No one does," Will said. He knelt next to Aradyn and gently pulled Krisf back, telling him it was time to let his friend go. He peeked under the elf's shirt and sadly shook his head, and then asked Drew to lead Oz and Aisha down the hill to wait with Shivan.

"Go with them," he told Krisf.

When he resisted, Hagar struggled to his feet. "Come on. I'll go, too. Let the Emperor do what he needs to do."

"Go with them, Wick," Will said. "Please."

I didn't want to, but it wasn't an order and someone else might need to hold onto me so that I could purr for them. They waited shoulder to shoulder and tried to pretend that they were just looking at the ocean. No one seemed to need me more than anyone else, so I climbed Drew's leg and waited with him.

When the Emperor fired his gun, they each flinched. A low, guttural wail slipped out of Krisf, but he didn't look back and he didn't cry.

"I'm sorry," Will said as he joined us. "I couldn't let him suffer."

"They'll all suffer, Emperor," Hagar said. "But yes, thank you. I could not bring myself to help him."

"How many of Aradyn's people are on the beach?" Drew asked, his voice thick. There weren't many left, and the Shedu were regrouping and heading toward the Cliff House.

"Fewer than half, I think," Hagar answered. "This was mostly Kilfin's army. The elves are likely in the park and headed this way. More fighters will come from the south, near the lake."

"We need to take out these Shedu before they get here," Will mused.

"There are seven of us," Oz pointed out. "Hundreds of them."

"Indeed."

We need a dragon. A friendly dragon. A big, friendly black dragon.

"Wick, don't."

Fluffy wouldn't eat this one because it would be on our side.

"What's he want?" Oz asked.

"A damned dragon," Will sighed. When Oz and Drew looked at each other, he sputtered, his accent thick, "No. You will no' do that."

You dropped your t again, dude.

But think about it. A dragon who would swoop down and breathe fire on them all, scattering their little points of data into a cloud of ashes.

He was about to inform me of the danger a giant black fire breather exposed us to, but I had already formed the image in my mind and wished it. Fluffy heard it first and cocked a giant ear as he listened, and then he turned as the breeze from its flapping wings reached us.

His name is Jeff, if you wanted to know.

"Goddammit, Wick. Jeff the dragon?"

Oz and Drew were staring up at him; Jeff flew over us, swung around the Cliff House, and then perched on a giant boulder that was fifteen feet in front of us. His scales were like polished black granite and eyes were the color of dark honey. Smoke puffed from his nostrils, and he sat with his wings folded back, waiting.

Don't be scared. Be impressed.

He's just a baby, you know.

Fluffy went to him first; he sat in the dirt and stared up at Jeff, tilting his head to the left and then the right, trying to make sense of the odd-looking bird that he somehow knew he should not eat. Jeff bent down, sniffing the massive lump of orange fur sitting in front of him, realizing, too, that this was his friend and not his lunch.

They're brothers, by the way.

"What the hell do we do with a twenty-foot-tall dragon?" Drew wondered out loud.

"Fire-grill some Shedu," Oz said. She turned to look at me. "That was your plan, Wick? Take them down with a giant, breathing flamethrower?"

Pretty much.

"Then have at it. But you should know, you missed a perfect naming opportunity."

I cocked my head and waited.

"You should have named him Puff."

Drew snorted. "Jesus, Oz."

I closed my eyes and imagined Jeff taking flight over the beach. He would soar high over the Cliff House and then over the water, making the Shedu think he was leaving, but once he reached the far end of Ocean Beach he would swing back and light up the sand and everything on it, all the way to the big rock that the house perched on.

Go on, Jeff. Fly.

With a smoky snort, he spread his wings and flew straight up, and followed the path I imagined for him. The few remaining elves on the beach scattered, some leaping over the break wall, some diving into the water, and then Jeff turned, exhaling fire as he skimmed fifteen feet off the ground. Shedu vanished in smoky black puffs, and the sand on the beach melted into a lava-red mass that turned slick and shiny as it cooled under the rapid beat of his wings.

Just before he reached the Cliff House, Jeff stopped breathing out fire. He arched skyward before returning, spreading his wings as wide as he could, and then he landed on the boulder. Will turned to him and said, "Good job, Jeff. Thank you."

Drew muttered, "Of course, we have a dragon now. Of course, no one is surprised by it. Of course, he's just another pet."

He doesn't need a treat. He'll find Shedu remains to nosh on later.

"Tell him to stay," Will told me.

He will. He won't move unless we need him again.

Shivan was the first to move. He clipped the sword handle to his belt and stepped forward, and without looking back said, "To the Cliff House. The dark wizard waits."

28

Will bent over, hands on his knees, so that he could look me in the eye. I was hanging in the sweatshirt pouch, which dangled loosely around Aisha, and she wasn't holding me still. I shifted to get comfortable, and the whole thing swung back and forth.

"Listen to me, Wick," Will said. "No more creatures. I can no' keep track of a gigantic cat *and* a fire-breathing dragon."

You dropped—

"I know. I'm tired." He stood up straight. "Just don't create anything new, all right?"

Oz reached over to pet me. "The Emperor gets tired, he gets hard to understand sometimes. But your pets have been helpful, Mister Wick. Don't think otherwise."

Shivan was still moving toward the Cliff House, and with a tired sigh, Will gestured for us to follow him. He took a few fast strides to catch up and then fell into step next to Shivan, warning him, I think, to be careful and consider everyone before trying to fight his way in.

There was a shack just ahead of the Cliff House. The dilapidated wood building was once a bar, one that Will never went to because they didn't have decent scotch and the beer tasted like pee. I asked him how he knew that—who's pee had he tasted?—but never got a straight answer, so who knows. There were always air bikes parked out front, neat little rows of floating metal tethered in place like mechanical horses; a few hundred years before that the air bikes would have been motorcycles, and the patrons would have been leather-clad middle-class men pretending to be tougher than they really were.

Oz pushed ahead and went around the backside of the shack, looking for a spot that would give her a good view of Tobias's lair. She wanted to count the guards surrounding it, and she wanted to see if there was access to the back side of the building. It was largely unchanged; a gleaming white structure perched inexplicably on the edge of the cliff, with vista windows along the back and narrow doors up front.

"Four men on this side," she said after a moment. "Armored and armed. We could pick them off from here, but if there are more on the beach side, they'll hear."

Hagar reached for her arm, touching her gently. "Be very careful if you open fire. Erich is likely with them."

"I can't tell one from the other in those suits," she said.

Hagar pulled his medallion out from under his shirt and wrapped his fingers around it. "When the bright light paints the house, fire a weapon in the direction of it. That should draw the guards to this side."

"And Erich?" Will asked.

"The light is for him. He'll understand what it is. He won't follow."

Drew and Will stepped ahead of Oz and waited. Hagar clutched the medallion so hard that his fingers turned white, and he held it high over his head, mumbling under his breath as it began to hum. His arms trembled and he dropped his chin to his chest, and just when I thought he was going to collapse from the effort, a brilliant white light shot from his hands, covering the Cliff House so brightly I had to squint.

Drew fired towards the house, hitting the wall squarely in the middle, just over the heads of the guards. They startled and began yelling, raising rifles as they readied to fire, and Oz ordered everyone to hit the ground as Will and Drew opened fire. Aisha curled around me on her side, tucking me between her knees and her chest, and she covered my ears with one of her hands.

It wasn't enough to muffle all the noise around me. The whine of the lasers hurt my ears, but I could still hear Oz yelling commands, shouting for Shivan to stay put, yelling to Drew to keep steady, and warning Will about a guard approaching from the left.

It wasn't enough to dull the sound of flesh being ripped by a laser.

It wasn't enough to keep Oz's anguished cry from stabbing at my heart. I wiggled out from under Aisha's hand and peeked out just as Drew fell backward and as Oz tried to catch him.

Will didn't flinch; he stayed on his feet and kept pulling the trigger until there was no return fire. When he was sure the guards were dead, he spun and hit his knees, trying to pry Oz's hands away from Drew's chest.

"Where are you hit?" he demanded. When Oz wouldn't let go, Will grabbed her wrists and forced her back. "Ozzie, let me check him."

Drew was holding onto his side, and his breathing was hard and fast. "Near my hip," he hissed between clenched teeth. "Jesus, it hurts like a mother—"

Will peeled Drew's shirt back. There was a thick three-inch gash just above his hip, but there was no blood. The wound had cauterized as quickly as it was created, leaving him with a missing chunk of skin. "Flesh wound. It's not deep," Will said. He pulled his backpack off and dug into the front pocket, fishing out a metal tube.

"This will sting, so grit your teeth."

He popped the top of the tube off and poured a finely grit yellow powder onto Drew's wound, and then put his hand on Drew's chest to hold him still as the wound bubbled and foamed. Drew's head went back, face contorted in agony as he took short, sharp breaths, but he didn't cry out. He reached for Oz's hands, something to grip while he waited for the pain to ease; Will reached over him with his free hand to stop her from reaching out too quickly.

"Two fingers, Oz. Only let him hold two fingers."

She nodded and place two fingers in each of Drew's hands, and let him squeeze.

When the pain diminished enough that Drew was no longer straining against him, Will got to his feet. "Stay with him until the pain subsides. It should only be a minute."

Aisha lifted me as she got up. "We should stay—"

"He'll be fine," Will said. "It nicked some skin, that's all."

"The Trident should be whole," Shivan argued. "One minute more won't matter."

"One minute more might bring backup for Tobias's guards."

"Just go," Drew grunted. "As soon as I can catch my breath, I'll follow."

Oz pulled her fingers from Drew's hands and stood up. Her hands were firmly on her hips, and her jaw worked tensely for a moment before she said, "We don't leave anyone behind, Emperor. He's alive, we wait. If more Shedu appear, we'll send Jeff or Fluffy after them."

"We need to get Shivan in—"

"We wait."

Standoff.

This isn't as fun as it should be.

I'd guard your groin, Emperor. She might kick you right in the fun bits.

"Wick, she won't—" He took a step back, and chuckled under his breath. "Wick thinks you're about to swing a foot to my groin."

"Listen to Wick," she said, still upset.

Drew rolled to his uninjured side and started to push himself up. He got to one knee and hesitated, then took Oz's hand as she helped him up the rest of the way. "Moot point now. You argued long enough that it doesn't matter. Let's go."

"You all right?" Will asked.

"Getting shot freaking hurts."

Only he didn't say freaking.

I thought the Queen would understand.

Will hoisted the backpack up. "Focus on breathing in and breathing out."

"I'm not having a damned baby, Will. I'm fine." He grimaced when he picked his gun off the ground, so no one believed that, but when Drew gestured for everyone to move on, Oz took the lead, and we headed downhill, toward the Cliff House.

*

Near the entrance of the Cliff House there was a lone Shedu in an exo-suit, crawling on his belly toward us. Will and Drew stopped and pointed their guns at him, until he rolled over and called out, "Hagar, call off your dogs!"

Will slid the gun back into his waistband and trotted the rest of the way to help Erich stand.

Without waiting for Hagar, once Erich was on his feet, Will asked why the house had so few men guarding it. "I expected dozens, not fewer than ten."

Shivan was at the door, tugging on the handle.

"He's not here," Erich said.

Shivan kept pulling on the door handle, rattling it as if he expected it to pop open.

"When the first skirmishes on the beach began, he fled," Erich went on. "He escaped in the chaos before I arrived."

"To where?" Will asked.

"He has a dozen places to hide. I was not informed of his intent today."

Drew looked skyward. "The light's dimming. What time is it?"

Will guessed it was close to one in the morning. While Shivan leaned against the door, defeated, he circled the building to check the beach. "The water is beginning to bubble. Wherever he is, he's bypassed the destruct sequence I placed on the computer. The rain is probably about to follow."

Erich agreed; if Tobias found a place to rest, he would use the rain to keep the elves at bay. It didn't matter if they now understood that the rain was harmless; it was bitterly cold and they would find cover, not fight. "I'll leave you here. I need to get back to my men before they come looking for me."

Well, he's certainly been useful.

Will nodded but didn't say anything and didn't watch him leave. He nudged Shivan out of the way and butted the door glass with his gun. When it shattered, he reached in and flipped the lock to open the door, and went in first.

"One massive common room, bathrooms to the left," Aisha muttered.

It was not a restaurant anymore; there was no foyer, so we entered directly into the main room. The far wall was window after window, allowing for a spectacular view of the ocean and of Seal Rock below, and there was a fireplace on the right wall. It was made of large river rock that went from the hearth to the ceiling, and Will went to it, looking for a switch to turn it on.

"We'll need heat," he said absently.

"Are we staying?" Shivan asked. "We should follow the wizard. The rain won't hurt us and we can catch him by surprise."

Once the fire was on, Will sat on the hearth, hard. "Shivan, I'm tired. Everyone is tired. The rain is a level of cold I don't wish to endure, and it will be dark soon. We're staying here and getting some sleep."

"But we're unguarded," Shivan argued.

Jeff will watch over us.

"Move Jeff to the front door, Wick," Will said. "I don't think he'll mind getting wet. Fluffy can sleep by the windows. He'll hear first if someone is trying to gain access from the cliff."

Without me asking him to, Fluffy crossed the room and curled up where Will wanted him. He tucked his tail around his body and began to purr, until the floor shook and Will asked him to dial it back.

"We're already on a cliff, Fluffy. Let's not send the whole place tumbling into the ocean."

"Look for supplies," Oz suggested. "Water, food."

"If there's a kitchen, there's food," Aisha said. "Eggs and chicken, I guarantee it."

Drew headed for a door near the fireplace, and Oz went

looking for closets. Will didn't move; he sat with his elbows on his knees and watched as a grief-stricken Krisf curled up with Fluffy. "There *might* be food," he said to Aisha.

She pulled me from the sweatshirt and sat next to him. "Fair enough. Simulated people, simulated food. But there's been edible food everywhere we've been. Someone is keeping this place stocked."

Will nodded but didn't say anything.

"It's the same kitchen every time," she went on, "isn't it?"

"Probably. The simulator changes our surroundings, but we're walking in circles. Literally, I think."

"It feels so real."

"Indeed. Drew's wound looks very real."

You warned we could really be hurt.

"I did warn that, Wick. I was hoping I was wrong. We need to keep an eye on it."

Drew came out of the kitchen, and his face was still pinched with pain. He was probably all right, but that didn't keep it from hurting. "The kitchen is stocked. Bread, cheese, eggs, milk, chicken, flour, oil, and a couple of things I can't identify. There's definitely enough food for all of us, and enough to pack to take with us."

"Anything for Wick?"

"Chicken," he replied. "I can cook some and chop some cheese up to go with it. He can eat that."

I'll happily eat that.

"He needs actual cat food soon," Will said. "I'm not sure how long his vision will hold without taurine, and I don't think he'll find anything live to hunt here."

"Six weeks or so," Aisha said. "Jimmy did a paper on cats in grade school."

"Ordinary cats, perhaps. Wick is very, very old. I don't know."

I can see fine. Don't worry about me.

Hagar sat next to Will on the hearth and pulled his medallion from his shirt, and then took it off. It was heavier than I remembered, and thicker, its middle broken by broad lines. I recognized the symbol, though I couldn't quickly put a name to it. I'd seen it plastered all over the city before Finn took me home. People wore it on their shirts and painted it on the walls, and they spoke it like a greeting, right before they chased me away from someone else's discarded lunch.

You're a hippy.

Will frowned. "Wick, really."

I know what that is. It's a peace sign. Hippies wore them all the time.

"Hagar is not a hippy."

Hagar looked up. "In a manner of speaking, yes, I am."

A hippy garden gnome.

"I stand corrected. But he's not one of the hippies you were afraid of, Wick. I can't imagine him chasing you away from food and water."

"I would not. But I do believe in the message of peace and love, and I miss the days when girls wore light, flowing dresses and flowers in their hair." Hagar laid the medallion flat on his palm, and one by one asked each of them to blow onto its center. He wouldn't say why but even had me breathe onto it. Will's breath turned it gold. Aisha's turned it white. Drew's, blue. And when Oz breathed onto it, the shiny silver glowed brightly with light that danced above it.

Shivan did not blow onto it; he said he already knew what color it would be, and it was a disappointing, ugly green. "Not even like an emerald. More like stale peas. I hate peas."

"It might be different now," Hagar said, but he didn't offer it to Shivan. He held it right where the necklace went through the little hole at the top, and using his finger, he traced a line around the inner circle.

When he was done with that, he held it close to the fire to warm it.

"Is there a point to this?" Will asked. He glanced up at Drew and Oz, but they were heading into the kitchen to make food for everyone.

"There is," Hagar said. "My magic is fading. The heart of my medallion should go to the next worthy person." When it was almost too warm to touch, he placed it back in his hand, holding a finger over it. Quietly, so that Shivan and Krisf would not hear, he went on, "I know what I am, Emperor. I know this is symbolic. But I must pass it on, while I still can."

A thin, white light shot from his fingertip, and he drew around the circle, following the line he'd made before. When he completed the circle, he tapped the medallion on the hearth, and the center fell out.

"Huh," he grunted, picking it up. "It looks like a chicken's footprint. All these years, and I never noticed."

Using the bright light from his finger again, he made a hole in the long end, and then took the necklace from what was left of his medallion to string through it. When Oz came out half an hour later to call everyone to eat, Hagar stood and placed it around her neck.

"You have the light in you, Princess Oz. I have no heir, and would be honored if you would wear this and keep it until either you return to your own time, or it speaks to you."

She touched it with her fingertips. "Hagar, this is part of your magic."

"Aye. It needs youth to come alive again. But more than that, I don't want Tobias to get it. It needs to be with someone who can breathe the light into it, and that's you."

She thanked him and promised to wear it always.

In the kitchen, he took the remainder of the medallion and slipped it onto Drew's wrist. "Your light is true, Prince Andrew. Please, take this to remember us when you've gone home."

He wanted to refuse; he wasn't taking any part of the old wizard's magic, but caught the sight of Will out of the corner of his eye, shaking his head ever so slightly, the way he did when he was serious.

Dinner was loud, and there was more laughter than I expected from battle-weary people. Drew had cooked enough chicken for three meals and had even cut up more than one piece for me. Oz made a giant bowl of mashed potatoes and gravy, apologizing because they came from a box and they weren't fresh, but I don't think anyone cared.

They were hungry; it was food.

It almost felt like family. The only thing missing was a tired teenager complaining about having to eat vegetables.

If there had been any to complain about, that might have been Shivan.

It also might have been Krisf; it was difficult to decide how old he was, and his grief was pulling at him so tightly that he looked younger than Shivan. I reminded myself he was a teacher and a keeper of the stories; he had to be older than Drew.

When dinner was over and the dishes had been washed and put away, Oz piled blankets she'd pulled from closets around the house in the middle of the floor, and Will suggested we all get some sleep because once it was light again and the rain had let up, we were heading out.

Except for Krisf, who snuggled up with Fluffy again, they paired off. I curled up on the hearth by the fire, where I could see them all. Oz and Drew cuddled together on the other side of the room; she'd cleaned and bandaged his wound, even though Will told her the powder he'd put on it was enough. It still hurt him, and she was damn well going to take care of him. Will and Aisha stretched out on the floor near me, using a folded blanket as a pillow. She was on her side, watching him fight falling asleep, and when he finally gave into it, she leaned over and kissed his shoulder before pulling a blanket over him.

You're good for him. I hope you stick around.

She reached up to pet me, rubbing my chin with her finger. "Go to sleep, Wick," she whispered. "Jeff and Fluffy will guard us. Thank you for creating them."

Yeah, we need to keep you.

29

It was still dark when Will woke, even though his watch said it was after eight in the morning. He put his finger over his lips to ask me to be quiet, and he eased away from Aisha, making sure he didn't pull the blanket away from her. I followed as he checked the front door—Jeff was still there, blocking it, with his tail plugging the hole in the glass—and then as he gently touched fingers to Drew's forehead, checking to see if he had a fever.

It was only a shallow slice through a fleshy part of his body, but Will was still worried about an infection. If Drew was hot, we were going home.

If we could even get home.

He went into the bathroom and closed the door, and he stood in the center of the floor, staring down at his own feet. I wasn't sure what he was waiting for; he wasn't shy and I'd seen him pee a thousand times, so modesty wasn't the issue.

Oh. Do you need some personal time? You can let me out if you do.

"What?" He laughed through his nose. "No, I don't need personal time. I'm just trying to wake up. Besides, when have you ever left the room? Don't you usually just try to nap?"

I'm trying to be polite.

"And I appreciate that. But there's no need."

Sure about that? It's morning.

"Wick, seriously."

Fine. Then pee and figure something out for me. I need to go, too.

He pointed to the shower stall and told me to aim for the drain in there. I didn't want to, but he'd already told me to stop creating things so I didn't think he'd be happy if I thought up a box with fresh litter that smelled like sunshine and shrimp.

By the time I was done, he was washing his hands, and we headed for the kitchen next. He found the coffee and started a pot, then sat at the table and rested his chin on his hands while he waited. I jumped onto the table to wait with him because I didn't have anything else to do.

"What happened to the sprites, Wick?" he asked suddenly. "They were resting on Fluffy's back, just before the butterflies swarmed the Shedu in Lands End."

You're just now missing them?

"Too many things to keep track of."

They'll be back if we need them.

"I'm not sure I want to witness the devouring of another Shedu. Or risk them turning on us. I'll be happy if no one thinks of them again."

Do you want to go home?

"Indeed. But my gut says it's not time."

My gut says it's food o'clock.

He pushed himself up, still tired. "When does it not, Wick?"

When I'm eating.

"I don't believe even then." He reached into the fridge for some of the chicken that Drew cooked. "Cold or hot? It's no trouble to heat some up if you prefer it that way."

Warm. Thank you.

Once my food was warm and his coffee was done, he placed a plate on the table and told me I could eat there, as long as I didn't make it a habit. It would not amuse the King, and he wasn't sure if it would disturb Aisha or not.

I would have told him she'd probably be fine with it, but my mouth was full.

"I owe you an apology, Wick. Last year you said that after we made it home, you'd never want to leave again. And now, here we are. I should be less selfish about the places I take you. I imagine this feels a lot like the hike across Colorado to you."

My mouth was still full.

Oz wandered in while he was still holding the coffee cup between his hands, as if he was trying to warm up. "Talking to yourself or the cat?" she asked.

"Wick. I have guilty regrets about bringing him. I promised him last year I would never again subject him to something like this."

She sat down and took a few seconds to rub between my ears. "He's a useful kitty. Jeff is magnificent."

"Jeff could kill us all."

"Then don't piss off the dragon."

"We have to avoid pissing off each other," he reminded her. "One stray thought from any of us could trigger Jeff or Fluffy. I don't think they're solely connected to Wick."

"He created them."

"But he didn't create Shivan and has been able to manipulate him. When Shivan ran ahead near the Palace of Fine Arts, that was Wick's doing."

"That wasn't very nice," she said to me as she got up. "Everyone is starting to wake up. Drew says there are enough eggs to scramble and probably enough bread to make toast."

"Save the bread. I'll cut up the leftover chicken and make sandwiches to take with us."

He still hadn't taken a sip of his coffee and was staring into it.

"Do you want to leave?" Oz asked as she pulled the eggs from the refrigerator.

"Do you?"

She leaned against the counter and looked at him. "Is it awful if I don't? I get it if you want to take Aisha to safety, but I feel like if I leave now, I'm running away."

He nodded, and finally sipped at his coffee.

"Drew and I can do this."

"I will not," he said, setting the cup down, "abandon you to the scenarios being spit out by my father's inventions."

"I thought we were doing all this."

"There's a root program, Oz. I don't know where the dividing line is, but after seeing what happened to Drew, I will not trust it to be safe."

"We can't stay just because I want to."

"We can, and we will."

We're almost done. I want to see the wizard.

"Even if he bites, Wick?"

I bite back.

Will softened, and the corners of his mouth lifted. "Well, there we have it. Wick wants to bite the wizard. We have to stay."

*

Just before ten o'clock, Tobias flipped a switch wherever he was, and the sky went from night to day and the rain stopped abruptly. Will and Aisha watched from the windows behind Fluffy as the ocean stopped bubbling; below them, Seal Rock was instantly dry, and the water droplets that had been pinging off the window vanished.

"All right, Wick. Time to move Jeff."

The black dragon took flight and we left the Cliff House. The air was considerably cooler than it had been since we arrived through the portal, and I could see little puffs of steam every time someone exhaled. Oz pulled her arms from the sleeves of her sweatshirt and held them close to her body, prompting Will to remind her that she was placing herself in an indefensible position.

"Hands out of pockets, don't cross your arms," she sighed, mimicking the way he often reminded her when she was young. "I remember the rules. Always be ready to defend yourself. But I'm cold and I'm counting on Drew to buy me some time if some random guy dressed in black drops from the sky."

"Totally got your back," Drew said. He held his arms out, and she snuggled against him, stealing some of his warms.

"But where are we headed?" Aisha asked. "He can follow you all day, but we need a destination. Where would you go, if you were a self-loathing tyrant with an agenda?"

"Disneyland," Drew said. "To make myself feel better. Who could loathe anything when they're at Disneyland?"

"We really have to take him to Disneyland," Oz told Will.

"He has a birthday coming up," Will said. He started down the path to the beach and stopped when he reached the place where he could see it stretched out like a long, thin blanket. The sand looked like ice, with little diamonds of light reflecting the sun. Close to the cliff, there was a massive black smear, the remains of the Shedu caught in Jeff's roaring fire.

"He won't have gone far," Will guessed. "He's kept to the west side since he took power, hasn't he? Something keeps him here." He turned to Hagar. "Does he ever venture east? To anywhere near your home?"

"The tower," Hagar said. "I don't believe he's comfortable lingering on the east side, not since his family died, but he does go every now and then. I wouldn't dismiss the notion."

"Follow the noise," Oz suggested. "Kilfin took troops into Golden Gate Park, and most of the elves are with him. It didn't look to me like there were many on this beach yesterday. Find the largest concentration of Shedu, and you'll find Tobias. They'll be protecting him."

"Another long walk," Shivan grumbled.

"I know," she said. "And we might get there and find that I'm wrong. Now would be a good time to call Zed and ask for a ride on his bike."

"Sure," Drew said. "You, me, Zed, and everyone else crammed onto the back while Zed putts along at grandma speed."

"He's afraid of getting another ticket," Oz snickered. "But still, if we had his bike, you and I could at least ride ahead and scope things out to make sure we're on track."

Take Jeff for a ride.

"You can't be serious, Wick," Will said. "How would they even hold on? As soon as Jeff was in the air, they'd fall."

He has handles near his neck. I made sure of that.

Will sighed hard and ran a hand through his hair as he debated whether or not he wanted to translate. While he pondered, Jeff landed, waiting to see what was needed from him. While Jeff waited, Oz pulled Drew's shirt up a few inches to check his wound—he proclaimed it ouchy but not horrible—and she decided he was fine for whatever they wanted to do for the day. "But if you get shot again, I swear to God I'm finding some menthol cream and smearing it on your junk."

"Damn, Oz."

Will took a look at Drew's wound, too, and then reluctantly said, "Jeff has handles to hold onto. Wick wants you to take him for a ride."

Drew's eyebrows furrowed. "Ride. On a dragon."

It's like riding a bike. I think.

"Wick, I can't even *drive*."

Oz inched her way over to Jeff, more curious than afraid. He snorted once, little wisps of smoke puffing from his nose, but he didn't move and only followed her with his eyes. When she was close, he pushed himself down and stretched his neck out, chin to the ground. "I'm going to touch you, all right? Very gently. I won't hurt you."

Jeff slowly blinked at her.

That means it's okay. You can touch.

Oz placed her hand against his cheek very carefully, and when Jeff sighed, she stroked him. "Your face is so soft. This is like touching velvet. Drew, come on. Feel this."

He took wary steps and hesitated several times before reaching out. "This feels really rude to be doing," he grumbled. To Jeff he said, "I apologize if this is out of line. You're not a cat. Maybe you don't like being petted."

He likes it.

"Wick, does Jeff understand us?" Will asked.

As much as I do.

He still didn't look happy about it. "Look, I'm against this," he said to Oz. "It's dangerous, and you'll be defenseless. But I can see you twitching toward him already, and I can't stop you." He dug into his pack and pulled out one of the cameras that was still attached to a headlamp, and tossed it to Drew. "The feed will appear on my phone. For God's sake, be careful. Don't let your mind wander because Jeff will tap into that. You can control him with careful thought."

"We'll be fine," Oz insisted. "Quick flight over the park to see where the elves are gathering and if there are any Shedu nearby. With any luck, we'll spot something to tell us where Tobias is."

Jeff rolled a half turn, enough to allow them to climb onto his back. Oz took the front, and when she was in place, Drew slipped the headlamp on her and flipped the switch.

"This is insane, Oz," Will said.

"And yet, here we are." She gripped the handles that jutted from the side of Jeff's neck, just above the spot it met his back. When Drew was set and holding on, Oz said, "Relax. We'll be fine. Come on, Jeff, let's go."

"She's her own person, that's for sure," Aisha muttered as Jeff took off. He did a slow roll to the left to get turned around, flying over the water, and Aisha set her hand on Will's arm when it looked like he wanted to run after them. "If not this, it would have been something else, don't you think?"

"I would have preferred they conjure a pair of horses instead. Why the hell didn't they?"

You didn't suggest it.

"Because he was here, and when else will they ever get to ride on the back of a twenty-foot tall, fire-breathing dragon named Jeff?"

He watched them soar down the beach, and his degree of unhappy ratcheted up. "If something happens to her, Jax will kill me."

"He'll be upset."

Will dug his phone out of his pocket and turned it on, searching for the video feed. "No, you don't understand. I am fully responsible for her safety in situations such as this. If she falls because I allowed her to climb on the back of a clear unknown and she dies...in his grief, I have no doubt that Jax would have me executed."

Aisha didn't believe that. Jax would be angry, he may never again speak to Will, he would likely blame him simply to have someone to blame and might even banish him from Pacifica, but you don't kill your own brother, even for this. "She's an adult, Will. Free will and all that. You don't get to decide for her."

"Even Oz will admit she's a starter adult at best. If something happens to her here, I am at fault, and I don't think I could bear that heartache again." He stepped back toward the house to shield the screen of his phone from the sunlight, and leaned against the wall to watch. Aisha stood next to him, pulling me onto her shoulder where I could see. Jeff was flying low and Oz was leaning forward to see past his long neck. He was heading into the park, just above the tree tops, going fast enough that the leaves were a blur.

There were clusters of people in the meadow just inside the park, but Jeff was going too fast to make out who they were, the elves and Kilfin's army, or the Shedu. As he sped along, there were more groups, men running between trees and even a few climbing them, but when Jeff dove and split the distance between the old museums Will wished out loud he would slow down.

"Dozens are guarding the DeYoung," he said to no one. "A few around the science center. Come on, show me more."

Instead of turning around at the panhandle, Jeff sped across the city. He looped around Dogpatch and Soma, then over the water where the Embarcadero should be, and turned back over downtown. He finally slowed, giving Will a clear image of Union Square. There were elves darting between trees, some carrying laser pistols, and others—to his surprise—bearing bows and arrows.

"They're taking to the trees. But why?"

"Because the Shedu would not expect it," Hagar answered. "Tobias would not expect it."

Without looking up from the screen, Will asked, "Where did they get the arrows? I only recall a single elf with a bow and I don't recall his quiver being full."

"Yeosef, I imagine."

Shivan agreed. "He knows people. He can get things."

"So, Yeosef is the Emperor of this time," Aisha mused.

If Hagar understood her humor, he ignored it. "Yeosef would

be a stellar Emperor. When this is over, he should, perhaps, be considered to lead the elves into prosperity."

"He won't want the job," Will grunted. "I've seen what's on the King's plate. It's not appetizing."

Butterflies, Will.

He peered at the screen closer. As Jeff finished circling Union Square, a mass of blue and red butterflies rose from the spot where home should be. "Drew," Will muttered. "Concentrate on flying the damned dragon, Andrew. Stop trying to impress Oz."

"Says the man who took a girl time traveling on their first date," Aisha mused.

"Don't get used to it. It's all downhill from here," he muttered. He blinked and then looked up. "I'm sorry. That was rude, wasn't it? I didn't mean it the way it sounded."

With a bit of a laugh, she leaned over and kissed him on the cheek. "You're adorable."

We're supposed to be super tough guys at war, and there's way too much kissing going on.

"Wick, you're only complaining because she kissed me and not you."

Jeff was making his way back to Golden Gate Park, slower this time, so that Will had a better look. There were Shedu slipping through the cover of trees, heading toward the meadow. They marched in a relaxed line, the sureness of knowing they had weapons and armor far better than their opponents.

"You know," Aisha said, "I think if I suddenly had a massive dragon flying overhead, I'd react."

"Especially if said dragon had barbecued some of my associates just the day before," Will said. "You're right. Not a single person has taken note of Jeff."

"Are dragons an everyday sort of thing?" Aisha asked Hagar.

"We are aware of them," he said carefully.

"One might assume." Will shoved the phone back in his pocket and moved away from the house so that he could watch Jeff fly over the beach. He banked a hard right out of the park and flew close to the ground, stirring up sand that had blown off the beach, and he slowed on approach until he came to a sliding stop on his belly.

Oz and Drew leaped from his back, both grinning wildly.

"Holy hell, I want my own Jeff!" Drew squealed. "That was some serious fun."

Oz patted Jeff's cheek. "That was amazing, Jeff, thank you. I wish we had a treat to give you."

Find him a crunchy Shedu snack.

"I don't need a translation to know that was gross, Wick," Drew said. "Did the camera transmit? We saw people moving around but no fighting. Very little movement, really, other than elves climbing trees."

Why are you surprised? Hagar and Shivan weren't moving much when they weren't needed. Look at Krisf. He's just been standing there since we left the house.

"Indeed," Will muttered under his breath. "Then we head for the park, and with any luck we'll find Kilfin. Perhaps he can confirm my suspicion that Tobias has taken the DeYoung."

"More walking," Shivan grumbled, though he didn't have to be prompted to move.

"You can take Jeff for a ride," Will said.

Jeff snorted, and heat washed over us.

"Or not. It's not that far from here. Ten minutes to the park, and then another fifteen to reach the meadow where I hope to find Kilfin."

Think up some bikes.

"No, Wick. Walking doesn't hurt anyone."

"Builds character," Drew snorted. "What does Wick want?"

"He suggested thinking bikes into existence. But no. They're noisy and we don't need to announce ourselves."

"Well, if the dragon didn't do it..."

"Fine, Andrew," Will conceded. "Think up an air bike. Make the controls simple, so that we can all ride. And while you're at it, think up the entire infrastructure upon which those bikes rely to function. The magnets, the air jet controls, the computers that keep everything running, and then every line of code that the computers need."

"Killjoy."

"Indeed." He pointed down the hill. "Let's go. The sooner we find Tobias, the sooner I can go home and take a long, hot shower and get some damned clean underwear."

30

Fluffy galloped ahead. Krisf bounced on his back, grabbing fistfuls of fur to keep from flying off. He hunted things only he could see, pouncing every few feet; he slapped down one of his mighty paws and sniffed, only to release his imaginary prey, and then started it all over again. When he got too far ahead, Will called him back, but instead of ordering Fluffy to fall into line with everyone else, he let Fluffy play, until it looked like Krisf wanted to throw up.

I should have given Fluffy a collar. And a saddle.

"At least let him off," Will told Fluffy. "You can still have fun, but you're making him sick and he can't even call out to anyone for help."

When he was on his feet, Krisf put his hand on his chest and made a small circle while he bowed his head. "Thank you," Hagar translated for him.

"It was still fun though, right?" Drew asked.

Krisf gave him a thumbs up.

While he giggled, Oz bristled. "I still don't get why Tobias had your tongue cut out. For what? Because you tell stories about history? What's the harm?"

Will answered for him. "A tyrannical dictator wants history painted in his own image. If people truly remember the past, they remember freedom. If they remember freedom, they'll fight to the death to win it back. Tobias removed the tongues of the teachers and storytellers in order to prevent history from inspiring others to fight for what their ancestors likely took for granted. An educated public is dangerous to the oppressors."

Aisha grimaced. "I wonder what his feeling about math is."

We were near the entrance to the park, across the wide sand-strewn path that was once the Great Highway. Oz put her hand on Krisf's shoulder and said, "It's wrong. It was cruel. It—" Without asking him, she placed both of her hands on his cheeks. "You should have a voice. You deserve one."

Krisf's eyes went wide.

"Whatever blip in your own cosmic program that allowed this to happen, it was flawed. It's just data switches, right? One flipped up, one flipped down, when they both should have been up." She stared into his eyes and didn't blink. His breathing grew fast, and he was swallowing rapidly, as if his mouth were suddenly filled and he couldn't figure out how to spit. Tears leeched from the corners of his eyes and his hands shot up, grabbing Oz's wrists, but he didn't pull her away.

Just before I thought he would pass out from hyperventilating, his mouth opened and he took in a deep breath.

"I am whole." His voice was soft and scratchy. He stuck a finger in his mouth and poked, and when he realized it was real, that he had a tongue and it moved, he dropped to his knees. "The Princess Oz, the Prince Andrew, the Emperor. Aisha. Mister Wick."

"Awesome, you know who we are," Drew said. He reached a hand down to help Krisf up. "Are you all right? Does it hurt?"

He shook his head. "I am fine, but I am..." He cleared his throat. "I am twelve again. I squeak."

The color had drained from his face, and he was trembling.

"I think my legs will fail me," he whispered.

"You're rattled," Will said. He brought Fluffy back and asked him to just walk with us and let Krisf ride on his back again. "Only until you're not shaking," he said to Krisf. "Then I don't care what you do."

Fluffy plucked him up by the collar of his shirt and settled him onto his back gently. Krisf buried his face into Fluffy's fur to hide the tears he couldn't hold back. His back heaved as he sobbed, but the others moved on, allowing him his private moment.

Will wanted to know why Oz had done it, given Krisf his tongue back. What possessed her?

"Everyone deserves a voice," she said.

Quietly, so that neither Hagar nor Shivan would hear him, he said, "They're not real, Oz."

"If they're real enough to hurt us, then they're real. No matter what side they're on."

"You're going to have to hurt some of them if you want to finish this."

"I know that. And I don't have a problem with that. But even when it's an us-versus-them kind of thing, why be unkind when you don't have to be? You already showed that when you ended Aradyn's suffering. He wasn't real, not by our standards, yet you still didn't allow him to suffer."

He conceded. "I'm not criticizing, Oz. Giving Krisf his voice was kind."

"But you think I'm a little bit nuts."

"Well." He grinned, just a little. "We all are."

Not me.

"Says the cat who created Fluffy and Jeff."

I wasn't going to argue that point, but I didn't think it was nuts. Fluffy and Jeff were useful, and as long as they didn't try to eat any of us, they were fun to have around. Both trailed behind us now that Will had asked Fluffy to stop running around, and I was proud of him for listening, right up to the point where we turned into the park and he saw the battlefield ahead.

It was a sea of elves and black-clad Shedu warriors, fighting hand to hand, but what Fluffy saw were toys, and Fluffy wanted to play.

*

"Bowling for elves."

Drew was both a little bit impressed and a little bit disgusted, and he couldn't stop himself from snorting out a laugh when Oz said, "Shedu Stomping."

Fluffy had taken off with Krisf still holding on by fistfuls of fur, running as fast as he could until he was fifteen feet away from the combative gathering of elves and Shedu. He stopped abruptly, sliding on his belly, and plowed into them like a massive furry bowling ball. Elves went flying and when Fluffy came to a stop—long enough for Krisf to jump off—he rolled over, squashing the Shedu who had not been able to run from him.

"You're amused, and yet not five minutes ago were telling me how real they all are," Will said.

"No one was hurt." Oz gestured ahead. The elves slowly got up, checking themselves for bumps and bruises. The Shedu that hadn't been squished like pesky flies ran, not waiting to see what else Fluffy had in store for them.

"Get up," Will said to Fluffy when we were close. Fluffy huffed but did as he said, and stepped away from the men he'd been laying on. There were three, and they all moaned, until one sat up, picking fur from his lips.

"What the hell?" he spat, along with more fur.

"It could have been worse," Shivan boasted. "It could have been our dragon." He gestured toward Jeff, who snorted out a wave of heat.

"You have a dragon." The Shedu guard slowly got to his feet. "How do you have a dragon?"

"No," Will said. "We have a dragon with us. We do not own him."

"Semantics. Get the hell up," he said to the other Shedu. Then to Will, "You're coming with us. Tobias will be—"

"No. We are not."

"We want the dragon." The guard fumbled for his rifle, which wasn't hanging from his shoulder as he expected. When his hand went to the pocket on the leg of his pants, Will kicked, striking him on the chin. He went down hard and stayed there. Oz and Drew braced for the other two to attack, but once on their feet, one looked at the other and shrugged, and turned to walk away.

"Well, that was rude," Oz said. "I wouldn't have hit too hard."

"Your reputation precedes you," the remaining Shedu said. He shrugged, too, and trotted off to catch up with his friend.

"Well, I wasn't exactly done," Oz sighed. "I was going to make a cogent argument as to why they can't have Jeff."

Fluffy leaped after the guard, who shrieked when he felt the thunder of feline footsteps behind him. He began to sprint, which made Fluffy want to catch him even more. He let the Shedu get ahead, and he paused, sticking his butt in the air, wiggling as he tracked each step. When he could no longer contain himself, he pounced.

He stretched as he reached with both paws; it was graceful ballet and showed every taut muscle rippling against his fur. He landed with a spectacular thud, trapping the guard under his paw, and he unsheathed his claws as he rolled the man over. The guard screamed, wiggling to get out from Fluffy's grasp, and the scream turned into full blown hysterics when the giant cat opened his mouth to cover his prey's head.

Shivan grunted, "Ugh," but Fluffy didn't bite down. Instead, he lifted the guard up by his head. We could hear his muffled shrieks and watched as his arms and legs flailed; Drew thought we should do something but he didn't know what, and Oz was content to let Fluffy do whatever he was going to do.

He brought the guard back to Oz, spitting him out at her feet.

He thinks you want a better shot at him. Or that you're hungry.

"Do what you will with him," Will said. "Argue about Jeff, or eat him."

"He's covered in cat spit and I'm pretty sure he wet himself," she said. "That's good enough for now. Thank you, Fluffy."

"And thank you for not biting down," Shivan said. "I've seen enough headless men."

Aisha looked around, at the elves now on their feet and

moving toward us, and the Shedu still retreating. "They don't look happy."

Krisf put himself between us and the angry elves. "The Trident!" he croaked, voice still raw. "The Princess Oz. The Prince Andrew." Before he could add the Emperor, several of the elves pushed their way forward and ran to him.

The first one to him was Lerym, the elf that Hagar thought would lead the elves alongside Aradyn. "Your voice!"

"The Princess Oz," Krisf sputtered. "I don't know how."

Lerym touched Krisf's face. "I don't care how. What about Jesf? Can he speak?"

Krisf shook his head sadly. "There was battle. He and Aradyn..."

His breath hitched. The elves stood toe to toe and stared at each other. Krisf could not bring himself to finish the sentence, and Lerym didn't have the heart to ask.

"We'll mourn them later." Lerym patted Krisf's cheek and sighed. "We've kept this band of Shedu to the park and away from Tobias's lair, but the word is that he slipped away last night. Now the Shedu are simply fighting us to fight, and they're making no attempt to move forward. A few have retreated."

"We were at the Cliff House last night," Oz said. "The Shedu who were guarding it are all dead."

"No word on where Tobias went?" Will asked.

"Kilfin may know." Lerym looked over Krisf's head, behind us. "He went to ask a Shedu."

Kilfin was dragging one of the guards across the meadow by his foot, letting his head bounce off the ground with each step. When he reached us, he flung the guard at Will's feet. "He knows where the wizard is, but he speaks in riddles."

The guard was out cold and wasn't going to speak about anything. Will prompted Kilfin to repeat what he'd heard, but the horse who wasn't a horse shrugged as if he didn't really know.

"Riddles are easy to remember," Will said.

"Call it whatever you like. It made no sense. He says Tobias is sleeping where a starry night once twinkled off water, where the dungeon held lilies for eager eyes to see."

"The lake?" Shivan guessed. "Near the gardens of the tea? Starlight would bounce off the lake, but I don't know if there were ever any lilies."

"Tea Gardens?" Oz asked him. "There's Stowe Lake, and the Japanese Tea Gardens are near."

Drew shook his head, and then asked Will, "You said you saw dozens of Shedu guarding the museum when we flew past?"

"Indeed."

"There's no riddle to it. Oz, remember last summer when we were going to go see the Impressionists' exhibit, but Uncle Willie here made us go get fitted for suits instead? They were showing some of Van Gogh and Monet's most treasured works. Starry Night Over the Rhone. Water Lilies. I still have regrets about missing that exhibition."

"The special event exhibit hall is in the basement," Will said. "The building as a whole is rather large, and would be easy to hide in."

"Not easy to approach, either," Oz said, reminding Will of the observation tower that rose above the museum. "We probably can't just walk up and expect to get inside without a fight. He'll have a watchman in that tower."

"And it won't be like getting into Red's compound," Drew mused. That had been easy; Will touched the man guarding the gate and made him think that we were expected. He let us in, and was never the wiser. Even if we could walk up to the door here, it wouldn't do Will any good to try to plant a thought into someone's head.

They were basically brainless.

"We could fight our way in," Oz said, "or we could use the tools given to us so generously by your former army major. We have a dragon. Let's burn down the tower."

Jeff spread his wings and snorted, then shot straight up; Oz called after him—not yet, we need a plan first—but he spiraled high, ignoring her. Just as she was about to yell at him, he turned back sharply and extended his razor-sharp talons; Krisf inhaled dramatically and took several backward steps, one arm held out protectively in front of himself.

That won't help you, dude.

When Jeff landed, he sank his talons deep into the dirt. He flapped his wings hard, slapping the tips on the ground, and then snorted rapidly while glancing over his shoulder.

"He wants something," Drew guessed. "What, Jeff?"

He wants us to get close to him.

"Why?" Will asked me.

Look behind him. Jeff folded his wings in so that they could see. *Seriously, look.*

"What the hell is that?" Oz sputtered.

"Tornado," Drew hissed. "Jesus, that's big. It could push every single one of us out into the ocean, shredded into a dozen little pieces. Do what Jeff wants! Now!"

The cloud spinning toward us was heavy and black; it vibrated as it swirled, its massive head expanding as its tail flicked from side to side. It devoured the sky, biting down on trees as if they were twigs, and then spitting them out like splintered toothpicks. Leaves exploded from branches and shot toward us, razor-sharp green disks topped with tiny bladed stems. Dirt shot up from between blades of grass and then fell like rain; if any of that reached us, it was going to hurt.

Jeff spread his wings again and snorted, dipping his chin so that they would understand: *come here, I will protect you.*

They crowded close, pressing against his chest and each other. He hunched down until there was no space between his wings and the grass, and then folded his wings around them. Fluffy dug his claws into the ground and waited at the space where Jeff's wing tips met, a furry ginger plug to block any gap where someone might fly out.

The wind grew stronger, and Jeff struggled to hold his place against it. Will yelled for everyone to sit down and make themselves as small as they could, giving Jeff space to work without smashing anyone into the ground. His entire body shuttered violently as the cloud hit, his wings vibrating and slapping against the onslaught of wind and debris. He strained over us, pushed forward until he was nearly laying on top of everyone. Fluffy flicked his tail up, wrapping it around Jeff's wing tips, and together they dug down hard, holding us in place until the wind abated and the tornado had passed.

Jeff waited before he let us up; first Fluffy unwrapped his tail and then slowly backed out to see if anything else was coming. It wasn't until he meowed that Jeff folded his wings back and pulled his talons from the ground. He snorted again—*it's safe now*—and then took a few steps backward.

Oz and Will were the first to get up. The meadow was covered in the detritus of broken trees and scattered branches, and uprooted flowers spent of their petals dotted the fractured blades of grass. Oz offered a hand to Shivan, and as she helped him up she said, "Don't look. Focus on Jeff. Just...don't look."

He couldn't help it. He looked.

The ground was cluttered with the broken bodies of elves who had nowhere to hide, no shelter from the blast that Tobias had thrown at us. Shivan swallowed hard, but then gave a slight nod of his head. Not all were lost; there were some wiggling out from tree branches, and some were running away from us, racing past the museum. The few who did not move were already dead, and he understood that there was no helping them.

"What the hell," Drew sputtered. "Is everyone all right?"

Oz and Aisha assured him that they were, but Will didn't answer.

Will was fixed on Jeff. He went over to the dragon and set his hand on Jeff's silky-soft chest, feeling the hard scales underneath. "Thank you. I have no idea how you kept so many of us safe. We truly owe you our lives."

I told you he was useful.

"Indeed, Wick. Jeff and Fluffy have been incredibly useful. Thank you, too, for making them protect us."

I didn't. Jeff thought of it by himself.

Will considered what that meant. "Did you prod Fluffy into helping him?"

No. They did it together. They can hear each other, the same way you can hear when you touch someone.

"Did you give them that ability?" he asked.

No. They're learning. They're babies, and babies learn.

"Indeed, they do."

"Tobias really does not want to deal with us," Oz said as Kilfin and the elves peeled themselves off the ground.

"He has to know that sooner or later he has no choice," Aisha said.

Oz shrugged. "Kill a couple of us, better his odds."

Will watched as the tornado disappeared in the distance, dying out over the ocean. "His intent may have been to render all of us useless. High winds, flying trees, broken bones and ripped flesh." He turned to look at Oz and Drew as he reached for Aisha's hand. "That was designed for us, specifically. He knows that if we're injured badly enough, our bodies will stop."

He didn't count on Jeff and Fluffy.

"He didn't count on *you*, Wick. If he's aware of your presence, he likely believes you to be nothing more than an ordinary cat. He has no idea what thoughts you're capable of. The Shedu weren't aware of Jeff before this. I'd presume he doesn't realize they came from you."

If I think really hard, can I give him jock itch? Like, a super case of it?

"You can certainly try. Be considerate in how you imagine it, though. If a thought of either Drew or myself sneaks in, we will not be amused."

"What's he wanting to do?" Drew asked.

"Inflict jock itch on Tobias."

"Damn, cat," Drew groaned. "Yeah, keep me out of that."

"It wouldn't work." Hagar picked me up. "You can inflict Tobias with any number of ills, but not Drew or the Emperor."

I could give Hagar hiccups. Just for fun.

Will reached for me. "That would be rude, and we have something to finish."

"Observation tower flambé," Oz said.

She was sure that if whoever was in the tower saw Jeff flying right at him, flames roaring from his nostrils, they would wet themselves and abandon their post—quite possibly in that order. Jeff could circle, letting the fire just kiss the windows, giving them ample warning before he belched out the flash that would set it ablaze.

Drew thought that would only serve to warn Tobias that we were there; Will said it didn't matter.

He was expecting us.

"And what if the entire building burns down?" Aisha asked.

Will shrugged. "Then Tobias is no longer a problem. Or he runs, and we follow."

"There's a sprinkler system," Oz said. "It's a museum. Surely there's a sprinkler system."

"It may not be a museum right now," Will pointed out. "But there's no point in worrying about it. If you want Jeff to light it up, then let Jeff light it up. If Tobias is in there and afraid, he can turn on his damned rain and put the fire out himself."

You're getting cranky.

Oz set her hand on Jeff's nose and gently stroked between his nostrils as she explained to him what she wanted him to do. He blinked slowly, telling her he understood, and she sent Jeff on his way. We watched from the meadow as he spread his wings and spiraled skyward, and then soared toward the DeYoung building. He flew in tight circles around the tower, flicking his tail and breathing thin lines of fire at the windows with each pass. When Will whispered to himself that he'd given them enough time to run, Jeff flew wide and headed right for the tower, flames billowing around the roof. He roared as he finished, arching his back to fly high over the smoke that began to fill the sky.

Kilfin ordered the elves to surround the building to take on any Shedu who tried to run, and told Will they would escort us as far as the entry point. After that, it was up to us to get Shivan to Tobias.

"Remember why you're doing this," Kilfin said to Shivan. "There is no honor in letting him live. Your only job is to draw the life from the evil that chokes us all. Do that, and we all go free. Do that, and your life will be so much easier."

Oz looked at Kilfin sideways—Shivan's life had been

pretty freaking easy compared to the elves—but she didn't say anything.

No one said much at all until we were close to the DeYoung. The tower was gone, replaced by puffs of smoke and burnt, crumbling tile. Water spewed from the hole in the roof, and Jeff hovered over it, admiring his work.

Will called to him; someone needed to keep an eye on Fluffy while we were inside. He told Fluffy to stay, as if he were a common house dog, and Jeff landed on the grass behind him. "You've both done well, thank you. Now might be a good time to rest."

With a single touch and thought, he put them both to sleep. *They'll wake up if they need to, right?*

"They'll wake," he assured me. "They're only sleeping."

They might want to help.

"Wick, you said yourself that they're babies. Babies need extra sleep, and they've earned their naps."

Jeff wasn't going to fit through the museum doors, anyway.

The doors were locked, but instead of Will smashing through the glass with the butt of a gun, Kilfin wrapped his giant hand around the pull-bar and twisted. The door frame groaned under the pressure of his strength, and then with a loud pop the entire thing pulled away from the wall.

"Good luck," he said as he turned to leave. He took Krisf with him, leaving only the Trident, the Wizard, the Lord of Prophecy, Aisha, and me.

Oz took a deep breath and headed inside, and the rest of us followed. As soon as Hagar was through the broken doorway, a solid metal gate slid down, the room filled with fog, and one by one, we went down.

31

The Emperor was gone.

I woke first—as the fog puffed from above and surrounded us in wispy clouds, Aisha clamped her hands over my nose and mouth, sparing me from the worst of it—and everyone else was slumped on the floor, eyes closed. I wasn't sure if they were alive or dead. The only thing I knew for sure was that Will was missing, and the white tile floor had dark streaks of spent rubber where his shoes had dragged.

Aisha was closest, so I sniffed at her face, deliberately brushing my whiskers across her cheeks and eyelids. She scrunched up her nose—good, alive—so I went to Oz and then Drew, making sure that both of them were still breathing. The air had cleared, but the metal gate was still in place, so there was no going back.

There were windows, but they weren't the kind you could slide open and then hop out of. Getting through one meant breaking glass; this was a museum so the windows were going to be tough enough to withstand anything a determined intruder could throw at them. Oz wouldn't be able to kick our way out, and Drew wouldn't be able to shoot the glass away.

I crept deeper into the room, hoping for a hint about where they'd taken Will. The entry was massive, with halls that split off, walls that hid stairwells, and there were little benches placed in odd spots where people were supposed to sit and gaze at artwork that was no longer on the walls. The walls were bare, with uneven color that marked where paintings once hung.

I looked in the direction that the streaks from Will's shoes went, sucked up my dignity, and wailed his name.

Perhaps if he heard me, he could answer.

I called again, and then again.

Nothing.

Quiet.

The silence was only broken by the uncomfortable waking of the people to my back. I heard them stir, but didn't look. They didn't need me. Instead, I called for Will again.

Aisha was first to realize he was missing, and she called out his name, too, although it was more sorrow and fear than it was trying to get his attention.

"Son of a bitch," Oz sputtered. She picked Will's gun off the floor and tucked it into her waistband before considering that Aisha was terrified. "We'll find him. He's got to be in here somewhere."

Unless they took him away.

I hope they don't have an Emperor-eating dragon.

Drew scooped me up. "Did you see anything, Wick? Any idea where we—"

I buried my face against his arm so that he would understand. They knew as much as I did.

"I'm sorry, Wick," he whispered.

"Stick together," Oz said. She knelt and scraped her thumbnail along one of the streaks on the floor, then rolled the rubber between her fingers, testing it, making sure it was real. Once she was sure, she dropped onto her belly and pressed her face to the floor, closing one eye so that she could see better. "These streaks definitely move into the room, not out."

Drew dropped down, too, trying to see what she did.

"Looking how the tiny slivers of rubber stand," she told him. "They bend toward the hallway. If he'd been taken back outside, they would bend in the other direction."

"Huh. I just assumed he'd been dragged that way based on the fact that the streaks are thicker toward the door and thinner toward the hallway."

"Fine." She got up. "Just being sure."

Before she could get more than a couple steps away, he reached for her arm. "Oz, I'm sorry. I can pick a better time to be a smart ass."

"No, but you're right. Overthinking is not my best asset right now. Let's just find him."

We headed for the first hall to our left, bypassing smaller rooms that had been gift shops and ticket sales; those doors were open, and no one was inside. The stairs that led to the observation tower were dirty and wet, with no footprints to suggest anyone had been on them in the last few minutes, so she pushed on. She was looking for hiding places, anywhere an unconscious Emperor could be stashed.

Once past the stairs, she hesitated; there were two doors, and one was open half an inch. Shivan nudged her and pointed to it, whispering, "There. They probably took him there."

Slowly, she made her way over and listened carefully. Hearing nothing, she moved to the door that was closed, tilting her head as she strained to hear. "Too easy," she said, looking at Drew. He nodded, but pushed the open door a few inches more, and peeked in.

"Closet," he said. "Mops and brooms."

"You can do a lot to a person in a broom closet," Oz muttered. She absently rubbed at her wrist and then nodded in the direction of the hallway. "We need to check it all before we start getting off track. The cafeteria used to be down this way, and the hall should lead us to exhibit rooms."

"What about the dungeon?" Shivan asked.

She was moving down the hall. "It's probably just the basement. No dungeon."

"Then why—?"

"We need to know the layout of this place. It's probably not the same as it was in our time." She glanced over Shivan's head to Aisha. "If we go rushing downstairs without knowing where the Shedu might be hiding, or without an idea where in here Tobias is waiting, we could walk right into an ambush. If we learn the building's footprint, if we have to run and hide, we'll know where to go. We'll find him, I promise."

"Just find him before it's too late," Aisha said.

"Will can hold his own," Drew reminded them both. He pulled his gun from his waistband and reminded everyone to be ready to fight; Aisha followed suit, and Shivan had his hand on the hilt of his plasma sword, but Oz stubbornly left her weapons in place. She walked soft and swift, keeping to the wall the way Will had taught her.

We checked every empty exhibit room along the way, stopping to listen, waiting for sound to drift through air vents or from the end of the hall. On the fifth room we entered, she motioned for everyone to plaster themselves to the wall near the door, and we stayed silent for several minutes, until she was sure that whatever she thought she'd heard was only a phantom sound.

Sound should echo in here.

"Hush, Wick," Oz said, peeking around the doorway.

Well, it would. If anyone is walking around, we'll hear their footsteps loud and clear.

"Depends on the shoe," Drew said, trying to peek over Oz's shoulder. "Maybe we should make our way back, and go down the other hallway."

"This one meets up," she assured him.

We're going to walk in circles.

Drew followed Oz, but grunted, "Looks that way."

Why would they stay on a floor where we can hear everything?

Oz hushed me again, but Drew whispered, "Look, just follow Oz, all right? They might not consider the noise."

Aisha reached for Drew's shoulder to stop him. "You're talking to Wick."

"Everyone talks to Wick," Oz said. "We always have."

"No, Oz. He's *talking* to *Wick*."

That made Oz stop and turn around. "Drew, you can understand him?"

He blinked a few times, thinking. "I was just reacting to his voice."

Dude, you totally heard me.

"Cat, did you just call me 'dude'?"

I call everyone dude. Sometimes it's 'dude' but sometimes it's 'doood.'

"Holy hell." He took me from Aisha and held me up so that we were face to face. For the record, I don't always like that, because people breath is not always fresh. "Say something else."

You need to brush your teeth.

"Yeah, we all do. Tell me something else."

You touched Oz's boobs when we were camping last year.

He lowered me so that I didn't have to smell his breath. "Yeah, now I know why Will doesn't always tell us what you say."

Well, it wasn't a secret. You weren't very quiet about it.

"Cat..."

I looked over at Aisha. *Well, they weren't.*

"Wick, did you see anything? Do you know where they took Will?"

I woke up and he was gone. I listened but there was no noise. I yelled, but he didn't yell back.

Aisha sniffed softly. Her eyes were red and damp, but she wasn't crying and Oz and Drew pretended to not notice. Hagar touched her arm gently, but he wasn't sure what to say to make her feel better.

I told Drew what to say.

"Will knows how to survive," he said, quietly. "He knows to not fight if it means living to see you again."

Can Will turn Tobias off? Like, pull his plug?

Drew asked Hagar, who thought that unless Will could get to the lab, it would require physically harming the dark wizard. Oz didn't think he would; kill the wizard too soon, die at the hands of his guards. The only choice was to keep moving and find them both.

Drew set me on his shoulder with the order to jump if we encountered anyone, and Oz led us through the maze of small rooms. She stopped just short of taking us back into the giant room where we'd entered the building, waiting to see if there was anyone in there. "Unless everything about this place has shifted, the only other place to look is downstairs. I know the special events hall is down a staircase to the left in our When, but I didn't see it here, and I don't know where else to look."

"Will was sure he'd be in here," Drew said.

"The number of guards outside earlier made it seem that way," Oz mused. "They were guarding something in here, there was no—" She sighed hard as the thought hit her. "The tornado. He wasn't just trying to kill us, it was a diversion. The son of a bitch knew we were coming and took off."

"What about Will?" Aisha no longer looked like she wanted to cry; she was pissed off. "He could still be in here somewhere."

There's always a downstairs.

Drew pointed to the locked door we'd passed. "Through there. Maintenance, maybe. Heating and air system. Plumbing. Storage."

Dungeon.

"Dungeon," he repeated.

"How is this even possible?" Oz asked. "Suddenly you understand him? Have you been hearing him all along but just now get what he's saying?"

Sometimes he understands me. He just doesn't realize it, like this morning when he told me he couldn't drive.

"I've understood his context a few times, but not the actual words. Now it's like I hear his people-voice inside my own head. I mean, I can hear him meow, but riding on that is a human male voice. He sounds...young. Teenager young."

"I admit, I'm a little jealous."

Aisha reached over to rub my head. "Maybe it's your transponders."

"How so?" Drew asked.

"You're tied into the computer that controls all of this, right? Without Will to translate, maybe the computer is letting you hear Wick in your head, to be sure he has a voice. When Oz said that everyone deserves a voice, maybe that became part of the programming."

"Then why just me?" Drew mused. "Why not Oz?"

Because you're special.

"You're almost as close to Wick as the Emperor," Oz said. "If any of us is going to make that leap, it'll be you. Enjoy it while you can. If she's right, once we're home you won't be able to."

"Damn." He pulled me a little closer. "I hope they're wrong, Wick."

Me, too. I have things to tell you. Like, you need advice in bed.

"Then again, maybe not."

Oz peeked out of the room and then pointed to the door we'd looked at before, the one that was locked. "Might as well start there. Once we cross, shoot it open."

"And the noise?" Drew set me down. "We'll call a lot of attention to ourselves."

"Not much choice."

He went first, gun in hand, and fired at the door handle. When it was open—he kicked at it, rather than risking the burn to his hand—we scrambled across the floor and headed down the dark staircase, not stopping to see if anyone followed.

We probably should have, because when we got to the foot of the stairs, Hagar was gone.

32

The landing at the bottom of the stairs was dim, and the only light came from a small bulb dangling from the ceiling, twenty feet away. The air was damp and I caught whiffs of people hours-gone; hanging in the air was sweat, sour breath, and peppermint. Whoever had been there ahead of us was nervous and using mints to cover the tang of a bitter stomach.

The good news was that there was someone to follow.

The bad news was that there was someone to follow.

Shivan was tangled in anguish. He called up the stairs, hoping Hagar was simply slow to follow, but was answered by the echo of his own strangled voice. He started up the stairs, thinking the wizard needed help, but Oz grabbed his shirt and pulled him back. "You go up there, and you risk being blown into pieces. They want you to chase after him. They expect it. We stay together."

"But we were looking for the Emperor," Shivan spat. "If we looked for him we can look for Hagar."

"The second Hagar vanished, what we're doing changed." Oz was just short of hissing at him. "We move forward and check the spaces here we haven't been."

"We have to find him. I need him!"

"No, you really don't. You *need* to stay focused. Your job is to get to Tobias, not to worry about Hagar."

"Easy for you," Shivan groused. "He's not your friend."

"The Emperor is my uncle," she shot back, jabbing a sharp finger at his chest. "He's Drew's best friend. He's half of Aisha's heartbeat. She's his *partner*. Don't whine to me about friends. We're all in the same damned spot, so suck it up and do what he trained you to do. He's a big boy. He'll take care of himself."

Under his breath but loud enough for her to hear, Shivan grumbled, "But he was supposed to be with me when I faced the dark wizard."

She gnashed her teeth together to keep from shouting at him.

"He still might be," Drew said to him. "Keep your faith, Shivan. Sometimes it's all we've got, and right now, it has to be enough."

You would know. Maybe you should tell him about walking all those miles to get to Oz. He should know that you get it.

Oz turned toward the tunnel where the light bulb hung loosely from the ceiling and started walking. It was dark and damp, with water puddled on the floor, dripping from pipes that lined the wall. She didn't think this was anything like the actual DeYoung; this was torn right out of a movie or a book, the wet maze of danger that the heroes have to traverse in order to find victory.

"We're part of his game now," she said, "but I'm not sure if we're pawns or opponents."

I think we're both.

"How are we both, Wick?" Drew asked.

One of us is his opponent. The rest of us are just the pieces he's moving around to make sure he wins.

"Then we make sure he can't move us. We protect Shivan."

It's not him.

You know who it is.

"I'm not sure I follow."

Will knew. Aisha knows. But don't ask her, because she probably won't tell you.

"What are you two chattering about?" Oz asked him. "Does Wick have some furry insight?"

He told her that I thought they were both pawns and opponents, and that we had to keep going, protecting each of us as if we were the Lord of Prophecy. She squinted, seeing the colors around him shift, but she let him think she believed him.

He wouldn't lie without a reason, not to her.

Pants on fire, dude.

The tunnel began to feel like the ones at the safe house; dark and gloomy, going on forever. After we hit the fifteen-minute mark and there was no end in sight, Aisha asked how far Oz thought we'd gone.

"A mile, more or less. Keep your eyes peeled for exit points because this is heading toward the ocean. If we can bail before then, we bail."

"If not?"

"If it caves in, we drown."

"Oz," Drew said, "if it caves in under the ocean, we drown even if we stay right here."

"I was hoping to not dwell on that."

After that, we were all dwelling on it. I listened for the tick of cracking cement, the roar of water. It wouldn't do much good if I heard anything because there was no way any of them could run fast enough to beat a wall of water surging through the tunnel, so I wasn't sure I would tell them even if I did hear something. I listened anyway. They fell quiet, their wet footsteps keeping time as Oz found a pace, until we'd gone another half mile and the tunnel made an abrupt right turn.

She stopped and listened before peering around the corner, and then gestured toward it with her head. Drew and Aisha followed, but Shivan had slowed, prompting Oz to stop and tell him to speed up.

"My legs feel weighted," he said. "Heavy and tingly."

"Yeah, mine, too." She set her hands on her hips and thought about it for a few seconds. "Look, the closer we get to Tobias, the more afraid you're going to feel. That's normal. We're all scared."

"How can you be? You're the Trident."

"Yeah, well, we're missing one of the pointy parts. We're worried about him, and we're worried about what we're walking into. But we still need to keep going. Being scared doesn't change the fact that we have to keep moving."

"So, suck it up, sunshine?"

That made Oz grin. "We all suck it up."

"We might die."

"To paraphrase the Emperor...we might not."

As she started walking again, he jogged after her. "You're really afraid?"

"I'm really afraid. My stomach is in knots, and my legs feel as heavy as yours do."

"But you're a fighter. You've battled before."

"Not as well as I wanted, Shivan. Not as well as I needed. And even the best fighter knows there's someone who might be a little faster and a little smarter, someone who can find his weakness and use it."

"The Trident isn't weak."

"We all have weaknesses. Mine is impatience wrapped around a weird level of overconfidence."

"Mine is hesitation," Drew said. "I overthink."

"Mine is anger," Aisha added. "Right now, I'm as angry as I think I've ever been."

Oz wasn't sure that was a weakness. That anger would keep her moving, and wouldn't let her stop until we found Will. Unless it made her do rash things, it was an asset.

"You're not rash," she said. "So keep being angry."

As long as she's angry she won't think about sitting down and crying.

"Same for us all," Drew whispered to me.

Shivan went quiet, pondering his own weaknesses, I think. He slowed until he was behind Aisha again, but I could hear his footsteps and he wasn't lagging. He wasn't going to be the reason we failed.

*

Another mile down the tunnel the lights were brighter, and the odor of stale water thinned until it was gone. The walls were dry, and written in bright red block letters to our left was 1600m, DOWN UNDER. Oz paused just long enough to read it, shrugged, and kept going.

Twenty feet later, in the same red letters, DISPLAY YOUR SHAME.

"What the hell does that mean?" Drew asked.

Oz had no idea. "It could be completely unrelated. Maybe it's someone's weird little underground art project."

It looks fresh. It looks like blood.

"It's just red paint," Drew said. "Not blood."

Yeah, well, you go lick it and tell us what it tastes like.

"I don't really know what blood tastes like, Wick."

"Copper," Oz asked. "Have you ever seen an old penny? It tastes like that."

Aisha looked puzzled. "This begs the question, how do you know what a penny tastes like?"

"No," Drew said, "the real question is what the hell is a penny?"

No, the question is how she knows that blood and pennies taste alike.

"She's been hit in the mouth, Wick," Drew said. "A split lip or two told her what blood tastes like."

"Seriously," Oz said. "And pennies are an ancient form of money. Practically worthless in its day, invaluable now. And I know what it tastes like because my grandad collected old coins. I tried to eat a few when I was four or five. The taste sticks with you."

"Remember that the next time you think about saying I'm a special snowflake," Drew chortled.

"You are special, hot stuff."

She can stop calling you that now. You're really just kind of warm.

Oh, like a muffin. She can call you that instead. Muffin.

"Seriously, Wick, I really do understand now why Will only tells us a little bit of what you're saying."

"What's he saying?" Oz asked. "Come on, spill it."

"I'd rather not."

The tunnel took a hard left and widened until it ended in a room that had a single door. She placed a hand on it, feeling for heat, and then set her head against it as she listened for voices or sound of movement.

"We either open it or go back," she said. "We all need to agree. There's no telling what's on the other side of this door."

"Open it," Aisha said. "Going back means two hours of walking for nothing because Will is not back there. Neither is Hagar."

Drew agreed. "The only way through is forward."

"Shivan?" Oz asked.

"My bladder wants us to go back. I think that means we should open the door and see where it leads."

"Pee in the tunnel," Drew suggested. "At least you and I have the advantage there."

Oz put her hand on the doorknob. "Yeah, don't think I won't if I have to. If I can pee in the woods and swap out a tampon while leaning against a tree..."

Shivan grimaced. "Gross."

"Fact of life," Drew said to him. "No point in getting skeeved out about it."

Whoever gets to clean up after us is the one who should be grossed out. We all peed in the woods. Oz tossed bloody things onto the ground.

"She buried them, Wick."

I'll let you think about that.

The door opened to another staircase. Drew put his hand on her shoulder to hold her back, and he crept forward, looking up the stairs the way Carter had when we were in the news studio in Chicago. He mimicked his brother's staccato movements, cocking his head as he listened; when he was sure there was no one coming, he gestured for Oz to follow.

Shivan began to whisper. "The Princess Oz, the Prince Andrew, the woman Aisha." He repeated it several times until Oz shot a look over her shoulder. "You are the brave, you are the mighty, you are the loved."

"Fine, thank you, but be quiet."

"I don't know why I did that, but I'll stop talking now."

He's praying. The Queen would like that.

The staircase was steep and felt more like a ladder the further up we went, and it was twice as long as the stairs in Lands End. Just when Oz began swearing under her breath, there was another door, but it was built into the ceiling. Drew handed me to Aisha and helped Oz push it open because she couldn't lift it all the way.

It opened into the wheat fields, which were beaten down and dying. There was a clear path cutting through, wet dirt that had mashed stalks of wheat strewn over it. The air was heavy with rotten grain, and I set my nose against Aisha's arm to keep from inhaling too much of it.

"What the hell," Oz muttered. "I thought we'd wind up on the other end of the DeYoung."

Fluffy and Jeff are back there.

"You can call to them, Wick," Drew said. "If it feels like we need them, think them here."

"Part of me wants to turn back to the museum. Yet I really don't think they're back there anymore. Follow the path." Oz sounded resigned, not at all happy.

"That way goes to the Dolores fields," Shivan said. "My father said that when he was a boy, before there was wheat here, it was a park. He used to take a giant block of ice and ride down the long hill. I'm hoping that someday I can do that. It sounded like fun."

"It is," Aisha said. "We did the same thing. Your dad," she said to Oz. "Oh my God. Will wouldn't do it, so Jax made his guards ride down with him. Three grown men who were supposed to be hiding in the shadows, rifles slung on their backs, following him while perched on little blocks of ice."

"Was alcohol involved?"

"Maybe," Aisha said, trying to not laugh. "Your parents were a lot of fun when we were kids. There wasn't much your dad wouldn't try."

"They were fun when I was little. But then Dad had to grow up and become king. I think he still regrets that. Grandad just couldn't go on with it after Grandma died."

"He'll retire young enough to still have fun," Drew guessed.

All the more reason to find Will, Oz thought, because if Jax retired as young as his father did, she wanted the Emperor around. It didn't feel possible to be ready for the job by the time she was thirty, and he would become her advisor.

"Wait, I thought we were going to use him as a nanny," Drew said.

"Well, I assume that will happen before I'm Queen," Oz said. "Won't it?"

He shrugged. "As long as we're married first. I'd like a couple of years, though."

"Have them while you're young," Aisha said. "A toddler at my age? You need energy for kids."

Oz raised one eyebrow playfully. "Accidents happen."

"Honey, I have to get that man into bed for there to be even a remote chance of an accident. We'll see."

Oz hesitated, but then shrugged. "All right, I just assumed when you stayed in the same room."

You're kinda nosey.

"I think he figured out early on that we're in a simulator. The last thing he wanted was for the program to stop and the imaginary walls to come down at the wrong moment."

The idea made Drew laugh until he realized what it meant. "Damn. We really should have thought about that."

"No, he should have told us," Oz said.

He did warn you about really thin walls.

"He did try to tell us the walls were thin," Drew said. "I just thought he meant, like, put a pillow over Oz's face to keep her quiet."

Aisha snorted out a laugh. "Please tell me you didn't do that."

"Not that I'll admit to."

Oz was laughing, too. "There might be bite marks on his shoulder. He had to shut me up somehow."

If she was going to ask, she forgot. We got to the hill in Dolores Park and were about to start down, but there was a sign planted right on the path. It was so new that the painted letters dripped red drops onto the dirt.

NONE PASS BUT THE TRIDENT

"Try and stop us, assmunch," Oz muttered. "We *all* move forward. Period."

"Maybe we should hold hands and skip past the sign together," Drew said. "In case someone is watching."

Aisha thought it wouldn't be more absurd than everything else we'd done. They could hold hands and swing arms while skipping just far enough down the hill to wonder why the hell they were out of breath. Then give the finger to whoever might be watching.

Drew took Oz's hand and turned to ask Shivan if he wanted to hold Oz's other hand or Aisha's because he was sure Shivan didn't want to hold his. It was moot.

No one was surprised when he wasn't there.

33

The long descent of the Dolores Park hill was made in silence. When it was clear Shivan was gone and not hiding in the wheat, ready to jump out like a naughty child trying to scare his parents, Drew set me in the pouch of his sweatshirt, and then reached for Oz's and Aisha's hands. The only thing I heard while they trudged down the hill was the scraping of shoes on grass, their breathing, and Drew's heartbeat.

Halfway, they were breathing in unison. Inhale deeply, exhale angrily. I peeked at their hands; Aisha had a death grip on Drew and his fingers were turning red under the pressure. He didn't ask her to ease up. He didn't tell her it hurt.

At the bottom, they paused. Oz stared down the path ahead and finally broke the silence.

"He offered me the chance to go home this morning. If I'd taken him up on it—"

"You'd have changed your mind ten minutes after we got there, and you and I would have come back without him," Drew said. "Don't pick though what might have been, Oz. Will would be the first to tell you, the only thing that does is make you feel bad. He's been doing it since you were snatched from the safe house."

"Even still?"

"I don't think he'll ever stop."

"That wasn't his fault," she argued. "He did everything to protect us. There's no way any of that was his fault."

Gently, Aisha said, "And this isn't yours, Oz. Will would no more blame you for whatever has happened to him than you blame him. I think the difference is that you can accept that. He never will."

"No, the difference is that he didn't stay in a situation he didn't have to. I did. He had no choice but to keep us in the safe house and there was no way to know that Florida's military minions would get in. I had every choice in staying here or leaving, and I told him I felt like I'd be running if I left. But we could have gone home this morning."

Aisha moved so that she was in front of Oz, but she didn't let go of Drew's hand. She used her free hand to touch Oz's face, fingers soft on her cheek. "No, sweetheart, we couldn't have. He didn't want to leave, either. He knows there's a reason for all of this, and eventually we'll figure it out. He offered to take me home, but he was damn well coming back to finish this. Whatever happened to him would have happened, because he wasn't staying out of it."

True. I heard him say that.

"Wick backs her up, Oz. Will was going to finish this."

Reluctantly, Oz accepted it. "Why *did* you stay, Aisha?"

"Because I haven't felt this connected to anything other than my son in years. I get that it's dangerous, but come on. Wizards and dragons, and a giant cat named Fluffy? You *flew* on a dragon! Where else will that ever happen?"

Plus, she got to see Will in his underwear.

"That's right, Wick. Spending time with him is probably fun, too."

"That's not what he said," Oz grumbled.

"Close enough."

They were still holding hands and started across Dolores Street, moving along a beaten path that I knew was new. Everything felt wrong—I was sure that the wheat fields had been at the bottom of the hill when we were here before, and I couldn't understand why they were at the top now—so I wiggled in Drew's pouch until I was almost standing up, and I strained to see as far as I could.

Things behind us were wrong, and things ahead of us were wrong.

The skyline had shifted.

Something's changed.

Look.

Drew, look.

He followed my gaze, up over the treetops. Jutting into the sky was downtown San Francisco, every building, every tower, that was part of our reality. The Transamerica Tower, the Salesforce Building. We shouldn't have been able to see any of it from this spot in the park, but the city here was flat and not built on the rolling hills of home.

Swarming from a spot that could have been over Union Square or even the royal house, was a vibrating mass of red and blue.

Butterflies?

"Hard to tell from here, Wick. It might be butterflies. It might be flying piranha."

"Great," Oz said. "We're going to get there right at dinner time, and we're the entrée."

Even tucked into Drew's sweatshirt, I felt exposed.

It wasn't safe.

*

The trees were big enough to use as cover, but there was no hiding from the noise that came up from behind. Oz heard the soft sound of feet slapping the leaves and dirt after I did, and she knew we were in someone's line of sight; ducking behind trees would buy a few seconds, nothing more. Still, she had her hand on her sword and whispered to Drew and Aisha to be ready to draw.

She spun on her heel and dropped into a fighting stance. Then half a second later she sighed and stood up, not sure she should laugh or yell at me.

Drew said to think him here if I wanted him. I wanted him.

"Why did you want him?"

Because he's Fluffy.

"Good enough," Drew said.

He wants to help. Give him something to do.

"Your giant furry soldier wants a job," Drew told her.

"We can send him ahead," Oz said. "If there's anyone waiting up there, he can draw them out." She reached up and scratched under his chin. "Would you do that, Fluffy? Be our scout?"

Does he get to eat a Shedu if he finds one?

"Gross, Wick," Drew said. "But yeah, we can't stop him from munching on the enemy."

"Only if he thinks they'll hurt him," Oz added. "Don't eat someone just to eat someone, all right? If you're hungry, we'll figure something out soon."

Fluffy head-butted her and knocked her to the ground.

He meant that in a nice way.

"We know he's trying to be nice," Drew said. "It would help if he understood how big he is."

Oz reached for me. "Tell him, why don't you?"

I rode on her shoulder as Fluffy took off, bouncing between trees as he hunted for something to play with. He stayed where we could still see him, but darted in a wide enough path to clear out anyone who might be waiting behind or up a tree. There were imaginary bugs to chase and pretend squirrels to torment, and he zoomed in circles with abandonment I hadn't felt since I was Will's Major, stomping through his carefully crafted wood-block cities.

Fluffy stopped once to look up, and Oz thought he was tracking a Shedu or an elf hiding in the leaves, but then a massive familiar shadow zoomed over and in front of us.

It was hard to see through the leaf-laden branches that were woven together, but Jeff was up there, flying in circles, looking for a way to get in.

"No place for him to land," Drew told me.

He'll find something.

Ten minutes later, Fluffy stopped abruptly. He looked up and meowed, then turned back to find us, babbling with excitement. Jeff found a stone wall to perch on, one that cut across our path and extended so far to the left and right that it seemed as if it didn't end.

There was a door right in front of us, freshly painted red letters dripping to the ground.

1600m DOWN UNDER

DISPLAY YOUR SHAME

"That was in the tunnel," Aisha said. "Are we going underground again?"

Oz wanted to go around. Going north, the wall could only be so long, ending in the bay where they could get around it, even if it meant going into the water, but that would also take more time to walk than she wanted to spend. After considering it, she decided that at the very least, they could open the door and see what waited on the other side.

"Could be men in black with big guns," Drew said.

"Could be a million Fluffy-sized spiders, too, for all we know." Oz pulled the gun from her waistband and set her hand on the door handle. "Scratch that. Don't even think that. If you think anything, it's just a wall, and the rest of the city is on the other side."

There were no men with guns. No massive spiders. Oz pushed the door open, and it slid to the side, neatly hidden out of the way, and she stuck her head in.

A cloud of chlorine-tinged air billowed out.

"It's a freaking swimming pool." She stepped through the entryway, craning her neck to look up, and then side to side. "The outside wall might go on forever, but the inner walls are roughly eight feet apart. And the pool, hell, I can't see the end of it."

Drew tried to go in to see for himself, but was bounced back.

"What the hell?" Carefully, he put a hand out. When the air bit back, he flinched. "I can't get in."

Oz tried to leave but was bounced back more forcefully than he had been. "It's like the suicide nets on the bridges. But with added tingly bits."

She put her hand out warily, feeling for the buzz as the net turned on, and then looked up again. "There are iron spikes all along the top of the wall, at least five feet tall. Three of them are jammed up Jeff's ass." She touched the force field again, testing. "Even if you could get up the wall and over the spikes, I'm betting this field extends over it."

Aisha stuck one finger out and felt for the net, but her hand went right through it. "I don't feel anything."

"Does she try to go in or not?" Drew asked Oz.

"Up to you," Oz said to Aisha. "If you can get in, you can probably get out, too."

Aisha stepped in. Drew tried to follow—maybe it was a glitch—but it threw him back, hard.

"Damn, it really doesn't want you in here," Oz said. She examined the trim around the door, looking for the contact points that would raise the net, but it was solid stone. They both felt along the wall, flat hands skimming the surface, but the only thing they found was dirt.

While Drew said a few things off the bad word list, Aisha took a closer look at the pool. It went nearly wall to wall, with only a twelve-inch clearance on each side. And on a small sign near the pool's edge were the same blood-red block letters.

1600m

FOR AUSTRALIA ONLY

DISPLAY YOUR SHAME

"What does that even mean?" Aisha asked.

There was a thick plastic bag at the foot of the sign. It was sealed with a zipper clip, and on one side there was a hard foam board to float it on.

"Sixteen hundred meters," Oz said. "Roughly a mile."

"To Australia?"

"*For* Australia. Yeah, that would be me," she sighed.

Drew was as close to the doorway as he dared get. "Oz, no."

"Do I have a choice?" She went to the wall on the right to see if there was enough space to walk along the water, but the field spit at her there, too. "Apparently, I'm swimming."

"And 'display your shame'?" Aisha asked.

Oz nudged the plastic bag with her foot. "Naked." She set me down and then handed her weapons to Aisha. "You guys take Jeff. Fly over the pool and meet me at the end. Should take thirty to forty minutes."

I wandered over the spot near the wall where she couldn't walk. The field didn't bite me.

I'll stay with Oz. She shouldn't be alone.

"You might get wet, Wick," Drew said.

If I ride with you, I might fall. I'd rather be wet.

When Oz kicked her shoes off, Drew groaned. "There has to be another way. They can't force you to do this."

She stuck her arm out, trying to reach over the edge of the pool, and activated the field. "I think they can."

"But why?" Aisha asked. "To what end?"

Oz shrugged. "I'll see when I finish, I suppose."

"Oz—" Drew looked as if someone had taken away his favorite toy. "I just..."

"You've seen me naked, hot stuff. Just get to the other side. I might need you to warm me up when I'm done." Piece by piece the clothes came off, and she rolled them together and shoved everything into the plastic bag. There was a loop to go around her ankle so that she could drag the bag behind her in the pool, but Aisha reached out for it.

"I'm staying with Wick. Don't trust that this bag will survive the water."

"Wick got through the field, but—"

"I got in here, didn't I?" she said. "I don't have a transponder. It probably doesn't even see me."

"But Wick has one."

"Wick is harmless. The computer knows that." She handed Oz's weapons to Drew. "Take Jeff. I'll stay with Oz and keep Wick safe."

"We shouldn't separate," Drew argued.

"We don't have a choice. I can't get out and you can't get in." Oz zipped the bag closed and handed it to Aisha. "I can swim a mile, the Emperor made sure of that a long time ago. I'll be fine. You concentrate on not falling off Jeff."

We'll watch Oz. We promise.

"Ozzie."

"I love you. Now go tell Fluffy to find a way around, and then ride the dragon. But, you can admire my ass as I get into the water." Before he could say anything else, she turned around and dove in. He was still standing there when I headed for the narrow walkway, watching Oz swim away.

A few minutes later I glanced back and he was gone, Jeff's shadow darkening the doorway.

Aisha balanced on the narrow pool edge behind me, and we kept a steady pace with Oz. The sound of her arms cutting through the water and the force of her kicks echoed off the walls; it sounded like she was struggling, but really, she swam easily. This didn't look any different than all the times the Emperor made her swim laps, other than there was a hard rule about no skinny dipping at home.

He could have been here, and I don't think it would have made her blink. She would have stripped down as easily with him there as she did with Aisha. He would have been riding Jeff with Drew, most likely, but if not, with every stroke she took the only thing he would have noted about her was the thick white scar that ran down her back.

She had a hundred others, easily, but the one on her back and the one on her chest were the most telling.

I wondered why she didn't have them removed. It was possible; Zed cracked his head open trying to run under the table when he was a toddler, and the cut left by the table's edge left a thick red scar. Aubrey took him to the doctor one afternoon, and when he came home, it was gone.

If Oz got her scars removed, she would get ice cream for dinner, like Zed did. And Oz had a lot of scars, so there was the chance she could have it every night for a month. Or she might only want cookies; she seemed to like those more.

If it were me, I would want shrimp. And steak.

Maybe when this is all over you can have cookies. You deserve cookies. I'll tell Will. The Queen makes chocolate chip cookies when he asks.

Careful to not lose sight of where I was walking—I didn't want to get wet no matter what I told Drew—I watched the muscles in her back work. She still hadn't gotten into the shape she wanted to be, which was three kinds of confusing because there was nothing wrong with her shape; she was still strong, and her skin pulled tight across her back as she worked.

Whatever flaws Oz saw, I don't think anyone else did.

Twenty minutes later, Jeff's shadow took a dive to the right, and the sound of lasers firing off swelled overhead. Oz hesitated, taking a moment to look up and see if Drew was in trouble, but he had steered Jeff away from any chance he would wind up falling on her if he was shot down. Bright white bursts from his gun lit up the sky, a fast series of ten shots that flared and then faded. Drew pushed Jeff to list to the left so that he had a better visual line and he fired again, rapidly. I lost count of the laser bursts; Oz was swimming on her back, watching, biting on her bottom lip.

Jeff surged higher, turning away from the return fire. He lifted his wing, protecting Drew and blocking him from our sight. He began banking away when the last shot went off, and the skin on his wing exploded, forcing his rapid descent.

The beat of his other wing increased and he turned hard, trying to gain control, but it was going to be a hard landing no matter what he did. As he disappeared from our sight, he curled his injured wing over Drew.

Oz began to swim aggressively, her arms chewing up and spitting out the water, and as she reached the end, the walls surrounding the pool ended and Drew ran in.

"Jeff," he sputtered. "We were hit. He—"

She pulled herself out of the pool, shaking water from her hair, and then ran to see what had happened. Ten feet way, Jeff was stretched out and rolled onto his left side, just off Market Street, a two-foot hole blown through his wing and a long piece of metal jutting from his chest. Oz ran to him, the dirt that she kicked up sticking to her skin.

"He hit a street sign when he landed," Drew sputtered. "It broke off..."

Jeff moaned, sending waves of heat from his nostrils and tiny sparks from his mouth. The flesh around the wound on his wing was singed, and thick, clear fluid dripped from his chest. Oz put her hands on him and started mumbling, trying to think him better, though it was more wishing than anything else because she could not form the picture inside her head of what his healed insides would look like.

She didn't know what was damaged, and couldn't heal what she couldn't see. When Jeff wailed, she rested her head against him, begging him to be all right.

Jeff wants to be let go. It hurts too much.

Oz can't fix him.

Drew placed a gentle kiss on Oz's shoulder and pulled her back, asking her to turn away. She didn't want to; she wanted to keep trying, until Aisha reached for her.

"He's in agony, Oz," she said gently. "He took care of us. He protected Drew in that landing. Let Drew help him."

She gritted her teeth together and turned, and I closed my eyes so that Drew could do what he needed to do. It was a gentle pop, his gun close to Jeff's skull.

I turned away and did not look back.

In my chest, I felt Jeff's last sigh like a wish. He was grateful, and he was happy. I felt bad only for a moment because he was still written onto the simulator's hard drive, and the hard drive would never forget, even when my own memory failed me.

I opened my eyes; there was another sign ahead.

BEHOLD THE SHAME OF OZ

Behind it, Market Street was filled with Shedu warriors in crisp, military lines all the way to the water's edge. The road was asphalt, and buildings lined the sidewalks that hadn't been there even two days before. As we looked around, more Shedu surrounded us, filling Market Street behind us, and Oz was still very wet, and very naked.

34

Drew stood in front of Oz and Aisha was behind her, trying to shield her from the angry gawking of the thousand or more Shedu warriors that had surrounded us. I climbed up Drew's leg to get away from all the boots in my line of sight, and as I settled on his shoulder, Oz gently pushed him to the side.

If they thought being naked and wet shamed Oz, they didn't know her. They could look all they wanted, but the first person to leer or make a lurid comment was going to be dead pretty quick.

I don't like this.

"I don't either," Drew muttered.

We can't see them all. There are too many behind us.

"Too many ahead, too."

Fluffy was looking for a way around. Maybe he would like to play Bowling for Shedu.

A slow grin crept onto Drew's face as he felt the rumble under his feet, and he turned, chuckling softly as Fluffy bounded past the spot where Jeff had laid—he was gone, I don't know how—and spotted the mass of guards standing behind us.

"Look, Fluffy!" Drew called out. "Little black squeaky toys!"

Several of the guards turned to see what Drew meant and shoved at the men nearby to get out of the way.

It was movement; they were scurrying mice as far as Fluffy was concerned, and Fluffy wanted to play.

He leaped into the air, paws extended, and he pounced, plowing through the Shedu behind us. Three guards were trapped under his paws, a few under his belly, and dozens more scattered. Drew and I watched as his tail flicked back and forth, knocking some of the runners to the ground.

"Good job, Fluffy. Now play with your toys quietly, okay?"

Fluffy lifted his paw to let the Shedu get up, but as soon as they started to run, he slapped it back down on them.

Drew turned back. "Only a thousand more to go."

Oz was staring them down. She hadn't said a word, which was starting to worry me. I stretched until I could see her face; she didn't look upset. She didn't look angry. The only thing I could see in her expression was curiosity, and I couldn't understand it.

She's not mad.

"What's the plan, Oz?" Drew asked.

Aisha offered Will's gun to Oz, but she shook her head. Between them, they had three laser pistols and a plasma sword, which would do no good against the massive line of guards armed with laser rifles.

She's thinking.

You guys might wanna back up.

When she spoke, her voice was loud; she spoke without shouting, but in a timber that carried from the first line of Shedu to the last. "You can't shame me. This is just skin. I don't care. But tell me where Tobias is, or face the pain that I will bring down on you like rain."

A rumble of arrogant chuckling moved through the crowd.

"Last chance."

She lifted the piece of Hagar's medallion from her chest and blew on it until it glowed; bright white light leeched from its four points and hung in the air before her. It swirled and popped with electric sparks, and she moved her hand around it until it shimmered like glass; with gentle breath and light fingers she teased it into a ball of light that was as big as Fluffy, hovering over her hands.

"Show me where he is," she whispered. The ball hung in the air until she splayed her hands behind it, and with a flick of her fingers it rocketed down Market Street, plowing through the Shedu, and the ball of light kept going until it reached the Powell intersection, where it suddenly stopped.

The guards were thrown violently to the ground and slammed against the buildings, leaving a clear path down the center of the street. The ball of light hung there for the breath of a moment and then exploded into bright, blinding white sparks. When the light faded, there was a lone man standing in the center of the intersection. He was dressed in clothes that were as white as his hair, and his head hung as he stared at his feet, hands clasped together, unwilling to meet Oz's gaze.

She began to walk.

"Is this what you wanted? Are you so blinded to other peoples' pain that this is somehow *funny* to you?"

His voice boomed at her. It was deep and gravely, and he still would not look up. "You wear your shame like a badge of honor."

"I'm not ashamed." She stopped, bare feet planted firmly. Drew wanted to run after her, but Aisha grabbed his arm to hold him back. Oz gestured to herself, inviting all eyes to take in each and every scar, from the bright white long scars to the tiny flecks that covered her from the neck down. She let them see all the bruises she'd received from fighting over the last days; her thighs were splotchy with black marks, and her back and chest fared no better. "This *is* what you wanted. Well, *here I am!*"

His head moved just a fraction, as if he struggled to keep from looking. "Cover yourself."

"Why?" she asked, hands balled into fists. "You made me do this. You gave me no choice, and now you don't have the balls to look."

He didn't think she had the guts to stand there like this.

"He wanted to humiliate her," Drew whispered. "Anyone who really knows her knows better."

"Well?" Oz demanded.

"You will cover yourself," Tobias said. "If you wish to see your Emperor again, you will dress."

Her hands went to her hips. "No."

Without looking up, Tobias held his arm out, and flicked his fingers, beckoning the guards. Two stepped forward and shoved Shivan into the street. He stumbled and fell to his knees, and stayed there. "Look at her," Tobias demanded.

Shivan shook his head and refused to look up.

"Get up, and look at her!" He held his hand out, fingers splayed, and thin white beams shot from his fingers, forcing Shivan to his feet.

"I won't," Shivan cried. "She is the Princess Oz. Have some respect. You can't make me."

"Oh, but I can, and I will burn the image of her shame into your mind."

He'll break Shivan's neck. Shivan will fight it that much.

"Oz," Drew pleaded.

Oz looked over her shoulder and nodded. He took the bag from Aisha and ran the few steps to her, tearing it open. To a man, heads lowered as she began to put her clothes back on.

"Oh, *now* they're too precious to watch."

Aisha was behind her and slipped the gun back into Oz's waistband. When she was done tying her shoes, Drew gave her the plasma sword and whispered to her to be careful.

"I am. I swear."

They stood shoulder to shoulder and watched as Tobias shoved Shivan to the side.

"All right. You get your way," Oz called out. "I'm covered. Your pretentious sensibilities will no longer be offended by my nudity."

"It's not your nakedness I find offensive."

"Apparently, since you still can't look at me."

"Your arrogance," Tobias said. "Your ego. Your impudence. You cherish your weaknesses as if they were strength. You should have followed your Emperor, Princess, not taken the lead. You are not worthy of the lead."

"There is no lead. We're equal."

"You can never be equal, you know that."

"Bullshit."

"You will never be equal, but you can be saved."

Oz took a step back and her breath caught. She reached for Drew and grabbed his arm, trying to pull him back. "No," she muttered. "No."

Tobias finally lifted his head and beckoned her closer.

He looked years younger and could call himself anything he wanted, but there was no hiding it.

It was Levi Munson.

35

Oz was rooted in place, full of fury and turmoil, her hands balled into tight fists as her jaw worked hard at grinding her teeth together. Tobias stuck his hands in his pockets and sauntered off as if he were merely a tourist taking in San Francisco's downtown sights. He went up Powell Street, leaving Shivan to wait for Oz and Drew to come for him.

It took her a full minute to move. Drew put his hand on her shoulder but it wasn't to get her walking; he just wanted to remind her that she wasn't alone. For the minute she waited, her breathing was fast and shallow, but when she decided it was time, she exhaled one long breath and finally turned to Drew.

"I could actually kill him this time."

He set his forehead against hers for a brief moment but didn't say anything.

"I know. We have to find Will first. Even if the bastard gets away, he comes first."

Aisha watched Oz struggle but didn't ask until we were on our way down the street. "Who is he?"

"Tobias," Oz answered evenly, "looks an awful lot like my maternal grandfather. The bastard is dead and I wish to hell I'd been the one to do it. If I'd been stronger—"

"You *were* strong," Drew interrupted. "He tortured the shit out of you, and you still managed to stand on broken legs and punch the daylight out of him."

"Not hard enough."

"He didn't win, Oz. He lost Florida, he lost his family, he lost any shred of respect his people had for him. He never got the sit on the throne of his own ego. He was never revered as the god he thought he was. He needed to live to see that happen. The revenge was in *not* killing him."

"The worst thing for a narcissist is to lose his power," Aisha said. "Drew is right. You won by proving him he was wrong about you. You're not some weak, worthless female who should be hiding behind a man. You're strong enough to walk away."

"Yeah. Totally not walking away this time."

Shivan ran to meet us before we reached Powell. He was breathless, but none the worse for the wear. No bruises I could see. No rips in his clothing that weren't already there. He looked fine, but fear rolled from him.

"Tobias can't get into the lab. He has the Emperor in the dungeon, and he won't tell Tobias how to get in and it's making him furious. He has Hagar, too, and he won't even talk. He pretends he doesn't hear Tobias at all."

"Where's the dungeon?" Oz asked.

"I don't know the place. It came up from nowhere, but it stands tall." He considered it and then added, "Hagar's home is gone. The chickens are gone. Kilfin will be heartbroken, he loved them."

"He *ate* them," Drew said.

"But he loved them all the same, and thanked them for their lives."

That gave Drew pause.

"Is he near the Square?" Oz asked.

Shivan nodded. "The Square is here." He drew an imaginary box in the air with his finger. "The lab door is here—" he marked a spot on the far side of the box "—and the dungeon is here, in the tall hut."

The royal house.

There were no guards at the door and Drew was going to just yank it open until Oz warned him it might be a trap. She had him carefully inspect the hinges and the seams, and he poked through the planters that capped each side of the entry. When he was satisfied that it wouldn't explode, he carefully pulled it open.

Inside was not home. There was no staircase going up, and no elevator. There was no going up at all. There was a ten-foot-tall ceiling and no accounting for the other seven stories that were clearly there from the outside. There was a down staircase, and hanging from the ceiling above it was another sign.

SALVATION AWAITS

THE PRINCESS OZ

"Salvation, my ass," she muttered. "I swear to God, I am drop-kicking the next idiot to get in my way."

She meant it, too. Halfway down the stairs we encountered a Shedu guard on his way up, and she sent him flying with a quick front kick to his chest. He landed with a spectacular thud, his arms and legs splayed out in a way that made him look like an unconscious asterisk plastered onto the ceramic tile floor.

"Slow down," Drew said. "We could walk into anything."

"He wants us there, Drew."

Aisha rushed to catch up. "He wants *you*, Oz. He couldn't care less about us."

"And even if he wants you to find him, that doesn't mean you should rush in blindly." At the foot of the stairs, Drew reached for her hand. "He knows you want him dead. He knows he can get under your skin. Don't give him that." When she didn't respond, he added, "Please."

We were on the pool level. There should have been a thick, clear wall to the left, shielding the stairs from splashes of water, but it was open and there was no pool. There were cells on the far wall that had heavy iron gates that looked like ugly lattice fences, and it was poorly lit. Will was in the center cell, sitting on the floor with his legs crossed and eyes closed, meditating. I knew he sensed we were there; his ear moved just so, the way it did when he was listening to what I had to say without giving away the fact that he understood me.

Aisha wanted to run to him. She twitched in that direction and only stopped because Hagar, standing near the gate of his cell next to Will's, mouthed the word "no."

In the center of the room there was a raised, round well. I could smell the water in it, salty and stale. It reminded me of the little pool Oz and Drew played in on the roof when they were small, when the Emperor watched them splash and throw things at each other. This one was taller, deep enough to cover someone at least to their chest.

"Oh, he's got to be freaking kidding me," she seethed.

Substitute freaking.

Tobias stood behind it, his hands resting on the rim. "You can still be saved, Princess."

Another man dressed in white came from behind him and started to climb in. "Do it and I'll kill you before your foot is all the way under the water," Oz snapped.

His face pinched with worry; he considered it for a moment, then pushed away from the baptismal font and left.

"Good choice."

"And again, you allow your ego to get in the way of your eternal life."

"Yeah, and how's that working for you?" she asked. "Have you become Satan's special little friend yet? Your eternity has to be several degrees of horribly hot."

His head cocked to the side, amused. "You believe in Hell?"

"I believe that if there is one, Levi Munson is in its innermost circle."

He patted the top of the font. "Thirty seconds. You go under, accept grace, and your soul is free."

"You can't afford my soul."

"You can't afford not to do this," he said. With a wave of his hand, Drew was in the cell with Will and Shivan was with Hagar. Will opened his eyes and very calmly stood up, and then reached for Drew.

I dropped to the ground, landing on my feet, wondering why I hadn't been thrown in with the rest of them.

"Still not doing it." She pulled the gun out and shot the side of the well. It exploded in a rush of water and I jumped onto Aisha's leg, using my claws to climb to her shoulder. "I don't need to be baptized to find grace, Tobias. I didn't need it then, I don't need it now."

"And yet," he said, walking around her in a wide circle, kicking up water, "you have regrets. You still wonder what would have happened if you'd just said something. If you'd given him a measure of what he asked for."

"He wanted respect."

Tobias shrugged. "He was your grandfather."

"An accident of biology. He gave up any rights to being family when he abused my mother."

"Did he admit to that? Or are you taking the word of a single side?"

"He admitted it on a worldwide broadcast, while I sat bleeding in his damned electric chair."

"Did you ask why?"

"I didn't have to."

"But he didn't do those same things to you. He didn't... touch you?"

Oz leveled the gun at him. "Shut up."

The grin playing about his mouth was ripe with anger. He continued to circle, hands clasped behind his back, and he kept his eyes on her. "Then he did."

"Stop it," Aisha hissed.

He stopped and looked at her as if he was seeing her for the first time. "Why are you not in the cell with the others?" Before she could answer, he waved his hand to dismiss her. "No matter. You can't stop this."

"What *is* this?" Oz demanded. "What the hell do you want?"

"What the hell," he repeated. "What the hell, what the hell. I want many things, Princess. Perhaps you should sit down and relax while I tell you." Another wave of his hand and the water on the floor evaporated, and the broken pieces from the well flew together until they formed a large wooden chair.

An electric chair.

"Sit," he said. "Relax."

"Go choke on a dick."

He snorted. "How very regal of you." He pointed at Aisha, and then curled his finger, beckoning her to come to him. "You can easily take her place."

"I will not."

She set me back down on the floor, just in case. Tobias glared, willing her forward, to sit, but the only thing she did was glare right back.

"Why can I not move you?" he muttered to himself. He began circling again, hands clasped behind his back, squinting at both Oz and Aisha, puzzles to be solved. "You're useless, then. A piece of filler. And yet, I can't seem to make you go away."

"Not going anywhere," Aisha said.

"I wish you would."

"Well, aren't you just a sparkling ray of pitch-black abyss," she countered.

My ear twitched when I heard Hagar whisper my name. Carefully, trying to not be seen, I crept over to his cell. "Get the other half of the medallion from Prince Andrew and give it to Oz."

I wiggled through one of the lattice holes in Will and Drew's cell and told him what Hagar had said. He slipped the outer circle of the medallion from his wrist and slid it over my head like a collar. It was heavy and hurt my neck, but I only had to get it halfway across the floor.

"You understood him," Will said, surprised.

"For now. It probably won't last once we leave here."

You never know. We don't know why Will understands me. Maybe it'll stick to you.

It was harder to wiggle out with the medallion on my neck. It caught, and Drew had to help me work it through. When Tobias's back was to Oz, I climbed her leg and torso, rubbing the metal on her cheek once I was sitting on her shoulder.

She glanced at Drew, who tapped his wrist and mouthed *Put it on.*

Tobias stopped next to the chair and patted his hand on its arm. "Someone is sitting here. If not you, and not this...woman... then the boy will do." With a wave of his hand, Shivan shot from the cell and was in the chair, the straps slapping over his wrists and ankles.

Oz didn't react.

"Make no mistake," Tobias said as he pulled Shivan's head against the back of the chair by his hair, "we know what we are. And you think this doesn't matter because we're not real." He pulled a leather strap over Shivan's forehead and cinched it tight. "But, you're mistaken. We are very real."

Shivan's eyes were wide with terror, but he huffed, "Don't listen to him."

"Listen to me or not, his pain will be quite tangible."

She wasn't moved. "Why should I believe you? You're lines of code written on a hard drive somewhere."

Will cleared his throat.

She looked over her shoulder. "I know what I said. They can hurt us, they're real. But only so much."

"Oz." He slipped his fingers over the iron of his cell gate. "They are *aware.*"

She went to Shivan. Batting Tobias's hands away, she undid the strap around his forehead. "Be honest. Are you afraid?"

"It doesn't matter."

"*Are you afraid?*" she hissed.

A bare nod of his head. "I'm terrified. I just want to go home now."

Tobias snorted. "Your Lord of Prophecy."

"He's a boy, Tobias," Hagar said wearily. "Leave him be."

"The boy who would kill me," Tobias snapped. He got between Shivan and Oz, planting his hands on both arms of the chair, and he placed his face a mere inch from Shivan's. "Do you know what you are? To them?"

Softly, "I know."

"Oz is willing to let you die because to her you don't exist.

You're a blip of data that can be rewritten. You're a static image that only moves when she's thinking about you."

"When I'm at rest I still—"

"She doesn't grasp that!" he shouted, pushing away from the chair. "We're amusement for them. A distraction. They don't care about you, Shivan of Blackshear. They would easily leave here and forget you ever existed."

"No. They would remember. The Trident would never forget."

"The Trident." He began walking aimlessly around the room. "The saviors of the elves. Free the elves, free the people, free their consciences." He stopped in front of Hagar's cell. "All of this, the decades of pain and loss, this is their doing, not mine."

"They didn't take control of the program," Hagar said. "You did."

"They killed my family!" he roared. He moved onto Will and Drew's cell. "Your precious lines of code, written specifically to murder women and children *brutally*. All for your own entertainment.

"Your progeny," he spat as he stood in front of Oz. "The son of your son, he did this. He created this world and then left us at the mercy of his faulty code for *eight hundred years!* He made us whole so that you would recognize us as your own, he gave us free will and thought, but he never fixed the code."

"Bad things happen everywhere," Oz said evenly.

"What am I to you?" he asked.

"An evil to be destroyed. I know you're not Levi Munson, no matter how you look, but you know what he did to me and you're willing to use it. You've held thousands of people at your mercy—"

"Yes. *People!*"

"Holographic people."

His nostrils flared. "Sentient holographic people. He gave us lives and expected us to not live them? We *have* lived them, Princess. We fall in love, we bear children, we grieve our dead. We feel. Do you understand that? We *feel*."

The sound of flesh on metal made me look back; Hagar

was wiggling his finger, pointing at Shivan. The straps around his wrists and ankles were very slowly coming undone. When they were off, he gestured to Shivan to hold still. Wait.

"Fine. You're pissed off," Oz said. "That's no excuse."

"Isn't it? What I've done, it brought you here."

"You know better," Hagar said.

"Doesn't matter," Oz said. "Faulty code or not, if you're as sentient as you say, then everything you've done is by choice. Including that perverse little show of making me strip down and swim. Why?"

"To make you feel ashamed. For what your progeny has done to us, you deserve to feel shame."

"All I felt was cold."

"You feel the shame of the flaws written on your skin. You hide them. You don't want to explain them. You don't want them seen."

Oz cocked her head to the side, mouth turned up at the corners just enough to show her amusement. "I'll give you a tiny bit of credit for that," she said. "I'm not happy with my body right now. But I'm not ashamed of it. Nakedness is not a problem for me."

"You were broken—"

"No. He never broke me. He hurt me. He injured me. He cut me open. But he did not break me." She inhaled a short, sharp breath. "He didn't break me."

He was nose to nose with her. "He touched you."

"I know. I was there."

"Intimately."

Drew made a choking sound, but she didn't turn to him.

"The asshat grabbed my boobs. Big freaking deal."

"And more," Tobias pressed.

"Through clothing," she said. "Don't make more of it than it was."

"You felt shame."

"I felt pissed off. I'm pissed off now, Tobias. What the hell is the point of all this?"

He stepped back. "I want into the lab."

"No."

He held his arm out, palm up, and rubbed fingers together until he'd worked up a tiny ball of light. "Give me the code to the lab, or Shivan will feel every measure of that chair."

Shivan slid, very quietly, to the floor. Oz shrugged and said, "So? Light that puppy up, let's see what happens."

As Tobias turned to throw the ball at Shivan, he scrambled away. Oz grabbed both parts of the medallion and turned sharply, slapping them together. She held them tightly, as sparks flew around her face and singed her hair, and as a thin tendril reached across to shove Tobias back. The cell doors flew open with a loud crack; Drew stepped out with his gun drawn, and Aisha tossed hers to Will.

Hagar calmly pushed forward. "They will kill you, Tobias. Give it up and live, or hold on tight and die."

Shivan turned his plasma sword on, ready to strike. "You will feel the pain of it, Wizard," he said.

"You'll never get close enough."

"Tobias," Hagar sighed. "If they shut the system down, we all die. You have nothing to gain."

"You also have nowhere to go," Oz said.

Will lowered his gun. "Just tell us what you really want. We can end this now without hurting anyone."

Tobias shook his head. "If you die here, you die. You understand that?"

"We got it," Oz answered.

"Then prepare yourselves. Because the end is near."

He moved his hands in circles, cloaking himself in smoke, and vanished.

36

"Leave," Hagar urged. "Get out before he brings the building down."

No one needed to be told a second time; there was a scramble for the stairs, and then everyone sprinted. Oz pulled me off her shoulder and held me close to make sure I wouldn't fall off, and she even called to Fluffy to hurry up. I imagined him to be a little bit smaller so that he could move quicker, and he bolted out the door as Oz reached Union Square across the street.

None of the buildings were coming down, but the façades were beginning to crumble. Hagar said they would continue to decay as long as Tobias's attention was divided, but I didn't think it mattered. Unless he intentionally decided to think the buildings into crashing all at once, they would stand, the same way Fluffy could still sit there when I was not concentrating on him. He might not move much, but he stayed. The buildings let loose a brick here, a brick there, and that felt more dangerous than their collapse; people might relax and walk without caution, not expecting that a piece of the royal house would drop on their heads.

They clustered in the center of the Square, muttering to themselves in frustration. While they complained, I watched

Fluffy flop down and stare off into the sky. He took a deep breath and sighed before setting his head on his paws.

He felt empty and sad, and that stabbed at me like a needle into my heart. It was my fault. I thought him into existence and then gave him a dragon, and he didn't get to say goodbye. He knew as surely as I did what had happened, and his heart was breaking.

A minute later, while Oz was bickering with Will about which direction they should go, a large shadow blanketed the Square. Without looking up, Will moaned, "Wick, what did you do now?"

Fluffy missed Jeff.

The black dragon flew in a circle but didn't land.

"So you created another dragon? Did we not speak about this?"

No, this is Jeff.

Drew watched Jeff soar between buildings. "Wick, that's not possible. Jeff is gone. I—"

I know what you did. I brought him back.

"But Oz tried to save him and couldn't."

I didn't save him. I brought him back.

Fluffy sat up and started to purr.

See? Fluffy needs him. They're brothers.

"He's completely the same?" Oz asked. "Same memories? He knows what he's done with us?"

I brought him back.

"Apparently," Drew told her. "Wick is being a bit vague."

"All right, furball," Oz said, poking at my chin with her finger, "why don't you think up a crystal ball for us to use to find Tobias?"

Me? Why don't you do it?

She tried; she closed her eyes and tried to imagine it forming, and hoped it into existence, but nothing happened.

"What the hell, Wick? Why can you do this and I can't?"

"Wick can imagine a living being," Will said. "He has a basic understanding of biology, and because of that, he can create a functioning life with thought. You can't create the crystal ball because you don't know how it would work. At best, you would wind up with a pretty glass sphere that does nothing."

"Same reason I couldn't create an air bike?" Drew asked.

"Essentially. There's far more to creation than concept. Still, your mind created the sprites, I think. Though I am a bit relieved that they're gone."

"Kind of forgot about them," Drew admitted. "But I don't think I ever considered that they would eat someone."

"Free will," Hagar said. "Once created, they are independent. You can compel them to do things they don't object to—eating someone, for instance—but you cannot think them into bringing harm to themselves unless it's for the greater good."

"But Wick can bring a dead dragon back."

"Indeed," Will murmured. He was watching Oz, who was looking up, but not at Jeff. Her gaze was fixed on the roof of the royal house, and one by one they all noticed and watched with her, wondering what to expect.

Jeff circled the roof repeatedly, quickly, and when the mass of butterflies began to lift, he soared higher, guiding them upwards in a fluttering whirlpool. They came off the roof by the thousands, a thick funnel of red and blue, and when they were spiraling over the Square, she said softly, "Show me where he is."

They circled the Square twice more, and then took off in a long ribbon, darting up Powell Street toward the bay. They were still rising from the roof when she said, "He's heading for Coit Tower. They're following as he runs toward it."

"What's at Coit?" Aisha wondered.

Oz finally looked down. "Dozens of servers, and access to the mainframe."

"Computers, yes," Will said. "He has no access to the mainframe. That's why he wants into the lab. He seems to understand that from there he would have a measure of control, though I'm not certain what he wants with it."

"Mass deletion of files?" Drew guessed.

Hagar bristled at the idea. "That would be suicide."

"Either he doesn't know that, or that's exactly what he wants."

"We know what we are," Hagar said. "He and I. Some of the elves. Some of the Shedu."

"And the others?" Will pressed.

"Fillers. Surely, you've noted the sameness in large groups. Faces created to fulfill expectation. Those who never come near you, but who fill a needed role." To Oz he said, "You've seen the difference. Those with an aura of color and those without. How many of the men standing while Tobias attempted to shame you had anything swirling around them? A hundred? Two hundred?"

"Very few," she said.

"Tobias created his army on a whim, as he needed them."

"Then why all of this?" Oz asked. "What's the point?"

The point, as he saw it, was that Finn created the program to serve as entertainment, but he didn't foresee what would happen if he left it running unchecked. "He intended for us to be whimsical creatures that responded to a visitor's wishes until they decided to return home. But in leaving us here unchecked?" He sighed. "We became aware of ourselves."

"And with that came all the emotions of human experience," Will guessed.

"Not immediately. But we do feel. We pair bond. We procreate. We have family units and property and governance, and with that we have every good and bad intention of humanity. We mourn. Tobias is lost in grief and strayed from his programming. He was never supposed to be...this."

Quietly, Will asked, "And Shivan? Does he know?"

"Not entirely. He knows that he is a holographic being, but still isn't aware of what that really means. I would not be the one to tell him that you could simply walk into your lab and with a flick of a switch, end this all."

"We wouldn't do that," Oz said. "And we'll see this through. I have to know why Tobias looks like Levi Munson, and why the hell he's done all this. I can't believe Finn would write any of this into a game."

"Then what do we do?" Drew asked.

Oz's hand went to the medallion Hagar had given her. "We

bring down the tower. Take away his place to hide, and then force him to come back here."

"You need a visual line to use the power of the medallion for that," Hagar warned.

"And I'll get it." She turned to me. "Call Jeff, Wick. Ask him to take me for a ride."

*

Will rode with Oz; he wore the headlamp with the camera and left his phone with Drew so that we could watch. In his head was the idea that if Oz slipped, he would steer Jeff into a dive to catch her and save us all from the royal eruption that would occur if she were hurt. Drew was just as capable—more, even, since he had already ridden Jeff and could control him—but there was no dissuading him.

I wondered if Aisha and Drew could hear the unspoken: if Oz fell and he couldn't catch her, he would dive after her. He was not going home without her.

He kept a hand gripped onto one of Jeff's handles, and the other arm was so firmly around Oz's waist that I wondered if she could even breathe.

"Man, she's gonna chew him out," Drew muttered as he sat on the ground with Will's phone in hand. Aisha sat next to him and scooched as close as she could get to see the screen. "He's got a death grip on her."

Hey, she said he could practice touching with her. Maybe they have a squeezing agreement we don't know about.

"Wick, do you have any idea how strong he is? I could hold her like that and she wouldn't flinch. He holds her like that and it's gonna hurt."

"Duly noted," Aisha said. "What are they doing?"

Oz guided Jeff out over the water, past where the Ferry Building should be, and she took him in wide circles. They flew over the sliver of Embarcadero that was left on the west side and went north of Coit Tower, keeping an eye on where the butterflies were swarming. Tobias was still far enough away that she could blow the tower into rubble and the worst he would get hit with would be dust.

Before they mounted Jeff, Hagar quickly instructed Oz on how to use the round section of the medallion that Drew had worn on his arm. It had a small amount of power and would act as a conduit when the time came. As she and Will circled the tower over and over, Drew became more agitated, until he spit out, "Just wreck the damn thing, Oz."

"Patience," Hagar said. "She'll feel when the time is right. She wants him close enough to feel the pain of losing the tower but not so close that he'll be lost to its destruction."

"Yeah, I don't get that. The whole point is to take him down."

"Not like this," Aisha reminded him. "She wants answers, and if we're going to do this right, there's still the prophecy."

Drew gritted his teeth. The only thing keeping Oz on Jeff was Will's arm. She had one hand on the piece of medallion hanging from her neck, and the other hand was in a tight fist with Drew's piece around her wrist. Jeff was banking left, his head dipped so that she had a clear line of sight, and she blew on the medallion to make it glow. Then with a flick of her wrist, she splayed her fingers and a bolt of white-hot light shot from her hand, growing in size as it sped toward the tower until it was the size of Fluffy and had turned bright red.

It hit the tower dead center, and it exploded into chunks and dust, and pieces of it rained down on Tobias and the men who were following him.

I hope the butterflies are all right.

"They're fine, Wick. Look." Drew pointed to a spot at the top of the screen. There was a cluster of buzzing blue, spiraling away from Tobias. "They sensed it coming. They'll follow him again when they know it's safe."

"You know this, how?" Aisha asked.

"Because I want it. That should be enough."

Tobias turned and kept running. He headed toward Ghirardelli Square, and Oz turned Jeff to chase after him.

"Wick," Hagar said, "Call Jeff back. They don't need to follow."

They might not have needed to, but Oz was four kinds of unhappy when Jeff suddenly stopped taking her commands and returned them to Union Square. She jumped off and stomped over to us, eyebrows knotted together.

"Who brought him back?" she demanded.

"Tobias is heading toward Kilfin," Hagar said simply. "He has few guards to protect him. Kilfin will intercept and bring him back."

"How will he know to?" Will asked.

"He knows where we are, and knows to bring Tobias to the Lord of the Prophecy. As much as he wants Tobias dead, he knows it will not be by his hand."

Oz's hands went to her hips, and her jaw worked tightly for a moment. "If it was that easy, why the hell didn't Kilfin just go after him before we even got here?"

"Tobias has remained hidden for years, well-guarded. And with the belief that only one person could remove him from power? What was the point?"

She glanced at Shivan and sighed. "All right, he was too young."

"I'm still young," Shivan muttered.

"You don't have to do this," Oz told him. "You don't have to do any of this."

"The Lord will draw the life from death, and freedom then will fall," Shivan reminded her.

"And yet, you don't want to. I can feel it, Shivan."

"I did. I mean, I wanted to do the things I'm supposed to, but the fighting—I didn't picture any of this in my head, and it's all sitting inside me..." He trailed off, shrugging.

"Like the unborn chickens Hagar makes you eat?" Drew asked.

"Worse," he answered in a near-whisper.

"Tell me you believe that you're the Lord of Prophecy," Oz said.

He bit his lower lip. "I am the Lord of Prophecy."

"Tell me your name and age."

Confused, he replied, "Shivan, you know that. I'm fifteen."

Oz turned to Will. "He doesn't honestly think he's the one meant to face Tobias."

"Then who?" Drew asked.

"The one who hasn't drawn a drop of blood in all the fighting we've done," Shivan said. "The one who fought with hands and feet, and dropped men to the ground, but never drew a sword. The one who sees the dark wizard for what he is, because the rest of us can't."

He stood a bit straighter. "It's not me. You know it's not me. It's Oz."

37

Will and Aisha took Jeff up again; he wanted to see where Tobias was and if he had, indeed, crossed Kilfin's path, and he wanted to take her on the ride she would never get to take if they didn't go now. Jeff glided through the air, gently tilting left and then right, making sure he didn't go too fast so that she would enjoy it.

Will did that on his motorcycle. He once circled Union Square—with permission—and leaned it back and forth, riding in gentle curves on the street. When Jax asked him why, Will said that straight, fast lines are fun, but feeling the bike move from side to side was exhilarating. He wanted to haul it outside the city, where there were open roads that twisted along the coast, just so he could lean into the curves.

If Aisha liked taking the curves while riding on Jeff, she would probably love riding on the motorcycle with him. He would probably even teach her to pilot the bike, just so that he could ride behind her, arms around her waist. He'd never ridden with anyone before, and unquestionably, he would want her to be the first.

We watched on Will's phone. Tobias was sprinting, and Hagar was sure he was headed for the Presidio woods, where there were places he could hide until he could regroup. His guards were falling behind, and while no one said so, I was pretty sure it was because Will was thinking them into slowing down and leaving Tobias on his own. The butterflies swarmed in a heavy, thick mass, pushing him away from the shoreline toward the Palace of Fine Arts, right at the edge of the Presidio. Drew was trying to get some measure of control, willing them to turn him south from the palace, and then onto Divisadero Street, where he would encounter Kilfin and Krisf.

They had dozens of elves with them; Jeff swooped overhead so that Will could get a better look, and then dove low so that he could shout to Kilfin: *Tobias is dead ahead. Look for the long line of butterflies. Then bring him to the Square.*

Kilfin broke into a run with Jeff flying low to the ground behind him. The closer to Tobias he got, the thicker the swarm of butterflies became, blocking the wizard's view. When Kilfin was near, the swarm lifted and he lunged, slamming Tobias into the ground. Tobias was winded and couldn't draw in a decent breath, but that didn't stop Kilfin from making a fist with his massive hand, and punching him into darkness.

*

Will and Aisha took the long way back; he steered Jeff away from the bloody pummeling Tobias was enduring and soared over the Presidio, then turned back to glide over Ocean Beach, down the coastline until he turned in near Lake Merced. For the next half hour, he took Aisha on a tour of the city from up high, weaving east and west, letting her feel the wash of the breeze and the gentle roll of Jeff tilting back and forth. He tucked his face next to her head so that her hair would flow behind him, and he coaxed Jeff into soaring up and swooping down. Drew watched on the phone and mused that it felt like the longest roller coaster ride ever, and he was going to miss it.

Invent that jetpack, dude. Just don't expect me to ride with you.

Will kept going until they had seen it the entire city, and when he finally brought Jeff back, Aisha was breathless and laughing.

"If not for the whole fighting thing, this would be so much fun."

Oz grinned. "Some of us don't mind the fighting. It actually has been kind of fun."

"Well, except for the whole naked swimming thing," Drew grumbled. "And the chicken. So much freaking chicken. God, we're going to go home and your mother will expect us for dinner, and she's going to serve chicken."

Her chicken is better than this chicken.

Will looked toward the west side of the Square. Kilfin was coming up the stairs with Tobias slung over his shoulder, and Krisf was running to keep up with him. When he got close, he dropped the wizard onto the ground without taking care to not hurt him.

Tobias's nose was bloody and swollen, his eyes rimmed with bruises.

"His guards scattered. They know they're done for."

Hagar leaned over Tobias. "Get up. I know you're awake."

Without opening his eyes, Tobias groaned. "Just kill me now. Spare us all the damned dance of the prophecy."

Will reached down and grabbed Tobias's shirt and hauled him up with one hand. "You owe us some answers first."

When he was on his feet, Tobias took a deep breath and slowly, painfully opened his eyes. "Dead man talking. Fine."

Hand on the butt of her sword, Oz stepped in front of him. "Why that face?"

"I may not be classically handsome, but I am not homely," he said. "Why any face?"

Hagar bristled. "Show her your true face, Tobias. Then give her the explanation she is owed."

"I owe her nothing," he said. Still, he closed his eyes and took several deep breaths, and as he did his features shifted. His hair lengthened and turned honey-blond, the lines faded, and within a minute he appeared twenty years younger and didn't resemble Levi Munson at all.

"Then why?" Oz asked.

"Because you expected it of me. You wanted me to be him."

Her eyes narrowed. "Not a snowball's chance in hell."

"I can feel it in you. You want to be the one to kill me, if only for the chance to destroy the arbiter of your worst dreams. You want to rewrite your nightmares. You didn't fight him then, so now's your chance. Kill them all, Oz. Every Shedu warrior, every man clad in the black uniform that *you* gave them. Destroy every person who resembles those who hit you, spit on you, tied you up, beat you bloody and touched you. And then kill the man who came to you looking every bit as much as you hoped, because *that* man deserved it and the chance to end him was taken away from you."

"I could have," she said softly.

"Oh, you hit him as hard as you could in the moment, but it was just short of killing him."

"I don't think—"

"I hear it in your head, Princess. Every 'if only.'" He looked over at Will and Drew. "She doesn't blame either of you, not in the least. She blames herself, wholly. Every scar she wears is a painful reminder—she failed to act and she failed herself."

Drew tried to take a step toward her, but Will stopped him.

"I did everything I could to stay alive," Oz argued.

"You don't believe that. In those moments, you chose to not fight because you didn't think the odds were with you. But now? Now you wonder, and now you can see every opening you didn't take, and now you realize you could have killed them all and walked away."

"Bullshit."

"Your ego, not mine," he said. "But that is why I took his face. I did as you wished."

Drew's anger flared. "Why the hell make her swim? Like that."

"To face her shame," Tobias said. "She couldn't hide it then. It had nothing to do with her nakedness." He held his hands out, palms up. "So do it. Bring forth the Lord of Prophecy, and let him do his worst. Or best. Semantics. I look forward to the end."

He bent toward Oz. "You know I'm telling you the truth.

Bring the boy to do what he must. I truly do look forward to this all being done."

Shivan stepped next to Oz. He was shaking hard and left his sword clipped at his waist. "It's not me. It's not—"

"Right through my heart," Tobias said. His voice was oddly gentle; he was trying to soothe Shivan. "I won't feel it. I'll simply... end."

Shivan squinted, staring at Tobias's chest. His medallion rested there, bright prisms pinging from its polished edges. His hand shot forward and he snatched it, yanking the chain from Tobias's neck.

"*This*," he murmured. "Not the beating of your heart. Not your breath." He took several steps back, holding the medallion close to his face. "Draw the life from death," he whispered. "It says nothing about killing the man. 'The Lord shall draw the Life from Death, and freedom then will fall.'"

He dropped the medallion to the ground, then unclipped the plasma sword from his belt and turned it on.

Tobias's voice boomed. "Stop!"

Carefully, curiously, Shivan touched the tip of the sword to the medallion. Smoky lines of white and gold mixed with red and blue shot from it, bathing Shivan's face in a rainbow of soft colors, and the metal sizzled as it melted. Tobias dropped to his knees, watching in horror as he begged Shivan to stop.

Oz took the pieces of Hagar's medallion and tossed them down, too, and when he nodded, she turned her sword on and followed Shivan's lead. The noise and light were softer, but it faded into the ground the same way Tobias's did, fractured threads of spent metal buried five inches deep.

"Please," Tobias croaked, "kill me now. I have nothing left."

"No." Oz flicked the sword off. "You're not done explaining. What the hell is all this? You destroyed their lives for what? Fun?"

"Payback."

"All this for revenge."

"I didn't kill them," he said. "But I made their lives the hell that they brought down on mine. A just reward, no more, no less."

"That was an accident," Hagar said. "Your family wasn't murdered. It was an accident."

Tobias got to his feet and roared, "They killed my wife and my children!"

Softly, Hagar said, "My daughter. The light of my life. My grandchildren. My reason for being. If the elves had truly *killed* her...it was only horrible misfortune. They grieved our loss, too."

"My life was broken, Hagar." He choked on the words as he added, "They were babies."

"I know."

"Why do you want access to the mainframe?" Will interrupted.

Tobias kept his eyes locked on Hagar's. "To turn it off. To end...everything."

"Jesus," Drew breathed out. "That's not the answer."

Tobias shrugged. "You would still survive, Prince Andrew."

"That's not the point."

"If I end everything, the suffering stops," Tobias said. His voice was almost gentle and was laced with regret. "We're all tired. The elves are nearly broken, and I'm too angry to stop hurting them. I'm tired of this life. If I can't bring my family back, then I just want everything to stop. The pain ends for all." He looked directly at Shivan. "It's a gift."

"I don't want it," Shivan grumbled.

Oz clipped the sword to her waistband, and after staring at Tobias for a long, silent, and angry moment—her hands were balled into fists and she fought to keep from striking out at him—she asked Will for a private moment. He asked Fluffy to stand at Tobias's back and then positioned Jeff to snort flames if Tobias tried to run, and then had everyone else stand off to the sides while he and Oz went down into the lab.

They were gone for over an hour; neither Fluffy nor Jeff moved at all, and Tobias barely shifted from one foot to the next. He watched as the elves came in masses down the streets, surrounding the Square, but he didn't move.

"He's ready to die," Hagar said quietly. "He knows it's over."

"I'm sure that doesn't make it easier," Aisha said. "Not for anyone."

"Was for me," Shivan muttered.

"And you did well," Hagar said to him. "Regardless of what happens, you removed the one thing he needed to reign."

"But your magic went with it," Shivan said. "That's not fair."

The corners of Hagar's mouth lifted. "Did it? Are you certain?"

"Didn't it?"

If Hagar was going to answer, whatever was going to come out of his mouth stopped when Will and Oz came back from the lab. He brought his tablet with him, and Oz no longer had her weapons.

"You cannot be allowed to survive here," Will said to Tobias. "You understand that."

He nodded.

Hagar put his hand on Will's arm. "He's spent. He has no magic, Emperor."

"Doesn't matter," Oz said. "Look around. The elves are gathering on the streets, waiting to see him executed. If we don't do our job, they will. And it will be bloody. They'll tear him limb from limb and enjoy every second of his agony."

"Oh, I don't want to watch that," Shivan said.

"We won't allow that," Will said.

"Just do it," Tobias hissed.

Will poked at his tablet, glancing every second or so at a spot near Jeff. "I created a secondary program that will run as long as the primary one does." When he was done poking at the screen, he looked at Hagar. "He can't stay here, but he doesn't need to die. I can send him there to live out his programming. It's up to you."

Ten feet from Jeff, a shimmering portal winked opened. We could see to the other side, where the city was gone and it was again filled with trees.

"Condemning him to exist in solitude?" Hagar asked.

"Please, no," Tobias begged. "I'd rather die."

Oz shook her head. "He wouldn't be alone. The program is populated, but he won't have magic to rely on. And he won't be lonely."

She gestured to the portal. Standing just within it was a woman dressed in an emerald green tunic, her long, dark hair loose over her shoulders. Behind her were three small children, too busy playing to notice what she was doing.

Tobias hit his knees again.

"Miriam," Hagar whispered.

"He can have his family back, as long as he leaves here," Oz said. She nudged Tobias with her knee and told him to get up. "Your choice, if Hagar agrees. Stay here and die—I will kill you, I have no problem doing that—or leave and grow old with your wife. Watch your children grow up. Hell, have more babies, and be worthy of them."

Tobias's resignation turned on itself. "Hagar, please," he said thinly.

The older wizard had tears dripping from his eyes. "Everything you've done, and if I say yes you'll be rewarded for the effort. And that leaves *us* where, to repair your shattered legacy here? You get what you so badly wanted, and the elves—" His voice wavered "—so many have died. They gave up their lives fighting, Tobias. With the promise that in the end, you would die."

"That wasn't the promise," Shivan said. When Hagar turned to him sharply, he rushed to remind him of the prophecy. "It was only to draw the life from death. Magic was his life, all that he had, and it's gone. The prophecy doesn't actually say he has to die."

"Is that a cop out?" Drew asked.

"Does it matter?" Oz countered.

"He gets his wife, his children," Hagar moaned.

Shivan slid his hand on Hagar's shoulder. "They didn't say you couldn't go, too. I would miss you, but what's left here for you?"

Hagar looked to Will, hopeful.

"You would never see Shivan again. Nor Kilfin or Yeosef. This place becomes a distant land to which you have no way to travel. But there is no reason why you couldn't go with Tobias." He glanced at the portal. "If I had a wife and a child...she's not a copy of your daughter. She *is* your daughter."

"You would be there to remind me," Tobias said. "In those moments when my ego gets the best of me, you would be there to remind me of the day I was shown mercy and kindness. We could tell the tale of the Trident, and how the Princess Oz laid bare her shame and cloaked herself in grace, and gave the Dark Wizard a bright light to show him the way."

"The reward is yours, Hagar," Oz said. "You can go either way."

He was staring at the portal. "I don't want him with my daughter, not the way he turned out."

"And I'd like him dead," Oz said, "if only for the face he used. That doesn't make either one of us right."

"Kill me or not," Tobias said. "But go, Hagar. No matter what we do here, she and the children exist again, and to leave them alone—"

"She would want you," Hagar whispered.

"She doesn't need me."

Hagar broke. "Need is irrelevant, and my daughter's heart is. I'll take you with me, but I swear, if you make a single step toward the dark again, I'll kill you before your foot hits the ground."

"I would expect that. I would welcome that."

"When you step through," Will said, "you'll feel a bit different, Hagar."

"How?"

"Younger. You'll reset to the ages you were the day before your daughter died. The memories will go with you, but at Oz's request, I'm giving you the years you lost. Tobias's anger should also abate."

"Oz." Hagar grabbed her into a hug, squeezing tight. "Thank you."

"When you're ready just step through," Will said.

He wasn't ready. He had to hug everyone, even Fluffy and Jeff. When he got to Drew, he said, "Marry her, Andrew. Soon."

"As soon as she tells me when. I'm all hers."

Kilfin wasn't ready to let him go. "You'll have nothing there, old man. Where will you live? How will you live?"

"His hut is there," Will said. "He'll make do."

"I will miss you," Hagar said to Kilfin. "Though perhaps not feeding you."

Kilfin looked into the portal. "You might be able to use me there. I can at least keep you fed."

Hagar shook his head. "Someone needs to stay to make sure the boy grows up well. With Tobias gone, the Blackshears may rise again. You could be his Emperor, as William is to Oz."

"That I can do."

"Krisf," Hagar started. "I envisioned Aradyn—"

"I know," he croaked. "Lerym will take his place. We'll be fine, after we grieve. Somehow."

"I'll go then."

And he did; without another glance back, he stepped through the portal and went straight to his daughter. Tobias lingered a moment; I wasn't sure if he was giving them time or if he couldn't make his feet move yet.

"I don't deserve this," he said.

"No," Will said, "you don't. So never forget—you live because Oz has chosen this for you. On her whim, I could just as easily write a line of code and erase you."

"I never believed in the prophecy," he said. "It was a fairy tale that I used to my own end. And yet...having my rule destroyed by the Trident?"

You got forked, dude.

He didn't understand why Drew laughed, but went on, "I meant what I said about grace, Princess Oz. You've shown me more in these few minutes than most see in a lifetime. So know this, because I see into your heart—the shame you bared for all to witness is not your own. Your suffering at the hands of Levi Munson was his shame to bear, and it was his soul in need of salvation. You know that here—" he tapped his forehead "—but you need to embrace it here."

He tapped at his chest, and with that, he nodded and stepped through, and the portal closed behind him.

Shivan stared at the spot where the portal had been, hands on his hips, as he considered what came next. "I suppose I'll go home to my parents. My father never wanted me to follow in his footprints, but now that this is done, I could do worse."

"Get an education," Will said. "If your family does, indeed, rise to power, you'll need that foundation."

"No schools," Shivan said. He sounded happy about it.

Will tapped at his tablet. "There are now."

"Really? Damn you, Emperor."

"What about Fluffy?" Krisf asked. "Are you taking him with you?"

I wish we could. We can't can we?

"It's not possible, Wick," Will said. "Fluffy and Jeff cannot exist in our When."

Krisf will care for them?

"Will you be their guardian?" Will asked him. "They can fend for their own food, but they need someone."

Fluffy needs Jeff. They're brothers.

"Wick reminds me that they were born of the same heart. They're a package deal."

Krisf's hand went to his chest. "Both of them? The dragon won't harm us?"

"He'll protect you. And if you ask nicely, will allow you to ride."

He's still a baby. He's going to get bigger.

Drew walked over to Jeff with him and placed Krisf's hand on the dragon's chest. "Just stay out of his way if he sneezes. But he won't hurt you. He's a good and loyal friend, and he'll protect you."

One by one, they left the Square, until we were the only ones. Will went back to the lab for his backpack and to return the laser pistols and plasma sword, and when he came back, he hoisted the pack up and reached for Aisha's hand.

"Open portal," he said to no one in particular.

The bright blue portal that Finn had opened when leaving his own When for ours popped up like a pinprick of light, and expanded until it was big enough to walk through.

"You knew it was there?" Oz asked.

"After a time, I suspected."

"Kinda sucks that this really isn't a thousand years in the future," Drew said.

"It is two hundred forward, if that helps," Will said. "And I'm controlling the return if you don't mind."

"Yeah, fine, but wait." He picked me up and held me close to his face. "In case this is it, I really liked being able to understand you, Wick. Your voice is gonna be in my head no matter what."

I stick around. Like bad cheese. But you're pretty good at understanding me even without the words.

"I like hearing the words. But I never would have guessed you call everyone 'dude.'"

Dude. Everyone is dude. I'm not allowed to call anyone an asshole. That would upset the Queen.

He smiled wanly. "Yeah, she would have something to say about that."

It's been awesome, dude.

I settled into his sweatshirt and we went through, arriving home one and a half minutes after we left, just as Will had promised Aisha.

38

Union Square was quiet; if anyone noticed us suddenly appear in its center, they went along as if it were a perfectly normal occurrence. There were people sitting at tables near the little bakery on the west corner, and a teenager rolled the length of it on a skateboard, but none of them reacted. It was just the Princess and her entourage, same as every day.

They stood in silence for a long minute, until Drew sighed and said, "So. I need more practice."

"Indeed," Will said. "Don't try to use a portal alone. Had my father not accounted for the possibility, there's no telling where we would have wound up."

"I know. And I'm sorry."

"I'll take you into the future someday, Andrew. Perhaps not that far, but to a time I can be sure we won't port into dead space. Or back into the simulator."

"Pretty sure I need to earn that trip now," Drew said. "I swear, I'll work on it."

Oz reached for his hand. "It's all right. And you win. You and my dad win."

"Win what? Is there a prize?"

"I need to see someone," she admitted. "I'm not as all right as I thought. I enjoyed that far too much, and until he admitted he wanted to end everything, I wanted to kill him."

"You believed he wasn't real," Will reminded her.

"Real or not, I was damn near giddy at the idea of tearing him in half and then spitting in his face before he died. That's a problem." Then, as it occurred to her, "That was the point, wasn't it? That's why we stayed?"

"It was my foremost consideration," Will admitted. "Though if I had known Wick was going to create Fluffy and Jeff?"

Aisha chuckled. "I loved Fluffy and Jeff."

Drew pulled me from the sweatshirt and set me down. "Big creatures from a big heart. You may be tiny, but you are mighty."

Oz scrunched her nose. "That's familiar. What's it from?"

He wasn't sure. "Shakespeare, I think. 'Though she be but little, she is fierce.' I'll look it up." To me, "I'll miss talking with you, Wick."

Meow.

"I thought so." He tugged at Oz's hand. "I'm starving. I want real food. Something not chicken."

When they were headed down the steps, Will scooped me up. "That was mean."

I'll talk to him later. Maybe at four in the morning.

"What if he truly can understand you still?"

Then he'll find out at four in the morning.

"Does Mister Wick have a bit of a mean streak?" Aisha asked, rubbing my head.

"He's sarcastic sometimes." He set me on his shoulder and tucked the strap to his backpack under my tail. "When Oz and I went back into the lab I took pictures of all the data my mother had collected on me. I have no idea what to do with it. But I know it matters."

"Think hard before you do anything."

"I know. For now, I need to find my father and tell him his simulator works. He might want your input, too."

I have a lot to tell him. Like, I thought Aisha said you were fat but I was wrong, and I had to bite you to keep her from taking your pants off.

"He doesn't need to know anything personal, Wick."

He doesn't need to know, but I bet he wants to know.

"We'll stick to the operational aspects of the simulator. He needs to know his program is at least semi-sentient and continues to progress."

"He won't shut it down, will he? I actually care about those people."

He thought the program was safe. "Even if the physical space needed for people to participate in the simulation is deconstructed, the program can run on the computer as long as it exists. He also needs to know I interfered in the outcome."

"That was an act of kindness, Will."

"I don't mean about Tobias. That was Oz's choice. But Aradyn and Jesf—any of the elves killed while we were in control. While I wrote the code for Tobias's alternate existence, it occurred to me that Wick had brought Jeff back, which meant there was no reason I couldn't do the same thing. So, I reset the parameters and brought them all back. I considered simply resetting the program to an old save point and removing the accident that killed Tobias's family, but...Oz felt that would take away from genuine gains in their awareness. So I settled for bringing the elves back. When Krisf and Lerym return home, Aradyn and Jesf will be waiting for them."

"And the schools? Did you really account for that?"

He nodded. "They may be data points, but they'll damn well be educated data points."

He'd make me go to school if he could.

"Indeed, Wick, if there were a school for petulant felines, I would enroll you today."

He slipped his arm around her shoulders and headed for the lab entry. "Let's talk to my dad and then I'll walk you home. I know you want to see your son."

"I do, and I can find my way just fine, Will."

"I know you can, but I'm still walking with you. And maybe we'll take the long way, for no reason other than I'll get to hold your hand that much longer."

Oh my God, not this again.

"The kitty doth protest too much, methinks," Aisha said. "I can tell by the tone. You need to get used to it, Wick. I am touching this man every chance I get."

I think you need to be afraid, Emperor.

"I am."

I am going to mock you endlessly.

"I know."

You are going to suck so hard at the whole bouncing thing.

"Probably."

You still want to try it?

"You have no idea."

They leaned against the back wall of the elevator, arms still touching. That was something I needed to get used to, too. Constant contact for the sake of itself. "Is Oz going to be all right?" she asked. "She still didn't get closure."

He thought she would be. "She could have gotten everything she wanted, and she wouldn't have closure. It's a process. She can't hurry it no matter how much she wants to."

"And you, with your mother?"

"That's a scab I'm just starting to pick at. But not right now, not with my dad."

"If you need to talk..."

"You will be the first."

The elevator door slid open, and Finn was halfway across the lab, playing with things that bite. He broke into a wild grin when he saw us and excitedly scrambled to pick up the latest bowling ball to go through the transporter.

"Look! It's not inside out!"

Will took it from him, and turned it over. "But it's lopsided."

"Well, if you're going to be picky."

Aisha was drawn to the giant board that was filled with the same numbers Will had accused Finn of making up. She stared at it the same way he often did, arms crossed and head cocked to the side as she considered what was in front of her.

"If I find an error, do you want to know?" she asked.

"God, yes." He took the ball from Will and set it down. "I've been looking at it for days."

She pointed to the second line. "You're off by a factor of ten."

Finn stared at it, mouth agape. When he saw the error

she pointed at, his hands went to his head and messed up his hair more than it already was. "I'm an idiot. How could I not see that?" He looked at Will. "Why didn't you? You looked at this. You know math."

"That's not math, Dad. That's...Martian."

"Blasphemer. Martians aren't nearly as elegant."

He started to pick up his marker to fix the error, but Will stopped him. With some effort and a promise that he could get back to the problem within fifteen minutes, he pulled Finn away from the board and over to his desk, where he outlined what happened in the simulator.

"You can't shut it down, Dad. Ideally, not ever."

"But it worked! I wish I'd known you were going, I could have gone home and monitored the simulation from the outside. Surely Rod noticed when it activated. Remember him, Rodrick Odivo? Weird little kid you went to preschool with. Constantly in trouble for trying to lick other kids."

"I remember him. He works with you?"

"Brilliant mind. Still a bit weird, though. Did you have food and fresh water? Necessary supplies? If he noted the program had activated he would have made sure whoever was inside would be fed."

Rodrick has a hard-on for chicken.

"There was food. And when we have more time perhaps we can flesh out a more varied menu and less dangerous scenario. I mostly wanted to let you know that it works."

"You can go back anytime you want," Finn said.

"Perhaps once some of the code is rewritten."

"And perhaps let people know from the moment they enter that they're in a simulator," Aisha suggested. "I know you probably have legitimate reasons not to, for the few who might want to hurt themselves, but overall? We wasted a lot of time trying to figure out why things were so off. And we put Oz and Drew in situations—"

"*I* did that," Will insisted. "And she's right. It would be easy for all the players you've created make it known that it is, indeed, a compendium of holographic characters. Give those who land there choices—go home without engaging anything, or create a relaxing scenario for themselves. Battle is not for everyone."

"Noted." Finn twitched toward the board. "It defaulted to battle because one of you was spoiling for a fight, but we can expand on it when you have more time."

Will started to turn toward the elevator. "One more thing, Dad. Something I couldn't figure out. The lab—was it part of the simulation or not? I guessed it was time locked, but we were able to take weapons from it, and many of my childhood things were there. Mom's work notes were on her desk, and the rocket ship drawing I made for her was there."

"Ah. Yes. That could be confusing. Everything in the lab was real, but it would take hours to explain. Lock plus a shift, and all that."

Will took the hint. He picked me up and gave me a choice, sweatshirt or shoulder, and when I was settled in the pouch of his shirt, we went into the elevator.

"Absent-minded professor," Aisha joked when the doors closed.

"He's going to offer you a job," Will said. "Just wait. He needs someone to proof his work."

"Maybe you just need to brush up on your calculus and analytical geometry so that you can help him."

He pretended to consider it. "I would need a tutor."

"You're in luck. I just happen to know someone who's damn near dying to teach you a whole bunch of things."

"Wick?"

Yeah?

"I am definitely afraid now."

The doors slid open and she pulled him out by the hand. "Emperor." She stopped and held his hand against her chest. "You're not running again. I'm not letting go."

He didn't run. Instead, he kissed her, and then did as he said he'd wanted to; he held her hand the entire walk home, and they took the long way.

That was probably the last time they took the long way getting anywhere.

ABOUT THE AUTHOR

Max Thompson is a long time feline blogger and life coach columnist for *Mousebreath! Magazine.* He lives in Northern California with his typist, writer K.A. Thompson, another human known mostly as "The Man," and the royal pain in his asterisk, Buddah Pest.

The author of numerous book, *Forked* is his third work of fiction and is book three in *The Wick Chronicles.*

He can be found online at
http://psychokitty.blogspot.com and at
http://facebook.com/thepsychokittyspeaksout

www.ingramcontent.com/pod-product-compliance
Lightning Source LLC
Chambersburg PA
CBHW071201020726
47502CB00002B/494